The Truth About Myths

By Giovanna Siniscalchi

"Step through the castle gates and journey into the opulent world of Portuguese royalty. She's the prudish princess. He's the rake with a devil-may-care grin. Together, they're the last pair anyone expected. Can these opposites overcome their clash of wits for the sake of a nation?"

Praise for The Winemakers

"Siniscalchi's compelling characters and propulsive plot create a warm romance that goes down easily and does not hesitate to explore the difficulties of a cross-cultural relationship." ***Kirkus Reviews***

"Giovanna Siniscalchi scripts scenes that will make readers feel they are there in person—drinking the full-bodied wine, feeling the port's luscious burn, smelling the lemon trees." ***The Chick Lit Cafe***

"Rich historical detail, vibrant prose, and engaging relationships." ***Booklife***

Dedication

To my unwavering family whose love and support have illuminated my path as I navigate the realms of story-telling, thank you for always believing in me. To the incredible readers who embraced "The True Purpose of Vines" and continued this journey with me, your faith and patience inspire me every day. And to Gareth, whose expert editing hands sculpted this tale, any re-maining mistakes are mine. With gratitude and heart-felt appreciation, this book is dedicated to all of you who have made "The Truth About Myths" possible.

Prologue

Ajuda Palace, Lisbon 1860

T he garden door was enchanted. Isabel's mother used to say it granted a princess her heartfelt wishes. As a ten-year-old, Isabel should have stopped believing in myths. She was, after all, at that season in life where princesses shed fantastical beliefs like trees dismiss leaves before fall. Still, Isabel clung to hers, each a ticket to the past, a thread of memory she had no intention of letting go.

Enchanted or not, the door was exquisite. While closed, light filtered through the stained glass, pooling over the aquamarine tiles. When opened, it framed the queen's secret garden, an invitation to explore the exotic fruits and flowers.

Isabel clapped her hands twice and pirouetted, the necessary ritual for wishes to come true, and closed her eyes firmly.

I wish to see them.

Tugging her governess' hand, Isabel crossed the threshold.

Ripened peaches and wet earth perfumed the air. Feathery leaves swayed to a gentle breeze. Isabel skipped through the fountain and the oriental pagoda straight to the pond. Mist floated above the lake. Their calling drew near. Shielding her eyes, Isabel peeked at the sky. They lived there between the clouds and all that blue—a castle of ice and feathers, where all the boys were princes and waltzed with princesses to the tune of heavenly chords. Once upon a season, they visited her in the garden.

Swinging her straw basket, Isabel scanned the line of trees. "Where are they?"

The governess glanced behind them and tapped her foot on the grass. Poor Marion hated to stand. It made no sense, as Isabel knew it was impossible to die while standing. When her mother and father died, they were lying on their beds.

Isabel whistled as her brother had taught her, then clutched her pinafore, waiting for a reply.

Pitter patter. A splash. A duck left the gnarled oak. Flapping its white wings, it entered the lake and glided toward Isabel.

Sighing, Isabel dipped her hand into the basket for the bread. "Can we come every day?"

"Oh dear, your schedule is full."

The ducks came only once a year. She couldn't miss their visit. "At least while they are here, please?" Isabel curled her lips into her most winsome smile.

The governess sighed an enormous sigh. "If I consult the French teacher, he could arrange for the art history lessons to begin later—"

"Thank you!"

Isabel hugged the governess, the scent of church incense making her nose twitch.

The duck paused below the willow's leaves, mere feet from Isabel, and arched its neck. Eager for a closer glimpse, she stumbled forward.

The governess held her arm. "My, such excitement will see you dunked. A lady should learn restraint."

Cooing gently, Isabel chose the softest part of the bread. "Do you think it's a girl?"

"It's just a duck, dear."

Isabel huffed. Just a duck? To Isabel, she was a lovely princess, owner of silvery dresses and tiaras. "I'll call her Alva."

With a swish, a drake landed in their circle. Big, bulky, and brown, it flung itself atop Alva, shanks digging into her folded wings. Alva protested, trying to unseat the brute, but it chomped on her delicate neck with its red bill.

"The beast will kill Alva." Isabel shooed and shrieked, to no avail. Lifting her hand high, she hurled bread missiles at the demon duck.

Crumbs peppered his ugly feathers, but the drake shrugged them away. Beady eyes glittering, the duck pounded its tail in quick motions. Poor Alva tried to resist, shaking her wings, but he forced her head down until her crown vanished under the water.

Out of bread, Isabel grabbed her governess's hand. "Marion, do something, please. Alva will drown."

The governess shook her head, eyes the size of her brother's tennis balls. "Come, the piano master must have arrived."

"No!" Isabel vaulted into the pond, her feet sinking into the mud. Before she could reach the evil duck, the beast jumped from Alva's back, leaving the poor creature disheveled and no doubt bruised. Cackling, the drake flaunted his wings menacingly. Isabel stared, open-mouthed, cold water seeping into her pinafore as the drake stalked another victim.

Marion pulled her from the pond. Limbs lax, Isabel let herself be dragged away.

"I'll go for Luis. My brother will know what to do. That animal is mad—"

The governess dug her fingers into her arms. "His Majesty is extremely busy—"

"I will speak with my brother." She spoke through clenched teeth and stomped her feet. "You can't stop me."

A flush rose on the governess's round cheeks. "You must forget about the ducks. Oh, don't you see? This is nature's way of... They were mating."

Chapter 1

Lisbon, twelve years later

"The excess of a virtue is a vice." Greek Proverb

"Dear clock on the wall, if you don't speed your turns, tonight you'll sleep without a cog," Isabel muttered under her breath and tore her gaze from the ornery Swiss piece. Facing her audience, she affected a warrior pose, bracing her feet and inflating her chest. "Who am I?"

"I know!" Lady Philipa said, bouncing on the upholstered settee. "Artemis, Goddess of the Hunt."

There. This was fun. A quiet night with her maids of honor, tucked into her private wing, playing games...Who needed her brother's revelries? "Close, but no," Isabel said.

"Give us another hint." Lady Anne Daun clapped her hands, a smile lighting up her gentle blue eyes.

Isabel tapped her chin. What else could she say without spoiling the fun? Before she could think of the next clue, discordant notes invaded their privacy. It sounded suspiciously like an orchestra warming up. Not fair. How could she compete with professional musicians? Clenching her hands, Isabel raised her voice, hoping no one else had noticed it. "I lived in the Middle Ages."

Lady Dolores rose from the settee. "Ha! The hero of the Great Navigations—Vasco da Gama."

Isabel lifted her brows at her youngest maid-of-honor. "Dear, the game's name is Guess the Powerful Woman."

Dolly pouted, patting her blond curls and fluttering her eyelids. "Oops."

The orchestra turned louder. Her ladies talked in parallel, glancing at the door. Isabel was losing their attention. No, she refused to forfeit this battle.

Frantically, she gazed at the drawing-room walls, searching for a distraction. Light glinted off the ancient coat of armor. Thinking fast, Isabel raided the steel knight for a breastplate.

Sorry, El Cid, but my brother has an orchestra.

Donning the rusty protection, she cleared her throat. The famous quote came to her in a flash of memory. "They admonished me to adopt feminine clothes. I refuse. As for other duties of women, there are plenty of other women to perform them."

Her ladies-in-waiting eyed her from their perches, their eyes round, their murmured voices punctuated by the tick-tick of the Swiss clock. Lady Dolores yawned.

As a last resort, Isabel went to the hearth and placed her foot inside. "Oh, please don't burn me. God sent me to make France independent from English tyranny."

"Joan of Arc," Lady Anne Daun said.

Isabel laughed. "You are very right."

Everyone clapped.

The music outside turned louder.

Philipa glanced at the door, her embroidery forgotten. "What do you suppose they are doing tonight?"

Dancing, smoking, drinking, making illicit assignations... Who knew what else? Her clique of maids of honor was the crème de la crème of Portuguese society. With her guidance, they would set the standard for high morals, and no group of carousing rakes would corrupt them. "Nothing appropriate for unmarried ladies, I assure you."

"I heard His Majesty invited Madam Gardenia to sing. She canceled her nightly performance just to indulge him," Dolly said in a stage whisper.

Ohs and *Ahs* burst from all around the room. Isabel hoped her brother's taste for music was all the virtuosa indulged.

Dolly smiled wistfully. "I would die to meet Signorina Gardenia. We have so much in common. Messier Dumas told the world she was the best soprano, and Vermeil said my nose is Portugal's most beautiful, well, nose."

When Vermeil painted Dolly's portrait last season and uttered such an epithet, he did Dolly a disservice. She didn't need her already-inflated vanity pushed to new heights.

A churchly silence descended upon the room. Competing with a world-class opera singer was unfair. The lantern clock chimed the half hour. Still half-past nine? Isabel glared at the offending piece, promising swift retribution. Glancing away, she released a strained breath. She could keep the ladies here until ten o'clock. Then they would retire, safe for the night.

The music got louder, the soprano reaching the aria's allegro.

Dolly perked up. "What if we went there... Just for a peek?"

The ladies dithered in their seats as if they all needed to visit the garderobe.

Why would they want to mingle with her brother's court? Rakes, liberals, artists, foreign *bon vivants*... Isabel could imagine their ranks closing in on her private rooms, like wolves circling prey, sniffing fresh meat. Instead of being thankful for her protection, her ladies had sullen looks on their faces, as if Isabel had kept them from a tasty treat.

A knock at the door brought her heart to a stuttering halt. Isabel rose, half expecting a drunken fellow to breach their retirement.

The equerry bowed deeply. "Your Highness, the queen wishes a word."

Queen Maria Pia of Savoy swept into the room. The blue and white of her ball gown accentuated her dark hair and fair skin. Still, why not adopt Portugal's colors?

The company of ladies curtsied. Black eyes shining feverishly, the queen waved her hand in dismissal and glided to the windows, where the heavy drapery allowed some privacy.

Isabel pitied her new sister-in-law. Settling in a foreign court was challenging. To make matters worse, her brother continued his dissolute ways. While she loved Luis dearly and respected him as her king, she could not help but fret. Yesterday, she had witnessed a terrible scene between the royal couple. She didn't want the same fate and would avoid marriage for as long as possible. Like all of history's powerful women—Queen Elizabeth I, Joan of Arc, Cleopatra—Isabel would remain unwed. With her fortune and influence, she could do charity, set an example of morality, and do her best for Portugal.

Isabel lowered her gaze respectfully. "Your Majesty."

The queen had calmed herself, but her smile was strained and did not reach her eyes. Could it be true? Was her brother unwilling to visit the queen's bedchamber? But why?

"I thought we were going to enjoy your presence tonight," the queen said, gazing at her fingernails.

Isabel deployed expression number three, gentle but resolute. During her years on public display, she'd learned to control her facial movements, maintaining a refined and poised demeanor no matter the situation. With a subtle brow lift, she could convey an appreciation of flattery, greet newcomers, show mild displeasure, and even refuse rancid sardines. One never knew the well-meaning presents a subject offered their princesses. "I apologize, but I must wake up early for my weekly visit to the orphanage. The girls would love it if you could come—"

"How adorable. But I don't rise before noon."

"Of course. How could I have forgotten?" Isabel sighed, crossing her arms above her chest. "You requested to speak to me. May I help you?"

Hurt flickered in the queen's eyes. "About last night, what you saw in my bedchamber..."

Isabel clasped her sister-in-law's gloved hands and pressed affectionately. "Is there anything I can do? I could—"

The queen yanked her hand away. "Just be sure to keep your mouth shut." Queen Maria's nostrils flared, her eyes flashing. She grabbed her skirt and stormed out of the alcove.

Isabel watched her leave the room, worrying her lip between her teeth.

Her ladies circled her, not even ashamed of their eavesdropping.

"Oh, that Italian is cruel. She is only jealous of you because you are so popular." Lady Philipa tittered, her chin trembling. "And prettier."

Isabel lifted her palms and bade them back to their chairs. "That Italian is our queen, Philipa."

At least the appearance had diverted them from the party. Still, the room had turned quiet. Too quiet.

"Where is Lady Dolores?"

The clock started beating the tenth hour. Isabel glared at the offending piece. *Now you will do it?*

Lady Anne accompanied Isabel to the door. "Dolly meant nothing untoward."

"I know she didn't. I'm sure she is just peeking at the opera singer from the ballroom's fringes. Still, I better go retrieve her."

"Isabel," Anne said, "what the ladies want..."

She caught Isabel's hands and stared into her eyes as if she had an important thing to say and couldn't fathom where to begin. As if Anne already knew how something momentous would play out. Was it because of her marriage to the Count of Almoster last summer? Though Anne was three years younger than Isabel's twenty-two, married women regarded themselves as the keepers of a coveted wisdom denied to maidens. No... Anne's earnest blue eyes held no conceit, just concern. It reminded her of Fernando, Isabel's deceased brother. He, too, had this foresight aura about him. Her new friend and her favorite brother shared another trait—the rare inclination to do right no matter the personal cost.

Tears clogged her throat, and Isabel forced a smile to dispel the gloom. How she missed Fernando. With a heavy sigh, Isabel pressed Anne's hands affectionately. "What?"

Anne shook herself and took a step back. "Just be careful."

"Always." Isabel smiled reassuringly. "Please stay and hold the front."

Isabel started in the ballroom's direction, pushing the strange interaction from her mind. She knew Dolly meant well. If she had too many hearts in her eyes and nothing in her head, it wasn't her fault. Poor Dolly. Her father had abandoned the family to live with a courtesan, and the mother had died of a broken heart.

The music got louder, string notes interspersed with laughter and clinking glasses. A volume littering the carpet caught Isabel's attention. When she bent to retrieve it, a gasp escaped her lips. A collection of Sappho's poems. The Greek poetess' work had resurfaced a few years before and caused a furor. Several countries had forbidden it.

Looking at both sides to assure herself she was alone, she opened it, half expecting exotic dancers to tumble out, wiggling their hips and shaking their cymbals.

"With sweet myrrh oil worthy of a queen,
you anointed your limbs..."

Cheeks flaming, she ripped her eyes from the lines and searched the front matter. A scrawled dedication read, "My lovely porcelain Doll, meet me tonight."

She turned the book around and located a name—Charles Whitaker. She had never forgotten a rake, and that one she had seen several times in London. The Englishman, not much older than she, belonged to the Prince of Wales' set, partaking in his debauchery. What did he want with Dolly? As if Isabel didn't know. He would either rob her fortune or her virtue.

The book alone could ruin a girl's reputation. Isabel concealed it inside her skirt pocket and hastened through the dimly lit corridors. More than ever, she needed to find Dolly. Heart speeding, Isabel lifted the hem of her gown and maneuvered between the furniture.

A shadow shifted five paces ahead. The door to her mother's garden lay open, a soft breeze blowing through the curtains.

Foreboding rippled through her stomach, lifting the hairs on her arms. Isabel had avoided the garden since she let go of her childhood. What nonsense, she told herself. Her body is only aware of brute urges. Her conscience ruled her. Gingerly, she opened the glass panel.

Cool night air touched her cheeks with invisible hands. Moonlight washed the tiled floor, casting shadows over the pathways. A single cicada sang. Water flowed in a soothing cadence.

It took a few moments for her eyes to adjust to the darkness, but when they did, her steps faltered. The silvery leaves of an olive tree concealed the dark shape of a man. The stranger lounged on the fountain's rim, his frame so still he could be one of the statues. Isabel tiptoed closer and crouched behind the begonia bush. Could it be Mr. Whitaker? Waiting for an amorous tryst?

Wings flapped, the sound coming from the pond's direction. Isabel inspected the surface, unable to glimpse any feathered creatures. When she gazed back at the fountain, the stranger had disappeared. She bent over the rim, inspecting the rose bushes and the oriental pagoda—all empty.

"Where is he?" she muttered.

A smoky voice sounded behind her. "Who are we looking for?"

Isabel jumped, the top of her head colliding with an object as hard as marble. She lost her balance and flailed her arms, dreading the encounter with the chill water.

Something caught her waist, pulling her backward. With a swoosh, she landed on her posterior, her crinoline taking the brunt of the impact. Isabel blinked at the starry night, her breath stuttering. The petticoat moved underneath her. Gasping, Isabel rolled to the side.

A silhouette materialized on the floor.

It groaned.

Isabel's cheeks burned with mortification. She had felled a stranger. How... how undiplomatic of her. Well, he shouldn't have startled her in the first place. He unfolded himself to a considerable height. A garden torch cast flickering shadows over his full dress attire. He sported the black and white finery with the ease of one who wore it every night, unlike others who only succeeded in looking like overgrown penguins. When her perusal arrived at his face, jewel-blue eyes returned her gaze, the color made riveting by his tanned skin. His hair fell in waves over his ears and collar as if windswept, the style too messy. She preferred the neatness of the pompadour, but at least the dark color ruled out Charles Whitaker.

"Pardon me. It's not my custom to startle fountain sprites." His voice belonged in the opera, not singing the heroic tenor, but graver and more velvety, like the seductive baritone who always tried to steal the heroine.

The stranger bowed and offered his arm. He seemed contrite, and it had been an accident, so Isabel used expression number five, meaning she was mildly aggravated but willing to forgive, and allowed him to help her stand. A little shaken by the stranger's regard, she smoothed her skirts. They were considerably less weighty.

The book! It must have slipped during the fall. Biting her lip, she scanned the tiles.

Lo and behold, the volume lay sprawled near the begonias, less than two feet from her. Her determination flared, and she reached down, her fingers poised to grasp it. Swift as a meddling hawk, the gentleman swooped in. His gloved hand met hers in a burst of electric energy. He came out with the prize, and Isabel clenched empty fists.

While she mentally berated him for his sharp reflexes, he took his time bringing the proof of Dolly's indiscretion to the front of his nose.

Isabel swallowed a groan.

A devilish grin transformed him into an overly handsome satyr.

Who had dimples like that? A hazard, they were. One could get lost inside them. She bet many did. The humane thing to do would be to send an expedition. Women must be trapped there, dazzled. They were lured within and vanished without a trace.

Lowering the book, he aimed his gaze at her, raking her from the hem of her gown to the braids crowning her head. His demeanor changed from solicitous to speculative. It didn't take telepathy to see the wheels turning in his head. He found a lady alone carrying erotic tales. What would he do next? Assume she was fair game?

He gave her no alternative but to use her expression number seven, the one she'd been grooming to repel rakes. Lifting her chin as high as it would go, which was a lot given her flexible neck muscles, she looked down at him. Well, she pretended to look down at him, his lofty height making it deuced uncomfortable.

He tilted his head to the side, unaffected by her efforts. "Have I died? Are you here to take me to my heavenly abode? If so, lead the way, lady knight."

Isabel's chin dropped to her chest, and she stifled a groan. Why in Athena's name had she not removed the breastplate? "I played charades. The armor was part of my costume."

"I see... What were you? Penthesilea, the Amazon queen?"

"Joan of Arc," she said, hoping the martyr would cloak her in respectability.

"Saintly Joan carrying Sappho's poems... Interesting."
He shrugged and leaned back over the garden wall.
"Should we play a charade for your real name?"

He had not recognized her, even though her life-sized
portrait crowned the gallery not a hundred paces from
here. But the light was dim, and she wasn't wearing
her tiara. Perfect. She would just retrieve the book and
leave.

Isabel sucked in a breath, but before she could speak,
he placed his finger atop her lips. "Don't tell me. Are you
one of the princess' Vestal Virgins?"

Beneath his touch, her face flushed. Did they call her
court The Princess' Vestal Virgins? "How dare—"

"Did you leave Olympus on a night of revelry? I can't
say I blame you. And if you ask nicely, I might be of
help. Gardenia's performance was quite entertaining,
but I'll make an exception for a lady in need."

This was getting out of hand. She gritted her teeth.
"Your Excellency—"

"Call me Henrique. I don't stand on formalities." He
shrugged his broad shoulders, flaunting protocol with
the same ease he flaunted his... his taunting male grins,
and expertly cut male clothes, his male squinting eyes,
and his gravelly, absurdly low male voice.

"Pity. I do." Isabel presented her hand, palm poised
up. "I require the book. Now."

He seemed taken aback by her curt reply but then
gazed at the cover. "Is it everything the critics claim?"
Frowning, he flicked through the pages until one
caught his interest. A devilish smile lit his face. "Come
to me and loosen me from blunt agony. Labor and fill
my heart with fire."

The words brushed against her, the breastplate no
protection against such intimacy.

He closed the book. "I can see the appeal."

"It's not mine," Isabel blurted and cringed. Why explain herself to this man?

He studied her. "It isn't yours, but you want it back?"

Isabel raised her brows. "At least your observation skills are better than your literary taste."

He chuckled, and the sound lifted pinpricks on her skin. "Thank you. I'm proud of my senses. Especially touch."

Isabel crossed her arms above her chest. "Careful. Words enlighten the spirit, while the senses can lead you astray."

He came closer. "I've been allowing the senses to lead me astray for a long time now, but I would gladly give you the reins."

Was this the sort of banter that enthralled other ladies? "You should return to the opera singer, Your Excellency. Your company is quite tedious."

"Ouch." A rakish grin lit up his swarthy face. "The princess is doing us a favor by keeping you locked away. Your tongue can crumple a male's pride."

Isabel ground her teeth so hard her jaw hurt. She didn't imprison her ladies. She protected them from males like him! "If your pride can crumble so easily, then it was not much to begin with, was it?"

His chin dipped low, and he lifted his dashing eyebrows. "Do you blame the moonlight? Or is my presence enough to ignite such passion?"

"I don't allow passion to rule me."

"I know passion when I see it. Right now, it is staring at me with flaming green eyes."

Controlling her breaths, Isabel pretended to clean a speck from her bodice. "Flaming? Sir, your senses are running ahead of you again. Where you see fire, there is only ice. Nothing you do or say affects me."

"No?" His gem-like eyes sparkled, and he bent forward.

His cheek brushed against her, the bristles of his stubble tickling her skin. Locking a gulp of air in her lungs, she mentally slapped her hand. Why provoke a reposing rake? Warmth wafted from him in waves, and her nostrils flared at the citric spice of his cologne. His gaze drilled into hers, consuming her space. Unnerved but unwilling to lose the advantage, she stared right back. A mistake. Up close, the curves drawn into his irises had a hypnotic symmetry—a maze seen from above. One more inch, and they would trap her.

Pulse speeding, she arched her back. "Release me."

Her glance shifted from his bottom lip to his heavy-lidded eyes. Quite suddenly, he dipped his nose to her collarbone and sniffed her—neck to earlobe—waking up the down covering her skin.

"Are you sure, Joan?"

She was sure her heart had become a treacherous belly dancer, as it literally danced in her belly. "Yes?"

"I'm not holding you." He stepped back.

The heat engulfing her vanished, replaced by the drafty air.

Disoriented, Isabel blinked once, twice. Indeed, he wasn't. Then how? She had felt trapped by him as clearly as if he had woven a web of crystal threads around them. Was it all in her head, an illusion? Or did he possess a hidden power of seduction?

He eyed her expectantly, smirking, and she realized he had proved his point. How easily he affected her.

"Keep the book." Clutching her skirts in her clammy palms, she brushed past him.

He grabbed her arm, his black-gloved hand shockingly hot. Isabel sucked in a breath.

His eyes twinkled mischievously, and he placed the book into her hand. "You should read a few verses, little Joan. Perhaps it can thaw ice maidens."

Her wrist tingled where he touched her, and she jerked free from his hold. Panting, at a loss for a proper set down, she watched as he swaggered away.

Chapter 2

"Never let a fool kiss you, or a kiss fool you." Joey Adams

"What you did yesterday put your reputation at risk," Isabel said, sitting on her bedchamber window seat. A woman's reputation compared with a Fabergé egg, precious and, once broken, irreplaceable.

Dolly poured forth sobbing excuses, but Isabel could not face her. Had she not placed herself at risk too?

The chilly north wind invaded the bedroom, ruffling Isabel's hair. Lisbon stretched out in front of her, its red roofs and whitewashed buildings crowding the Tagus bank. Relentless, the gale shook the pines and the cypresses, making the river surface crisp like a startled cat. Suppressing a shiver, Isabel shut the window. The night encounter had left her a tad brittle. Thankfully, her agenda included only a photo for the newspaper and a public building inauguration.

Dolly had stopped crying and now wrung her hands, rubbing her lovely nose. "The book isn't mine. I swear I went only to get a peak of the singer, Your Highness."

"Of course, I trust you will practice restraint from now on."

The book was still inside her drawer. The verses didn't interest her in the least. She simply didn't have the opportunity to burn it, that's all.

Sighing, Isabel traced the rosewood of her escritoire. Dolly's singsong tirade faded into the background, cut off by that man's voice. Gravely and low. As if Sapho had conjured the perfect narrator for her erotic poems. He was dangerous. Isabel had misjudged her own susceptibility. She couldn't name the symptoms, possibly because she hadn't felt them before—a lack of breath, an awareness of one's own heartbeat... And the heat? As if embers had been strapped to the tip of her ears. Isabel shuddered and covered the evidence with her palms. No one was immune to a rake's charms. Not even her. She needed to be more vigilant.

Her lady's maid approached and climbed atop the stool, lifting Isabel's petticoat above her head. Pink slippers peeped from beneath the hem of her austere gray gown. "Mind the coiffure, *s'il vous plait*, Citizen Isabel."

Isabel's gaze strayed to the other ladies and then back to the French maid. "Sophie, not when there is an audience," she whispered.

Today, Isabel hadn't the stamina to deal with Sophie's political inclinations. Sophie was... Well, there wasn't a nice way to say it. She was a Republican. Sophie's family had a long lineage of French rebels, but tragically, they had all perished during Bismarck's siege of Paris. Others might consider it imprudent to keep a Republican close, but in Sophie's defense, she had delicate hands, and Isabel's scalp was excruciatingly sensitive. Once, her mother's staunch royalist maid braided Isabel's hair so tightly that tears streamed from her eyes. And Sophie's loyalty transcended political regimes, so the French Republican stayed.

"Your Highness," Sophie said, her lips curling.

Nodding, Isabel lifted her arms. The crinoline passed over her torso to settle at her waist. Sophie did the buttons, and then three more layers of petticoats landed over the cage.

All this, the dress ceremony, the protocols, the ladies, and the servants, and all her entourage, and charities, and obligations—they were valid and genuine and made sense. Until, at odd moments, a shiver coursed through her, like water scraping from the riverbed to show the rocks beneath, revealing an unpleasant truth she would rather not see. After a minute or two, the current rushed out again, and all was normal, as it should be.

While Isabel adjusted the front fastenings of her corset, Sophie retrieved Worth's latest delivery. Isabel's ladies-of-honor halted their chattering, and a hush fell over the silk-paneled bedroom.

Helped by Sophie, Isabel donned the gown and posed before the Venetian mirror, turning to check her profile. The green accentuated her eyes, and the bodice hugged her torso without revealing too much skin or curves. The colors were flattering yet demure. Why had the gentleman perceived passion in her? Why was she even worrying about it? He must speak the same lines to every woman he meets.

Her tiara had been returned from the goldsmith, and she placed it over her hair. More than the sparkle of the princess cut diamonds, she relished the slight weight atop her head. If she'd had it yesterday, the rake would not have dared to... She wasn't sure what he did, but he certainly would not be so effective in doing it.

"Your photograph will be on the first page of the newspapers tomorrow. Every baroness, countess, and duchess will want a Worth dress for herself," Philipa said, fussing over the gown's train.

Isabel shrugged. To influence her subjects with what was inside her, she needed to impress them with what was outside. "Remind me to use a local dressmaker next time."

The footman opened the door, and the equerry entered, bowing at the waist. "Your Highness, His Majesty requests your presence."

Isabel stood by the music room, composing herself before talking to Luis. What could he want with her? She hoped it didn't involve the queen. A cello overture spilled from the half-opened door. The mellow notes of Saint-Saens' *Carnival of the Animals* filled the corridor as they did when they were children. If she closed her eyes, she could see her brothers wrestling atop the old chaise, feeding the parrots, talking about the day's lessons. The scents of tobacco and beeswax tickled her nose, the same as when she skipped through the palace's corridors, the youngest of five siblings. More than a princess, she had been the only girl, a friend, an accomplice, a sweet stealer... Only Luis and she remained, Mother and Father long gone, two brothers lost to typhus, one to an assassin. Isabel brushed away a stray tear. They either learned to live with death or died trying to live a lie. Life was fickle, and passions were only passing storms. True meaning could be found only in a person's deeds to her country, in her legacy.

Gliding inside, she placed her hands on the closed piano. "You still keep your elbow too high."

Luis stopped playing and rested the bow on his knee. "A man has only so many things under his control."

"You requested my presence?"

"I wanted to see you, yes." He took an envelope from the side table. "This arrived for you."

She picked the heavy vellum from his outstretched hand. "An invitation?"

"Our cousin Rafaela is having a party at her summer residence in Comillas, on the Spanish seaside."

Isabel traced the gilded letters. "I haven't seen her since she married Lord Canastra. It is a kind offer, but I must send my regrets."

"Why the prompt refusal? It's a lovely opportunity to escape the Court and enjoy a waterfront resort. Mingle with people your age."

The hospital, the orphanage... She couldn't indulge in a vacation and leave her duties behind. Isabel had helped double Lisbon's institutions, but she wanted to build others in Oporto and Aveiro. If it depended on her, no Portuguese girl would remain on the streets, easy marks for exploitation. "I'm perfectly rested."

He narrowed his eyes. "I strongly advise you to go."

Why was he so adamant? Her summers had never concerned him. Could it be the queen who wanted her gone? Her chest contracted, and she bit her cheek to keep him from seeing her reaction. "I've barely arrived from England, and already you want to send me away?"

"I just thought it would be—"

"My presence here will help to... You know the royal family image is not the same after Mother's death." She refrained from blaming his lack of restraint and unsavory friendships. Marriage had failed to reform him.

His hand contracted over the cello's neck, and the strings groaned in protest. "I do what I can. I'm just a man."

"Except you are not." A rake could indulge in a life of passion. A king had to conform to a life of duty. Luis wanted both—an impossibility.

"I wish everyone could be like you. Some of us are human."

First, she hoarded Vestal Virgins, and now she was inhuman? Heat rose on her cheeks, and she flung the invitation at him. "Is that all?" Tossing her head, she grabbed her skirt to leave.

"Wait." He brushed his hand over his thinning blond hair. "I didn't mean to offend you. It's more than a vacation, all right? I need to gauge the mood of Spain's politicians. My refusal to be their king could have implications."

Two years before, the Spanish army had forced Queen Isabella II into exile. Their general invited her brother to be their King. Luis' denial came as a relief. The Spanish throne had the reliability of a quicksand pit. The Duke of Aosta, Queen Maria Pia's brother, had accepted the offer and moved from Italy to Spain to be their monarch. So far, he had one crowning achievement—he kept his head above his shoulders.

"What implications?" Isabel frowned.

"Nobody can read the aristocracy like you. Portugal's political instability is enough to rob me of sleep. I cannot deal with foreign threats." He exhaled loudly—the sound he made when defeated.

He dragged himself to Saint John's altar. Her mother had built the wooden devotional after the death of her heir. The Braganza's curse became an unwanted presence in their lives then. While peasant children behaved under the threat of werewolves and phantom Moors, she and her brothers had grown up dreading a friar's words—'No first son of their lineage will ever live to inherit the Portuguese throne'.

Isabel brushed her arms, suddenly chilled. She hated the curse, hated how it had made her mother sad, how she spent most of her free time trying to find the friar's grave so she could atone for their ancestor's sins.

Luis lit a candle. After crossing himself, he touched the Saint's feet. Her brother seemed tired, his face aged beyond his thirty-five years. Isabel hoped he didn't allow groundless superstitions to worry him.

Sighing, she clasped his hand. "You look terrible."

"You never looked better." He kissed her cheek. "I've missed you, Bel."

Warmth radiated from their joined fingertips, and she sighed, leaning her head over his shoulder.

"You are a Portuguese princess, but in this chess game, you are the queen. While a king has limited moves, one square at a time, you go wherever you wish."

She had to agree. Kings had to obey protocol. Their strategies were carried out by ineffective diplomats, who acted in their own interests. How many wars could've been avoided if women could interfere? "How should I use my influence?"

"To support my brother-in-law."

She gazed into her brother's eyes. Did he believe in the Duke of Aosta's capabilities as sovereign? Or did he support him because of family ties? Luis was her king, and she must accept his judgment.

Isabel retrieved the invitation, tracing her cousin's signature. A stay in Comillas was abrupt, but she couldn't shirk from duty. Plus, if she went to Spain, she wouldn't risk meeting the garden rake with his twinkling eyes again. Dolly, too, would be far from Charles Whitaker and his inappropriate literature.

"I must have total command of the trip. Including who accompanies me and how long we stay there."

Chapter 3

"It is absurd to divide people into good and bad. People are either charming or tedious." Oscar Wilde

The automobile sputtered two times and came to a dead halt at Santo Amaro Avenue. Pedestrians passed, turning their heads to gape at the vehicle. Henrique jumped out of the driving seat and opened the engine. The exhaust had clogged again. He pulled on his fob. Five-thirty. Forty minutes to fix it and arrive at the hotel in time for dinner. A minor setback wouldn't sour his mood. The evening demanded celebration. His business in town had been highly successful. The Italian count had made an exorbitant offer for his Braganza estate. Before embarking on the steamer to Liverpool, all that remained was to ask the king to sign the deed and say goodbye to his friends. He would tackle both tonight.

"Gardenia, thy mouth blooms in exquisite delight." Sprawled in the passenger seat, Dio pulled a pencil from his meticulously disheveled locks and scribbled on a notebook. "She loves my poems... Said I was her blond Byron." He smiled self-deprecatingly. "I'm glad she has no literary taste."

Henrique shook his head, laughing. Diomedes da Veiga, Marquess of Faial—assumed *bon vivant*, a passable poet, as entertaining when drunk as in a hangover... Of all Henrique's friends, he would miss him the most.

"She loves your money." Not that Henrique judged it. As long as both parties understood what they got from a relationship, they could enjoy themselves without the added burden of unfulfilled expectations. Henrique cleaned sweat from his forehead. "Can you give me a lift here?"

"Of course. How lazy of me." Dio straightened and looked at him, all seriousness. "You are the greatest scientist this country has ever known. Handsome, too, if a little long in the tooth. If those scurvy politicians ignore your work, the fault is in their shriveled minds. Is that enough, or should I write an ode to your twinkling blue eyes?"

"I'm thirty-two, hardly older than you." Henrique lifted his brows. "And I need a literal hand."

"I would lend it to you, but I cannot possibly do it without ruining my clothes." Dio leaned back and crossed his ankles. "Why did you leave the palace early last night?"

Henrique stopped rattling the manifold, gazing at nothing in particular. Mossy green, the Tagus River flashed at him from gaps in the two-story buildings. The color of the frosty lady's eyes. "I was ambushed by a dangerous species."

Dio sighed dramatically. "What was it this time? A nasty disease you spotted in your microscope?"

"This species is glaring to the naked eye, I assure you. They stalk their prey and disorient them, using their venomous tongue to administer the final blow."

Dio glanced at the Rocio square as if it were the Serengeti plains. "Do we have a loose viper in Lisbon?"

"Worse. A virgin." Virgins were a bachelor's natural predator. Especially a green-eyed one with a *retroussé* nose and a cutting wit. The temptation to prove how much passion she had underneath her breastplate had been so strong he almost forgot his vow to restrain his amorous conquests to the married variety.

Dio laughed. "One of the princesses' maids of honor? That's rich."

"Why does the princess keep them in chains?"

Dio avoided eye contact, polishing his nails on his superfine coat. "Some blame her time in Victoria's court. That it turned her into a prude. Others say she hates women. Who knows? She could be the priestess of a cult to the hymen."

Dio was being cryptic on purpose. If anyone knew about the princess, it was him. As the son of the Duke of Palmella, the country's top diplomat, he grew up with the royal brood... Until he refused a post as an attaché in Geneva to pursue his literary vocation and became his family's *bete noir*. No news there. In this country, you either followed your aristocratic father's footsteps, or you received said foot in the arse.

"Hymen cult? What nonsense."

"Careful, a feminist might call you a misogynist."

Of course not. Henrique loved women. "Society is misogynist. I'm merely prudent." He pointed at Dio with his screwdriver. "I find it hard to understand all the fuss around the hymen. Women cling to it as if it were their Achilles' heel, while men venerate it like the holy grail. The body possesses countless membranes, synovial, cutaneous, connective, mucosal... Among all those, society chose one to determine the fate of fifty percent of the population—the hymen. Is a one-inch membrane sealing the vagina more important than its five-foot owner? Nature tried to lock the vulva from bacteria, but it locked women in a lust-free prison."

Dio's face flushed bright red, and he glanced at the crowded street. "You love to squander scientific terms, don't you? Was she attractive?"

He shouldn't have mentioned the girl to Dio. The sudden light in his black eyes meant trouble. And Henrique didn't find her attractive. Too thin and stiff, she had swaddled herself to the neck with starched cloth and piled up her hair atop her head like chains. High-strung. That was the right word. High-strung like a mountain lioness. But then he witnessed her combustion. His provocation had been the catalyst for a thermal reaction. Her eyes... Her eyes burned.

She'd singed him.

If he was frustrated, it was not attraction but the futility of it all. Why should a healthy woman be kept from nature's pleasures? A ripe grape forcing herself to be a raisin? What a waste.

"I never saw your interests engaged so." Dio smoothed his goatee and eyed Henrique thoughtfully. "The muse came to you at last. Will you forget England? Will this *belle dame sans merci* settle your quest for meaning in life?"

Henrique scoffed. "If you are searching for meaning in life, you better find yourself a microscope." True happiness lay in hunting for pleasure and avoiding pain. All else was mental masturbation, and he much preferred the physical kind.

Henrique gave one last shove, and the engine sputtered awake. "If anything, it means I must leave with all haste."

By the time they neared their destination, Henrique had pushed thoughts of the green-eyed she-cat to the recesses of his mind. He breathed in the afternoon, the river's breeze mixed with the gas lamp's oil. Sunset shone copper on the mosaic walkway. The golden hour. When the hard-working city sighed, doffed its uniform, and went back home, while the fun-loving city yawned awake, donned its finery, preparing for the opera, the Fado taverns down the Aterro, the cabarets.

"Won't you miss Lisbon?" Dio asked, lifting his hat to greet the Count of Burnay. The older man stopped chatting with clients in front of his double business—Burnay Bank and the Havanesa House. "Where else in the world can a gentleman enter the bank, contract a loan, and, on his way out, buy Cuban cigars?"

"They have cigars in London." As Henrique watched people strolling, their faces illuminated by the last traces of sunset, an empty feeling swept his chest. Why this now? He had experienced Lisbon to its dregs, bedding all available women, tasting every wine and pleasure. Now, to ladies plenty and pastures new.

The church bells started their six o'clock toll as they climbed the steps to the Grand Central Hotel. When the old doorman opened the oak portal, a cough racked his torso.

Henrique reached inside his coat pocket and passed him a package of mints. "Here, Damião." Poor man suffered from the luxurious hotel's constant drafts.

His rheumy eyes lit up. "Oh, Your Excellency, always so kind. Your guests have arrived already."

"Did the chef manage the *paio* with peas?"

"It came all the way from Quinta do Lobo. The *Ananás* soaked in rum the whole day."

"Terrific. Same table?"

"Of course. Only the best for Your Excellency."

Henrique tapped Damião's bony shoulder and strolled over the crowded saloon to the separate room reserved for his dinner. A single candelabra cast shadows over the oak-paneled walls, adding to the cozy atmosphere. His friends occupied the round table. Griffin Maxwell and Pedro Daun were under the same roof, if not chatting amicably, at least tolerating each other. Whoever saw them like this couldn't guess that only last year they had been mortal enemies.

Pedro Daun clasped Henrique's shoulder, and Henrique pulled him in for a hug. It took a damn slave trader to make them close. Pedro dressed informally, a black velvet coat over a plain white shirt. At first glance, he seemed the same, with blond hair tied behind his neck, the old-world elegance that could turn into deadliness in a heartbeat. Still, after that horrible day at the bullfighting arena, his gaze was no longer haunted. Marriage to Maxwell's sister suited him.

"How's the sweet Anne?"

"Engaged with society functions."

Maxwell rose to greet him, his lean frame encased in the staid frock coat preferred by the British community. "Won't you ask about Julia?"

"I don't have to. I've seen your lovely wife today." Julia Costa blended the best port in the Douro, and he admired her tremendously. He had stopped at Maxwell's townhouse to give her one of his latest inventions, a steam machine to separate stems and seeds from grapes, reducing the wine's bitterness. Obviously, he omitted the business-like reason just to aggravate his friend.

Henrique ignored Maxwell's angry retort and turned to his last guest.

Charles Whitaker didn't bother to stand. He lifted his eyes from a full glass of Scotch and shook Henrique's hand distractedly. The lad also seemed different. And when Henrique sat by his side, and alcohol fumes didn't attack his nostrils, he understood why. Charles was sober.

Dio greeted the others and slouched by Henrique's left.

The waitress brought his favorite dish—*paio* with peas. He would miss the sausage filled with pig blood after he moved to England. While they attacked the food, they talked about wine specifically and politics in general. Henrique noticed with amusement that his friends avoided the subject of his departure with the same effort as the picky eater Maxwell avoided the *paio*.

After the plates were cleared, they covered the table with green baize. Pedro chose dice to begin their game night.

A few rounds later, thoughts mildly murky after a bottle of Vesuvio's Port and pockets considerably lighter, Henrique leaned back. "I should give up. I have the devil's luck tonight."

Maxwell collected his earnings, his gaze straying to the mantelpiece clock.

"I know my charms are feeble compared to the lovely Julia, but can't you keep your eyes on the table for a change?"

Maxwell bristled. "To watch your ugly face? Shut up and play."

Henrique would miss flustering the stoic Englishman. Finding another uptight friend who put up with his provocations would be a hardship.

Pedro Daun collected the dice. "I thought Dom Luis would be here tonight."

"He sent me a note. He will arrive later. Couldn't leave the palace before dinner." The man led a country and still had trouble leading his own household. He'd better come, though. Henrique needed the king's signature to conclude the sale of his estate.

Dio looked both ways and lowered his voice. "Rumors have it he does not visit the queen's bedchamber."

"Who told you so?" Pedro speared Dio with a stare.

Since Pedro became the king's chief adviser, his power in court had grown exponentially. Still, Henrique had high standards for after-dinner chat. "Why, I beg of you, did Luis' activity between the royal sheets creep into our conversation?"

Pedro gave each one of them an accessing gaze. All eyes were on him, except for Charles, who kept mumbling to his glass.

"The ministers are restless. Until Luis produces a male heir, the monarchy is vulnerable. His hold on the throne is secure while his popularity is high, but the populace is fickle."

"Another blight on the Braganzas," Dio said, lowering his voice and brushing his goatee. "The family is cursed."

Maxwell snorted. "What in Hades are you speaking about?"

Dio pulled in a long breath. "It all started with Dom João IV in the seventeenth century. He kicked a Franciscan who asked him for alms. The monk cursed the king, saying no male firstborn of the Braganza house would ever live to inherit the throne. Since then, all the firstborns of the dynasty died before they could rule. Dom João VI and his wife tried to revert the curse to no avail... They never found the monk's grave."

A moment of silence descended. Against his will, Henrique's thoughts climbed the royal family tree for the past two centuries, and in fact, he could not remember a single firstborn who had lived long enough to assume the throne. Dom Luis himself had been a second son, his older brother, raised to be king, had died when he was nineteen, forcing Luis into a commitment he neither wanted nor had been prepared for. Henrique couldn't fathom what had shocked Luis the most, the death of his brother or the need to give up his devil-may-care life in the navy.

"Curse or no curse, Luis better produce an heir soon. Otherwise, his reign is at risk," Pedro said, genuine concern weighing his voice.

Henrique wouldn't want to be in Luis's skin or other body parts, for that matter. Being discussed by his friends as if he were a stud? "I'm sure he will apply himself to it in due time. Now, did we come here to speak about the royal cock or play dice?"

Dio chuckled, and Maxwell wrinkled his nose at the crude joke. The seriousness dissipated, and the air of camaraderie returned.

"Seven." Pedro flung the ivory cubes. The lucky bastard hit a four and a three. "When do you plan to leave?"

"Next week. First, I need to conclude Braganza Castle's sale."

Maxwell shook his head, looking aggrieved. "You will dispose of the Princess Tower?"

"The Italian count will turn the property into a luxury hotel. He will even hire a writer to embellish the tower's myth."

At the word *princess*, Charles startled from his tête-à-tête with the untouched brandy glass.

Henrique turned to him, as Charles didn't know his estate's story. "According to legend, my ancestor used the tower to lock his wife in so she would not pester him over his mistresses. The gruesome tale will scare tourists, so the buyer will make it more romantic." Why didn't the medieval Penafiels keep their wives well-pleasured instead of in chains? Sad brutes, one and all. More intent on warring than lovemaking. Perhaps their wives were green-eyed vixens. The stray thought brought images of naked limbs, iron fetters, and much better uses for her sweet tongue. Cursing under his breath, Henrique swallowed the port.

Charles frowned and returned to the perusal of his glass. His shock of russet hair caught the light from the lamps as if his head had caught fire.

"Knowing these Italians, he will write an opera about it," Maxwell said, disgust seeping into his voice.

"Unlike you, I like a romantic story." What was the harm in giving the tower a happy ending?

Maxwell lifted his brows. "Just like that, you will sell the property and tamper with an age-old legend. Have you no love for our country?"

There. It took them two hours to breach the subject.

"Our country? First, you are British. Second, I am as patriotic as everybody else—I keep a flag stored in the attic. In the improbable event of war between Portugal and another nation, I will know who to cheer for. Third, I can't help it if I lack my friend's marital bliss. If I had Julia for a wife..."

"Leave Julia out of it."

Henrique grinned. "When will you forget it? It was a good-natured flirtation, nothing more."

The Englishman glared at Henrique. "I know your problem—Don Juan's fever. You have a pathological need to search for the ideal woman, chiefly among other men's wives. Like Don Juan, as soon as you attempt one, you flash your unrepentant smile, say, 'Sorry, my mistake', and move on. Acting like this in Spain, Don Juan tried one thousand and three."

Henrique laughed, lifting his palms. His conquests weren't so numerous. "What can I say? As a scientist, I must apply a method of trial and error. One day, the system will prove effective, and I will find my better half."

Not that he was in a hurry. Of all types of love, men and women could only share one. Eros, alias lust. But lust, like any combustible, flared brightly and died quickly. In Aristotle's own words, the only lasting relationship was friendship. Friendship only existed between equals, something women and men were not.

Pedro Daun rolled the dice between his fingers. "Chasing your fated mate is pointless. When the timing is right, she will come to you. You are here at Chiado, and she may be in Ceylon. While you are the country's most celebrated scientist, she could be an exotic dancer. Like two armies charging a mountain pass, you are both irrevocably, irresistibly, marching one for the other."

Henrique gaped at Pedro. When had the cynic Count of Almoster developed such eloquence?

Maxwell grimaced. "Bank the stars in your eyes, will you? You are thinking about my sister, for Christ's sake."

Charles shot to his feet. "That's it! I won't let the prudish princess keep me from my dove. Goodbye."

Charles had been so quiet, Henrique forgot his presence. Charles Whitaker strode to the exit, his steps sure and his posture erect. Who would have thought he could walk in a straight line?

"What bit his ass?"

"I don't know who that was," Pedro said.

Maxwell frowned, staring at the door. "Charles is being most peculiar since the king's musicale. His father is worried. Asked me to look after him."

Dio rose and adjusted his coat. "I'll go with him. If his dove needs saving, who knows? She might have a friend or two in the same predicament."

Henrique watched both men leave and lifted his palms. "Listen, gentlemen. The fairer sex did not affect my immigration. Director of Oxford's Life Sciences studies? How could I refuse?"

A commotion was heard outside their private room. The waiter opened the door and admitted Dom Luis, who strode to their table, bulky frame clad in civilian clothes. So he was not king tonight, but Dr. Tavares. He used the alias to take a breather from Court life.

Griffin made his excuses and rose. Pedro did the same and pulled the king to a corner. After some whispered words, he also left. Married sheep they were, no doubt their ladies awaited outside with their leashes.

Dom Luis enthroned himself in the armchair. He tugged his neckcloth and reached for the card deck. Henrique stifled a groan. If they started playing whist, Luis would get carried away, and Henrique would have better luck extracting a signature from the king of spades.

He took the estate deed from his briefcase and passed it to the king. "We should sign this before the brandy blurs the paper's lines."

The king ignored the documents, a flush rising on his fair skin. "No risk of that happening."

Why the reticence? The signature was a mere formality. A relic from the feudal system.

The king shuffled, gaze fixed on the cards. "I have a favor to ask of you."

"As the king or as Dr. Tavares?"

"As a friend."

"I'm listening."

The king exhaled through his mouth. "I need you to accompany my sister to Spain."

Henrique laughed. "Is this my surprise? Are there dancers hidden somewhere?"

"I'm not jesting."

"You cannot be serious. My ship sails next week."

"Postpone the trip."

And they wondered why he wished to leave? He could be one microscopic step away from finding the cure to typhus, and yet, his king wanted him as a babysitter. Henrique gripped the dice, pressing the ivory against his palms. "Why me? Ask for your equerry, or even better, Santiago." If the princess were the stickler for morality the rumors implied, she would appreciate the priest's company much more than his.

The king dabbed at his forehead with a handkerchief, his eyes going to the door and back to Henrique. "I can only trust you."

Trust. He should be flattered. The king or any of the country's politicians never recognized his research. Some sneered he shunned a public life to become a natural philosopher, no better than a sawbones in their narrowed minds. Henrique lifted his brows. "It's only Spain. What's the worst that can happen?"

"Since the Spanish queen was exiled and the army placed my brother-in-law on the throne, their political situation has deteriorated. That hapless Italian doesn't even speak their language. Their aristocracy is cooking something, and it is not paella."

First, the king's marital affairs, now this. And Henrique had hoped for a pleasant goodbye dinner. "You could have accepted the throne yourself. The Spaniards asked nicely."

Dom Luis straightened, his face turning somber. "My ancestors shed the country's blood to maintain Portugal's independence from Spain. If I had agreed to become their king, the next generation would see Spain and Portugal united. I cannot allow it. I wasn't coined for this." His gray eyes turned humid like they always did when he spoke about his deceased older brother. "No matter what happens, I will not be the king who loses Portugal's autonomy."

"If the Spaniards are troublesome, I have a much simpler solution. Keep your sister in good old Lusitania."

Glancing away, Luis tugged his cravat. "I... can't. You haven't met her. Isabel has a mind of her own."

"And you are king. Really, Luis, you shouldn't let the girl decide important matters." If Luis had put limits on this princess, she would not try to keep women in the Middle Ages.

Dom Luis snorted. "You don't live with them. My wife knows how I value punctuality. Do you know what she does? Runs late on purpose for every function requiring her presence. Not to mention her unbridled spending—"

"Women do not control my life because I don't give them the opportunity. You should try to be a king inside and outside your palace. My answer is no."

Dom Luis swept all semblance of friendliness from his face. He placed a hand over Braganza's unsigned deed and pushed it back to Henrique's side.

Henrique lowered his voice, gripping the port glass with enough force to shatter the crystal. If the king was not already cursed, Henrique would do it now. "Damn it, Luis. I won't be manipulated."

Crossing his arms above his chest, Luis lifted his brows in an imperious display of kingly demeanor. Dom Luis was more than willing to forget he was the king... as long as nobody else did.

Henrique drained the port. The liquid went down his throat with the ease of a struggling frog. "Curse you. I'll go. But I won't be ordered about by a spoiled princess. You'd better tell your sister who's in charge."

Henrique entered the Bacchus Club. Smoke clung to the wine-colored leather coaches like past patrons fighting for the best place. Sirens and satyrs frolicked over the arched ceiling. He found Dio lounging at his customary stool, scribbling on his notebook more fervently than usual.

Rolling the tension from his shoulders, Henrique massaged his temples. Worse than cheap brandy, the king's blackmail gave him a sour mouth and the devil's headache. But he wouldn't cry over the spilled experiment. What was done, was done. Henrique had a journey to plan, and Dio would have to help.

"I see you found your muse. Charles' Dove, perchance?"

Dio lifted his eyes from the paper. "No. I left him at the palace, of all places. Forget Charles. I decided on a subject for my literary masterpiece. I want to write Hercules' biography."

"What?"

"No, before you object, listen to this. I will do it in twelve cantos, heroic verses. It will be brilliant. I've penned the first stanzas already. It begins with our hero dwindling on a farm, raising bovines. He is visited by Lady Virtue and Lady Vice. They fight for his allegiance until he follows the path of greatness."

Henrique drummed his fingers over the bar, wondering how to stop Dio's nonsense about Hercules and breach the subject of Comillas. "The poor fellow should have stayed at the farm. What boon came from his toil? His only rewarding labor was the thirteenth."

"Hercules did only twelve."

"Chronologically, it should have been his job zero, but the Greeks lacked the concept of zero as a number. I'm talking about the impregnation of fifty girls in fifty nights while hunting lions. Before your man became a hero, he became a danger to the fathers of teenage daughters."

Dio laughed. Henrique shared his friend's mirth, and after the humor faded, he rubbed his hands and eyed him askance. Henrique only had to ask. Dio would pester him but would relent.

Dio pushed away from the bar stool. "You look like the proverbial horse manure. What's the matter?"

"I need you to take care of my bacteria."

Dio batted his eyelashes. "You flatter me, Your Excellency. I thought you would never ask."

"It's only for a few weeks."

"Aren't you moving to England for good? Why leave your research behind?"

Henrique sat on the bar and poured himself a liberal dose of port. "The king asked me a favor. I must become the princess' escort. Luis and his damn problems."

"He should count himself lucky... Modern-day monarchs only have to keep an eye on aggressive neighbors and ensure their subjects pay taxes. A king in Hercules' age had to deal with monsters roaming the countryside and the constant worry Zeus would rape his daughter—"

"Would you drop the mythological crap? This is serious. Luis blackmailed me into escorting the prudish princess to Spain, of all places, and avert some peninsular crises—"

"Spain? Crises?" Dio frowned, his heavy-lidded gaze lighting up. "This is your hero's call."

Dio could utter the most absurd nonsense with a straight face. Henrique didn't need a call, heroic or not. What should a fellow do in this country to get on with his life? Henrique massaged his forehead, the pain drilling into his skull. He was so close to finding a microorganism capable of killing typhus. "I came here to ask you to take care of my colony. They need to be fed twice a day and—"

"When I met you, just out of Sorbonne, you had this passion for science. A curiosity to know all about the world, including how we fit into it, the wholeness of nature, the harmony of its patterns... It's all in the past, isn't it? You've been complaining about ennui since that terrible business with Pedro Daun. This is your mythical awakening."

"The only thing resembling a myth in this is the Trojan horse Luis gave me as a farewell gift. After I'm back, I'll return to my plans." By God, if the princess turned out to be a bore of herculean proportions, he was doomed.

Dio snorted. "So typical. Every time a hero receives a call to action, he refuses. This is a chance to make your life interesting."

"You've been reading Hesiod? It makes you delusional."

"I don't know why you hate myths so... Mythologists and scientists are both in the same business—explaining cause and effect so people's lives can be more predictable. You explain wine as the nasty byproduct of yeasts digesting sugar. To me, wine is Bacchus' gift, a delicious elixir that helps humankind escape their worries." Dio tapped his chin with his aristocratic finger. "Who has the more captivating story?"

"Myths are nothing more than society's way of forcing poor males to do things they don't want to do in exchange for a transcendence that does not exist."

One had to wonder if the whole concept was not invented by females.

"And accomplish the greatest deeds humanity ever accomplished. Think about it. You could be our Portuguese Hercules."

Henrique gasped. He? A hero? "I fail to see the similarities."

"Hercules is prickly and proud. So are you."

Henrique would not bite Dio's bait. "Hercules' problem-solving skills are faulty. The chap is always ready to fall back on his core strength, which is, well, his strength. I shun violence."

Dio laughed. "Well... Your articulation has a mighty punch."

"Hercules is inconsiderate, willful, and impulsive. He will chomp something off first and see if he can chew it afterward."

"But his impulsivity is freeing. Whether Hercules is right or wrong, he is never uncertain." Dio wiggled his brows. "Existential fear is unknown to him."

Henrique had no existential fear. He had no fear. At all. "Dire traits in an ungovernable train." Henrique threw a cork, aiming at Dio's head.

Dio ducked before it could hit him. "True, but one thing you two have in common. Hercules is intelligent. He starts each of his labors with careful research—"

"Tricks from a trickster." Henrique sank into an armchair, suddenly tired. The weight of responsibility settled over his shoulders with the finesse of Hercules' clubbing. Tomorrow, he would escort a prudish princess up north. His heart sped up for no reason. Anticipating meeting Joan again? Nonsense. He had no interest in green-eyed viragos. Henrique stared at Dio, passing his hand through his stubble. His friend might pretend to be a dissolute poet during evening hours, but by daylight, his blood ran as blue as the sky. "What is she like?"

"The Princess?"

"No, the Hydra of Lerna. Of course, the princess. Who else? Is she a dried-up maid with long teeth and short-sighted views?"

Dio choked on his wine, coughing his lungs out. "I wouldn't put it into so many words, but as always, my friend, you have an interesting way of stating things."

"I knew it." Henrique groaned. It was just his luck. Spending his summer babysitting a shrew. "Will you take care of the bacteria or not?"

"Of course I will. Pack the nasty bugs! A hero needs a faithful companion, and today, my affair with Gardenia made the news. A spell away from Portugal will take my father off my heels. I'm coming with you."

Chapter 4

"They both distrust the advice of heaven; but what harm will it do to try?" Ovid, *Metamorphoses*

The Ajuda Palace's courtyard soaked up dawn's first sun rays. Outside the gates, the crowd awaited to see their princess off. Musicians entertained with mouth organs and concertinas. Hawkers sang of their fresh fruit, their voices rising above the swallows' excited chirps.

"Diomedes Da Veiga, I hate to keep my subjects waiting." Isabel tapped her boot on the graveled ground.

His eyes rounded in feigned innocence. "Why, Viscount Penafiel must have had an emergency, I assure you. His philanthropy knows no bounds. If you had lived here in the past four years, you would have known how people come from far and wide to ask for his help. I'm sure he is solving one of the world's greatest problems right now."

She eyed him askance. Could it be true? With Diomedes, one couldn't be certain. Still, she loved science, and a dutiful subject was an asset to his country.

"Perhaps I'm lucky Luis found me this paragon." She chanced a peek at Viscount Penafiel's entourage—a black lacquered Landau and three Lusitano horses.

The chestnut stallion stomped his hooves, no doubt more impatient to start the trip than Isabel. Why had she not thought to bring her mare from Mafra Palace? Riding would undoubtedly make the carriage portion of the journey to Comillas livelier.

"Indeed, you are, your Highness." Diomedes bowed, and a smile lifted the corner of his lips.

"Do you know him personally or just his fame as a scientist?" She grew up with Diomedes, but that didn't change the fact he was a rake. If Viscount Penafiel frequented the same fast set, he must be cut from the same cloth. Nothing would be worse than spending her summer with a dissolute escort, no matter his scientific accomplishments.

Diomedes sighed. "Hardly. Viscount Penafiel wouldn't deign to frequent the same shady places I do."

Her shoulders came down a notch. "Is it true he is a polymath?"

"Gospel truth, my dear."

"What type of scientist?"

"Exactly the one you are thinking of."

Isabel smiled. "With a lumpy beard, thick glasses, and hair sticking out from his head?"

"You bet he is. Funny chemical smells adore him, and he doesn't survive outside the lab without his case of experiments and potions."

"And is he old?"

"Definitively. A cantankerous old man, he is. Likes to grumble and has bouts of moodiness..." Dio eyed the gate, furrowing his blond brow. "And sleeps late in his dotage, it seems."

Isabel nodded, relieved.

Another thirty minutes passed, and no one arrived.

Isabel could no longer wait. "Tell the Viscount he can meet me midway."

Diomedes frowned. "Why the haste? What if you forgot a bauble or two?"

"I've all I need," she said pointedly. For the past week, she had prepared herself for this mission. She studied history, from the rise of the Spanish Empire and the death of the last Habsburg monarch to the first Bourbon to assume the throne, the Napoleonic invasion, and Queen Isabela's forced abdication two years before. She went to sleep early and woke before dawn to ensure everything would be done correctly.

Clicking her tongue, she called for Sophie and Dolly to enter the coach. Dio caught her hand in his. Isabel lifted her brows. Lean, with tight blond curls and soulful black eyes, he was a very handsome man. Still, while all of society looked at him as prime groom material, she only saw the gangly youth who had pulled her braids when she was ten.

"He will arrive, I assure you."

"The time for reassurances ended fifteen minutes ago."

"What about your brother? Won't he object if you take off by yourself?"

Luis valued punctuality, too. And she didn't mean to pull rank, but a viscount shouldn't leave a princess of the realm waiting. Not even an old scientist. It was not done.

She had placed her feet on the stool to climb atop the carriage when a honking made her pause. The crowd lining the palace gate parted, their cheers obliterated by a blaring horn.

A dreadful roaring came next. The horse flanking her coach pranced and reared, almost toppling the cavalry guard.

Isabel craned her neck to see the motive of such a ruckus. An automobile sped through the driveway, lifting pebbles in its wake. She had seen the fanciful model once, in possession of a railroad magnate in London.

A gentleman occupied the burgundy bench. He drove, eyes protected by green-tinted glasses, a red scarf flying behind him like a castle's pennant, his gloved hand gripping the wheel, a wicked smile on his lips.

Isabel clutched her parasol as a fuzzy feeling invaded her stomach.

The coupé vehicle came to a screeching halt, blocking the exit.

Dolly gaped at the man, her fair cheeks turning crimson. "Oh, my. I think this is my cue to swoon..."

Sophie's eyes rounded, and a little sigh escaped her mouth. "If all aristos are *beau gosse* like this, the Republican cause is hopeless. *Totalement désespérée.*"

The stranger approached their small group. His dinner jacket and wine-colored silk vest were mussed. No doubt the same clothes he had worn the night before.

He took off his glasses and hat. Isabel blinked several times.

It was the garden rake!

Her back went straight as a rod, and Isabel gasped. "What is he doing here?"

Diomedes laughed. "And this, my lovely Isabel, is your stuffy old escort."

Chapter 5

Twenty minutes before...

"The natural desire of good men is knowledge."
Leonardo da Vinci

H enrique drove through Ajuda's crowded streets, pitying the poor sods who climbed out of their warm beds to glimpse a woman just because she carried a crown on her head and blue blood inside her veins.

Henrique felt his grip tightening on the wooden wheel and forced his muscles to relax. Princess or not, she was a woman like all others. How hard would it be to woo her a little? After living cloistered her whole life, she must be starved for male attention. Charm and finesse could go a long way to convince her to curtail this blasted trip.

Soon, he would be back in Portugal and his plans. With this gratifying thought, he halted outside the palace's gates, honking to alert the guard of his presence.

The crowd opened, revealing a courtyard filled with nickering horses, traveling coaches, and humbled servants. His heart picked up speed, anticipating seeing fiery Joan, but he squelched the perspective. When he asked Dio if the ladies-in-waiting would accompany them to Spain, his friend told him the princess had dismissed them so they could return to their country abodes for summer. Some people had all the luck.

Henrique parked the car, blocking the aligned coaches. A trio gathered in front of the royal carriage. Dio waved at him, his expression relieved. A plump blond girl tumbled out of the coach, her eyes openly admiring him. If this were the princess, Henrique would accomplish his goal with minimal effort.

She curtsied, bending her torso until the ostrich feathers on her bonnet licked the ground.

Sparks flashed behind her.

Frowning, Henrique vaulted from the driver's seat, riveted by the Tyndal effect—the scattering of light by tiny particles suspended in the air. He searched for the cause, usually diamonds, and found a tiara. He lingered over the colors, half mesmerized by the precious stones, half afraid of what he would find if he acknowledged the owner.

Dio cleared his throat.

Henrique's gaze crashed from the crown to a pair of flashing green eyes. His heart ricocheted against his ribs, and he stepped back. His mind took longer to process what his body already understood. The princess was his midnight Joan of Arc.

Her eyes locked into him, more striking than he remembered, broad daylight emphasizing their liquidness. The absence of a rusty breastplate revealed a slender torso. She looked every part a perfect princess. Fashionable, hair done the right way, skin flawless. Hers was the beauty women marveled at, poets fawned over, but hot-blooded men should be leery of. Despite the necessity of being leery of her, a lightness buoyed his chest, and his mouth turned dry. If he didn't know himself, he might believe he was excited about spending weeks in her presence.

Dio flashed a wicked grin.

Henrique glowered. A dried-up maid with long teeth? He hoped his friend had enjoyed the joke. During the first stop, Henrique would douse his friend's hair with phosphorus and set it on fire.

Ignoring Dio for the moment, Henrique turned to his charge. A ruby-colored blush and a murderous grip on her parasol were the only telltale signs little Joan had recognized him. Had their garden tête-à-tête ruffled her feathers the wrong way?

That wouldn't work now, would it? Time to woo her properly.

Henrique bowed and flashed a grin. "Princess Isabel, daylight pales compared to your beauty."

She tilted her head, impervious to the innuendo about their midnight encounter. "Thank you. We are extremely late, so—"

"The trip will be awfully long, I'm afraid. I hope you brought some reading material. Greek poetry is perfect for passing the time." He winked.

"I've packed the complete history of Spain. Three volumes, two thousand pages," she said, her expression turning glacial.

"How... entertaining." Henrique narrowed his eyes. Well, the teasing had no effect. Perhaps some bribery. "It's such a lovely day. Your brother advised me how much you love horses. Do you wish to ride? I've selected one of Pedro Daun's prized Lusitanos for your pleasure."

She let out a little gasp, and then her gaze escaped to the horses. Henrique pressed his lips not to smile. She was mellowing already. Who wouldn't want to ride on such a fine day?

"Oh, Your Excellency. I get terribly sick inside the coach. A tragedy, really. I'll accompany you." Lady Dolores pawed his jacket.

He had been so engrossed by Isabel he forgot the girl.

"My pleasure," Henrique said and turned to Isabel. "Your Highness?" Henrique kept eye contact, glad he didn't choke on the formality of the address.

"It looks like rain. I'll travel inside. Thank you for the kind offer."

So, that's how she wanted to play... Henrique nodded, making sure his expression was as blank as hers. "We've dallied enough here. We better depart."

When they finally approached the hotel, Henrique couldn't recall a single idea, original thought, or coherent opinion passing through Lady Dolores' mouth. His ears had absorbed so much inane chatter they had become numb. The only thing he could fathom from her chitchat was her boredom. Princess Isabel kept her ladies from mixed company unless she had vetted the guests first. They couldn't stroll unescorted and had a strict diet and exercise routine.

He glanced at the royal coach. Could the princess believe in such rules? Why would a woman with her wit keep herself so restrained? Henrique shook his head and dismounted. After enduring thirty miles of dusty roads and Lady Dolores' frivolous conversation, Henrique arrived at this conclusion—he didn't understand Princess Isabel de Orleans. No matter. The princess was a puzzle he had no intention of solving. He decided upon a course of action. If the princess could act the Antarctic glacier, so could he. He would be perfectly civil. Warring didn't go well with summer.

The Copa Hotel, a pleasant neoclassical building in Beira's central square, opened its doors to receive them.

The princess alighted from the coach and sped to them, sniffing over Lady Dolores like a lioness with her cubs. What did she think he would do with the girl? Debauch her in plain sight of three carriages while being assaulted by her chatter?

Henrique rolled his eyes. "Are you done?"

She bestowed upon him a gelid smile.

He preferred her disheveled and wearing a breastplate. Even armored, she had been more approachable. In full princess regalia, she was too perfect, and her perfection rubbed his skin like pollen, making it itchy. He'd bet it had the effect of turning the male public into contrite schoolboys. A glimpse of Isabel's perfection worked as a schoolmaster's ruler, compelling them to keep their eyes to themselves and their hands above the table.

But not him.

Growing up, he'd been immune to correction, and in fact, his rebellion grew exponentially with the threat. Right now, his fingers tingled to muss her hair and steal her tiara just to hear a perfect gasp. His devious mind conjured all sorts of pranks, including attaching it to a peacock or hiding it inside his mattress so she—the image of Isabel wearing nothing but the crown assaulted him, and desire pulsed through his veins. He mentally bashed his palm. She was his friend's sister, for Christ's sake. Better keep the schoolmaster's ruler close by.

She linked her arm through Dolly and deigned to look at him. "Since you've stopped at this inn and not the hotel I had chosen, I must assume you've informed the establishment of our arrival?" she said in cool, cultured tones.

"They are expecting Viscount Penafiel and Baroness da Beija."

She frowned. "Why use my lesser title?"

Any of the twelve would've done. "Do you mean to cause a stir every time we stop?"

She lifted a dainty shoulder. "The country should be able to see their princess, don't you think?"

Is Portugal obliged to endure her, too? "I'm sure most are not ready for such honor and would expire in ecstasy. Shall we?" There, he had acted civil enough. He offered his arm and escorted them to the reception area.

Though it was not the Hermitage Hotel, the rosewood furniture and *toile du jouy* tapestry gave it a charming hunting lodge atmosphere. Not even a princess could find fault with it.

Piano music floated from the restaurant, and the scent of roasted pig flavored the air. His stomach rumbled. A hearty meal and some rest would restore his temper, and acting cool with Isabel in the morning wouldn't be as straining as carrying a boulder uphill.

At the reception, Lady Dolly toyed with a silver candle holder, attracted to the shiny object. The princess tapped her impatient feet on the parquet. The hotel clerk gave them the room keys and beamed, offering a place in the restaurant.

Henrique nodded. "I'll escort the ladies to the table. Their *açorda* dish is famous in the region."

Dolly licked her lips, her gloved hand extending to Henrique's arm. "How delicious. Thank you."

"The common room isn't appropriate for unmarried ladies." Isabel turned her nose up as if scenting an offensive smell.

Henrique counted to ten and forced a diplomatic smile. "There are families inside, surely—"

"Lady Dolores and I will have dinner in our bedchamber."

Henrique gritted his teeth. "Why deprive the girl of such simple pleasures?"

Isabel glared at him. "Lady Dolores, please accompany Sophie and the porter to our room. I will join you momentarily."

The girl dropped her shoulders and sulked. "If I must heed the curtain call, I bid you good night." With a parting sigh, she dragged her feet to the stairs.

"I would appreciate it if you stopped interfering in my household." Isabel's silvery voice could cut steel.

Someone opened the restaurant door. Upbeat notes of a *modinha* floated to the reception, cheery and inviting.

Isabel gasped. "Must she make a spectacle of herself?"

Henrique followed her ominous stare, expecting to see an odalisque shedding her seven veils. Inside the restaurant, a voluptuous woman danced with a coarse man. What could've shocked Isabel? The poor lady's sin lay not with her choice of conduct but with her partner.

Cool, remember? "The lady is just dancing."

Pressing her lips into an unforgiving line, Isabel averted her eyes. "A woman need not lose her virtue to dance."

Perhaps it was the long day of hearing about modistes and fashionable gossip, or that his stomach protested its emptiness, or the minor detail that Henrique's whole life had been put on hold to accommodate Isabel's wishes—whatever the catalyst, he'd had enough.

"Here is a new concept for you. Some people enjoy having fun."

"Fun can be had in less public venues."

Henrique smirked. "I assure you, it can."

"Use as many innuendos as you please. Not every woman cares about the type of fun you flaunt."

Chill and detached, Isabel behaved as if she alone belonged to a different species, immune to the principle governing all beings under the sun—seek pleasure and avoid pain. But she was wrong. Evolution overruled a barely out-of-the-schoolroom princess.

"Don't you? And must you keep your ladies from life's pleasures?"

The top of her ears went fiery red, and her nostrils flared. "Leave them out of this."

A sore point if she had any. "Why, so you can continue bullying them into doing your bidding?"

She bristled like an eagle defending her chicks. "Dolly is perfectly content, I assure you."

He snorted. "Of course. Content as a nun in a convent."

"Nuns have higher callings. At least their lives are meaningful." She gave him a pointed look.

The innuendo hit him in the chest. So she thought life as a scientist was frivolous? Henrique locked his jaw. "You are right. The ladies are better off living in your household." He leered at her, his smile showing too many teeth. "Much worse to kiss the mother superior's hands than your royal rump."

Isabel speared him with a stare deadly enough to smite a lesser man. Her alabaster skin became as red as any common Douro wine, her eyes flashing like amethysts in a jackal's statue. "Viscount Penafiel, my brother made you my escort, but he could not make you a gentleman."

She tossed her beautiful hair and stormed past him.

Panting, Henrique watched Isabel climb the stairs. Somewhere, his ancestors were hooting at his atrocious manners. Good God, she had dropped the icy breast-plate, hadn't she? What a sight to behold.

Clapping came from behind him. Dio sauntered to the light. "For a second there, I thought you had lost your finesse with the ladies. Old age and all…" He drawled, cleaning tears of mirth from his eyes. "But then you ended your couplets with 'royal rump.' You managed alliteration, consonance, and personification, all in two words. No wonder Isabel is so smitten."

"Shut up."

Chapter 6

"We men are wretched things." Homer, *The Iliad*

I sabel knotted and re-knotted the bows of her night-gown, unable to calm her nerves. Why had Luis saddled her with such a disreputable fellow? An escort should protect her from precisely the kind of threat Viscount Penafiel represented. They had engaged in a tap room argument. In public, no less. What came next? A brawl? Steam built up in her chest, and smoke would certainly escape through her ears if she didn't vent it. Why could she not control her reactions when *he* was near? It would be a nuisance being this aggravated for weeks on end.

"AHRG!" Dolly let out a series of mouse-like squeaks and jumped atop the four-poster bed. "A troupe of spider eggs is hatching in the armoire!" She covered her nose with both hands as if afraid they would choose that specific body part for dinner.

Isabel gritted her teeth. It was the libertine's fault. If he had revealed her identity, they would sleep in the hotel's best room, not in this dusty, insect-filled closet.

With the help of a letter opener, Isabel scooped the tiny spiders atop an envelope. Careful not to drop them on the faded carpet, she placed them on the flowerbed hanging from her window.

"Are they gone?"

"Yes, you can sleep now."

Dolly bounced on the mattress and pulled the covers atop her head. Isabel settled beside her, already missing her own bedchamber.

A door banged. Muffled voices, raised in anger, breached their corner room. Burrowing in the pillow, Isabel closed her eyes, but the bed wavered as if she still jostled in the carriage.

When sleep came, music invaded her dreams like an uninvited gale. She wore the same low-cut red dress as the woman downstairs and danced, her feet moving against her will. The notes increased their tempo. She wasn't alone. The viscount pulled her close, his laughing eyes daring her to refuse. A tingling spread to her limbs and gained intensity. She averted her gaze. When she looked up again, the viscount had vanished, replaced by a hulking brute, saliva dripping from his mouth.

A scream brought her swiftly awake. Perspiration dampened her nightgown. The candle had burned out, leaving the room in shadows. Disoriented, she touched the other side of the mattress and sighed with relief when she felt Dolly's lumpy form.

She found and gulped a glass of water from the bedside table and fell back onto the pillows. What a horrible dream.

Turning on her side, she forced her eyes shut. A crack sounded outside, followed by shouting, an angry male voice, and a woman's plaintive one.

Isabel shot up in bed. Holding her breath, she pressed her ear against the wall. The strident noise of a hand hitting flesh made her grit her teeth. Her body tensed, her palms closing into fists. Who dared abuse a woman under the same roof as a princess of Portugal? Isabel donned her robe-de-chambre, placed her tiara atop her head, and marched out. In the long corridor, the shouting struck her anew. Slurred voices and a woman's moans. How could the other guests listen and remain passive?

Yelling for help, Isabel thumped on the doors closest to her room. A negligent silence was all the answer she got.

If a gentleman screamed, help would be swift. But a woman was a man's property to hold and abuse. Many would think she deserved the rough treatment.

A shriek, loud and filled with pain, congealed Isabel's spine.

This wasn't acceptable. Isabel forced her panic to recede. She straightened her dressing gown and strode to the couple's room. Heart beating in her throat, she knocked.

The shouting ceased. Isabel's legs barely supported her weight, but she stuffed her chest with all the pride of her ancestors. A Portuguese woman would not be hurt tonight.

The door was flung open.

The awful man from downstairs polluted the threshold. While the room's shadows concealed his face, they revealed his yellowed eyes. Isabel cringed at his stale breath.

The woman cowered near the bed. Her red dress was ripped in the bodice, and she hugged herself, tears streaming from her downcast eyes.

"What do we have here?" His gaze traveled from Isabel's ankles to her breasts, and he whistled, spittle forming at the corner of his mouth. "Come inside, precious. There's room for another."

Isabel didn't need a man. She could handle this by herself. All she had to do was draw strength from her expression seventy-four, the one she reserved for anarchists, angry taxpayers, and rabid dogs. During emotional confrontations, confidence and authority were the secrets of success. Isabel ignored the drunk's stare and advanced inside the room.

The woman's cheek had a red mark, her left eye too swollen to open.

"What's your name?"

"Carlota"

"We will leave here, Carlota, together." Isabel pressed her hand encouragingly. Supporting the woman's weight on her shoulders, she dragged them to the exit.

The stranger stepped back to give them space, and relief washed down Isabel's limbs, turning her legs into rubber. Not now. Later. When they were both out of danger, she could crumble.

The man stirred from his stupor, narrowing his eyes. "The bed's over there."

"If you interfere with our departure, sir, you will face grave consequences." Isabel's voice cracked.

His face contorted in a mask of anger. He grabbed Carlota's arm and shoved her to the floor.

Carlota fell to her knees, sobs racking her torso.

"You stinking animal!" Isabel screamed. "*Maldito, desgraçado!*" Words that would shame a dockside worker spilled from her mouth until her throat ached.

"I teach you to curse, whore."

The man lifted a club-like arm above her head. Isabel's breath caught, and she scrunched her shoulders.

His hand descended on her. Before the blow connected, he was flung backward. From the blur of shadows and limbs emerged Viscount Penafiel. Isabel staggered back from the melee. The viscount punched the drunkard's face. His devil-may-care insolence slipped, exposing a swarthy stranger, his shirtsleeves doing a poor job of concealing menacing muscles.

Panting, she cradled her cheeks to reassure herself she still had all her teeth. The bedroom swam before her vision, and she watched the fight with a sense of detachment. All of a sudden, it seemed to her that Viscount Penafiel understood a thing or two about handling a crisis. His fists were quite... diplomatic. Perhaps she had been too hasty in condemning her brother's choice.

The viscount's white teeth flashed against his bronzed skin. "Your Highness, please lead the lady from here. The chat I'm about to have is inappropriate for women."

Chapter 7

"Flaming summer charms the earth with its own fluting, and under leaves the cicada scrapes its tiny wings together and incessantly pours out full shrill song." Sappho

Henrique thanked the tavern server and swallowed the port. A second more, and the princess, his friend's sister, would have sported bruises on her royal face—a purple testimony to his lack of care. He stared at the swirling liquid until his vision blurred. What in Dante's many hells was she doing in that room?

Henrique would have better luck solving the Riemann Hypothesis than understanding his meddling princess. One moment, she disparaged the woman for dancing too close to her partner. In the next, she turned her cheek to receive a blow in the woman's place.

The door swung open. Dio strolled inside as if presenting himself to court, his posture erect and his face impassive. A challenging undertaking with his coat wrinkled and splattered by blood and his curly hair sticking out of his head like a magpie's nest.

Henrique kicked a chair for him to sit. "And?"

"I've locked the fellow in his room. The hotel clerk will release him in the morning after we leave. It's not as if he could compose a pastoral and break out into verses. Your goodnight swing put him to sleep."

Henrique gripped the stem of his glass. "And the princess?"

"The pretty maid wouldn't let me inside the chamber. She informed me Isabel was resting and in perfect health."

Henrique exhaled heavily and leaned back in the chair. The movement upset his sore shoulder, and he winced.

Dio eyed his bloodied knuckles. "Shouldn't you clean your battle wounds?"

"It's nothing. You know her better than I do. Why was she there?"

"Maybe she does it for sport. Who knows, you could've interrupted the performance of a pugilist."

Dio laughed at his own joke, and Henrique glowered at him. He usually went along with his friend's ability to find humor in the most gruesome of situations, but tonight, he had no stomach for it.

"I'm serious."

"Look, she might or might not be the adopted little sister I grew up with, and you might or might not be the much older brother figure who gave me liquor and the odd aphrodisiac, but it does not mean I will carry tales back and forth between you two."

"I'm only four years older than you."

"If you say so." Dio's chuckles dwindled to a stop, his gaze turning serious. "Talking about performances... You should have told me you embraced the hero's quest. I would've come to your first battle. Instead of Hercules defeating the Nemean Lion, we had Henrique beating up the Copa's drunk."

Henrique pushed the glass away and crossed his arms. "Leave it be."

Dio lifted a brow. "Seriously, though. If you had invited the chap for a drink, told a joke to dispel the gloominess... Violence is not your style."

Indeed, it wasn't. But when he saw the swine about to hit Isabel, he became a savage. Luckily, Dio had arrived before he could do more damage.

"Good night." Henrique grabbed the bottle and stood, leaving behind the tavern and Dio's unwelcome questions.

Outside, the hotel stared at him, a gray lump of concrete sticking from the ground, beams of light escaping from the closed shutters. He lifted his gaze to the third floor, the fourth window to the right. Dark. She must be sleeping. Excellent. At least one of them would rest.

He crossed the empty square and neared the entrance. A pitiful whine—midway between a broken steam valve and a wheezing dog—made him halt. Would there be no end to the night's pitfalls? He followed the sound around the building. The pebbled path opened to a kitchen garden, the scent of rosemary thickening the air.

It was her.

The bane of his existence huddled against the graying wall, the tiara at odds with her old-fashioned dressing robe. A shaft of moonlight gave her a translucent and altogether vulnerable aura. By Saint George, what the hell was she doing there?

Henrique came closer, the grass muffling his steps. She startled, her head lifting, a gasp escaping her lips.

He shoved his hands in his pockets and gazed up at the light spilling from a single window above them. "I can't say it's a lovely night."

She brushed at her tears and raised her chin, fixing him with a defiant gaze. "If you came here to reproach me—"

"For almost getting your beautiful face smashed? No, never crossed my mind." He dropped by her side. With a heavy sigh, he leaned on the icy wall and stretched his legs.

She shifted away, studying him with her usual intensity. At least this side of her was predictable. "I wonder if making fun turns everything easier."

"It is an acquired art... But I must admit, not for everyone. Some find better solace in wine." Henrique smiled self-deprecatingly and placed the port bottle in the space between them. She looked like she needed a bit of Bacchus' oblivion.

Her eyes widened, and she stared at Vesuvio's best vintage as if he had offered her vulgar *aguardente*. "I don't drink port."

Another of life's delights she avoided. He shrugged and reached for the bottle. She beat him to it and, placing her lips over the rim, gulped it down like the last drop of water before a drought.

"Easy there."

She grimaced and returned it to him.

Henrique rested his weary bones on the wall and sighed. It was one of those nights where the cicadas' song rose in waves, lifting to a melodious pitch and then lowering in unison.

"Their call reminds me of Braganza. I used to sit close to the river, listening until my mother herded me to sleep."

"Why do they sing?" she asked.

"They spend seventeen years underground, and on one special night, no one knows why, they emerge and shed their carapaces to experience flight."

She took a shuddering breath. "Isn't the carapace safer?"

Henrique tugged off his coat and placed it around her, careful not to touch her. Somehow, he knew she would flee if he did.

It shifted something inside him, seeing her engulfed by his coat. "Do you think you could fly with a carapace?"

She observed the movements of his hands, her lips pressed firmly. "I don't care much for flying."

"That's a pity. I would love to see you fly." For a quiet moment, their gazes met, and Henrique knew his words to be true. He would love to see Princess Isabel de Orleans fly.

She broke eye contact first, staring at his bruised knuckles.

"You are hurt." After producing a handkerchief from somewhere in her voluminous clothes, she grabbed his wrist. His protest fell on deaf, delectable shell-shaped ears. She wet the cloth on his best port. He stiffened, reading for pain, but she was delicate, dabbing at the dried blood with angel-soft hands.

"I must thank you... I didn't know you could, you know..."

Hurt another? Lose his temper? Neither did he. He pulled away from her tender ministrations, flexing his fingers. "Why were you there?"

"I wasn't negotiating a treaty, I can assure you." She blinked at him, those green eyes flashing as if she spoke with a nitwit instead of the country's most sought-after scientist. "He abused her. Couldn't you hear her screams?"

His face grew warm, and he looked away. "I went down to the stables. The groom thought my horse had colic. When I returned to my room and heard the screams... It was too late."

The cicada's quieted, leaving only the rasping sounds of his failure.

She shifted closer and sighed long and deep. "You were not too late."

Henrique snorted. "Luis shouldn't have trusted me to—"

She placed her fingertips on his lips. Henrique froze. "The king would have been proud of you."

She removed her fingertips, her gaze softening. Henrique needed no affirmations, but her praise was port wine-sweet and appeased the worry inside his chest better than alcohol. Did Hercules feel the same when he defeated the Lion? As if to prove him right, the constellation of Leo, named after the hero's first task, winked at him from its place in the sky.

They leaned their backs on the wall, gazing at the valiant effort clouds made to cover the moon. Still, the silvery disk prevailed, bathing tomatoes, cucumbers, ripe melons, and a lonesome grapevine in a soft glow. A dog howled in the distance. Somewhere in the hotel, a door opened and closed. If someone had told him he would end this day seated on the grass, posterior soaked, knuckles bloodied, drinking with the princess, he would have the fellow interned.

He fingered her tiara. "Is there a protocol? A princess must not be seen in public without her crown? So no one forgets your status?"

"It keeps *me* from forgetting it." Her voice became frail and transparent.

Henrique didn't like the bleakness in her eyes and changed the subject. "What did you do with... What was her name?"

"Carlota. I helped her clean her bruises. She is resting in Sophie's bedroom."

"Good."

"She trained to be a ballerina. The monster lured her from Theater San Carlos with an offer of marriage."

Certainly, she would show some disdain for the woman's profession. Though many ladies in the theater led respectable lives, most people thought they earned their livelihood not on the stage but on their backs.

Henrique studied her. "What will she do now?"

She shrugged, her hands fiddling with the grass. "For ages, Sophie has been asking me for an assistant. She complains about how I rip my gown's trains, and she barely has time to sew them with all her other duties. I offered Carlota the position."

Had he heard her correctly? She would employ Carlota, the ballerina with a shady past? His theory of a moralist prude who hated her sex had just been ruled out. Had he misjudged her? Instead of disdaining women, she wanted to protect them—an armorless Dom Quixote. God save them both.

She leaned forward, her eyes searching his. "Why do men hit women?"

He sustained her gaze, cursing the drunkard for exposing her to violence, and yet, he sensed her question had a deeper root. Isabel de Orleans had a lousy view of males. "Not every man uses his fists. Some prefer a subtler seduction."

She tilted her head to the side. "Is there a difference?"

He was tempted to show just how different it could be. His fingers tingled to touch the slanted corners of her eyes and the little dimple she had on her left cheek. To brush the tears and kiss the corner of her lips until her gaze lit up with lust, and they forgot what happened. He settled for tucking a strand of silky hair behind her ear.

Her breath caught, and she gazed at him, a question in her lovely green eyes.

Henrique drank the port. He shouldn't entertain unchaste thoughts of his friend's sister. "So, my valiant Dom Quixote, how many more women will you take in until we arrive in Comillas?"

"How much space do we have?" Isabel smiled, unleashing a chain reaction. It sparkled her eyes, glowed her cheeks, glistened her lips.

Henrique brushed his chest, staring at her face. Isabel's smile was one of those events a man caught once in life—discovering a new species, a total sun eclipse, or losing one's innocence. She had smiled for the first time, and he understood why she reserved it for special occasions—it must be a political decision, magnanimous and charitable—to guard males' hearts.

With reluctance, he stood up and offered his hand. "Come, Your Highness., For the safety of the other men in this hotel, I must bid you retire."

She placed her palm atop his. "Call me Isabel."

He stilled, her hand grasped in his. "I will do nothing of the sort."

Her eyes widened, no doubt startled to have her words flung back at her.

He grinned. "I'll call you Isa."

Chapter 8

"It is not difficult to govern. All one has to do is not wish to appear wiser than the laws, nor richer than the country, nor more noble than the citizen."
Queen Maria II of Portugal

"My Lady, your entourage awaits."

Henrique's grave voice startled Isabel, and she gripped the railings. What would she see in his eyes this morning? The tender understanding they shared in the garden? Or mockery? She cared not for how they treated each other before last night's incident. The veiled insults, the need to keep her guard up, the fluttery feeling inside her chest every time he came near. It would be exhausting to spend the summer in opposing trenchers.

They had different points of view, it was true. But two parties could coexist without constant altercations. She had selected a medal from her jewelry box—the Viana's heart—as a peace offering. Ready for a unilateral compromise, she clutched the small parcel.

Now, facing him in the crowded hotel lobby, her grand idea, the perfect way to appreciate his bravery and seal their newfound friendship, made her cheeks burn and her neck prickle.

She met his eyes, searching for something... What? He was back in the skin of an aristocrat-about-town—well shaved, hair combed, his light grey morning coat matching his striped trousers. When she found no traces of the disheveled hero who had saved her last night, Isabel stuffed the velvet pouch in her jacket's pocket.

He had renewed his invitation for her to ride with him. Perhaps the right moment to give him the medal would present itself later. "Will you show me this mare you've been bragging about?"

"I'm waiting for your pleasure." He gazed at her expectantly, as if he too wondered where they stood, and offered his arm.

He escorted her to the hotel courtyard. Word had come out of her true identity, and people leaned over their windows and porches, watching the liveried servants and the lacquered carriages lining the street. The cheers and smiles on her subjects' faces warmed her heart. Isabel waved graciously while Henrique waited patiently. It took fifteen minutes for them to cross to the two saddled horses waiting behind her coach.

"Is it always like this?" He glanced beyond his shoulder, where the crowd still cheered.

"Not always. But, yes, whenever I'm recognized."

"Doesn't it bother you?"

"I'm a princess. Women look up to me as an example of moral conduct. It is my duty to inspire." She took pride in being an asset to the Royal Family.

"And you shape your life around this duty?" He studied her, his head tilted to the side.

For the first time, she felt in the presence of a scientist, not a rake. It gave her a fuzzy feeling in her stomach, not at all unpleasant. That's what his experiments must feel like—not judged but analyzed.

She forced herself to respond truthfully. "It is my obligation, and serving my country makes me happy."

His lip lifted, flashing a dimple. "Aren't you a patriotic princess?"

"At least of this crime, I cannot plead innocence. I've traveled the world, but this... this is home. Don't you love our land?"

"They have rugged cliffs in other places, too." He looked away, and the dimple vanished.

Other places? None of them as majestic, for sure. Isabel was about to admonish his lack of love for Portugal but swallowed her words. His neck and shoulders were stiff. She wouldn't start another conflict.

A neigh from the waiting steeds pulled him out of his musings.

He exhaled and steered her toward the horses. "This is Dulcinea."

Isabel chuckled. "Don Quixote's dream lady? So this makes your horse the intrepid Rocinante?"

Henrique patted the stallion's chestnut coat, a grin crinkling the corners of his eyes. "You wound this steed with such dastardly a name. Can't you see he would put the knight-errant's nag to shame? This, my lovely princess, is Incitatus."

Isabel feigned shock. "Caligula's horse? Careful, sir, beasts show their owner's true character."

"Caligula so loved his horse, he made him a senator of Rome." He lifted his brows. "Madness runs deeply in royalty."

"That's hardly fair. As a scientist, you should know it was never proven madness is more frequent among royal families than common folk."

He studied her, his eyes glinting. "Has anyone ever said you have a fetching logical mind?"

She was rarely admired for her intellect and batted her eyelashes playfully to conceal her reaction. "Cease, sir. You will make me vain with your flirtation."

"When common people go mad, they are locked in sanatoriums. When royalty goes soft in the head, they run rampant, impaling their enemies, planning a winter invasion of Russia, or living to please others. Now, enough dawdling. We better move if we are to reach Tavora before nightfall." He bent, linking his fingers, and gave her a suggestive look.

Did he expect to help her mount? Climbing a sidesaddle was no easy feat. The lady depended on her helper for the right amount of push—too much, and she would topple over the horse, ending up flattened on the other side. Too little, and she wouldn't make it. Where was her groom?

"Come on. I won't throw you off."

"Sir, you seemed ready to do worse yesterday." To her shame, she couldn't conceal the hurt in her voice.

"I was an ass, wasn't I? Can we start anew?" He looked at her openly, no jests.

Despite the crass word, she felt the sincerity of the apology and placed her right foot over his palms. Before she could spring, he lifted her effortlessly.

Her chest became level with his face, his breath warming the velvet of her gown. The invisible threads came alive, connecting them as if they were tied with hemp rope. Her heart leaped to a double measure, and her stomach stirred.

His smile faded, and his eyes focused on her lips. "Isa..."

"Hmm?" She had the baffling impulse to trace his cheek and feel the grains of his shaved skin.

"After last night, I—Are you all right?"

Cheeks flushed, Isabel adjusted herself over the saddle and made a show of concealing her legs below the folds of her woolen skirts.

He pulled her chin up.

Her heart bruised her ribcage, and she sensed he expected something from her, and it maddened her that she didn't know what. The little medal burned inside her jacket. Should she give it to him now? Just so she could occupy her hands?

"I'll be fine, thank you."

He kept eye contact. By daylight, his irises weren't a maze but two fathomless lakes. She was glad she had never learned to swim. Otherwise, she would be tempted to dive.

Around them, horses snorted, jingling their bridles. Wheels scrunched gravel, and birds chirped.

"Should we go?"

He pulled away from her, walking backward until he reached his horse. As Henrique mounted his steed and signaled the guards to proceed, she admired the ease with which he carried himself and the husky timbre of his voice. Last night had vanquished the animosity between them, but it had done nothing to control the fluttering inside her stomach.

Távoras's inhabitants had decorated their village square with lavender and hydrangeas. Still, little effort was needed to make their city inviting. Whitewashed buildings lined the narrow streets, and bougainvillea adorned the simple but charming cottages.

Isabel's cheeks hurt from the smile she kept on her face, her right shoulder sore from waving at villagers and accepting gifts. None of that bothered her. It was the least she could do after learning about the ravages of phylloxera. The wine plague had curtailed their livelihood. She would write about their plights to Luis. Even with the rightful complaints, an aura of cheerfulness prevailed. She had been correct to arrive as the princess and not mask her identity. People needed to see the royal family. It gave them hope and made them feel special.

Henrique stood at the fringes of the small group. He had been silent during the trip, and his introspection increased with each flower given to her or the children she embraced.

"Can we retire now? The sun is burning my nose," Dolly whined, pressing Isabel's arm.

Isabel nodded and said her farewells. When the royal entourage returned to the carriages, Henrique took the opposite direction, his gray coat vanishing into a side street.

Isabel told Diomedes to proceed with Dolly to the hotel. Escorted by Sophie and a guard, she followed Henrique. The walled city was tiny, and she had no difficulty trailing his steps to an ancient house.

A plaque read Cister Monastery. Isabel asked her maid and guard to wait outside and, ignoring their protests, crossed the copper gate. Stillness pervaded the moss-covered stone walls, the kind present only where no one had lived for generations. The main entrance opened up to an inner courtyard. Isabel shuddered at the sight of a greenish pond, half expecting to see a drake landing in its depths. Should she return? But Henrique had not been himself. What if he fell ill?

Rubbing her arms against the sudden chill, she followed the path until she arrived at a stair leading down. Curiosity piqued, she descended the stone steps, holding the granite wall for support. The passageway opened to a cavernous space with an arched ceiling. Water dripped. The scent of wood and mold mingled with wine. A cellar. Blinking to adjust her eyesight, she crossed the threshold.

A gigantic log occupied the center of the room. Dust-covered bottles protruded from the contraption like the needles of a porcupine.

Henrique had his back to her, studying the apparatus.

Her breath caught, and she paused. The inconvenient flutter started anew.

When a minute passed, and Henrique didn't move, she gripped her elbows, her eyes straying to the exit. Why had she followed him here? He must have wished for a private moment. She picked up her skirt to leave.

"Do you know what these are for?"

He stood several feet from her, but the vaulted ceiling echoed his voice as if he had spoken near her ear.

"To store wine?"

He chuckled, closing his eyes. "No."

"I shouldn't intrude. I just wanted to—"

"The Cister Order arrived in Portugal in the twelfth century. They brought their methods of winemaking from France." Holding a bottle with his bare hand, he turned it on its axis like a faucet. He then moved to the next in line and repeated the same gesture. Slowly, reverently, he played glass against wood, evoking a mournful chime.

"Are you familiar with winemaking science?"

Isabel shook her head and stepped closer.

"After the grapes are macerated, wild yeasts on the skins attack the juice, turning the sugar into alcohol." Like when he spoke about cicadas, his voice became lower and graver. It held a hint of wonder, of deep curiosity that made her want to partake in his science as if it were delicious food or a ticket to an exotic place. "Because of Távora's colder temperature, the yeasts don't complete the fermentation in the pipes. They go to sleep. When they wake up in summer, the process starts again, this time inside the bottles, trapping the carbonic gas. The result? Bubbles."

"Champagne?"

His smile didn't reach his eyes. "Sparkling wine. But the gas comes with an unwanted byproduct. Do you see? This mossy powder inside the glass? It's the dead yeast. The monks built these racks to turn the bottles a few degrees every month, sweeping the powder closer and closer to the bottle's finish. This way, when the dust reaches the cork, they can extract the yeast with minimum loss of bubbles."

Awed, she touched the rack, and the raspy wood caught on her glove. "I didn't know Portugal produced such wine. Why is this place deserted then?"

"After the liberal revolution, the monks were expelled. I'm not a religious man, but did we have to forget the process along with the tonsured folk? And now, fifty years later, France sells champagne for fifteen *Reis* a bottle. Portugal peddles a full casket of red wine for five."

"I will write to my brother. Certainly, he can do something—"

"Why not? Let our King Luis resolve everything." His voice changed, becoming cool and detached.

The loss of wonder disturbed the air, making it thick and uncomfortable.

Isabel felt inside her skirt pocket until she clutched the gift. Her cheeks grew warm, and she extended her arm before courage deserted her. "I've brought you this."

Frowning, he opened the package and stared at the gold piece atop his palm.

"It's a filigree heart. The symbol of Portugal. For what you did yesterday. A token of friendship." She delivered the words in short bursts.

His virile hand closed around the medal, engulfing it. He averted his eyes, his attention back on the bottles. "I'm sorry. I'm dreadful company for princesses today."

She took a step closer. "Does it have to do with the vineyards?"

He exhaled loudly. "The cure for phylloxera was found last year, but winemakers are still trying the most outlandish methods to get rid of this plague." He jerked the bottles.

"Do you know how many types of grapes are only raised here, in this country that fits six times inside France? Over two-hundred-fifty. Much more than the forty that exist in Bourdeaux and Burgundy. Do you know what will happen? No Portuguese native vine will survive." The bottles shrieked in the rack as he turned them violently.

Isabel covered her ears.

"After the grapevines are destroyed, we will have to import them from France. Stupid villagers."

Isabel flinched. How could he speak as if the problem didn't concern him? "You are the wine expert. Why don't you do something?"

He halted. The last screech echoed on the stone walls and vanished, leaving in its place a pointed silence.

"I won't be here."

"I don't understand."

"After this little trip of yours, I will leave Portugal."

"But when will you return?"

"Emigration, have you heard of it? It is permanent."

Isabel crossed her arms above her chest and took a step backward. How unfair to criticize the peasants when he couldn't wait to turn tail and flee. She grabbed her skirt and strode to the passageway.

"Isa?" His voice came from too close behind her.

Isabel halted.

"You should keep the medal." He pulled her hair above her left shoulder, brushed the naked skin above her collar, and pinned it to the lapel of her jacket.

The gesture, too intimate, lifted the hairs on her arms, and her eyelids fluttered shut. His presence hummed against her spine, insistent, impossible to be ignored.

She turned to face him. His eyes lulled her, the blue of Portugal's sky reflecting on the ocean. Isabel pulled in a shaky breath and held the air inside her lungs like a swimmer who realized the water was too deep. Except she had never learned how to swim.

"There." He took a step away from her. "You will care better for Portugal's treasure."

Isabel covered the jewel with her palm. His voice had the same note of despair she'd heard last night when he blamed himself for not arriving in time to protect her.

She placed a hand over his forearm. "You can do so much for Portugal. If only—"

"Do you believe men and women can be friends?"

The sudden change of subject startled her, and she smiled nervously. "Why, yes? If a rider can befriend his horse, and a lady can befriend her maid, surely—"

"The rider wants to ride the horse, and the horse wants to be fed. The lady wants her hair dressed, and the maid wants to get paid." He gave her the sardonic smile she despised. "Are you seeing a pattern yet, Isabel?"

Chapter 9

"All these Portuguese Princesses are demons either in politics or in love, and sometimes in both." The Duchess de Dino

The Canastra coat of arms flashed atop the pedimented gateway, signaling their destination. Isabel's carriage left the main road and lumbered through the path cut through a sprawling plain. She lowered her embroidery and chanced a look outside. Henrique and Diomedes rode behind their coach.

Henrique spoke, and Diomedes laughed. She could bet he had made an outrageous remark, dripping with his dry, witty humor. After their encounter in the cellar, he hadn't invited her to ride with him... Not that she wanted to. In fact, she could hardly wait to arrive at Comillas so she wouldn't have to see him as often. She had no intention of preoccupying herself with a man devoid of love for his country. A rootless tree, ungrateful to the earth sustaining it. She pierced the cloth with more force than necessary and poked her fingertip. Muttering a curse, she flung it away.

The coach halted.

Sophie stored their books and embroidery in a basket, and the ladies adjusted their bonnets and gloves. When a footman dressed in the ochre and carmine of the Spanish flag opened the door, they were perfectly composed.

Isabel alighted first, expression number six in place—a greeting smile and upraised brows.

A marine-scented breeze brought laughter from the beach. Emerald lawns reached to the glittering ocean, the perfect green peppered by carnation and pomegranate flowers.

Dolly shaded her eyes. "By the bard almighty, how grand it is."

A palace perched on the hill, flanked by towering cypress trees. The apricot-colored stones stood in sharp relief against the bright blue sky. Atop the minaret, the Spanish flag trembled under a light breeze.

Rafaela, the Duchess of Canastra, fluttered closer and kissed Isabel's cheeks. "My dear, dear cousin. I'm so happy you came. I promise you will not regret it." She stressed each word with a fluid hand gesture, exposing multicolored gems on her fingers.

Rafaela was every inch as vivacious as Isabel remembered. Spain had colored her skin to a lovely olive. Her black hair was arranged atop her head, and a handsome bonnet perched rakishly over her curls.

Isabel introduced Dolores.

"What a delightful girl." Rafaela inspected Dolly at arm's length. "Why, I must take you both under my wing."

Henrique cantered into the courtyard and halted not fifteen feet from them. The sun kissed Henrique's skin, shining over his windswept hair. With the ease of a brilliant rider, he vaulted from Incitatus' back. Grinning at something Diomedes said, he flung the reins to a liveried groom and patted the horse's neck. As he swaggered to their group, the silly beast followed his master's every move, undoubtedly as eager for the man's crumbs of attention as everyone else in their entourage.

Everyone except Isabel.

Diomedes cleared his throat and gave Rafaela a polite bow.

Henrique swept into their midst and introduced himself with the savoir-faire of a man who exuded self-confidence. The days riding outside the carriage had made the laughing lines around his eyes more pronounced.

Rafaela curtseyed deeply, showing a blatant amount of decolletage. "Welcome to our country, Your Excellency."

"The Viscount of Penafiel has no trouble embracing any country he is in," Isabel said, plastering a sweet smile on her lips.

"I am easy to please." He addressed Rafaela, but his eyes flashed at Isabel. "Unlike some others..."

The Duke of Canastra cleared his throat. The middle-aged aristocrat towered over the courtyard's center, two Galgo hunters guarding his legs.

Smiling, the duke bowed over Isabel's hand. "Princess Isabel. More stunning than I recalled. You are an asset to our humble home." A white streak marked his black hair, giving him a severe countenance. The red and ochre military uniform emphasized his lean figure, but the epaulets seemed too large for his shoulders. Was he an officer now? How odd. Canastra came from trade, and gossip had it he bought the title with shipping money.

"The pleasure is all mine. It's been ages since I came to Spain. Your country is lovely in summer," Isabel said.

Rafaela cut in front of her husband. "You arrived just in time. We're having a *fiesta* on the beach. Today is *Cavatast*, and we will honor the tradition of tasting the year's first *cava* wine."

Guests talked in small groups or lounged around cocktail tables. Games of shuttlecock, lawn tennis, and cricket made the grass colorful and alive. Paper flowers in yellow and rose decorated a trellis. The ocean glittered, the blue interspersed by pointy sails.

"Your Highness, I was waiting for your arrival." Canastra pointed to an austere portal leading into the house. A stuffy butler held the door open. "If you can forgo my wife's frivolous party, I would love if you could attend a meeting with me—"

"*Por favor, Ignacio.*" Rafaela sidestepped the growling dogs and placed her bejeweled fingers atop her husband's arm. "Isabel and our guests just arrived. Allow them to have fun before you accost them with politics."

Isabel gazed from the party to the portal. Laughter floated with the breeze, and the scents of cotton sugar and currant jam wafted to her nose.

Still, her brother had asked her to understand the current mood of their neighbors. Who needed a delicious and fragrant celebration when she had the chance to speak with tedious aristocrats? She gazed from the lawn to Henrique, and her mouth watered to join the fun. Why this now? She had never shirked her duties. Parties meant little to her. It was Henrique, she realized with dismay and the promise of laughter dancing in his eyes. What tempted her was experiencing the party with him.

Henrique lifted his brows at her as if aware of her weakness.

"I will be happy to join you," Isabel blurted and placed her hand above Canastra's forearm.

Rafaela shrugged. "Still the diplomat in the family."

Isabel watched her cousin collect a paper flower from the trellis and insert it in Henrique's coat pocket. Then, she playfully shooed the guests to the beach. They all laughed. None looked back.

Isabel lowered herself to a Chippendale chair in Canastra's drawing room. The effort to keep her attention focused on what mattered was fruitless. Every time laughter intruded from outside, her thoughts wandered. Isabel mentally shook herself. This was her chance to make a sterling impression and show her support for the Duke of Aosta.

She forced herself to notice the details. The ceiling rose as high as a cathedral, and Italian marble lined the floors, walls, and arched columns. Statues and mirrors adorned the niches. All attested to the rumors Canastra was the wealthiest man on the peninsula. As she expected, she was surrounded by the cream of the Spanish aristocracy. She recognized the Duke and Duchess of Montijo, one of the oldest lines in Spain, and the Marquiss of Albuquerque.

The table before her had a lavish tea service, including pastries, sweetmeats, and a *tarta de Santiago*.

Canastra offered her a plate. "Your Highness, do you accept a treat? You look a little pale."

Isabel's mouth watered, but she forced her gaze from the tray. She would not allow the temptation to control her. Isabel de Orleans was not governed by her senses.

"Thank you, but I must decline."

He lowered the plate. "How is your Spanish?"

"I hope not to disgrace myself with my poor pronunciation," she said demurely, omitting the fact that she spoke five languages fluently.

The duke fired a sequence of questions. Her upbringing, how many of her mother's progeny had survived infancy, the number of instruments she played,
and her exact opinion of their constitution. Bespec-
tacled and monocled eyes observed her from their
perches around the drawing room. Even a trumpet
was pointed at her, capturing her every word. Why
had she become the center of attention?

"I'm a decent chess player." Isabel lowered the cup
to the saucer. "Do you know who else plays a great
game of chess? The Duchess of Aosta. Will we have
the pleasure of her presence this summer?"

Disapproving murmurs rose from the assembly.

Isabel swallowed, and a prickle of unease climbed
up her spine.

Canastra stood and stared at a gruesome painting
lining the wall. Light focused on a Spaniard pleading
for mercy. Other dispatched souls sprawled on the
blood-splattered ground. A line of French hussars
pointed their guns at the unarmed man. In the background, Madrid burned.

"What a magnificent piece of art," she offered, her
voice strained. "Is it perchance a Goya?"

The duke clasped his hands behind his back, still
facing the carnage. "The Dos de Mayo. It represents
the Spanish fight against Napoleon's tyranny."

Napoleon's deranged passions ravaged the country
during the Peninsular Wars. Isabel hugged herself.
"Past feuds are a waste of a country's resources, don't
you think?"

He eyed her askance. "Napoleon is gone, but the
Spanish people have an Italian usurper on the
throne."

Well, then, he seemed quite happy to nurture past
feuds. Isabel sipped her tea to swallow her misgivings
and pasted on expression number fifteen, a raised eye
brow softened by a diplomatic smile. "Isn't usurper a

harsh word? I'm sure the Duke of Aosta is a dedicated ruler."

Canastra inhaled sharply, his olive skin turning red. "Dedicated to whom?"

"To the Spanish people, of course. I always say it's best to look at the future. Better unite with a less ideal king than have no king at all, don't you think?" And no king at all, to the aristocracy, meant only one thing—a republic. None present tilted toward a republican regime, so the Spanish aristocracy would have to accept him.

"Have you met the Prince of Asturias?" Canastra spoke casually, but his eyes roamed over her face, and she had the impression he studied her, noticing her minute reactions.

Of course, she knew of him. Royal circles were tight. Alfonso de Bourbon, the eldest son of Queen Isabela, had been exiled along with the rest of his family.

"Only his sisters. They are wonderful girls." She felt the need to add. Otherwise, he might take offense. She'd met them when visiting Paris last year. Alfonso had been studying in Switzerland. They lived well enough in the Rue de Rivoli. Still, she had sensed in the family a deep sorrow and fear. After all, a dethroned monarch led a risky life.

"He became a striking young gentleman. Honorable to a fault, bright, honest. Your views would match with his on many subjects," Canastra said.

An aura of expectancy descended upon the room. Several aristocrats nodded, leaning forward. Canastra exchanged a glance with the others, and she had the distinct impression they were up to something.

"What a shame he cannot return to Spain." Isabel paused. She must tread carefully. "Perhaps I can write to him."

"You won't have to."

"No?" She lowered her tea and lifted her brows.

"You will meet him in person." The duke placed his right hand atop his chest. "Alfonso de Bourbon arrives tomorrow."

Chapter 10

"Society is now one polish'd horde, Form'd of two mighty tribes, the Bores and Bored." Lord Byron

Henrique entered the palace, directing the footman to accommodate the box with his experiments and microscope. Isabel's maid paced the corridor, her expression bothered. Henrique could not blame her and glared at the door. Isabel had been locked inside it with Canastra for two hours. The princess should have stayed in Lisbon if she wished to bury herself in smoky rooms and drudging company.

He was about to return to the party when he heard a gasp.

Isabel stumbled out of the room. The maid hurried to her and grabbed her arm.

Heart speeding, Henrique strode to them.

Isabel seemed troubled, her skin pale. What the hell had they discussed? If they had been mean to her—Henrique pushed the thought away. Isabel could hold herself better than most people he knew.

Green eyes settled on him for a second, and then she fainted.

Henrique folded Isabel's weight close to his chest just as her legs melted beneath her.

"What is wrong with her, Sophie?"

"I don't know. She was fine when she entered with the Duke."

"Lead the way to her bedroom."

Henrique strode through dark corridors, his foot-steps clattering over the checkered marble, Isabel's long skirts tangling with his thighs. Her head lolled with each step, her lips white as the Greek statues lining the gallery. Henrique cursed the palace's gigantic propor-tions, counting six turns before Sophie threw open the door to the princess' chambers.

Brocade curtains hung from the windows, curtailing the light. As with everything else in the castle, the room was overdecorated.

Henrique lowered Isabel to the bed. To reach the skin of her wrist, he had to unbutton the glove and rip the lace from her long-sleeved dress. Her pulse beat erratically, her breathing shallow. Damn her prudish clothing. He could barely see her throat through the ruffles of her bodice, the taffeta stiff as armor. How could the woman breathe in the cursed thing?

"Help me remove her gown."

The maid wrung her hands. "But, sir—"

"Now, Sophie."

The tone of his voice forced the maid into action. With her help, Henrique unhooked the bodice's fasten-ings. The cloth gaped to reveal a corset hard enough to shame any breastplate. The top reached her collar, smashing her chest, and the other end nipped at her waist—too tight. Most women abused corsets for two reasons—to produce a cinched midriff or enhance their bosom. Not Isabel. Her corset did the opposite, flatten-ing her curves.

"Why in heavens do you pull it so?"

The maid sucked her lips in. "I'm a sans-culotte, sir. I follow orders."

Henrique grunted. Frustrated, he took a knife and cut the tapes. Isabel's chest inflated with the force of her inhale. His shoulders sagged, his eyes closing in relief. She still was pale and wan, but a monstrous corset coupled with Spanish heat could do that. Efficiently, they tugged the bustle from her waist and removed her petticoats.

From beneath layers of cloth and wire emerged surprising softness. Rounded breasts strained the translucent cotton of her chemise. Tapered legs stretched into arched feet. Without the armor, she was all woman. The knowledge would haunt him later, but he couldn't avoid feasting on the view.

Henrique took a step back, his breathing rough. He looked away, cursing his body's reaction, and focused on the ever-present tiara above her head. He better not forget who she was—his friend's sister, Princess of the Blood.

Color returned to her lips. Sophie moved quickly to cover her with the counterpane, no doubt conscious Isabel would rather die than be seen in dishabille.

"When was the last time she ate?"

The maid fussed with the pillows. "Sometimes she—"

"Should I send for the doctor?"

"No, they will want to bleed her, and... Well, some days she refrains from food, sir."

"She refrains?" Food wasn't superfluous, damn it. People refrained from gambling, champagne, or French courtesans, not food. "Why in heaven's name would she do that?"

The maid fidgeted with her austere gown, her discomfort palpable. Sophie was not at fault.

"Go to the kitchen. Bring back a light meal. Broth, bread, and tea."

She left, closing the door with a soft click.

Alone with Isabel, Henrique exhaled. His chest bothered him as if someone had filled it with cement. He wanted to strangle her for endangering her health. No, too quick. What she deserved was a good, long spanking—a tanning of her royal rump. Henrique sat by Isabel's side. A strand of hair had been lucky enough to escape her chignon and now rested on her cheek. He twirled it around his fingertip. So soft. "Foolish, foolish girl, what will I do with you?"

Isabel's eyes fluttered open and focused on him. Lifting her hand, she picked something from his coat. The paper flower.

She frowned at the wrinkled petals. "I'm sorry you had to leave the party to carry me here."

Her voice had a hurt, sad note, and damned if it didn't make him feel guilty. He shook away the feeling. If she wanted to waste an afternoon instead of enjoying herself, it was her choice, not his. "Why don't you eat, Isabel? Are you trying to kill yourself?"

"My eating habits don't concern you."

Henrique gave her a look to rival Hercules' wrath.

Biting her lip, she tugged the covers to her neck. "If you must know, I received some unexpected news. And the long journey... I'm perfectly fine now. You can return to your entertainment."

"Don't tell me you want to mimic those consumptive women." If this was a whim to follow a silly fashion trend, he would indeed thrash her, and then he would lock her up and feed her until she dropped the nonsense. "To starve is dangerous, Isabel, and you are barely above a wisp as it is."

"I'm not a wisp, and I have no intention of starving. I merely believe some indulgences should be restrained."

"Enlighten me, if you please." Henrique shut his eyes, knowing whatever she meant by including the word indulgences and restraint in the same sentence would make him groan.

She lifted a royal shoulder as if readying herself to impart common sense knowledge. "Food, drink, gambling, and other private pursuits overstimulate the senses. The senses can lead us to forget morality. When we forget morals, we lose track of our purpose."

Good God, did she believe this nonsense? What should people save themselves for? The grave? Stimulating the senses, living in the present, was the only fleeting happiness human beings could enjoy.

Eating, sleeping, and having sex felt wonderful because it ensured life's continuation. Fighting against it was unnatural, a testament to her twisted beliefs.

Henrique searched the room until he found a tray brimming with Spanish treats. He caught a *buñuelo*, the fritter dripping with powdery sugar.

Isabel watched his movements, her gaze alert.

Henrique lifted his brows and bit into the pastry. Closing his eyes, he threw back his head as the sweet melted in his mouth.

Even before he opened his eyelids, he could feel Isabel's stare.

"Want some?" he asked, sprawling by her side.

She tried to roll away from him, but his weight trapped her underneath the counterpane.

Isabel shook herself like a little bird after a bath. "No, I—"

Henrique painted her lips with powdery sugar. A pink tongue came out to lick the sweetness.

Breathing heavily, he broke the pastry in two and pushed it under her nose. She gave a dainty bite. A little mewling escaped her throat.

Her eyes widened, and startled, she covered her mouth as if ashamed of her pleasure.

He hated her restraint. Her warped worldviews would make the Inquisition proud. "You just indulged in sugar, Princess. Ready to lose your morals? Invade another country?" He clasped her delicate wrist and traced her palm. "Kill with your bare little hands? Or worse, debauch an unsuspecting male? If it's the latter, don't forget this dutiful subject."

If a pinch of sugar had such power, what would happen if he fed her a bucket?

"I don't think you need my help with debauchery. But I'll know who to assign if I ever want a volunteer for the gibbet." She pulled away from his touch.

A fire-breathing hoyden lived underneath her stiff, perfect carapace. How he was tempted to see her out of it, even if it burned him.

Henrique clicked his tongue. "Hateful words for a prim princess. Have you no royal restraint?"

When she opened her mouth, no doubt to shoot an angry retort, Henrique fed her the second half of the pastry. She chewed it murderously, her gaze never leaving his face, and he cringed to think what part of his body she imagined destroying inside those delectable lips.

A knock on the door startled them both.

Sophie entered, carrying a tray.

Henrique pulled away from the bed. "You better eat every crumb, or I will mouth feed you like a spoiled baby."

"I guess I should thank you for your assistance. I hope you don't expect a medal. I save those to people who do not abandon their country."

She could throw the damn medal into the garbage for all he cared. He shut the door and leaned his forehead against it, panting.

A medal? He deserved sainthood.

Even Hercules would have a hard time dealing with her. She was Luis' problem, not his. What was it to him if she wanted to live inside her carapace? He needed a plan to take her back to Lisbon. Then would he be free of her haunting green eyes.

Henrique selected an arrow from the makeshift table. The duke's guests came out to enjoy the morning sun on the lawn. All except the princess. Isabel no doubt campaigned against outdoor games. Who knew what depravities could happen? One risked tossing a ball and his clothes during the same match or dirtying his hands and his conscience. She must be solving the country's problems, armed with her exquisite brain and an embroidery needle.

The Duchess of Canastra strung her bow and loosed an arrow. The shaft flew ten feet and dropped onto the lawn, adding to the dozen already littering the grass. "So, what is in England? A sophisticated aristocrat? A lovely debutant?"

Henrique grunted. There would be several women and zero judgmental princesses with inquisitive green eyes and too-kissable cherry lips, whose naïve patriotic ramblings could vanquish all mills in the world. Henrique pulled the bow's string. The arrow flew in a perfect trajectory and hit the circle painted on the oak's trunk. "A chair at the university."

"I thought we had those in Coimbra."

Why did people find it so hard to believe he wanted to leave? "I won't bore you with the details. Science isn't run on good intentions. I need investments and long-term commitment." And peers who recognized his profession as an honorable pursuit.

"Don't we all..." She sighed, a wobbly smile on her lips. "Speaking of Portugal, How is Dom Luis? Some *hidalgos* here weren't pleased with his refusal to assume the Spanish throne."

"I have many interests. Politics is not one of them."

"If only my husband had the same discernment." She lowered her bow. "Pity the princess could not join us."

Henrique looked at the palace's east wing. The window of Isabel's bedroom was shut. What's the point of coming to a beachside paradise if she would lock herself in stuffy meetings? He should be glad. Whenever she came near him, she caused an unwanted reaction. A rogue chemical waiting to blow up a man's carefully planned experiment. He gripped his bow and aimed. The arrow flew several inches from the target and vanished inside the oak forest.

Voices and rushed steps rose above the birds' chirping. Canastra and his buttoned-up sycophants crossed the veranda behind the lawn. Rafaela dropped her bow and rushed to Henrique's side.

"Oh, darling, another bullseye." Flickering her eyelashes, she laughed seductively.

The husband halted, lifted his brows at Rafaela's sudden performance, and after an awkward moment, continued on his way.

As soon as he left, Rafaela returned to her bow, her cheeks stained by a crimson blotch.

She fit his type—attractive, mature, and married. But he was not interested in her romantically, and unless he misread the signs, neither was she. Since their arrival, they had developed a friendship, nothing else.

Henrique narrowed his eyes, lifting a brow. "Care to explain?"

She shrugged, and her gaze wouldn't meet his. "You will excuse me. I need to oversee... the dinner preparations. Yes, the French chef cannot *pureé* without my help." She whirled on her heels. "Don't forget the yacht party tomorrow. Bring your swimming suit."

In her haste to leave, she bumped into Dio.

Dio bowed and ogled her retreating form. "I'll tell you, there's something fishy going on here. The women are curious enough to my tastes, but the men... Can't you feel their feigned tolerance? They have all the love for foreigners you have for dirty hands."

"Nonsense. The Spaniards are a proud and independent people."

"Oh, please. They stroll around in their military finery, unsure if they are characters in a doggerel or an elegy. They give me charged looks as if afraid I could escape with their house silver or their wives, maybe both. They are always plotting, but each pretends not to know the others are also plotting because the admission would have made the plotting absurd."

Henrique snorted.

"Something is rotten in the state of Spain," Dio said, his brows furrowed. "If you cannot feel the situation boiling, then you are not applying yourself to your hero's mission—"

"Not applying myself? Hercules had it easy. Half of his jobs summed up to carting animals across Greece. I would like to see him do the same with an obstinate princess. Hercules would have broken her pretty neck."

"Isabel is sometimes, well, difficult."

Henrique raced his hand through his hair and glared at the princess' window. "That, my friend, is an understatement if you ever uttered one."

Dio tilted his head to the side, caressing his goatee. "The hero doth protest too much, methinks. Care to explain?"

Curse his outburst. Like a hyena, if Dio smelled a carcass, he could not rest until he found it.

Ignoring his friend's curiosity, Henrique pointed at the envelope sticking from Dio's frock coat. "You've opened my correspondence again?"

Dio smiled sheepishly. "Is it not what sommeliers do?"

"Sommeliers test food and drink for poison. Nosing others' mail isn't in the job description." Henrique grabbed the letter and scanned the lines. "The Italian is pressing me to conclude the sale of the estate. But you already knew that, didn't you?" Henrique crumbled the paper.

"What will you do?" Dio fingered the bows and arrows displayed on the makeshift table.

While Henrique played the nursemaid to a prim princess, his future was at risk. "I need to convince Isabel to leave, but she is more stubborn than a mule. If she realizes I must return, she will plant her feet on the pasture just to spite me."

Dio chose a bow and tested the string.

"Don't—"

Dio had terrible luck with weapons. Before Henrique could take it from him, Dio placed it over his shoulder and aimed.

The arrow went flying.

Henrique grabbed the bow from Dio's hand. "Damn it, what if you hurt someone? The last time you caught a bayonet—"

A pitiful caterwaul came from the oaks edging the lawn.

Henrique held his breath.

A man staggered out of the woods. He had an arrow protruding from his top hat.

Dio jumped back and crossed himself.

Henrique swore, rushing forward. "Charles? What are you doing here?"

Charles' clothes were in disarray, his eyes red-rimmed. "I need your help. She doesn't allow me to see her."

Henrique pointed at his head. "You have an arrow on your—"

Charles removed the pierced hat and stared at it as if he couldn't decide what was stranger, the hat or the arrow. At least he wasn't hurt, thank God.

"Have you been drinking?"

Henrique examined the other man's preoccupied expression. To be honest, his jaws and nose had lost the bloatedness he sported back in Lisbon. He seemed bewildered but not intoxicated.

"It's Dolores, my lovely Doll. She is so sad... She fears the princess will never allow her to see me. The tyrant kept her under strict surveillance in the palace, but here is worse."

Was Dolly the reason Charles acted like a deranged fool? Henrique exchanged a glance with Dio, whose lips twitched with suppressed mirth.

Charles held his hands together in front of his face. "You have access to the princess. Help us, please."

Henrique frowned, not liking the direction of the conversation. "Help you with what?"

"I need to see Lady Dolores. You could arrange it if you wanted it." Charles kneeled and grabbed Henrique's feet. "I'll die if you don't help."

Henrique stepped away from Charles' grubby hands. Who knew what sort of bacteria they carried? While he disagreed with Isabel's way of living, he couldn't throw Dolly into the arms of a profligate like Charles Whitaker. "What are your intentions with this girl?" Henrique gagged over such damning words.

"I love her."

"That does not mean a lot, does it?" Henrique turned to leave.

Charles followed him. "I want to marry Lady Dolores. If you help us, I'll name you my best man."

"And what does the position entail? Should I drop by every week to bring you a fresh stack of cards and a pack of cigars?"

Henrique stared into Charles' earnest gray eyes. He could imagine the princess' panic if she knew a first-order wastrel pursued her precious lady. She would gather her bags and flee.

Of course, she would. And Henrique would be there to pile her trunks atop the coach.

Henrique's lips tugged up in a slow smile as the plan took shape inside his mind. He would love to see Hercules topple him now.

Chapter 11

"I have the simplest tastes. I am always satisfied with the best." Oscar Wilde

Henrique braced his feet on the yacht's deck and grabbed the railings. The sailing cruise presented endless possibilities. Recline on the silk pillows, savor fresh oysters and chilled champagne, and swim in the Atlantic. Perfect for Henrique's plan. A full day of seeing Dolly and Charles together would be enough to chase Isabel out of Comillas. He breathed in the brine-scented breeze and allowed himself a moment of self-congratulation.

Dio sipped his *sangria* and examined the apple bits floating in the white wine. "Delicious stuff. Where was I? Oh yes, he arrives this evening."

"Who?" Henrique's gaze traveled from the golden beach to the palace. Shouldn't Isabel have arrived by now? Most of the guests had already embarked.

"Have you been listening to anything I said? Alfonso de Bourbon, who else? It's all this Spanish folk talk about." Dio leaned closer, his voice lowering to a whisper. "Strange things are happening here. Too many secrets." He raised his brows.

Henrique waved away his concerns. Government stability in Spain had been in short supply since the Hapsburgs had inbred themselves into idiocy, ending their dynasty without an heir. Why meddle in their affairs when the effort would cause more uproar? "Tell me something new. They season their paella with political intrigues."

Henrique leaned forward but couldn't see the princess's room from the yacht. Would she use a bathing suit that left the arms uncovered? A detailed image of her body invaded his thoughts—alabaster skin turning peachy with the sun's kiss—and he loosened his cravat, suddenly overheated.

Dio cleared his throat. "One would think this Bourbon prince to be a demigod, for all folk are anxious about his arrival."

"Still rambling about this prince? He could be the Grand Calipha for all I care." Henrique had dealings with royalty to last him a lifetime. He only put up with Dom Luis because of their friendship, and now the little princess because of Luis' blatant manipulation. He had zero will to interact with a royal whelp with more conceit filling his head than gray matter.

"Where is she?" Henrique rubbed his palms together. *Come on, Isabel, I dare you to prove you have more than frosty blue blood racing through your veins.*

Dio watched Henrique with narrowed eyes. "If I did not know you so well, I would think you were eager to see her."

Henrique tightened his hold on the railings. "The plan won't work if she is not aboard, will it?"

Charles waved at them, his fair skin already an alarming shade of red. How futile to ask him to stay concealed until Isabel embarked. With his ginger hair combed up and his gaudy summer coat fighting with his magenta vest, he was as inconspicuous as a peacock hiding behind a maypole.

Dio sighed and shook his head. "Are you sure this is a good idea? Do you remember his affair with the baroness? People still talk about the duel and how the angry husband shot his buttocks."

"Charles promised to behave," Henrique said with less conviction than he should. What could happen in a confined yacht with Henrique and Dio keeping close watch? Charles would be let loose long enough for Isabel to see him pursuing Dolly and listen to a pathetic declaration or two.

Steps clattered on the wooden pier. It must be Isabel. Henrique straightened, his hands twitching to help her aboard.

Dolly crossed the drawbridge and ambled inside the deck. Alone. Henrique's arm went lax, and his shoulders deflated.

When the girl saw him, she lowered her head and increased her steps.

Henrique blocked her path. "Isabel?"

Her face colored, and she peeped at her pink skirts, the bonnet hiding her eyes. "I haven't seen her since last night."

Henrique exhaled and moved out of her way.

What had happened? As if he didn't know. The princess must have stayed locked inside, paying her respects to boring aristocrats and burying herself alive in the middle of this paradise. A wave of disappointment hit him in the guts. What a waste. All of a sudden, the pillows seemed faded and flattened, the champagne still, and the oysters spoiled.

Henrique twisted the ropes of the yacht as the hull rocked from side to side, the rhythm morose.

The duchess emerged from the downstairs cabin, straightening her naval officer's jacket. Her loose skirt caught the wind like a sail, emphasizing her ample hips. She came closer, a bright smile showing her teeth.

"I thought you had invited everyone," Henrique said, unable to disguise the sullen tone of his voice.

"Good morning to you too, *querido*." She tapped his arm with her closed fan, her eyes glittering. "Isn't everything to your liking? You mentioned you were easy to please."

A crew member delivered her a note. She opened the piece of paper, and her smile wavered. She cramped it in her hand. "Canastra isn't coming. Lift anchor."

The boy hurried away. Shouts instructed to unfurl the sails. The wind picked up, animating the canvas like a dancer's veil.

"Make no mistake, I'm eager to start the journey, but won't Isabel be cross if we leave without her?" She would sweep down on them from her lofty heights, a vengeful pirate princess demanding they walk the plank.

"Isabel has no passion for sailing... And the tide waits for no one. Come, I have someone dying to meet us—the duke's private wine collection." She curled her hand around his forearm and licked her lips.

Henrique stared at the jewels bedecking her fingers. An emerald the size of a robin's egg flashed at him. The exact tone of Isa's eyes.

"You go ahead. The guests are waiting."

"As you wish." Tossing her head, she sauntered away.

Groups opened to greet their host.

She paused in their midst. "Welcome to the *Poseidon*. I have only one rule: the first who speaks about politics will be dunked in the ocean."

Claps and laughter followed the statement, soon engulfed by excited chattering and clinking glasses.

Henrique grabbed Dio's arm. "Keep an eye on the love birds."

"But what about you? Never tell me you will resist the duchess? She is riper than a grape in September. The plan can always start tomorrow."

A crewman released the rope tying the boat to the pier. The hull swayed and lurched to the sea. Henrique stared at the gap between the pleasure barge and the dock. Two feet now, and increasing.

Tensing his grip on the railing, Henrique leaped.

Dio gasped. "I'll be damned."

Chapter 12

"For the valiant, the world is as their own estate."
Miguel de Cervantes, *Don Quixote*

The day dawned blue and hot. Isabel tossed away the bed coverings and went to the window, pulling her nightdress from her perspiring skin. Strange dreams had bothered her all night. They all involved tasting sugar, and Henrique's lips. She shouldn't preoccupy herself with the libertine. A genuine threat lurked. Alfonso de Bourbon would arrive today. His presence could undermine the Duke of Aosta's hold over the Spanish throne.

Isabel flung the glass panels wide and supported her elbows on the windowsill, welcoming the sea breeze. The green lawn gave way to the beach, which, in turn, faded under the pressure of the Atlantic. A boat, its sails high and proud, braved the surf.

Shadows passed beneath the rippling water. What hidden threats lurked inside the blue depths? Seen from the safety of her bedchamber, the ocean breathed, a living creature waiting to swallow a person whole.

Why hadn't she learned to swim when she was a girl? At least it would have made her less fanciful. With a sigh, she shut the window.

Isabel stretched her arms and donned her robe. She needed to understand Canastra's intentions. Another day hearing the duke's guests' heated discussions... Better prepare her ears. It took a while for her to realize their raised voices and angry gesturing were not fighting but normal conversations.

Portugal and Spain shared a peninsula, and many in Europe couldn't understand why Portugal clung to its independence. The fact was that Portuguese and Spanish were as different as the Flamenco from the Fado. While Spain's cultural dance expressed emotion through passionate movements, the latter contained music with glorious feelings but little action.

She could ask for Dolly's help to uncover information. Since she loved to chat, Dolly could befriend other ladies, and they would open up to her. Isabel strode to the sitting room she shared with Lady Dolores.

A sliver of light peeked from the other bedroom. Was she still abed?

Isabel opened the door. "Dolly?"

The wind fluttered the gauzy curtains. Isabel pulled the sides of her robe close and padded inside. The room was empty.

Clothes lined the back of chairs, and stockings littered the Persian rug. A red garter decorated the recamier. She must warn the girl to get rid of such gaudy unmentionables.

Dolly's writing box lay open atop the escritoire. A letter had been left in the drying sand. Who could Dolly be writing to? Her father, the Duke of Chagas? Isabel doubted it. Prying was wrong, but what if it belonged to that rake, Charles Whitaker?

Gaze rushing to the door and back, Isabel swept the sand away. The revealed words were not to Charles...

but to Lady Anne. Why would she write to Isabel's most trusted confidante?

Isabel blinked, trying to make sense of the child-like handwriting. Dolly started by flattering Rafaela, gushing about the Duchess' sophistication, fashionable gowns, and delightful disposition. The sweetness burned Isabel's throat. Then came line after line of complaints about... about... Isabel. The travel and the days spent here in Comillas. How Isabel had made her suffer through bland tea parties and dinners with old, grumpy people.

Those were important meetings. Luis had entrusted her with understanding the mood of the Spanish aristocracy. How could Dolly ignore the need to sacrifice frivolous pastimes for the greater good?

They had an entire load of merriment in Lisbon, didn't they? Could Henrique's words be true? Did her ladies prefer the convent to her household?

The unwelcome thought washed down on her, and she gasped, dropping on the chair and lowering the letter. Hugging herself, she closed her eyes. Joyful sounds pressed against her ears. Everyone laughed—the gulls, the children, the servants, even the sea.

The door swung inwards. Isabel's eyelids shot open. Henrique barged inside the bedchamber, bringing in the ocean's scent. He flung his hand at his windswept hair and scowled at her.

Isabel stood still, her heart picking up speed. "I'm not receiving visits today."

"Have none of your tutors instructed you on common courtesy? Do you take pride in dismissing invitations?"

Her chin weighed a ton, but she lifted it anyway, cloaking herself with all the composure a princess could muster while dressed in a robe and fighting back tears. "My education should not concern you. The only thing I plan on dismissing is you. Please leave."

Frowning, he paused and gave her a bewildered look as if only then noticing her dishabille.

For once, Isabel had made him speechless. She lifted a brow. "Well?"

He shook his head and averted his eyes. Was there a blush on his cheeks? "I came to... You didn't show up at the pier today. Some worried you were unwell."

"As you can see, I'm in excellent health."

"Are you, though? All the guests embarked on the yacht this morning. When Dolly boarded alone..."

Everyone except her? And no one thought to invite her. Of course, who would want a bore like her to ruin their fun? Mortification sank into her chest, robbing her of air. "How convenient. I hope they enjoy themselves then." For the first time since he had invaded her privacy, she felt naked in his presence. Isabel tightened the knot of her robe, her fingers clumsy.

Henrique advanced in her direction, examining her with his head cocked to the side. Isabel fought the urge to turn from the sarcasm he would no doubt inflict and stiffened her spine. Let him mock her. She wouldn't cower before him.

He came closer still and cupped her face. His palm rasped her skin, surprisingly warm. His nearness ignited the invisible tendrils, but today they were different. Not only did they make her immobile, but they singed her. When she lifted her eyes to his, Isabel's breath caught in her throat. His mask of cheerfulness had slipped to show the man beneath, and it disarmed her. He brushed his thumb over the corner of her lip, and tingles caused a riot in her chest. Isabel inhaled to speak, to say he shouldn't touch her thus, but her mouth wouldn't obey.

"I thought Rafaela had invited you."

So they were on a first-name basis already? Isabel jerked away from him, and her hands clenched, crunching Dolly's letter.

He perked up at the sound. "What do you have there?"

"Nothing." Under no circumstances could he see the cursed letter.

"Isa, Isa... What secrets do you hide?" His husky voice made the hairs on her arms stand on end.

"You have overstayed your welcome."

"But why? I'm getting comfortable." His lips tugged up, and he prowled closer. "I would rule out a love note. Is it perchance a political conspiracy?"

"Don't be ridiculous." She backed away from his advances until she stumbled on the escritoire.

A second sheet dropped from the tabletop and landed on the carpet between them. Why had she not checked for more correspondence? Isabel dove for the paper. The infuriating man launched himself forward. She expected him to go straight for the damning letter, but he tackled her. Panting, she tried to free herself, but he tightened his grip. After catching the paper with his left hand, he extended his arm above her reach.

In her struggle, the robe had gaped open. He stared at her decolletage, blatant appreciation heating his gaze. Cheeks flaming, Isabel shook herself from his hold and refastened the sash.

While he read the letter, Isabel contracted her shoulders, trying to disappear from his sight before he made sense of Dolly's handwriting. What kind of disparaging comments and complaints the girl had written this time?

"Attending the races, swimming with my new bathing gown, riding a bicycle. What is this? A to-do list?" He studied her with narrowed eyes.

Isabel grabbed it from his hand and breathed a sigh of relief when she noticed the lack of a signature. "Er... Why, I made this list to plan my day here in Comillas, but as you said, Dolly and Rafaela left on the yacht, and I am all alone."

"Are you sure you wrote this?"

"Can't you recognize my handwriting?" Fluttering her eyelids, she sustained his probing gaze.

He lifted his brows and circled her slowly. "I think the author has a shorter vocabulary."

"You are absolutely mistaken, sir."

He paused too close and leaned forward to speak in her ear. "Prove it."

"You want me to write a few words for you?" Isabel shivered and rubbed her arms, her voice coming out too breathless for her own taste. "So you can compare our handwriting? Even you must admit it is extreme—"

"No need. A child could copy such..." He scrunched his face, pointing his chin to the letter. "Markings. Today is your lucky day." He made a flourish with his right hand and bowed. "I'm ready to squire my Dom Quixote to all her earthly desires."

Isabel gasped. "I'm in no need of a Sancho Panza."

He chuckled. "Not Sancho. I'll be your handsome and more experienced knight."

She scoffed. "You, a knight? More likely a knave—"

He shushed her with a finger on her lips. With a firm leash on herself, she restrained the urge to bite him. She glowered at him instead.

"Before you deny me, I have a revealing story for you. Once upon a time, a proud princess lived in a castle. She was indeed charming, and her patriotism inspired the masses..." He placed his hand above his heart, his eyes twinkling mischievously.

She feigned interest in her nails. "Your point is?"

"The princess professed to the winds her court delighted all, but when one of her ladies decided to live in a convent..."

She glared at his smiling eyes. "Lead the way, Sancho."

The Turkish silk kept the sunlight from entering the bathing machine. Still, it did nothing to avoid the heat. What an awful contraption. Whoever invented these cottages on wheels just so women could bathe in the sea must be a sadist. Isabel wrung her hands while Sophie unbuttoned her morning dress. Would she go ahead with this? Swim with Henrique in the ocean? Her heart had yet to settle into its normal rhythm, stuck in an allegro ever since she accompanied him to the beach. Curse Dolly for being so sloppy with her things. Curse Henrique for riling her up. Above all, curse her pride. When she was twelve, her head tutor had waited an entire afternoon in her mother's dispatch room to warn the queen of Isabel's excessive pride, calling it hubris. Granted, her mother had laughed, telling him Portugal could use more pride in its princesses. But Isabel had countless opportunities to reform, hadn't she? But no, instead of giving in to Henrique, she chose to drown.

Sophie cleared her throat, presenting the shapeless trousers of her bathing suit. Isabel eyed the black garment with distaste but helped her maid settle the dress and adjust the belt over her waist. This entire business of sea bathing struck her as incongruous and unnecessary. Dressing in the middle of the beach while Henrique waited outside, only a canvas sheet separating them? To make matters worse, the bathing machine stood suspended on railings, waiting to be lowered into the ocean, like a sacrifice to Poseidon. All to enjoy the dubious pleasure of splashing around in salt water.

Hung over the opposite wall, Rafaela's bathing suit flashed at her like the costume of an odalisque. The outrageous sleeveless garment had short trousers!

Sophie followed the direction of her gaze. "It is all the rage in Paris."

"*Et tu*, Sophie? I thought Republicans shunned such earthly pleasures." She hoped Rafaela would get sunburnt and have wrinkles before her time.

"Republicans are not Puritans, I assure you. We enjoy earthly pleasures very much. Indeed, we would love it if they were not only for the aristos... The duchess's bathing machine is *très chic*. The ones used by the common folk are hay carts. They smell of seaweed and body odor."

Isabel laughed. "That sounds preposterous."

"Indeed, it is. Oh, dear. There are no towels here. I will retrieve them from the palace." She turned to leave but halted. "Will you be all right, Citizen Isabel?"

Isabel nodded once, twice. It was at the tip of her tongue to ask Sophie to stay, but she shut her mouth. "Yes... Yes, absolutely."

How hard could it be? Isabel would enjoy the water for a minute or two and then return, a small price to keep her pride intact and avoid Henrique's gloating for the rest of their stay. Many women didn't know how to swim and bathed regularly in the ocean. She eyed the ropes pending from pegs on the machine's wall. That's what they were for, were they not? When the lady couldn't swim, they tied her to those strings and dropped her... like an anchor. Isabel shuddered and looked away.

"When you are ready, just wave the flag. The dipper will lower the bathing machine. Citizen Henrique awaits outside."

"Thank you, Sophie."

The maid opened the canvas and left.

Chafing against the heavy flannel of the bathing costume, Isabel fanned herself. Was this supposed to be fun? Why did it feel like she awaited to enter a circus but was clueless about her performance? Wave the flag, indeed. They could wait there all day.

A loud clatter and a series of clicks came from outside. The bathing machine shuddered, rattling the Venetian mirror. Rafaela's indecent bathing suit quivered and jerked, the starlet of a bawdy show. The wheels groaned, and the whole wooden house shook. Clasping her hand over her mouth, Isabel opened the curtain.

They tumbled down the beach, the ocean looming closer and closer.

Her stomach dropped, and she held the hat peg for support.

With a last groan, the contraption stopped. The waves seemed louder. Isabel took a deep breath, but the stuffy air brought no relief.

"Are you sulking in there?" Henrique's voice boomed outside.

"I don't sulk."

"Why are you still inside? Oh, I know, you missed the heralds announcing your entrance."

A loud, blaring sound came from outside. Isabel realized he mimicked the sound of horns.

"Ladies and gentlemen, I announce Princess Isabel."

The man was impossible! And he made keeping her pique an impossibility. Against her will, laughter bubbled out of her chest. Isabel tiptoed to the canvas door and pulled the drapery. A gush of breeze greeted her. The ocean spread an inch below the bathing machine's front porch, submerging the steps she had used to climb inside. She lowered herself to a seated position, bending her knees to avoid wetting her toes.

Henrique moved his arms underwater, his hair slick, his shirt soaked, and then he inspected her, his eyes sparkling more than the sea. "By God, what a hideous garment."

Isabel crossed her arms in front of her middle. He would no doubt prefer Rafaela's daring bathing suit. "Always so charming. The dark flannel might be unflattering, but at least it keeps a lady's modesty."

"Of course, better to suffocate than show a little skin. The water is divine."

Indeed, it was so transparent she could make out the sandy bottom. But the calmness deceived. The sea merely slumbered, waves swelling and ebbing, the breaths of a mystical being.

"I'm perfectly fine where I am, thank you." Isabel touched it tentatively, sighing at the delicious coolness.

"If it is modesty you fear, no one will see. The beach is empty. Rafaela's guests are still on the yacht, and the duke's subjects stay inside the palace."

"You never give up, do you?"

He smiled sardonically. "I've heard Princess Alexandra of Denmark is a proficient swimmer. Once, she even attempted to cross the English Channel."

Her lips twitched at his feeble attempt to engage her pride. "Perhaps she just needed space from the Prince of Wales." Ignoring his bafflement, she closed her eyes and leaned back on her elbows, pretending she was enjoying the sun's rays and not cooking inside the black flannel.

A hand circled her wrist and tugged. She lost her balance and gasped. Henrique kept pulling until she verged on falling over.

"Stop! I can't swim." The words burst from her throat, and Isabel cringed at the shameful confession.

He released her.

She shuffled back to safety, hugging her knees.

He glared at her, his hands on his lean hips. "You can speak five languages, play two instruments, and discourse about literature, science, and philosophy like a scholar, but if your boat capsizes, you'll drown?"

If he put it that way... "Three."

"What?"

"I play three instruments."

"Come here. I will teach you how to swim."

She eyed the water wistfully. What would it be like to move inside it? "I'm not interested."

"You are an intelligent woman. This is a matter of safety. What if you had to save another? A child?"

"I don't think I can do it." By Athena, was that her voice? It sounded taut and thin and... weak. She gazed away from him.

Her admission drained his anger, and he smiled, treading the water until he was level with the bathing machine porch. "Nonsense. As an Orleans, you have French blood, have you not?" He caught her wrist and traced his fingertips over the blue veins.

His tanned hand against the whiteness of her skin blurred her recollection of the family tree. "I do? Yes... Yes. Of course, I do."

"Then, you are a descendant of Melusine, the mermaid who gave birth to French royalty. Therefore, you must be a natural swimmer." He released her wrist.

Isabel laughed nervously. "What kind of scientist spouts hereditary ties from a myth?"

"The very best. A natural philosopher embraces theories, no matter how outlandish. I must formulate a hypothesis, then devise methods to prove it."

"And how, pray tell, will you accomplish that?"

"By trial and error, of course." He splayed his hands atop the porch, wetting the wooden platform, and hoisted himself to her side. Grinning, he lifted her to his lap, one hand below her knees, the other holding her shoulders. Moisture from his shirt seeped into her bathing suit. Like a hulking stray dog, he shook his head, spraying her face.

Gasping, Isabel pummeled his chest. "I command you to release me."

"To hear is to obey." He lifted her high and let go.

Screaming, she plummeted with an undignified splash. The ocean swallowed her whole. She lifted her head, sputtering. "You... You madman! I'll drown."

"We are in the shallow," Henrique drawled.

Isabel anchored her feet on the sandy bottom and forced her eyes open. Her cheeks burned with her dramatic outburst. Cool water penetrated the heavy folds of her clothing. She took tentative breaths and relaxed. Confident in her safety, she moved her arms, enjoying the water's caress, and wiggled her toes in the sand.

Henrique dove and emerged near her. "Before we begin your lesson, I must warn you. Whatever you do, do not lower your head and put your feet up."

"Why would I attempt something so outlandish?"

He flashed a wicked grin, exposing white teeth. "Trust me, just don't."

Isabel rolled her eyes. "Fine. Now what?"

"We are governed by survival instincts. You will start listening to yours."

"That may be the truth for animals. I am ruled by my conscience."

He lifted his brows, patronizing her. As if he alone kept all of humanity's secrets. "Are you so in control then?"

She didn't care one whiff about the challenge in his tone. "Always."

"Then prove it. Control your body into swimming."

She glared at him and lifted her leg. "See, no fins."

He laughed, raising his palms in self-defense. "I'll demonstrate."

He opened his shirt and flung the dripping garment atop the porch. Isabel blinked, riveted by the expanse of bronzed skin and taut muscles. So this was a male chest. Had the temperature increased several degrees? Men swam bare-chested all the time, and she wore the most modest gown possible, but still... The moment felt too intimate. How could it not? The same water lapping her torso caressed his male nipples. Gasping, Isabel tore her gaze from his salacious body to his unrepentant grin. He winked and plunged headfirst. With fluid movements, he lifted his head above the surface, kicking his legs and pulling with his arms in perfect cadence, as if he alone listened to the ocean's music.

He flashed her a conceited smile. "Come here."

Isabel's heart drummed inside her chest. She remembered to put one foot in front of the other until she arrived before him. He lifted her, one hand under her knees, the other below her mid-back.

"Calm down. This is part of the lesson."

She curbed the instinct to plant her feet back on the sandy bottom.

"See how the water buoys you? It's natural."

Isabel relaxed her neck and shoulders and closed her eyes. The water magically lifted her. Still, she could feel his palms burning her skin. When she opened her eyelids, his gaze was fixed on her mouth. Isabel licked her lips, her pulse accelerating.

He released her and cleared his throat. "See how easy it is? Now it is your turn. Go."

"Can't you be more specific? Was this how your tutors taught you to swim?"

"My father used to take us to the river Tua in the summer, my sister and me. His teaching method consisted of dunking us first and then shouting to keep our heads up. Later, we would fish until the shadows of the Princess Tower were a mile long, and Mother shooed us back into the house." The memory softened his features.

His father spent time with him? "He seems wonderful."

"You would've liked the stoic old gentleman. He most surely would've liked you. A more patriotic subject this country never saw." His voice turned gruff.

Isabel had the impulse to massage the pleats on his forehead. "Does he live in Braganza still?"

"He passed away long ago."

"I'm sorry."

Their gazes locked. Emotions swirled beneath his surface. Should she ask what happened? When they seemed to haunt him so? Did she want to know?

He broke eye contact, his customary smile back in place. "We are here to swim, no? You are lucky because swimming is one of the many things I excel at. I've swum the Hellespont, the Seine, the Thames, the English Channel."

She lifted her brows. "I don't think your conceit will teach me."

He laughed. "You will push with your legs and paddle with your feet."

Determinedly, she gazed at the water. Everything she had attempted, she had succeeded. The ocean would be no different. Isabel mimicked his instructions and relinquished the safety of the bottom. The sea buoyed her.

"There you go. Now work those arms and legs!" he shouted.

She gritted her teeth at his military tone but sprang into motion, whipping her limbs. Up. Down. Up. Down. Her muscles protested the sudden sprint, and every time she lifted her head to breathe, the water tried to find its way into her tiring lungs.

"Come on. You can do better."

Isabel redoubled her efforts, battling the water with all her might. She gained traction and speed, her movements more coordinated. That would show him!

"Enough there. You can stop now." His voice came from far behind her.

But she was making progress. Ignoring his command, she trudged on. A wave hit her in the chest, lifting her high. Hazily, she fought the surf, but it crashed down on her, a waterfall of foam. She tried to kick the bottom, her lungs burning for air, but the wave twisted her, pulling her down.

Something gripped the loose folds of her gown, dragging her up, blessedly up, until she broke the surface, gasping for air. Henrique stared at her. Through her watery vision, the white of his eyes gleamed against his tanned skin.

"What were you thinking? Why didn't you stop when I asked you to?" he yelled, hauling her to the shallow.

"What? I didn't... The wave pulled me down."

He halted and whirled her to face him, clasping her shoulders. "This was a lousy idea if ever you had one."

She dared a step closer, inhaling the salty, sunny scent of his skin. "You, sir... are a terrible teacher."

He raked his fingers through her hair, forcing her face up. The heat of his stare sizzled her. "You, Princess, are no mermaid."

The sun cooked her back and the top of her head. His nearness dissolved her will. Those invisible bonds shimmered into life, drawing her near. Light-headed, she clung to him, waiting, wishing, craving, her fingers digging into the sinewy strength of his arms. A compelling force took control of her. The lack of air, the water—later, she could blame them. Now she only wanted.

"This is wrong. Tell me this is wrong, siren princess." His voice lowered to a husky whisper, his breath tickling her eyelashes.

Was it? He was too close. She couldn't think, much less form words.

"Wrong—right." Isabel went on her tiptoes, her hands clutching his shoulders.

Waves sluiced around them, bonding them.

He brushed her bottom lip with his thumb. "You madden me."

"I..."

He kissed her eyelid, her temple, the hollow of her cheek, and then her chin. His mouth was half open, painting her skin in salty water. Her heartbeats matched his too-slow explorations, pounding in her neck. When Henrique arrived on her lips, she was breathless, seeking his attention.

He stopped.

She inhaled to protest.

A rough exhale, a groan, and he meshed their lips, invading her mouth with his tongue. He tasted like the sea, forbidden and hypnotic. How could she have lived this far without knowing this flavor? He loosened his hold on her face and circled her spine, bringing her chest into contact with his. The heat of his skin seeped into the flannel of her dress, pouring into her nerve endings until her legs turned liquid.

Too soon, he pulled away from her, holding her at arm's length. Water dripped from his eyelashes, and she followed the tiny drops until they pooled near the corner of his lip.

He leaned forward until his forehead rested on hers. "I've told you we are ruled by animal instincts."

Isabel broke his hold and stepped back. The muscles of his neck and shoulders rivaled a marble statue for stiffness. He ran a hand through his face, his jaw locked. As an expert in expressions, she read the frustration in the tightness around his mouth and there, by the corner of his eyes, regret.

The mist clouding her thoughts dissipated. What she felt for this brute of a man didn't spring from her gut, as he implied.

Isabel clutched her hideous skirt, her chin trembling. "I see only one animal here."

Chapter 13

"Youth is wasted on the young." Bernard Shaw

Henrique paced the beach, fists on his hips, waiting for the princess. Isabel climbed out of the bathing machine. With her color high, the princess-turned-virago tossed her wet hair, lashing it against his chest, and spun past him in the palace's direction. The maid emerged from the striped canvas tent, gave him a startled, disapproving look, and sped after her mistress.

Henrique followed. What had he done? Luis should call him out. Henrique would not hesitate to pummel any bloke who dared the same with his sister. All was fair in the quest for pleasure. But crossing the line with a maiden? But all the chemical reactions he knew couldn't match the explosion of Isabel's kiss, an Amazon princess who knew what she wanted. He avoided self-deceit, and he would not start fooling himself now. The jolt coursing through him when their lips met had produced more electricity than a voltaic battery. A battery? Who was he fooling? Isabel hid enough passion beneath her flannels to light up an entire village.

And his lame attempt to justify himself? Flung it right back at his face. Still, should he be less than honest? All he offered was attraction, desire. Hot lovemaking and pleasant friendship when this journey ended. He rubbed his chest and exhaled. He couldn't trust himself around her anymore. The plan to escape Comillas took on a new urgency. His ill-begotten function as an escort needed to end before he did something both would regret.

Isabel hastened her steps along the graveled path leading to the palace door. He could tell she didn't lace the stiff corset, no doubt wanting to leave his presence with all haste. Her long strides emphasized her lean curves, a fresh reminder of treasures he couldn't explore.

A cold bath and a bottle of port would be in order. He would have dinner in his own room. He needed space. By the look of her, she would thank him for the courtesy.

Canastra sauntered out of the palace, interrupting her race toward safety. "There you are, Your Highness. I have someone to introduce to you."

A man of no more than twenty-five years old strode outside. With flaxen hair combed back severely and an unadorned black suit, the stranger stood in sharp relief against the duke's gaudy uniform.

Canastra beamed, eyes glittering like a besotted maiden, his chest gleaming with medals like a fanatic. "I have the honor of introducing His Highness, Don Alfonso, Prince of Asturias. The rightful king of Spain."

Henrique halted. So this was the prince Dio gushed about. He had the square Bourbon chin and the straight Bourbon nose. His mouth was an uncompromising slit topped by a waxed mustache. Dark eyes finished what was, he had to admit, a strong face. What lay underneath, though, he could not tell and had not the slightest inclination to discover.

Alfonso took hold of Isabel's hand and bowed at the waist. "I've been denied my home for long years, and when I return, it is to find the beauty of my Spain obfuscated by a Portuguese princess."

He spoke with the right amount of eloquence and surprise, as if he had just come up with that fanciful speech. He stared at Isabel with ill-concealed hunger. Henrique didn't like it and fisted his hands at his sides. Sure, the prince was handsome, in a predictable, staid way, but Isabel would not fall for his Romeo act.

Isabel curtsied gracefully. "I must discount your words as undeserved compliments, Your Highness. Your Spain's beauty gains on me by leagues."

She was wrong. With her flashing green eyes, alabaster skin, and regal posture, she put Spain's hills and golden beaches to shame.

Tilting her head, she wiped off all traces of the vengeful mermaid from her expression. "But I thank you for your kindness. It is a joy to find a gentleman with courtesy these days."

She didn't even deign to look at Henrique, but the barb hit home. He certainly deserved it. He took a step forward and cleared his throat.

The duke waved in his direction. "And this is the Viscount of Penafiel. A scientist," Canastra drawled.

Henrique ignored the petty slight to his profession, grabbed the prince's hand, and squeezed. Alfonso's grip wasn't the wishy-washy one he expected, but a firm handshake, returning the pressure Henrique gave.

Henrique sustained the other man's gaze until the prince's eye sought Isabel again.

"My sisters said wonderful things about you." Alfonso offered his arm, and Isabel placed her hand above his elbow.

Those fingers had just curled over Henrique's chest.

His gut tightened, and he started after the royal couple.

The duke grabbed Henrique's elbow. "Why the long face? Let's leave the young people to know themselves better."

Henrique gritted his teeth. "Dom Luis sent me here to protect his sister—"

"I can vouch for Dom Alfonso. He is a perfect gentleman. Isabel is more than safe with him as an escort."

The house party guests had abolished the siesta en masse to stroll around the garden. No one in their right mind would want to walk in the mid-afternoon sun under the Spanish heat. Still, the Bourbon prince had taken Isabel for a turn, and voilá, here Henrique was—following the royal couple, dragging an uncooperative Rafaela by the arm. The Spaniards watched Alfonso and Henrique's princess with barely concealed glee. Crap, she wasn't his anything. He shouldn't care if the prince drooled all over her. She could defend herself.

While Isabel sauntered on the arm of the Bourbon prince, Dolly chatted with Charles, their profiles partially hidden by a trellis. The rake's besotted looks would send any chaperone running for smelling salts, but not Isabel. How quickly she forgot her charge.

Without so much as a 'by your leave', Alfonso steered Isabel out of the garden path and into Canastra's maze. What a sleazy bastard. Taking a maid into the tall hedges, concealed from view, was the oldest trick in the rake's book.

Henrique increased the speed of his steps.

Rafaela pressed his arm. "Darling, if you go any faster, these slippers will torture my toes. Why race after the princess, anyway? My husband's protégé is a boring stick in the mud. He won't dishonor her."

"He can stay in the mud until it is dry. I'm curious about the maze, that's all."

She sank her feet on the grass and pointed to the Minotaur sculpture guarding the entrance. "My husband adores the myth of how Ariadne gifted Theseus with a spool of thread so he could defeat the monster and leave the labyrinth. Some say the Minotaur represents our deepest fears. I have nightmares about its hideous horns."

"Nonsense. The Minotaur is an allegory for humanity's basest desires." The creature was the son of a goddess and a bull. It didn't get baser than that.

"I won't enter."

"I've seen it from above. It is a spiral with branching exits every seven feet. I can navigate it with ease."

Canastra strolled along with his companions.

Rafaela threw herself in Henrique's arms. Canastra eyed his wife's spectacle and frowned. Then he averted his face and continued on the graveled path.

What in blazes was she doing, taunting her husband like that? The fiery duchess would get him expelled from the castle with her overtures. Frowning, Henrique planted her to her feet and stepped back.

Rafaela whirled to leave. "I bid you *adieu.* The laundry maid needs me—"

Henrique caught her arm. "Not until you tell me what is going on."

Her carefree smile faded, and she touched the paw-shaped leaves covering the maze's wall. "Have you ever been in love?"

Henrique had lost the royal couple and was fast losing his patience. "What does love have to do with this? The way you throw yourself in my arms every time your husband appears? If you are trying to incite a duel, you must know honor wouldn't allow me to kill him. Is this your plan? Do you wish to become a widow, Rafaela?"

"Of course not. I love him." Her black eyes turned liquid.

"Then why?"

She looked at him, and such hurt glimmered from her gaze that Henrique wondered how she managed her fun-loving façade.

Her chin trembled. "I love him, and well... my husband loves Spain."

Henrique brushed her arms and pulled her into a brotherly hug. Was all humanity blind? Rafaela was utterly different from Canastra. To think they could share anything more than a few grunts in an unlit bedroom was society's greatest lie.

"I'm sure he cares for you. Most husbands can be cold during the day, but at night, they—"

"He doesn't visit my room. I'm hopeless, aren't I?" She smiled, cleaning tears from her eyes and smearing her face powder. "Desperate for my husband's affection, trying to make him jealous when he clearly doesn't care."

"I would gladly help, but—"

"Thank you, oh, thank you! No one in Spain dares to come close to me. He is too powerful. But he has no power over you. I'm sure he will notice me if he thinks you are interested."

She kissed his cheek and skipped away.

Henrique's shoulder deflated. This stay couldn't possibly get more complicated. Shaking his head, he entered the maze. The evergreen walls raked his clothes. Their height was five inches taller than he, swallowing the sunlight. Closing his eyes, he visualized what he saw through his window. Right, left, right, center, three rights. Yes. He grinned. How easy it would be to surprise them in the center. Isabel's face would be priceless, with the bonus of curtailing their time alone.

Henrique's pulse quickened as he approached the last bend. Water dripping and murmured voices sounded closer. He was almost at them. Clenching his hands, he emerged at the central square.

A fountain gushed there, indeed, but its only dweller was a statue of Theseus killing the Minotaur. The royal couple had vanished. Henrique ran his fingers through his hair and clenched his jaw. Where did they go?

A shape detached itself from the shadows.

Henrique narrowed his eyes. "Almoster? Why are you haunting the maze like a golden-haired Minotaur?"

Pedro Daun strode near. He had ditched the military uniform and wore a black frock coat, his blond hair hidden underneath a tricorn. Anne wasn't with him. Still, Pedro didn't look like he was on holiday.

"Keep your voice down. I'm not officially in Spain."

"That, my friend, is a paradox. But making sense or not, you are a welcome vision. This place is a mad-house."

"Where is the princess?"

Henrique gritted his teeth. "She is with Alfonso de Bourbon."

"Shouldn't you be shadowing her?"

"Believe me, I've tried."

"I have critical information for you."

Henrique laughed. "You sound like a spy."

Pedro lifted an eyebrow. "Luis has been coerced into sending his sister here."

Coerced? The king had told him Isabel wanted a vacation. Of course, Luis had lied. Isabel was as interested in this loose seaside resort as he was in becoming a eunuch. Luis must have manipulated her into coming, just as he did with Henrique. Cunning royal bastard. "How can a Spanish duke force the Portuguese king to do anything?"

Pedro's look said Canastra could do that and much more. "At first, I suspected Canastra to be threatening Luis' finances. For a decade, the king overspent the annuity allowed by the Congress, contracting credit from the Rothschilds and the Burnay Bank in Lisbon—"

"And Isabel? Had he spent her—"

"The princess has a separate settlement. She keeps a tight financial rein over her household and wisely invests her mother's inheritance."

"That's my girl," Henrique said, his lips tugging up.

Pedro narrowed his eyes, no doubt processing Henrique's use of the possessive.

Why had he blurted the words? Isabel wasn't his anything. He shouldn't have kissed her. It was basic physics. Energy couldn't be destroyed. And they had created a lot of power with that kiss. Now it would walk with him, pestering him all day, with no chance of dissipating.

Pedro tilted his head to the side, his compelling gaze studying him closely. "If the problem was financial, the king would've come to me. Last month, I learned Luis kept a Spanish mistress, and she was selling his love letters. Before my aide-de-camp could retrieve them, Canastra bought the lot."

"What a sordid mess."

"Indeed. Before I go—"

"Go? How did you even get here?"

"The Angel is anchored in a hidden cove south of here."

"If Gabriel and Cris have returned from their grand tour, they can take my place."

"They haven't. I bought another yacht. Anne believes we are summering here."

"I have an idea. You stay here to clean up after the king's affairs. I will escort Anne to Biscay Bay."

Pedro laughed. The sound was still foreign to Henrique's ears, and in all their time serving in Mozambique and haunting Lisbon's hells, he never knew his friend had so many teeth. Marriage to Maxwell's sister agreed to him. The girl combined softness and courage, her strength so acute she could put a grown man to shame. At first, Henrique believed their marriage was doomed. Pedro and Anne were as different as combustion and photosynthesis. While the first released energy by breaking organic matter—or people's skulls—the latter consumed power to build matter. Who knew destruction and creation's final product were smiles?

"Even if I had the slightest inclination to relinquish my wife's company, she would balk at having me here with the princess. Despite her friendship with Isabel, I don't think she forgot Luis offered me the princess' hand last summer."

"Curse Dom Luis and his impulsivity." Pedro was a handsome devil, and the shrewdest bastard he ever knew, but a marriage between him and Isabel would've ended disastrously. They would clash day and night, both as bendable as a granite slab. "If you explain the situation to the princess, we could convince her to return to Lisbon." And then he could resume his life.

"I cannot be seen here, and before we discover Canastra's schemes, incurring his wrath would be a mistake."

But what of Dolly and Charles? The plan was already in place. In fact, Isabel would witness the couple strolling in the garden after dinner. If Isabel left because of a personal matter, Canastra could not blame Dom Luis. Henrique crossed his arms over his chest. "Why me? You are the politician. Every day I dally here risks my position in Oxford, not to mention the sale of my estate."

Pedro placed a hand atop Henrique's shoulders. "Your photographic memory and deduction skills will prove invaluable in bringing Canastra to the ground. I'm sure you will make your country proud. Your sacrifice won't be in vain."

Sacrifices of any kind left a bitter taste in his mouth. The Penafiel family perpetrated them as a sort of un-official motto. His father, with his fervent patriotism, was always ready to sacrifice for the sake of his country. Henrique should be excused if he had a distaste for the sacrifice chain. "Damn, you are good. You almost made me believe your crap. Save the haranguing for your soldiers, General."

"The country is counting on you."

"God have pity on their poor souls." Henrique turned to leave.

Pedro clasped his shoulder. "I need those letters. The king's popularity won't resist the scandal. You will help me recover them."

They had shared more than a bivouac in Mozam-bique. Pedro knew Henrique didn't care for politics, and few things would compel him to do what he had no interest in accomplishing. They were well-matched in stubbornness. "Impossible. Canastra has guards and is surrounded by devoted aristocrats."

Pedro's expression hardened. "If Luis falls, think what will happen to your girl. The best she could hope for is an exile to Prussia."

Henrique clamped down his retort so he wouldn't give Pedro more ammunition. He should not concern himself with her, and yet... Isabel, with all her sacrifices for morality's sake, should not pay for her brother's indiscretions. Henrique glared at Pedro. Almoster was not the most powerful man in the kingdom for playing fair, was he?

"What do you want me to do?"

Chapter 14

"It is not the man who has too little that is poor, but the one who hankers after more." Seneca

Isabel's calves burned with the quick steps she took to accompany Prince Alfonso's brisk walk. Was he in Spain to spend the summer? Or to threaten the Duke of Aosta? How challenging to glean his intentions while sprinting. Her skin was sticky from the ocean, and water dripped down her spine from her wet hair and her mind... Well, she forced her lips into a demure smile, hoping her appearance was composed while her insides had shifted. Sea bathing shattered a woman's inner world. The waves created extra space where she needed none, adding flashy colors to previously demure arrangements, exposing areas better kept secret. It was Henrique's fault. His and those squinting eyes and salty lips. Her first kiss, and he called it animal instincts. She stumbled on a loose rock and would have sprawled on her face if Alfonso had not caught her.

With a strong arm around her waist, he helped her regain her feet. "Am I walking too fast?"

Isabel peeked at him. When Canastra told her of Alfonso, she had pictured a conceited, self-important young man, much like other princes of her acquaintance. She had been wrong. Though he couldn't be a year older than her twenty-two, he wore sober clothes, no fancy uniforms or diamond studded links. The Spanish prince seemed reserved, serious even. She almost missed Henrique's quips and jibs.

"Racing can do wonders for a woman's constitution, I'm told."

Alfonso pursed his lips. "My legs are better suited to marching in a field."

"Fair enough. We should have Canastra level all the pathways and flowerbeds into a parade ground," she said teasingly. "Then ladies could run in their dresses and not disgrace themselves."

He smiled for the first time, and it quite softened his austere face. "Princess Isabel de Orleans, you have *gracia*."

"*Gracia*? Is that the Spanish word for short-legged princesses?"

He chuckled and shook his head. "*Gracia* is something everybody notices, but no one can explain. It's... A woman with *gracia* is more than beautiful. She illuminates her surroundings. She gives it character."

"Oh, thank you." Isabel gazed away. Everyone delighted in telling her just how dull she was. "I'm glad to learn the hidden meanings of Spanish words."

"I'll be happy to oblige. Especially if it will atone for tiring your short legs," he said solemnly.

Had he just made a joke? Startled, she glanced at him. Alfonso grinned and carried on.

They settled on a manageable speed, and Isabel felt her tension ebbing away. Despite the heat, or because of it, the scent of carnation and bluebells perfumed the air. Butterfly orchids poised over palm trees' trunks, giving the garden a fairytale aura. Walking with a gentleman without a constant flutter in her stomach was a welcomed reprieve.

"I didn't expect to have a screen of onlookers." Alfonso halted and glanced over his shoulder.

Isabel could well imagine the long line behind them crashing like domino pieces. "I'm used to it."

A veritable procession followed them, filling the walkways with pastel dresses and formal court attire. Henrique trudged the beaten path as well. Isabel ignored the cold shivers racing through her body whenever she heard his voice.

"I forgot about this lack of privacy. My family walks through Paris' streets undisturbed. In Sandhurst, I'm treated like a regular cadet."

"I'm sure it must be wonderful to avoid the headlines and live a common life," Isabel said, analyzing his reactions for any trace of his true intentions.

He frowned and searched her expression. She had the impression she, too, was being studied. But why? Without another word, he changed course and tugged her into the garden's maze.

A striking group of sculptures representing the Minotaur Myth guarded the entrance. Theseus' marble muscles bulged as he wrestled with the grotesque half-man, half-bull figure.

"As a prince of Athens, he could have had all earthly pleasures. But he abandoned his riches to stop the Minotaur's killing spree."

"He did his duty," Isabel said, and their eyes locked.

"You understand."

Did Alfonso perceive his duty was to gain the throne? While a man's duty boiled down to a 'do' or 'don't' type of decision, a woman's was far from simple. Isabel contemplated the third statue, the beautiful Ariadne. The princess admired Theseus. Would she have helped him flee the labyrinth if she knew the prince would seduce her and then leave her on a desert island, ruined? How easier would it be if women could remove feelings from the equation? Ariadne would then have stayed with her father, her heart intact.

Voices became louder as the onlookers approached, no doubt curious about their conversation.

Alfonso eyed them wearily. "Do you think they can follow us into the maze?"

"Do not underestimate human curiosity." Isabel glanced beyond her shoulder. Two couples had entered in their wake. At least Henrique was nowhere to be seen.

Alfonso increased his steps and took wild turns over the maze's path.

He halted. "Do you notice this scent?"

"What? I—"

He caught her forearm and guided her through a slit in the evergreen hedge. They emerged at the back of the palace, the stone structure crisscrossed by vines.

"Have you just cheated the maze?"

"I knew it." Smiling, he opened a door.

Then he took her parasol and, after folding it, escorted her over the threshold. Isabel scouted the path and, seeing no one, halted, reluctant to enter an empty corridor with him.

"You have nothing to fear from me. I'm a man of *pundonor*." He placed his hand upon his heart.

Though she had yet to discover what the Spanish word meant, she didn't feel threatened. The prince radiated an aura of righteousness. It radiated from his clear eyes and how he didn't lower them from her face.

A few moments alone with him could make him disclose his goals. Lifting her chin, she accompanied him inside.

They entered a kitchen, of all places. Alfonso tugged her through service stations, his excitement growing with each step. Copper pans and *jamon* haunches hung from the ceiling. Screams and hissing casseroles were punctuated by dough hitting and cutting.

Isabel took a moment to adjust from the peaceful rigidity of the garden to the aromatic chaos. Cloves and toasted chicory made her nose twitch. What could this foray mean? She'd been to a kitchen once in her adult life and doubted it was the natural habitat of an exiled prince.

He halted.

A maid rolled a white dough, and the scent of almonds and sugar made the air sweet. With their approach, the servant stopped and averted her eyes, her cheeks red.

"Turrons?"

She curtsied. "Yes, m'lord."

"Can we have some, please?"

The maid placed the cubes in a basket, and Alfonso took them. Another set of doors, and they left the crowded kitchen. The vegetation wasn't as well tended at the palace's rear. He lowered himself to a patch of grass and, hooking his arm over a bent knee, motioned for her to do the same.

The sun had started its descent. The golden light favored him, smoothing his lankiness. After Alfonso offered her one sweet, he bit into the white cube. His eyes closed, and a deep sigh escaped his chest. The breeze ruffled his blond locks, and in pleasure, he looked younger.

When he noticed her stare, a blush colored his fair skin. "I have not eaten a turron for years."

"Do you miss Spain?"

"With my every breath."

She couldn't resist feeling his pain. How horrible to be ousted from his own home.

Isabel twirled the turron in her hands. It tasted overly sweet to her taste. "Do you have plans for after Sandhurst? Will you take a grand tour? Imagine the freedom... Choosing wherever you wish to go."

"Duty comes above freedom."

"A little freedom has its uses. You will choose your own spouse." She kept her tone light and breezy. "No obscure German princess for you, or better yet, no one will force you to marry a cousin."

He fixed her with an unwavering stare. "Are we cousins, Isabel?"

A wave of heat covered her cheeks. "If you count Aunt Eulalia, who married Dom José in the seventeenth century... There is a reason Portuguese and Spanish royalty don't intermarry."

"Different tastes in music?"

Isabel discarded the *turron*. "Marriages entangle our royal lines and risk Portugal's independence. Portugal and Spain are different countries—different cultures, languages, everything."

"Of course. I admire your love for your country. I feel the same."

They were silent for a long moment. Chaffinches rustled about in the hazelnut trees, preparing for the evening.

Alfonso finished the sweets and brushed sugar from his hands. "What would you want to do if you were not a princess?"

The image of her kiss with Henrique came to her mind and, with it, those dreaded stomach flutters. "I love being a princess," she blurted. "It is an honor to represent my country. I strive to inspire my subjects. Especially the women."

"I'm certain you are a role model for Portuguese women." He gazed at her, admiration shining in his eyes.

Isabel couldn't keep his stare. Her skin was still salty from her ocean frolicking. She wasn't sure if she could be counted as an example of anything and wondered how to change the subject. "When you mentioned *pundonor*... I fear I missed the word's denotation."

He stood taller. "A Spaniard is nothing without his *pundonor*."

"Do you mean his honor?"

"Spanish has the word honor. The same as in Portuguese or English. But *pundonor* is different. How can I explain? *Pundonor* is a contraction of punta de honor—point of honor. Many things that a Portuguese or an Englishman can, in all decency, allow himself to do or to be done to him, the true Spaniard cannot." He punctuated the words with vigorous hand gestures. "If he is a man of *pundonor*, he must take action against insult. Otherwise, he is a *sinvergüenza*. A shameless man. An epithet worse than death."

The concept appealed to her in ways she could not explain. This sense of duty, of right and wrong, of morality should be present in Kings and subjects alike.

"Alfonso?"

"Yes?"

Isabel tilted her head to the side. "Why are you here?"

"I'm visiting friends, of course." He rose and extended his arm to help her up. "Will you be my friend, Isabel de Orleans?"

She sensed there was more to it, and still... With his dark clothes and serious gaze, he didn't look dangerous. He looked lonely. And terribly homesick. Sighing, she placed her hand in his. "I can be your friend, Alfonso de Bourbon."

Isabel sipped her wine. A gaudy arrangement of roses and crystals broke the dinner table in two. On her side of the flowers, Alfonso spoke about the future, his opinions enlightened and his face inspired. Below the flowers, the men guffawed, and the ladies giggled. One could guess which side Henrique occupied. Isabel tore her eyes from the merman-turned-Bachus reveler. She would show him she cared not if he kissed her and then flirted with Rafaela.

When Alfonso finished his speech about industrial progress, Canastra lifted his glass, his face showing great appreciation. "To Alfonso de Bourbon. *Dios, Patria, Rey.*"

Every guest repeated in unison. "*Dios, Patria, Rey.*"

God, Country, King. Everything the Spanish cared about in the world. All that 'Dios, Patria, Rey' stands for were male entities...

The Duchess of Montijo, mother-in-law to Napoleon the III and Alfonso's great aunt, tapped Isabel's arm. The elderly lady pointed an enormous ear trumpet in Isabel's direction. "Are you perchance the opera singer, the one who seduced my nephew when he was fifteen? Shame on you." Winking, she spoke in a lascivious side whisper loud enough to shake the dead.

The trumpet's silk fringe tickled Isabel's nose, and she sneezed. "Oh, no, I wouldn't. I'm—"

"Ha! Don't tell me. You are Maria Rattazy. The scandalous playwriter?"

Alfonso turned from his conversation with Canastra and caught his aunt's hand, pressing it affectionately. "This is Princess Isabel de Orleans."

"Dom Pedro's granddaughter?" Lady Montijo yelled and fished inside her reticule for a lunette.

Isabel felt her cheeks redden at the scrutiny. Lady Montijo thought fit to ask her to open her mouth and even lowered her glassy eyes to Isabel's hips.

Isabel caught Alfonso's gaze above Lady Montijo's white head, and he mouthed. "Ignore her."

While Lord Montijo gaped at Dolly's breasts, Lady Montijo turned to Diomedes. After her very vocal flirtation made Diomedes cringe, the old lady's hands vanished underneath the table. His face turned an unbecoming shade of red. Isabel could only imagine what sort of battle they fought beneath the pristine linen.

Meanwhile, laughter rolled out from the other side in shameless waves. When Rafaela's red lips touched the shell of Henrique's ear, Isabel gripped her knife with enough force to break the cutlery.

Would this dinner keep going forever? She had waited to be lulled in the rhythm of these affairs, the initial awkwardness of long silences and weather conversations turning animated, then argumentative, then wine-inspired, then finally sleepy. Instead, course after elaborate course, a stark reality mocked her. The Canastras, the Montijos... Henrique, with his squinting eyes. She knew this was the truth of aristocratic marriages, and yet... Why couldn't the vows spoken in a church carry more weight than a passing passion?

Rafaela clicked her glass, calling everyone's attention. "I'm so excited to receive you all here. I hope you brought some stamina because I've planned vigorous entertainment. We will have a hunt and boating on the lake, and to crown our summer, I'm organizing an amateur theater performance. Diomedes da Veiga wrote the play, and everyone must take part." Rafaela paused dramatically, waiting for the claps to end. "And that is not all. Tomorrow, we go to Sevilla. Matador Borriegas is in town. I'm sure our Portuguese guests will enjoy seeing how bullfighting is done."

Isabel had never attended a bullfight and intended to keep it so. "How considerate of you."

The duke lifted his palms. "Rafaela, don't make plans before consulting my wishes. I will take Alfonso to a political meeting—"

A glower replaced Rafaela's smile. "Always politics—"

"I thank you for the invitation," Alfonso said. "But I wanted to show a special place for Isabel on the morrow."

Henrique narrowed his eyes, and Isabel felt a frisson of excitement at his disapproval.

Her cousin seemed about to argue, but Canastra lifted his hand imperiously. "The young people should decide their entertainment."

Rafaela gave Canastra a malicious smile and turned to Henrique. She spoke something to him, and he laughed. The dinner participants resumed their parallel conversations.

Alfonso bent forward to whisper in Isabel's ear. "I hope you were not jealous."

A furious heat claimed her cheeks. "Why would I be jealous of Henrique? He is just the escort my brother imposed on me—"

"I meant of my aunt's ravings. The opera singer she mentioned and Maria Rattazy... Both belong in the past."

Isabel averted her gaze, cursing her wayward tongue. "Oh, I'm certain—"

His face turned serious, and he placed his hand above hers. "A man in my position is constantly besieged by the opposite sex, but I want you to know I despise infidelity. I will be as faithful to my wife as I am to my country."

Her eyes sought Henrique's, and her heart stung with pain. If only all males felt the same.

Isabel left the drawing room before the other guests. The dinner had drained her energy. She needed a restful night to collect herself. On her way to her bedchamber, Isabel was startled by a shuffling sound. She paused before a Venus statue, half expecting it to speak. A gigantic moth flapped its wings and flew to the ceiling. Isabel chuckled at her own jittery nerves.

When she resumed her steps, someone grabbed her forearm.

A scream rose in her throat. Henrique's eyes glittered in the dimly lit corridor like a stray cat looking for trouble. Isabel clamped her mouth shut. No matter what he did or said, she wouldn't react. From now on, he would only see temperance in her, royal indifference. She would snap the threads linking them for good.

"You must stop accosting me, Your Excellency."

"Follow me." He tugged her arm. "Your help will come in handy."

"No—" She was about to give him a tongue lashing but swallowed the angry rebuff. Instead, she glanced placidly toward her room. "I'm not a footman to be in hand for any of your troubles. Please treat me with a gentleman's courtesy from now on. I bid you good night."

He huffed and rolled his eyes. "Would your magnanimous Highness perchance concede me the grace of your help?"

"No."

He pursed his lips. "But I asked nicely."

She shrugged, smiled prettily, and whirled to leave.

"I need Joan of Arc tonight, not the smiling other half of the Bourbon Prince Charming. But if you rather risk your beloved country's fate, suit yourself." He brushed past her.

The words country and fate strung together in the same sentence triggered alarm bells in her belly. Clenching her jaw, she went after him.

He stopped before Canastra's study and wrestled with the door, twisting the knob.

What could he possibly want in there?

He removed a pointed instrument from his pocket and poked the lock open.

Isabel lowered her voice. "This room is closed to the guests. What if someone comes in?"

"We will invite them to our private party. What else?" He glanced above his shoulder briefly and strolled inside as if he had not just breached the duke's privacy.

Isabel should leave. The devilish grin on his face spelled trouble, and if he disgraced himself, it could brush on her.

Henrique pulled the lamp's chain. Hissing, light crawled through the dark paneled walls, revealing an assortment of... objects?

She shuffled to the nearest shelf. Saint images, in all colors and sizes, occupied every nook and cranny. To the side, an altar of sorts. "I did not know the duke was such a religious man."

Henrique whistled. "What if he harbors more than ships in his ports? A heavy conscience?"

"Nonsense. Like all Spaniards, Canastra is very Catholic."

"A reliquary, saints' bones, candles, skulls. Who believes this is real? And there are shelves for pagan stuff as well. Canastra isn't taking any chances with the metaphysical." Henrique attacked the duke's desk, rummaging through his drawers.

The position stretched his black evening coat, outlining his shoulders. Images of those muscles, glistening and salty, assaulted her, making her mouth dry.

Henrique raised his brows. "Will you stop gawking and start helping?"

"What are you looking for?"

He lifted his head, and a forelock covered his left eye. "Letters. Implicating your brother in a scandalous affair."

Isabel gasped. A denial sprang to her mind, but she rebuffed it. She had lived too long with Luis to doubt it. Curse her brother's imprudence. Didn't he know the press would love rolling their name in the muck? Just thinking about the wealth of disparaging newspaper headlines made her shudder. If anything of the sort reached their subjects, her effort to uphold the morals of the royal family would be for naught. Portugal didn't deserve such shame.

"Will you help now?"

Well, she could compromise. But help was all he would get from her. No more extravagant feelings. Isabel moved to the bookshelves. Gaze straying to the door, she palmed the tomes and shuffled through pages. Perspiration dampened her fichu. This business of espionage was better left to salty satyrs like Henrique.

When he reached the shelf above her, she inhaled. What was it with his presence? It steeped the air, demanding attention like a burning candle in a darkened bedroom. Sure enough, she could shut it off if she wanted to. Still, worse than seeing the flame was the knowledge of its presence, the awareness increasing until her entire existence focused on the unseeing pinpoint of light.

She looked at him askance. "Don't you think it best if we divide our efforts?"

He lifted a brow and moved on.

When the last book had produced no secret stash of letters, she turned to a niche below the window seat. Outside, moonlight washed the grass. The cicadas sang softly, less urgently. If she were fanciful, she might believe they no longer struggled with their carapaces. Were they enjoying flying to fresh adventures, or were they missing the protection of the known?

Isabel allowed her gaze to travel farther until it landed on the ocean. The waves reminded her of salty kisses, and she looked away. Quite by chance, she saw a tendril of smoke and connected it with a lit cheroot and an unmistakable redhead. Charles Whitaker leaned against a cork tree, a blight on the night's loveliness.

"What is that rakehell doing here?"

The air shifted by her side as Henrique moved to the window. His arm brushed against hers, and Isabel stepped away, the casual touch singing her.

Henrique peered outside and grumbled. Isabel squinted at a volume in his hand. Why would he carry the image of a dwarf? Protruding from the statue's belly, at least as long as the dwarf's height, was a giant phallus.

Isabel sucked in a breath. "What in heaven's name is that?"

"Haven't you heard of Priapus? The Greek god of fertility?" Henrique asked without bothering to look at her.

"What is he doing here?"

"Priapus? I guess Canastra must be having problems with his male potency—"

"I mean Mr. Whitaker!" she cried out.

"Yes, of course. He must have come to spread his body fluids in Spain. Who knows what sort of depravity he has in store under his flaming hair? The risk to Lady Dolores's reputation is immense." Henrique tapped Priapus's shriveled head. "As soon as we find the letters, we better leave Comillas."

Isabel stilled, narrowing her eyes. She didn't mention Dolly's infatuation to Henrique, and she could bet Dolly didn't speak of it either.

With a jerk, she closed the draperies. "My duty here is not over, but I can certainly send Dolly back to her father."

"Damn it, Isabel. I have a life. I—"

"Have you summoned Charles? To force my hand? Well, your efforts were pointless. I won't leave. But it's no longer safe for Dolly. I will inform her to pack her suitcases." Isabel shook her head. His selfishness knew no bounds.

"What are you, a schoolmaster? Let Dolly and Charles know each other, see if they suit."

"Charles will ruin Dolly."

Henrique clicked his tongue and stared at the indecent figure in his hands. "Did you hear it, Priapus? Ruin her? I'm not privy to Mr. Whitaker's staff, but if anyone could ruin a female, you are the fellow to do it with your mighty sword."

Isabel could not help it. Her eyes went to the statue's male appendage, and heat flooded her cheeks. "You would go to any length to shock me, would you not?"

"Length is indeed the point here." A satirical grin lifted his lips. "Why so bashful, Isabel? Every living creature with carbon in its composition and genitalia in its body does it. The bees do it. The birds and the trees do it. The horses and the hounds do it. Goats do it, and so do queens and little princesses."

Isabel gripped her skirts, crumpling the velvet. "If you have no respect for a lady's virtue, our conversation is over."

"My fiery princess, a maidenhead is only a membrane. I don't understand how losing it can be ruinous."

He robbed her of words. How easy for a rake like him to scoff over morality. While he lived in good society, enjoying all the benefits and none of the obligations, women had to conform or accept ostracism.

Tapping his chin, he addressed the dwarf. "If women were born without maidenheads, think of the fun—"

"Keep your sinful musings to yourself." She sucked in a breath. "My concern is Lady Dolores and Charles Whitaker—"

"Of course, the two lovebirds." Henrique brought the statue an inch from her face. "Priapus will help them tie their knots."

Isabel yanked it from his hands. "He will not!" She curled her fingers around the oversized genitalia and wrenched it. The old wood splintered. Jutting her chin forward, she gave him a smug look.

Henrique's hand went to his groin, and he stepped back. "What if Dolly is in love with him?"

"I know she is. A girlish, innocent, idiotic love." She punctuated each word by tapping Henrique's chest. "Why else would a young lady encourage Mr. Whitaker's attention?"

"Can you stop hitting me with Priapus' cock? It's unladylike."

"What?" She opened her hand and stared at the brownish stick. "Ew, Ew, what should I do with it?"

"The wooden or the real one?" He winked.

Glaring, Isabel shoved Priapus and his torn appendage into a shadowy perch where it could not cause mischief and cleaned her hands in her skirts.

"Look. Charles loves her. His intentions are noble. He wants to marry the chatter chit."

"He is a rake and a drunkard."

"He has not drunk since he met her. He changed."

She crossed her arms over her chest. "I hardly believe such to be possible."

Henrique exhaled through his mouth. "Whatever happened in the past to make you hate men, don't extend it to him." He dropped his voice as well as any hint of mockery.

She didn't hate men... She didn't hate the man standing before her, his face bronzed by gas lamps, his hair disheveled, his coat wrinkled from the search. A knot formed in her stomach, and she dropped her gaze.

He took a step closer. "I see you entertaining the prince all day. Just because Charles isn't royalty—"

"She can stay." Isabel blurted, hoping she was not making a terrible mistake. "But you must help me keep an eye on them."

He caressed her cheek. "Isa, Isa... We make a lovely team. When you are being all mellow and reasonable and not a royal shrew, that is."

Isabel danced away from him before the tendrils could work their treacherous magic. There. She had allowed her temper to get ahead of her with Priapus, but she regained control soon enough. "We should resume the search."

Applying herself to the quest, she left no rock—or image, for that matter—standing. The minutes ticked by slowly. Her fingers hurt from shuffling through Canastra's unusual possessions, her eyes gritty from reading correspondence in the dim light.

When the clock pounded midnight, Henrique cursed. "It's useless. The letters aren't here."

Isabel splayed her hands over the duke's desk. "Why the impulse to help my brother? I thought you couldn't wait to leave the country and all its problems behind."

He had the grace to blush. "Why, er... I'm more complex than you take me for... Surprised?"

"Of course. Men are notoriously complex. In fact, science should try harder to crack open the male brain. You should volunteer."

He laughed, and his eyes glinted predatorily. "You have a very cunning tongue, Your Highness. I wonder if it is as competent when it isn't protected by your sharp wit."

"You will never find out."

Henrique grinned. "No? You enjoyed sticking it into my mouth this morning."

Only her years of princessing restrained the urge to slap his face. "All it took was one kiss for me to move on. Is it not what happens with rakes? One taste of a woman enough to discard her? Chase the next target?"

He sucked in a breath, the sound barely audible in the hushed study, but she heard it as if it was an elephant stomping in a crystal shop. "Have you moved on, Isa?"

Isabel stepped back until her crinoline bumped the desk. "Yes. Yes, absolutely."

His eyes hardened. "Think you a pillow prince can kiss you better than I?"

Kissing Alfonso hadn't crossed her mind, but he didn't have to know that. Isabel raised her chin. "He would not dream of taking such liberties. He is a man of *pundonor*."

Henrique shuddered. "That sounds painful. Will he survive?"

"*Pundonor* is the Spanish concept of absolute honor. A standard for high morality and a life of duty."

"I hope it isn't contagious." He shoved his hands in his pockets, and a tic appeared on his jaw.

"Even if it was, you are quite safe from contracting it."

"Isa, Isa, you should know not even a rogue can accept a slight to his character. You leave me no alternatives but to take offense. A duel is what you deserve."

"Excuse me?"

He cradled her face. Isabel clutched both his wrists, but before she broke free from his hold, he advanced. She stumbled, her spine meeting the window's cold glass. Breathing heavily, he pressed his chest against hers and melded their lips. Blatant, insistent, his tongue invaded her mouth. A torrent of warmth consumed her, and she held on to him, afraid to dissolve, leaving a puddle on the duke's carpet. His heart pounded against her, the steady drum comfortingly exciting. Pulling in a deep breath, she held it in her lungs, savoring his decadent scent. Those tendrils climbed up her legs and found their way to her hands and around her spine, binding her will to him. She stopped fighting. She couldn't leave. She didn't want to.

He loosened his grip and pressed his hips against hers. Isabel's heart pumped inebriating liquid into her veins, making her vision swim. She dug her fingers into his upper arms, relishing his sinew and strength. Bolder now, she moved her tongue against his, tasting his taste, his texture.

He groaned and pulled away from her mouth. Chanting her name, he rained kisses down her cheeks and neck, and then he stopped.

Isabel opened her eyes.

He stared at her, his brows raised to his hairline. "And?"

Her knees threatened to buckle beneath her, and her breasts strained her corset. No matter what, she would not give him the satisfaction of knowing how much he affected her. Had he not said their attraction was nothing more than animal instincts? Stoically, Isabel smoothed her skirts. "Really, Henrique, you should improve your... your technique. I find it to be lacking."

He eyed her suspiciously. No doubt bemused why she was still standing on her own two feet, not leaning over his manly torso and running her hands over his close-cropped hair.

Well, Mr. Henrique's pride, take that for a change.

She brushed past him, rubbing against his chest a shoulder colder than a January evening. Few things could give her more satisfaction than the way his glistening lips fell open.

"Perhaps I should try it again. Practice makes it perfect."

Plucking her wrist, he pulled her against him, circling her waist and bending her torso backward until her heels no longer touched the carpet. Her breath caught, and her pulse beat in places it had no business reaching. Henrique's grin flashed at her, his eyes sparkling. Her center of gravity tilted, making her stomach flutter. She stared into eyes the blue of mythical places and instead of negotiating an armistice, she wondered what she had to do to lure his mouth closer.

The door opened with a startled swoosh.

They were caught. Gasping, she placed both palms on his chest and shoved. His hold on her gave away. She toppled to the floor, her bustle taking the brunt of the impact, and bit the inside of her cheek to muffle a cry.

"Can I help you?"

Isabel vaulted to her feet and stared at the duke's majordomo, mortification boiling her face and the tip of her ears.

Henrique stepped forward, covering her. "We are handling ourselves fine, thank you very much."

"Your Excellency, I must warn you this room is not open to guests."

She was about to acknowledge the *faux pas* and leave when Henrique laughed. "Closed, you say? Do you know who you are talking to? This is the princess. Nothing is ever closed to her."

The butler's eyes rounded, and he stepped back.

"What are you doing?" she mouthed furiously.

"Just play along," he whispered.

The butler lifted his white-gloved palms. "Oh, I didn't recognize Her Highness. Still, I must insist."

"What is your name, kind sir?"

"Pizarron de Moncayo-Tully."

Henrique opened the door. "Let me tell you something, Pizarron. This woman expects everything she wants to be delivered to her on a silver platter. Don't you, my dear?"

She didn't! "Do I? Yes, indeed I do," Isabel mumbled.

"And if lives have to adapt to her wildest desires, then be glad you could serve. But don't raise your hopes too high because soon she will move on, and you will be powerless to prevent her."

"What?" The butler looked extremely uncomfortable.

"I'm sure she'll let the interruption pass this time, but next, I'll advise you to be more diligent unless you wish to lose your head or even more important parts." He jerked his head toward the door, a clear signal for the butler to leave.

The poor servant gasped and whirled in fear or outrage, she could not tell in the dim light. Henrique closed the door.

Grinning like a pirate, Henrique raised his brows. "What do you think of my performance? Could Alfonso topple that with his *pundonor*?"

Isabel's face burned with shame. "You are a rogue and a blackguard—a sinvergüenza." One with shameless lips. She couldn't seem to tear her eyes from his shameless lips. "And I... I loath your hide."

Laughing, he sniffed her neck. "I'll take a princess' loathing any day. Smells much better than royal indifference."

Chapter 15

"You don't reason with intellectuals. You shoot them." Napoleon Bonaparte

The morning sky had no clouds, promising a sweltering day. A breeze shook the olive trees, making them shimmer. Henrique crossed his arms above his chest and glared at the palace's door. The prudish princess had the gall to pursue him into his well-deserved sleep. In his dream, instead of racing to her room in high dudgeon, she kissed him. He had peeled layer upon layer of clothing, never arriving at her pale skin. Just as he had reached her shift, a gull screeched outside his window, and Henrique woke up with a hard-on. No amount of ice-cold water would solve it, and he had to take matters into his own hands. A practice he had avoided since his randy teenage years.

Henrique cursed under his breath. Instead of lusting after Isabel, he should find the letters. As soon as the guests left for their outdoor entertainment, he would continue to search the palace. Hands crossed behind his back, Henrique paced to the Eros statue. The mischievous imp pointed its arrow at him, and Henrique stepped out of his range, an inch from crunching a couple of insects. The male praying mantis flapped its wings and swayed its abdomen to get the female's attention. The female stared, oblivious to his efforts. Henrique wanted to shout to the male that once it climbed on her back and mated, the female would bite his head off. How futile. He would do it regardless.

Males were all the same.

Foolish creature. Henrique kicked a pebble. Movement at the front door alerted him of their exit. His pulse sped up for no apparent reason. He spotted Isabel. Her hair was pulled up, so much so her already strong cheekbones stood out. Human nature was vile. Just because he'd never seen her hair down, he obsessed about its weight, its color, if it smelled of roses or jasmine. He hated her crown, not because it symbolized their different status, but because it forced her to pile up her hair mercilessly atop her head. What would it take to lift the weight of those diamonds from her temple and free her mane? He would do it slowly, kissing and smelling every strand. Lazily, he would massage her scalp, and then he would drink her thankful moans.

Alfonso's laughter pulled him from his revelry. The prince clung to her side. She rubbed off an air of royalty to the inconspicuous prince, a legitimacy to Alfonso's somberness that clashed with Henrique's breakfast.

Instead of the usual fichu, Isabel wore a scooped gown, chaster than current fashion but showing two inches of skin. A simple strand of pearls graced her neck. Alfonso laughed at something she said, and his eyes danced to her chest. Bastard. Henrique had invented the eye dance.

Dio elbowed Henrique's side. "Perfect, they are all leaving. Where do you wish me to start the search?"

The royal highnesses strolled along the trail to the beach, escorted by several couples, including Rafaela, Canastra, Charles, and Beatriz.

Before he could judge the sanity of his actions, Henrique jogged to their front, blocking the way. "Care for a tennis match, Your Highness?"

The couple stopped.

Isabel's smile was all teeth. "Alfonso planned to show me—"

Henrique shrugged. "Go along then. Prince Alfonso shouldn't risk losing face among such a glittering court."

The prince frowned, no doubt unused to being challenged. What did Isabel see in the guy?

Isabel patted the prince's hand. "I'm sure Alfonso would love to sharpen his technique, won't you?"

The prince took a measured breath and removed his gloves. "Of course."

Henrique stifled a laugh. Isabel had just met him and already knew how to manage him. Should he warn Alfonso of the female mantis mating habits?

Isabel glared at Henrique, all nasty and provocative. It promised a world of painful, hopefully sweaty, retributions.

After sustaining her look for a few seconds, he winked. The game hadn't started, and Henrique was already winning. He had disgruntled Isabel and prevented them from spending time by themselves.

As they convened at the tennis court, Dio pulled him to the side. "Why the change of plans?"

"You whined the Bourbon was dangerous, did you not? This is a perfect opportunity to study the prince. Wasn't it Aristotle who said a man shows his true self at play?"

They faced each other on opposite sides of the net. The sun shone behind Henrique, another of the advantages lady luck bestowed upon him. Slashing the air with his racket, Henrique waited for Alfonso to serve.

An itch of satisfaction coursed through him. Dio's talk about heroes must be to blame—he felt a primitive urge to trounce the foppish prince on the lawn of honor and prove to Isabel what a dunce he was.

The lad bounced the ball two times and threw it up in a flawless perpendicular arc. He swung, using his body weight in the attack. The leather sphere grazed the painted line, bruising the grass and isolating itself.

Hearty claps thundered from their small audience. The loudest of all was Isabel's.

"Fifteen zero," Dio declared.

Henrique's smile showed all his teeth. "So, just back from Sandhurst? When do you boys graduate?" Henrique slashed the air with his racket. "Eighteen years old? I don't remember."

The prince cleaned sweat from his forehead. "I've been told it often happens with age."

Henrique narrowed his eyes, his fingers flexing around the racket handle, and vowed swift retribution. The back and forth of the match heightened the tension. Henrique's muscles strained as he chased after shots, his mind focused solely on the game. When the ball flew at his side, he hit it at the right angle. It rolled and scraped the net, falling limply on Alfonso's side. He lifted his palm. "Sorry."

The lad nodded, a flat smile on his Bourbon lips.

They disputed the points thoroughly. Henrique had to admit the prince had some technique. After a pernicious forehand, Henrique veered to the left. When he realized the boy's intention, it was too late. Alfonso pitched to the right. Henrique could only follow the ball with his eyes. Point for Alfonso.

The prince smiled. "I apologize. My friends at Sandhurst are sprightlier."

Gritting his teeth, Henrique smashed. The ball hit the prince in the chest.

A deadly silence descended over the court.

Rafaela raised her arm. "How entertaining. But we ladies also need some exercise. What if we played doubles? I can play with Henrique and—"

Henrique shook his head. "I will partner with the princess."

Isabel frowned, her gaze shifting from Alfonso to him. "I don't know. It's been years since—"

"Portuguese versus Spaniards? But then... We are far from home, and I don't intend to embarrass our country with a lousy performance."

Isabel pulled herself up to all her diminutive height. "Why not?"

A thrill coursed through him when the proud princess abandoned the prince and glided to his side of the court, and he controlled the impulse to puff up his chest and make indelicate gestures at their Spanish audience. After a terse nod in his direction and a thorough inspection of her racket, she positioned herself forward and to his left, her stiff corset making her dress look like armor.

Henrique groaned. What had possessed him to incite her into this? He couldn't care less if they failed, but now he linked their game with her exalted country, he would endure her displeasure after they lost.

Rafaela threw the ball, a very mild, very gracious serve, almost as if afraid to hurt the leather sphere.

Isabel had no such compunctions and returned the ball with savagery, her arm as punishing as her tongue lashings. The ball zinged past Rafaela, who narrowed her eyes in a very feminine, very predatory way.

So the game began.

It was tight. Rafaela and Alfonso were well-matched, their technique flawless. While Isabel had no service to be proud of, her competitive streak could scare even the staunchest of generals. No point was lost for her, and the potential strength in that svelte body defied the laws of physics.

Rafaela won the point and blew Isabel a malicious kiss. The princess's face turned an alarming shade of red.

Henrique caught her arm and whispered in her ear. "Mind her not. You are superb. Portugal could not be better represented." He meant it as a joke, but it came out with a ring of truth.

Isabel searched his eyes and gifted him with a sweaty smile. "Thank you. You are not so bad yourself."

Henrique placed a hand above his chest and returned to his place, still not used to the power of those smiles.

For all their constant bickering, they made perfect teammates. Pride filled his chest at being on the same side as hers. As the game progressed, he knew what balls to go after and which were hers. He trusted her to do her best, celebrated her victories, and cursed their defeats.

It led them to the match point. The crowd hushed. Isabel moved with predatory grace and advanced toward the net, her hips swinging from side to side. Henrique's breath came in short bursts, not because of the physical strain but because her derrière was mere feet away from him. He shook his head. Cleaned sweat from his brow.

Rafaela, her face flushed and hair undone, followed the ball's trajectory with her chin. When she sprang to block Isabel's backhand, she missed.

"Match point!" Dio screamed.

The audience clapped half-heartedly.

Henrique found Isabel's gaze. A luminous smile lit her face, her green eyes flashing. Henrique felt her smile's power inside his chest as if she had charged it with electricity. His pulse sped, and he had this strange feeling of elation, making every single atom of his body alive. The cheers of the onlookers mingled with the rapid thud of his heartbeat. In four strides, he demolished the distance between them. He grabbed Isabel by the waist,

her small, beribboned waist, and swung her in the
air. Her eyes twinkled, and she hollered an unladylike
howl.

"We won! We won, Henrique."

She placed sweaty hands over his shoulders, and he
lowered her slowly. The crowd hushed. Victory was
heady, but Isabel's smile inebriated him. The pastel
gowns and flannel coats vanished, or they were still
there, but Henrique had stopped seeing them. He had
so much to say. If this was feeling patriotic, why had
he not enlisted sooner?

"We won."

He lowered his face, his lips craving her cherry-col-
ored smile.

A throat was cleared, and an outstretched arm
intruded on their private celebration. The crowd's
cheers came back in a hush, and with it, Alfonso's
breathless voice.

"Good game," Alfonso said.

Isabel shook herself, and in a dash, her composure
was back in place.

Henrique fisted his hands, a breath away from
punching the pompous prince. A need to crush Alfonso's face and then kiss Isabel, claiming her in
front of the audience, burst inside him, as primal as
hunger, thirst, pain, and desire. The violent thoughts
staggered him. What was he doing?

Panting, Henrique stepped back.

This whole patriotism had climbed into his head.
He hadn't come all this way north to despoil his best
friend's sister, his monarch, for Christ's sake.

After a brief handshake, the prince offered his arm
to Isabel. "Are you still up for our outing?"

She hesitated, searching Henrique's gaze, a shy
question hidden in its depths.

"You go ahead. I promised Dio to trounce him at
whist."

Hurt flickered in her expression, or he had imagined it. Isabel didn't spare him a second glance. She smiled at Alfonso, and the prudish princess and the pompous prince walked out of his sight.

Chapter 16

"Spain is a bottle of beer, and I am the cork; when that comes out, all the liquid inside will escape, God knows in what direction." King Ferdinand VII

I sabel crossed the formal garden and exited to a dry, rocky outcrop behind the castle. How quickly Henrique had dismissed her. Why had she fooled herself into expecting more from him? He had stayed for the entertainment. Woe to those who wanted more from him than fleeting pleasures.

Alfonso exhaled heavily. "I'm ashamed now... I've never been beaten so soundly at tennis. But this Henrique, he is quite good. Have you known him for long?"

"I met him on the day of the journey to Comillas. He is one of Luis's trusted friends." Debauchery cronies more likely.

"He seems like an odd option to accompany an *Infanta* of Portugal."

Isabel frowned. She could speak badly of Henrique but wouldn't allow anyone to do the same. "Viscount

Penafiel was my brother's choice, and I bow to my king's wishes."

"Your brother should have sent a royal. We have a duty given to us by God to rule, and it leaves the relationship biased. It is not fair to any of the parts. We must keep our distance from the rest of the subjects."

No! She would tear apart any barrier between Henrique and herself. Isabel sucked in a breath, her hand instinctively moving to cover her mouth. Where had such riotous thoughts sprung from? If she had any sense, she should be the one erecting those walls. "You are right, of course," she forced herself to say, her voice a dejected whisper.

They walked in silence. Isabel could not muster the will to ask him about his plans. A flock of shallows flew from cork tree to cork tree. The fluffy beings had the freedom of wings but couldn't escape each other.

Sophie and two of the duke's footmen trailed behind them. Her own guards had returned to Lisbon yesterday. Canastra bade them leave in a closed coach as the leader fell ill with the Typhus. She hoped they would recover. Sophie didn't trust their new bodyguard, that's for sure. ... Still, Isabel had no reason to worry about her safety. Canastra guarded his property well.

"Are you all right?" Alfonso asked.

"I'm just eager to see your surprise." The lie came out lamely, and she stifled a groan. "I'm glad you saved me from Rafaela's bullfight. I take it the sport isn't to your liking?"

He grimaced, and a sallow smile curved down his lips. "Canastra fears the Guardia Civil will be there. They are loyal to Aosta."

Isabel had read about the fearsome military police. They were both revered for keeping order and reviled for being too vicious in keeping such order. How dreadful to fear walking freely in one's own country. She touched his arm. "I'm sorry."

He dismissed the sadness like a puppy shakes water drops. "To be Spanish and not love *Touradas*? What kind of *sinvergüenza* do you take me for?"

"Now you will tell me bullfighting is a matter of *pundonor* as well?"

"Not quite. A *torero* without *pundonor* is not a *torero*, of course... But *Toradas* are Spain, and Spain is *Toradas*."

"I won't believe such a lovely country to be the same as the violent sport."

He placed a hand over his chest. "One day, Isabel de Orleans... I will make you like bullfighting."

Isabel caught a daisy in her hand. "I doubt it."

"You are looking at this from the wrong angle. Spain's story is linked to bullfighting in ways as ancient as the land." He peered at her briefly, and then his eyes lit up. "Have you been to the Jupiter temple close to the beach?"

"What does a ruin have to do with bullfighting?"

"Everything. During the Roman Empire, Spain garrisoned most of the legionaries. While common folk adored Jupiter or Minerva, soldiers worshiped Mithras. They believed this dark God to be responsible for creation. He killed a divine bull, and its blood originated all life."

"Gruesome," Isabel said, wondering where he was headed with his tale.

"The legionaries built temples to worship Mithras. Before a battle, soldiers huddled in its underground caves. A priest would slaughter a bull atop the grate, and the animal's hot blood would bathe them, making them invincible."

He paused, his voice solemn. "The *torero* fights the bull for this same mythical strength, giving immortality to those who fight the bull and those who watch."

Isabel smiled for his sake. "The history lesson was great, but I will keep to my lavender soap."

"Thank Mithras for that." Laughing, he kicked a pebble. "Isabel de Orleans, what would you do if you had absolute power?"

Isabel frowned, taken aback by the odd subject. "I believe in a constitutional monarchy."

"That's why it's a hypothetical question. If I were king and didn't have to bow to parliament, I would forbid exile. Spain for the Spaniards." His voice faltered a little.

It broke her heart how much he missed his home. But what could she do other than offer him empty platitudes?

"I would banish male debauchery. Enhance women's power," Isabel blurted.

"More power?" He halted and looked deep into her eyes. "Impossible."

Glancing away, Isabel kept walking. She had breached all her rules about interacting with males during this trip. Still, she didn't feel threatened, the way she advised her ladies would be when in the company of a man. Henrique aroused in her a palette of unwanted emotions, but fear wasn't one of them. And Alfonso... his were the manners of a true prince.

"It is here."

The olive grove parted to show a grassy ridge. She had not realized they had climbed so high. A plain stretched for miles and miles, the muted colors of earth, rocks, and sun-burned hay contrasting with the powerfully blue sky.

"That is the Ebro River. Since my family had to escape from everything we held dear, I didn't cross the river back to Madrid, to my home."

Caressing the horizon, the Ebro sashayed among rocky outcrops. The water was so incongruent with the dry land it was almost a mirage.

Isabel looked into eyes so black they resembled a fathomless pond. A shiver ran up her arms. "Why, Alfonso, are you in Spain?"

His face hardened, and he took a step away from
her. "I graduated from military school, and I'm not
allowed to wear the red and yellow uniform. I've
studied history, geography, and politics, but I'm not
allowed my opinion. My mind brims with ideas to
take Spain to the future, but my future was robbed of
me. I want to wear my country's uniform and board
a Spanish frigate while my subjects scream *Viva Es-
paña.*" He closed his eyes, and the wind whispered
through his hair. "I want to cross the Ebro to Madrid
and sit on my throne."

Isabel gasped. "Surely you know this is impossible."

"I'm the only descendant of Saint Louis. The legiti-
mate heir."

He talked treason. She turned to leave.

He held her arm. "Are you still my friend, Isabel?"

She shrugged away his touch. "I don't have dangerous friends."

"How would you feel if a power-starved general
banished your family from Portugal and installed
foreigners in your place? An Italian playboy who
doesn't even know your motherland's idiom?"

"I would not interfere if it was in my country's best
interests."

He grasped both of her hands. "I know you love
Portugal, and I admire patriotism. I wouldn't be
here if my presence weren't needed. Aosta is killing
my country. The economy flounders. The peasants
starve. Spain is in the Middle Ages, while Britain,
France, and Prussia have factories and progress. I
want to change the order of things."

A tightness spread from her chest to her limbs. For
the first time, she felt unsure of how to act. Her king
had given her clear instructions. Luis was back in
Portugal, secure she was doing her duty. But Alfonso?
Her instincts screamed he was ready to be king.

Alfonso smiled, his black eyes alight with shy mischief. "Come now. I'm not asking you to take arms with me and invade Madrid."

"What are you asking me? Portugal's support is not mine to give."

He shrugged. "If I can't have the support of the entire nation, can I at least have it from the one Portuguese who counts for me?"

Isabel stared at his outstretched arm. Could she deny Alfonso had the strongest claim to the throne? She placed her hand atop his. "You have it."

Chapter 17

"Vision without execution is hallucination."
Leonardo da Vinci

Henrique entered the conservatory, his eyes scanning for Dio. The scent of orange and greenery tickled his nose. In the far corner of the glass room, a stage had been erected, and servants bustled around, arranging chairs and various props. The clanking of a mallet hitting wood blended with Dolly's high-pitched voice, creating a lively cacophony.

Dio glared at the setting, a scarf tied around his forehead and an apron covering his clothes. With a brush, he assaulted a stretched canvas, splashing paint over the floor. His portrayal of Zeus and Olympus was unconventional, to say the least, likely to frighten small children.

Henrique raked a hand through his hair. "Can you stop for a second? I need your help."

"What a coincidence. I needed you as the star of *Hercules' Choice*. What did you say? 'I have no patience for amateur theatrics.' The performance is the day after tomorrow. This setting is dreadful, and now I'm stuck with Alfonso to play the hero. I doubt his eloquence."

"Alfonso is a man of *pundonor*. He won't have to pretend to be a hero. The prick merely has to be himself."

"Unless *pundonor* is a dramatic streak, I don't know how it will help."

"Oh, but trust me, it will. According to Isabel, *pundonor* is this exalted quality, a high honor only present in martyrs and Bourbon princes."

Dio chuckled. "If I had not crossed the Hellespont with you, I would believe you are jealous."

Jealous? He wasn't jealous. He had wanted to murder Alfonso only when the bastard placed himself between him and Isabel. But the feeling had passed. Now, he merely wished to slap him around and break a bone or two. Nothing too damaging, just his ischium or his scapula.

Henrique pushed aside those thoughts, reminding himself of his purpose for seeking out Dio. "Pedro Daun is pressing me about the letters. He will come tonight. To help search Canastra's bedchamber. The only place we didn't look."

Dio stopped painting, his face serious. "Does he know the room is guarded by the duke's militant footmen?"

Exhaling loudly, Henrique stared at his own hands. "Pedro expects me to deal with them before his arrival."

Dio nodded. "The usual way?"

Being a scientist had its uses, it seemed. "How can I dose two guards and the duke? I have no access to their food or cellar.

"I know how."

"Are you sure? They must sleep soundly. I don't want surprises during the search."

Dio inspected his painting and grimaced. "If I do this, you will help me with the setting."

"Fine."

"I know a chambermaid. She told me a pastoral story about how the master drinks peppermint tea every night before bed. He uses a carmine and gold cap and kisses the feet of all the images in his room. But that's hardly relevant..."

"A splash of chloral hydrate in the tea, and he will be as immobile as one of his statues." Henrique smiled and turned to leave.

"Where are you going? You said you would help."

Henrique groaned. "What do you want me to do? I'm a lousier painter than you are."

"Perhaps your brawn and latent heroic powers can be harnessed for the greater good... I need to add glamour to the last scene. When Hercules finally meets Lady Virtue."

"Who will play Virtue?"

"Isabel."

Henrique exhaled. Who else?

While Dio moved away to direct the rehearsals, Henrique inspected the makeshift stage. The remnants of previous productions littered the backstage area—costumes, masks, ballet slippers, mirrors, and sheer silk for light effects. Among the boxes, he discovered coils of rope. He touched tulle cloth so fine as to be the translucent wing of a dragonfly. A scaffold towered above the curtain line at just the right height to—no, she would refuse. But with pulleys and a strong rope, he could make a princess soar... like a cicada leaving its carapace.

He conjured alternate designs like people shuffled through book pages until he found a masterpiece. It would allow her to soar and experience the lack of gravity in the pit of her stomach. It would also be safe and sturdy to carry her weight. With pontoons and pulleys suspended from the ceiling, it would give her the freedom to stretch her wings. The sketch faded, replaced by a vision of Isabel floating above the audience, that heart-stopping smile lighting up her eyes.

With all his *pundonor*, Alfonso took her on garden strolls, but could he make her fly?

Chapter 18

"The strong did what they could, and the weak suffered what they must." Thucydides

The hunting party spread out across the marsh. A gust of hot wind swept through the foliage, lifting the women's riding habits and sending the gentlemen's caps flying. The scent of clay and decay caused Isabel to scrunch her nose, and she looked up as clouds raced across the sky. She held onto her bonnet and rubbed her arms, dreading the unease brought by the wind. If it rained, at least the water-fowl shooting would be canceled. Hunting, a habit mankind veneered as one of their last links to uncivilized roots, felt ungentlemanly to her.

"How many birds do they usually bag?" Alfonso glanced at the assembled aristocrats and then straightened his hunter's coat.

Of course, he was uneasy. Today, his hunting skills would be scrutinized. A virile young king should be the one to bring the better game.

Smiling, she patted his hand. "Most guests are here to court a prince, not kill fowl. Look, Canastra pays more attention to his hounds than his gun, so I guess he is not taken with shooting."

The duke petted his prized Galgo and glanced at them as if sensing their regard. At times, Canastra's awe of Alfonso slipped to show a patronizing attitude.

"How long have you been under Canastra's tutelage?"

"Long enough," Alfonso said enigmatically, color rising on his fair skin, and pointed to the other side of the meadow. "And your escort?"

Isabel glanced at Henrique, and a sigh escaped her lips. Instead of a shapeless hunter's garb, he wore a superb riding ensemble, the gray tone complimenting his sinfully tanned skin. Attention caught by some plant or bug, he bent, collected the lucky creature, and stored it in his coat pocket.

He loved nature, or at least was extremely curious about it, and even though he was a shameless pleasure-seeker, she doubted he would kill one of its denizens for fun. An idyllic image swept through her mind of a country gentleman strolling through the Portuguese countryside. He wasn't alone. His wife walked by his side. More than a wife, a partner. She would hang on his arm as he stooped down to inspect a new creature. Then he would explain to her it was an arachnid, not an insect. A child would bounce on its little legs, craving a look. The child would smile, a confident smile. The smile of a child who merited a place on her parent's schedule. Isabel bit the inside of her cheek to dispel the fierce longing burning in her chest. Henrique wasn't the faithful gentleman, just as she wasn't the bourgeois wife.

Forcing her eyes back to Alfonso, she lifted her shoulder. "I would worry only about the duchess. Of all present, she seems the more excited by the prospect of shedding blood."

For all her femininity, Rafaela had a manly liking for the sport and was once rumored to have killed a stag, and then watched in fascination as her dogs ripped it to shreds.

The gamekeeper sounded the horn, and groups were formed. Before the first shot could streak the sky, a guttural "took-took" rose above the hound's barks and excited chatter. It grew in timbre and volume until it obliterated everything else. The hunting group fell silent, and unease descended over the meadow.

Isabel inspected the willows and acacias, her breathing shallow. All was stillness, the lake, the leaves, the hunters, the insects, and then a black cloud flew over their heads. Ducks. Dozens, hundreds of them. They hovered, flapping their wings, black missiles with beady eyes and cackling beaks. The wind lashed out as they landed in the hunting party's midst.

By God, they were besieged by harpies. Isabel screeched, her hand covering her mouth.

All around them, the creatures stormed the hunters, their quacks obliterating the human shrieks.

Her limbs became useless clubs. This couldn't be true. They were ducks. Ducks! Her mind kept repeating the pathetic litany. A hound-sized drake charged Alfonso's saber. Yelping, the prince wrestled with the feathered beast.

Mouth gaping, she gave one step back and then another. A few gentlemen dropped their weapons and took flight, some waving their canes at the winged menaces, others flapping their hats.

Something grabbed her wrist, and Isabel jumped.

It was Henrique.

"They are attacking us. Why are they attacking us?"

"Remind me to take a survey later." Henrique pulled her away from the ruckus. "The ducks are harmless, but Rafaela and Dio are armed. I trust neither with weapons. The scene will fast turn deadly."

Chaos ensued, with men charging their guns, dogs barking, and women wailing.

A duck flew from an elm and bit Lady Dolores' nose.

Isabel planted her heels on the grass. "Dolly!"

Henrique circled his arm around her shoulder and turned her away. "Charles will help her."

The sky opened. Fat drops splattered over the marsh. Isabel shivered as her riding dress soaked and the dapper feather of her bonnet fell limply over her cheek.

They hurried across fallen logs, their steps skittering over the muddy ground. When they arrived at a Roman ruin, the crumbling columns jutting out from the soil, Henrique stopped and pulled her into a small wooden structure. The three-walled enclosure had only a partial roof. The rickety planks stood up thanks to inertia and a bush of vines with purple flowers.

Henrique deposited her on the bare ground and huddled by her side. His chest heaved with the force of his breaths.

Rain fell on a steady curtain by their feet, lifting mud and the scent of wet earth. Perspiration plastered her bodice over her breasts, and she hugged her knees to keep from sogging her boots.

"What is this place?"

"It's a blind. Hunters use it to shoot flyaways."

Isabel shuddered. "Flyaways? They seemed more like fly-right-at-you to me."

He took a heavy breath and groaned, the sound similar to a ship's hull braving a storm. Isabel gasped, her concern constricting her throat. Had he sustained any injuries during their escape?

He shook, indeed, but not in pain, the blackguard.

"Are you laughing?"

Henrique tilted his head back and howled, his mouth wide open, hands holding ribs that jutted out with the force of his guffaws. It wasn't the rake's sneer, the peers' polite chuckle, paired with his dark humor and double entendres, but a full belly laugh. Henrique Penafiel was an ugly laugher, and it made him even more beautiful to her.

He brushed away tears of mirth. "God, have you seen them? Fending off the fowl as if hellhounds were on their heels?"

"Why were the ducks misbehaving? They acted as if possessed by demons."

"Those were north shovelers. One of the few birds with the ability to team up. Flocks of them swim in circles to stir up food. We must have interrupted their courting season."

"Courting? You must be joking."

"Some animals have more rational methods of procreating than their human counterparts." He lifted his brows in a challenge. "They follow instinct instead of coating themselves in pointless rituals and expectations."

Expectations? Here he went again. Why had she given him ammunition to flaunt his ridiculous ideas? "Oh, let's all lose our well-bred façades and give vent to our, how do you put it? Yes, animal spirits. I guess humankind will revert to perfectly natural behaviors—braying, cackling, wallowing in the mud, howling to the moon..."

He considered the matter, and she hoisted up her chin in smug satisfaction over his loss of words.

But then his eyes narrowed, and he shrugged. "I don't know about mud, but braying and mewling... definitely possible. Howling to the moon? It depends on many variables, the position, the partner, the stamina... But I'm game if you are."

The indecent images flitted through her mind, and a fire spread from her belly to her core. Still, just as it ignited, it burned out, and a gloomy feeling invaded her chest. "Do you ever take anything seriously?"

As the ducks hovered over their heads, Isabel lowered her chin to her knees and shut her eyes. Cicadas called from somewhere behind the planks. The little creatures should be comfortable flying by now, shouldn't they?

The air shifted by her side. Her body knew Henrique was nearer. How unnerving. Her body shouldn't know more than her mind. A recipe for disaster. If it knew more, it would soon want more, and bodily cravings were dangerous.

He inhaled audibly, and then she felt a whimsical caress on her cheek.

"Can I tell you a secret?"

She stayed silent because she craved knowing all his secrets, and while his knee grazed her forearm, she couldn't be expected to form any words.

"I hate hunting. The senseless killing, the black powder and blood, the noises. I hate it."

"I hate drakes," she blurted out and cringed, wondering why her mouth was betraying her.

He eyed her with interest, the scientist with a new object. Would he put her in his breast pocket too?

Shielded by the blind, the rain acting like a drapery, Isabel exhaled, and the subject she had carried for so long climbed to the surface, pulling itself out from the secret garden's shadows. "I hate their mating. I hate how they treat the females."

The words hovered between them, waiting to bite whoever spoke first. She hiked up her chin, daring him to mock her.

"Monogamy is not a trait they possess. It's not in their nature." His voice was tender, filled with warmth.

She drew in a raspy breath. "And what is the female to do? Accept their loutish behavior? Swallow her pride and watch their philandering?"

"Can't she enjoy the same? Must she want more?"

Some principles she could never, ever relinquish. Fidelity topped the list. Their eyes met for an uncomfortable moment. His gaze wavered, almost pleading with her to let the matter go. But she wouldn't.

"How? If it is not in her nature?" she whispered.

His expression softened, unguarded for a change. His eyes shimmered, the blue of a blurred lake. If she stared at it a minute more, the water would settle, and she could see into its depths.

But then the surface rippled.

Henrique removed his hand, and his façade returned, the shutters closing and shifting, pulling the corners of his mouth and his eyes until his expression assumed the mask of rakish rapport.

"Are we still talking about ducks?" He touched her cheek.

Oh, his touch... a single brush of skin against skin and yet so sweeping. Isabel gripped her skirts, her heavy breathing straining her corset. She should get away from him. She desperately needed to get away from him. But her body became an unresponsive picketer.

"Nature is so efficient. It built us to avoid pain and embrace pleasure." He took her hand and traced the lines over her palm. A current passed through them, so strong it had a scent and a color, undoubtedly a color. Red—its color was red.

"Pleasure?"

"The drive to pursue pleasure is intense. It makes us want to do things."

"What things?"

He traced the corner of her lip, then brought his mouth close to her ear. "You have a constellation of freckles here, right atop the bridge of your nose. I want to study them, name them, and then hunt for strays down the column of your neck."

Isabel stopped breathing. The sounds outside faded until there was only them, the rain and wet earth, and his touch.

"Do you want it, Isabel?"

If she wanted it? Her heart pounded with the force of her want. But he offered pleasure, not himself. To give in to him was to relinquish all she held dear.

Shutting her eyes, she took a fortifying breath. "Is it safe to return?"

He exhaled, and his hand fell to his side. "Probably."

Isabel moved away from him, intending to stand, but a snap brought her back to a seated position, bumping her head on the wood. Stiffening, she tried to move her neck. Her hair was entangled. Isabel lifted her arm to inspect the cause, but her taffeta bodice would not allow her to reach beyond her ear.

She groaned. "I'm stuck."

Henrique cleaned the mud from his trousers, his back to her. "I know... if you only let go of the unreasonable beliefs—"

"I'm literally stuck. My hair. Something is fastening it to the planks."

He crouched by her side. "Bend your torso forward."

She did and flinched at the strain on her sensitive scalp.

"Don't move. Damn it, I can't see in this light." He flattened himself against the wall, his shoulder and face glued to the wooden slabs.

Isabel stood still, tears of pain coursing down her cheeks. Looking straight ahead, she tried to ignore him as he prodded and tugged behind her.

"It's a twitch-up snare. Two forked pieces of wood. The first is hammered into the soil, and the other is attached to the cordage near the noose. When an animal pulls, the twig is dislodged, flinging the sapling to its unbent position. Now it is holding its more valuable bounty. A princess's hair." He dried her tears with a handkerchief and then did something with the twigs that relieved the pressure. "Do you think the hunter will be overjoyed?"

She sniffed. "Can you remove it?"

He let go and stared at her, his brows furrowed. "With all due respect to your person, I must climb atop you."

"Absolutely not!"

"Do you prefer me to call someone?"

"Do not dare leave me," she blurted and took a deep breath. "You very well know I cannot be seen like this."

"Just relax." Grinning, he straddled her legs.

When his groin grazed her thighs, an animal sound escaped his chest. Or it came from her.

He reached behind her neck, his hands working her tangled hair.

Isabel shut her eyes firmly. The chill vanished as his body gave off the heat of a furnace. She tingled unbearably. He emanated a scent of earth, pines, and rain. This close, she could see the stubble breaching his tanned cheek and the contrast of his shirt with the rough skin of his neck. What would that abrasiveness feel against her lips?

"It's worse than I thought. I'll have to…" He bent forward, his chest coming in contact with hers.

She dug her fingers into the earth to keep from embracing him. They were in the open, protected only by a meager, treacherous fly, but her body cared not, wanting closer, resenting the cloth layers separating them.

Something shifted against her belly, a rugged ridge. It took her a second to realize the culprit, and she sucked in a breath as a wave of heat turned her legs into dough.

He made a sound like water dripping over heated stones. "Just ignore him."

Warmth colored her cheeks. "Is your male part always this unruly?"

"Male part? It has a name. Several, actually, and each less unflattering than 'male part'. You can't go wrong with the classic cock, dick, of course, penis—"

"Must be the sign of the times," she said, her cheeks burning. "Me, a princess from Portugal, depending on a rake's help with a penchant for vulgar vocabulary."

He paused and eyed her with interest, the frown he used for scientific discussions. "Don't you want to know how it goes? Between a man and a woman?"

"Why?"

"So, when the time is right, you can take pleasure in the act."

"Pleasure? Don't be absurd. Respectable ladies are expected to endure the marriage bed to produce offspring. It is only the male who craves such things."

"If women allowed themselves to experience pleasure, husbands wouldn't be so inclined to find it outside the marriage bed."

Isabel peeked at the place between them. "What if the problem is physical?" The image of Priapus floated inside her mind, and she quickly gazed away. "How could it possibly fit?"

He stopped working on her hair and considered her for a flustered moment. Then he plucked a bloom from the vine covering the shag. "This is perfect for an anatomical demonstration. The blue pea flower has two petals, an upside down heart-shaped one and a smaller one at the top, like a monk's hood."

He assumed a professor-like tone, and Isabel leaned closer despite the absurdity of being lectured among mud and snares.

"You must be pleased with yourself, are you not? Having a captive audience to your rumblings."

He shrugged. "The bluebell has a similar design to the female genitalia."

Isabel's eyes widened, and she could not muster a single retort. She hadn't peeped down there. Still, the flower looked delicate and lurid in his hands.

"If this were a vagina, this would be the labia majora."
He trailed his index finger from the top of the outside
petal down to the bottom.

The pitter-patter of the rain faded, replaced by her
strained breaths, too loud for her ears. The ancient
wood, the cicadas, and the towering temple dissolved
into blurred brown. All she saw were long, overly-long
fingers and a blue flower coming alive under his touch.

Her body trembled, and she licked her lip. The heat of
his chest and thighs seeped into her, leaving her breathless. He caressed the flower's left side—slow, impossibly
slow. The hairs on her nape and arms lifted, and she felt
phantom fingers flirting on her skin. Heat flooded her
as the threads connecting them thickened, spreading
like vines until she didn't exist apart from him. She
should push him away. Risking baldness, she should rip
her hair from the snare, place both her palms on his
chest and shove.

If he noticed her agitation, he ignored it. His voice,
smoky, husky, contrasted with the scientific quality of
his words. "When a male wishes to perform intercourse
with a female, he will caress her intimate lips and kiss
them."

Henrique's lips were firm and so movable in his words
and grins. How would it feel? This shocking kiss?

He is making me lose my mind.

She gulped, her mouth dry. "That seems hardly the
practice of a gentleman."

"Shove your breastplate at his head if he doesn't." His
voice sounded strained, and he leaned closer. "This
little hood is called the clitoris. Your body is especially
sensitive here." He circled there once, twice.

A languidness coursed through her limbs, and she
could not wrench her gaze from his fingers. Her legs
relaxed, parting under his weight, and he settled closer
in her lap. His hardness pressed against her, and her
hips had an urge to brush against him.

Now, Isabel, leave now.

"And then?"

"When she is pleasured, her inner muscles will relax, and penetration will not only be possible but pleasurable." He inserted his fingertip in the cavity below the flower's inner petal.

Isabel cried out, her tummy tensing. Overheated, thirsty, she splayed her hands over his chest.

Push him away.

Gaze hot on her face, his eyes flicked from her lips to her eyes and back. The muscles below her palms contracted. Isabel tensed her arms. A cicada called outside, and then another. They were preparing for their flight.

Isabel grabbed his lapels and kissed him.

Chapter 19

"The very essence of instinct is that it's followed independently of reason." Charles Darwin

Henrique endured her timid ravishing for a total of five seconds. Groaning, he plowed his fingers through her hair and pulled away. He stared at flashing green eyes, breathing her breaths. Heart racing, he kissed her like a man possessed, like a lusty god, like a crazed animal. Drinking her mewls and moans, he tilted her head for better access and explored her, his tongue sweeping inside. She relaxed the strain in her neck, and the snare gave way an inch. Impatiently, he shoved his hand into the wood plank behind her and maneuvered the trap, freeing her. He tugged lumps of hair from her ruined coiffure. When he finished, her mane hung around her face in a snarled mess.

He sniffed the strands and rubbed them against his cheek. It was silk. It was soft. Glorious. "I care not for politics, but I would learn it just to pass a law forbidding you to confine your hair in braids."

She gasped. "That's hardly useful—"

He hushed her with his lips. Spanning her waist, Henrique rolled her atop him, her legs straddling his lap. He never left her mouth.

She'd kissed him. Isabel had placed her hands on his lapels and pulled him in for this. He knew she hid a passionate side. But this? This wild fusing of mouths stunned him. What had she called him? A *sinvergüenza*. Oh, yes. That he was. His honor had washed away and now swirled in the mud as she strained against him, her inexperienced kiss inflaming his lips.

He dug his fingers into her bodice, knowing there was no hope of opening the tiny buttons but needing to. If he didn't have to worry about returning her later, he would peel the layers one by one until he found bare skin.

He settled for tugging her dress up, revealing her muddied stockings. When he placed his palm atop her thigh, she shuddered.

He had planned a theoretical education, but his body had overruled good intentions. Practical, it would be. "I'll show you a hint of pleasure."

She gazed at him, her green eyes troubled.

He drew small circles below her knees. "I won't breach your maidenhead, love. A lesson in pleasure, no consequences."

Biting her swollen bottom lip, she nodded. Her trust raced through his system, and a bolt of lust shot through his spine. Clenching his jaw, he reined in his desire. He could do this. Show her how wondrous a man's touch could be.

After pulling her skirts as far as they would go, he arrived at the naked skin above her garter. She panted, her gaze following his hands. A groan escaped his chest when he found the entrance to her pantalets. Her desire and dew coated the pad of his finger, and his hand shook when he traced her swollen outer lips. He needed a plan for this. Hopping in bed—or muddy ground, for that matter—without a strategy was a recipe for losing control. And without control, feelings and expectations could get out of hand. Surface caresses, no penetration. There. That would have to suffice. He moistened his fingertip on her desire and circled her clitoris slowly, gently. Her eyes closed, and she sighed.

He caressed her, sometimes giving her more friction, sometimes tantalizing her with the promise of more. Color rose on her neck and cheeks, her lips parting.

"God, you are so beautiful."

He brought her closer and licked her lips, moving his tongue in tandem with his finger. He always thought of the kissing and the preliminaries as necessary steps on a ladder, a ladder leading to his ultimate pleasure. But not with Isabel. Kissing Isabel had intrinsic value, and pleasuring her? Pleasuring her became his sole vocation. He would commit to studying all the ways he could achieve it.

She tilted her hips, seeking more friction, her breathing shallow.

"Easy, love."

Arching her back, she splayed her hands over his thighs, and her legs opened, revealing her sex. Henrique groaned, brushing his thumbs over her labia reverently. Having her in his arms, pliant, fragrant, uninhibited, unleashed something within him, a pleasure so acute it bordered on pain. She panted, her pelvis undulating. Her response electrified him. Plans be damned. He wanted to feel her pulsing against him.

Henrique licked rain from her skin, tasting her sweetness, and hand trembling, pushed a finger inside her. Her inner walls contracted, milking him, but her barrier curbed his penetration. Curse the blasted membrane. Some age-old instinct screamed for him to open his trousers and shove himself deep, claiming her as his. With a firm leash on himself, he curbed the impulse. Her pleasure would have to be enough for both of them.

Her hair tumbled down her shoulders in perfect disarray. She shuddered, and a glorious cry escaped her parted lips.

The orgasm transformed her. She was a goddess, and he, a mere mortal who dared touch her. Her bliss was his ache. And he would gladly sacrifice his needs at her altar.

Henrique savored the last waves of pleasure on his fingers and withdrew. Breathing heavily, he leaned his forehead on her breastbone, disoriented, not ready to put into words what had happened. What they shared went beyond the physiological consequence of friction, skin, and moist membranes. A fanciful bastard like Dio would start linking their experience with a mythical joining, earth meeting sky, and such nonsense. Henrique would have to observe and collect data and devise a replication model. Yes, experimentation and method—that's what he needed.

She dropped her face on his neck. Her breaths fanned his earlobe. He was painfully hard, but held still, listening to her heart, caressing her back with long, long movements. He liked her draped on his chest, the mythical princess exhausted by his lovemaking. He liked the sweet scent of her arousal mingling with the wet earth.

His mind raced, thinking of plausible ways to keep her in the shag. If he chopped wood, he could build a nest around the old blind. He would teach her all about pleasure. Just the two of them, no foppish prince, no string of courtiers.

Minutes or hours passed, he lost count. She stirred and splayed her hands over his shoulders. Now she would kiss him again, ask him to take her, to extend this. He wouldn't be strong enough to say no.

She pecked his cheek as if he were an aunt, not her lover. "We should go. If we hurry, the guests won't notice our absence, and we can change before dinner."

Using him for balance, she rose.

Guests? Dinner? Henrique stared as she primped herself into a semblance of order. She didn't meet his eyes. Without her straddling him, he became aware of the mud surrounding them, of his ruined coat and the bulge inside his trousers.

"I'll give you a moment to recompose," she said.

Grumbling to himself, he pushed to his feet.

She took her muddied skirt in her hands and whirled to leave. Then she stopped. "Henrique?"

He shot to attention. "Yes?"

A mischievous smile played at the corner of her lips. "Thank you for the lesson."

Chapter 20

"Wise men speak because they have something to say; Fools because they have to say something."
Plato

I sabel observed clumps of foam forming and ebbing in her bath. Heat climbed up her limbs, condensing around her neck and bottom lip. Her skin felt so sensitive... As if her consciousness had shifted from within her to the surface of her body.

Sophie hummed softly, arranging the fresh towels on a stool. When she left the bathing room, Isabel parted the foam until she could see her woman's mound. Holding her breath, she gazed at the tuft of hair, then allowed her knees to open. The pink flesh and the little hood blinked at her.

Should she feel guilty? Ashamed for allowing Henrique liberties? Isabel swirled her fingers over the water and sighed. She had been wrong about pleasure, wrong about relationships. All her life, she believed only men enjoyed mating. By Athena, the closeness of it, the absolute delight. It was dangerous. Her mother had taught her so, and her governess and her confessor. But was it? Why must women be kept from it? Nothing seemed transparent. Suds had found their way into her mind, clouding her thoughts.

The dinner bell rang, intruding on her musings.

How would she speak with Henrique now? Isabel covered her face with her palms and sputtered when soap stung her eye. He made her feel too much—worry, confusion, elation, irritation, jealousy... She shouldn't find him so appealing.

Did Henrique experience the same with other women? Had he been doing this with Rafaela? Her chest ached at the thought of him touching her cousin intimately. He must be glad she accepted his vow of no consequences, of a simple lesson. That she didn't fuss or ask for more of him. She could not bear it if he mocked her as he did on the beach. Still, his gaze had been so unguarded... She had been about to pour her own feelings when fear clogged her throat. No, it wasn't cowardice but royal restraint. She rose abruptly, and water sloshed out of the rim.

With brisk movements, Isabel dried herself and covered her nakedness with a robe.

When she entered her bedchamber, Dolly flung herself over the bed. Hiding her face, she moaned. "My life is over."

Isabel hurried to her. "What is it? Did Mr. Whitaker hurt you?"

Dolly shook her head. "Not him. The ducks."

Isabel had forgotten about the bite. "Let me see."

Shuddering, Dolly lowered her hands.

Isabel cringed at the red mess that had been Portugal's prettiest nose.

"I'm finished. If only the heavens opened and swallowed me whole."

With a heavy sigh, Isabel settled by her side and twirled one of Dolly's blond curls on her finger. "It's just a bit swollen. A day or two, and it will be all right."

"I don't think I can go through with it."

"Is this about the play?" Diomedes had given Dolly the leading part after her talent surprised everyone during rehearsals.

"What? Oh, yes. Silly me, of course, it is. What else could it be? It's not like I plan to go to Paris for a glittering debut..." Flushed, Dolly traced the roses embroidered on the counterpane. "I'll speak with Diomedes. I cannot perform like this."

"That's not true. Dear, you are so talented. Please don't give up. You are more than your nose."

Dolly tilted her head to the side, her gaze vulnerable. "You seem different. Is something wrong? You can talk to me. I'm your friend. Everyone needs a friend now and then."

Isabel shut her eyes. She wanted to say so much about Henrique and her fears. But Dolly didn't need her confusion. She gulped air and assumed expression number twenty-one, a confident smile and slightly condescending brows. "I am quite well, dear."

"You were right all along." Dolly sighed, cleaning her tears. "I'll conform to a life of duty. It's the only way to protect myself from hurt."

"No!" What was she teaching her ladies? Isabel straightened, pasting her most royal expression on her face. "I was wrong. You will go ahead with your performance, and the audience's applause will shake Canastra's palace."

"Oh, thank you so much." Dolly hugged her fiercely. "Your courage inspires me."

Heat climbed up her cheeks. Courage indeed. The thought of facing Henrique made her insides quiver like a cupboy serving the king for the first time.

Chapter 21

"To me there has never been a higher source of earthly honor or distinction than that connected with advances in science." - Isaac Newton

H enrique stared for the seventh time at the microscope. The bacteria colony had died again. Cursing, he rubbed his temples. How could he concentrate on typhus when his skull had been drained of brain tissue and replaced by an unresponsive slug? Henrique pushed away from the table with an oath. 'Thank you for the lesson,' Isabel had said prettily, perfectly polite. As if he had taught her a new tennis technique or a hairstyle. As if she had not milked his finger with her pleasure and made his cock painfully hard.

And then, after sprinting back to her room, she didn't appear for dinner. Henrique should find her. Teach her all sorts of pleasure. Let's see if she could stay detached then.

What the hell was he thinking? Pedro Daun would arrive tonight, expecting a slumbering Canastra so he

could break into his chamber. He had no time to fanta-
size over Isabel's orgasms.

But he was her escort, damn it. What if she fell ill?
Without giving himself a minute more to ponder the
ridiculous excuse, he grabbed his coat and hat and sped
to the door. When he placed his hand on the knob, a
decisive knock came from the outside.

Dio. Had he come to fret about their night raid? Pedro
Daun didn't become the most powerful man in the
kingdom by blundering his missions. Henrique flung
the door open.

He was greeted by a vision in white, crowned by diamonds. Isabel gasped and stepped back.

Henrique flashed an epic smile. "Couldn't stay away?"

"Don't flatter yourself. Come, Sophie." She jutted her
chin to the French maid and strode inside his room.

So she brought a chaperone? "Coward."

"If you behave mulishly, I can return later."

Henrique affected a perfect bow. "I'm always willing
to assist royalty."

"Liar," she said saucily, her gaze straying to his lips.

"If you came for another lesson, prepare to shock
poor Sophie."

Isabel blushed. Nothing more than a response from
her sympathetic nervous system caused by an emotional trigger, dilating the blood vessels in the skin. Yet, in
her, it was art that set his heart into a frenzy. He must
be falling ill.

"Diomedes sent me. Our resident playwright. He said
you needed to take my measure. He was cryptic, so I
hoped you could explain it better."

Henrique shook his head. Of course, the harness. At
least Dio had not ruined the surprise. Henrique wanted
Isabel to fly, but she would balk if she realized his plans
before the performance. He only needed her waist, but
after spanning it once, he knew it to be Pi times ten
inches. Last night he had tried squaring the circumfer-

ence but failed. Her shape was unique. But he could not say as much to her now, could he? Not with a chaperone eying him as if he was Zeus bent on ravishing her precious charge.

With a heavy sigh, he dropped the hat and the coat atop the couch and pointed to his working table.

Isabel followed. The maid ambled toward the window, giving them some privacy.

Like an obedient seamstress, Henrique stretched his measuring tape and came to her. He sucked in a breath, hoping he could store her fragrance inside, knowing it was just distilled alcohol, ambergris, and jasmine, but wanting it as if it was ambrosia. Pulse speeding, he circled the leather ribbon around her waist. When his hands met near her navel, he stopped. The twenty-five inches were there for all to see, but he refused to acknowledge the number. Henrique could only focus on the green of her eyes, challenging and pleading.

She licked her lips. "Is that all?"

He moved away from her, ostensibly to write her measurements.

She strolled to his desk and flipped through his notebook. What was she hoping to find? He crammed every inch of his pages with miscellaneous drawings and looking-glass jottings. Scribbled together were math calculations, sketches of birds, flying machines, theater props, water eddies, blood valves, microscopic organisms, siphons, plant stems, sawed-apart skulls...

Before he could stop her, she pressed her eyes to his microscope. He held still as she peeped at his life work as one visits the exhibits of a menagerie. He was used to it by now. The exclamations of admiration followed by a quick change of subject. Most people would pay to avoid going into the minutiae of his science.

"What is this?"

"You just saw a colony of typhus bacteria. For the past six months, I've been trying to identify an agent to kill it. As you can see from the plaques you inspected, the typhus thrives."

"Bacteria? Are you a disciple of Pasteur?" she asked casually, as if commenting on the weather, and placed her eye back on the lenses.

Frowning, Henrique took a step closer. "I trained under him in Paris. Won't you drill me on why I chose such a non-aristocratic pursuit? After all, science is neither wearing the military uniform nor the political toga."

She lifted her face and met his gaze. "I'm certain your work as a scientist is more rewarding than any contribution made by politicians or soldiers."

Henrique rubbed his chest, not sure what to make of her praise. Part of him wanted to shout with glee. The other had learned to search for hidden meanings. People usually recognized his work when they wished for something in return. "You'd be surprised. But not every place treats its natural philosophers as poorly as Portugal. In England, a scientist receives incentives, public acknowledgments—"

"Shouldn't the work and the benefit to others be enough reward?"

Henrique grunted. He wouldn't explain to Joan of Arc about a scientist's necessities.

She didn't seem to want to hear his justifications anyway and went to his second microscope. "When Pasteur published his manifesto on hygiene, most surgeons in Lisbon burned the papers. I helped Sister Agnes convince the midwives to wash their hands before birth, and the mortality rates were reduced by thirty percent. It struck me as common sense practice then, but looking at your bacteria... Is it true then? Is there a world of small beings we are completely ignorant of?" Her eyes flashed with interest.

Pulse speeding, Henrique took her hand.

She startled.

"Let me show you."

She hesitated for a second and then nodded.

He removed her lace glove, revealing bitten nails and white skin. He turned her palm up and placed it under the microscope, adjusting it to the highest possible resolution.

"It's amazing."

"The answer to our health is not on humors or bleeding, but here. In this microscopic world. If we conquer this world, like we conquered the way to the Indies or the colonies, we could reduce mortality rates during operations, avoid disease contagion, prolong life expectancy rates."

"The future," she said under her breath.

Henrique nodded. "The future."

Their gazes met and locked. She understood. Not the glazed eyes of desire or boredom, but... she understood. Of course, she understood. She was the most brilliant person he knew. He'd believed men and women were two parallel lines, never crossing in ways beyond the physical. And yet, here she was. Good God, he'd been an ass. Standing here, gazing at him expectantly, was his equal in intellect and wit and passion and everything.

He wanted to kiss her, to place her atop his shoulder and run away with her, to spread her on a table and devour her, to brush his head on hers and absorb all her ideas. He settled for removing her hand from under the microscope's lenses and pulling it close to his mouth. With deliberate intention, he kissed her palm.

"You have a beautiful mind, Isabel."

"Mind? I thought I was an animal like everybody else."

Dio was right. He resembled Hercules when handling subtlety, clubbing his own foot first and asking questions later. Zeus himself should smite his arse for spouting such nonsense.

"I said that, didn't I?" He lowered his chin to his chest and lifted his eyes to her. "I wonder how you still put up with me."

Sophie ambled closer, her gaze shifting nervously between them. "Your Highness, you promised Lord Diomedes you would rehearse your part today."

"Of course." Isabel stirred, breaking eye contact, and whirled to leave.

He was mentally cursing himself blue enough to make a fisherwoman proud when she paused, her shoulder touching his.

"I put up with you because you are a gifted teacher."

Chapter 22

"Now, now, my good man, this is no time to be making enemies." Voltaire on his deathbed in response to a priest asking him to renounce Satan.

"When did Canastra retire?" Pedro Daun asked while working on the door latch.

"One hour. I administered enough chloral hydrate to fell a horse. He should be sound asleep now." Henrique watched both ends of the corridor.

The palace was silent. Moonlight spilled from the mullioned windows, giving a sickly pallor to the slumbering guards. Dio's chambermaid had delivered the soporific wine to the duke's minions. Now both slept, their boots casting shadows on the hall.

He eyed Pedro's black-gloved hands as they coaxed the lock into revealing its secrets. For the tenth time this night, he wondered why Pedro bothered with the king's letters. Call him a cynic, but he didn't buy the whole 'the country's stability is at risk' speech. Henrique wouldn't be in Spain if not for the king's coercion. But Pedro?

He knew his friend well. Ambitious? Always. Patriotic? When it suited him.

The door gave in with a startled click. While Dio stayed outside guarding the corridor, Henrique and Pedro invaded the dimly lit chamber. A single lamp burned in the corner, giving a phantasmagoric sheen to the life-sized paintings. The air was as still as it was stale. While the four-poster curtains were drawn, the heavy drapery couldn't shield them from Canastra's loud snores.

Chests, an escritoire, bookshelves, two tallboys, and a Chinese commode cramped the space. Henrique shuddered at the infinite number of drawers, nooks, and crannies the deranged duke could have used to hide the letters.

After a silent exchange, Pedro took the shelves, and Henrique dragged himself to the Chinese monstrosity. Silently, he opened the first of the dozens of tiny compartments, half expecting to see another Priapus statue. Only the dregs of a lifetime collecting knick-knacks stared back at him.

Even now, ears assaulted by the duke's vibrating uvula, he could not stop thinking about his perfect princess. Somewhere inside the palace, she slept. Did she feel cold during the night? Would she kick her covers and curl her hands near her cheek? He would give up the right to name a new species just to open her door and nudge her aside. When she protested, and knowing Isabel, she would protest, he would tell her he always slept on the right side. That settled, he would pillow her face on his chest and—

"You didn't tell me Canastra was a collector," Pedro said, startling him from his awakened dreams. "He has three El Grecos and two Goyas decorating his bedchamber walls." A hint of bitterness colored his voice.

Henrique chuckled. "I forgot you enjoyed art in between training your horses and conquering the world."

"That's in the past."

When the clock struck one in the morning, Henrique closed the last drawer and paced away from the ornery piece of furniture. How futile. Since Canastra hoarded everything, they would find only moths and dust.

The duke moaned. Then, guttural words escaped his mouth, the Spanish too fast for him to understand.

Henrique stopped pacing. Perhaps finding the letters was one of the herculean jobs requiring more wit than physical exertion. If the duke was a night speaker... "I will ask him."

Pedro cocked his head.

"Canastra is drugged, but his subconscious is still working. If given the right incentive, he might disclose the location."

Pedro nodded. "He can recognize you. I'll do it."

Henrique walked to the bedside, his steps muffled by a tiger's skin.

Pedro covered his head with his mantle. Dressed all in black, feral eyes flashing through the hood's shadows, he could make Hades vacate the underworld.

Grinning, Henrique whistled under his breath. "You might succeed if you wish to kill him in fright."

"You said he was religious. A glimpse of the Devil will give him the right incentive to pray."

Pedro unsheathed his saber. Moonlight glinted off the steel. Countless men had seen the same shine seconds before their lives were snuffed. Henrique shuddered, glad his army days were long gone.

Pedro poised the sword above Canastra's head. "Awake, vermin, or be forever falling."

A quote from Milton's *Paradise Lost*? Clever touch, Henrique thought.

"Now."

Pedro's voice commanded—a general haranguing a lazy corporal. Canastra's eyelids shot open and then rounded with terror.

Clutching the sheets, the duke scrambled backward until the bed rail curtailed his escape. "I'm not ready to die."

"Prepare for the final judgment."

The duke scrunched his face as if readying for a blow. "No, no! So much to do. She... she needs me."

Pedro touched the duke's chin with the steel. "Say your last prayers."

"Please, not yet, my lord." The duke placed both his palms in front of his chest. "Spain needs me."

"Does she now?" Pedro sheathed the saber. "Never say the Devil is not a patriot."

The scent of hanging game and anchovies permeated the crowded tavern. A Flamenco musician, his bald head reflecting the crude gas lights, played his guitar while a dancer clapped her castanets. Henrique clinked his glass with Pedro's. Canastra had revealed the letters' location, and now the proof of Dom Luis' indiscretion lay inside Henrique's pocket. Not bad for a clandestine night's work.

If the king had been coerced to send Isabel here, they eliminated Canastra's leverage. Henrique had half a mind to haul Isabel and take her back to Lisbon tomorrow. Canastra's face when he spoke about his plans for Spain had been too devious for Henrique's peace of mind.

Dio clapped his hands when the couple finished their performance, his eyes admiring the woman's legs. On cue, a trio of doxies approached the table.

Pedro waved tersely, dismissing the company. Henrique smiled at the heavily painted girl but shook his head in denial. His hands had only yesterday touched a princess... He wondered if they would ever settle for anyone else.

Eyeing Henrique with shock, Dio rose. "Ignore my friends' rudeness." After flinging his arms over the girl's shoulders, he steered them to the private rooms in the back. "I'm enough to entertain a crowd."

Henrique cleared his throat. "Santiago should have been there. And Gabriel. They would've enjoyed your Lucifer impression. Your Latin is still top form."

"I had the best tutor." A shadow fell over Pedro's features, and he extended his hand. "The letters."

Henrique opened his coat but hesitated. What would Pedro do with them? More blackmail? Would it somehow threaten Isabel? "You are making a lot of effort for Dom Luis. I did not know you were close to him." As far as Henrique knew, Pedro had been Fernando's best friend, the king's deceased younger brother.

"I'm not." Pedro kept his arm extended, waiting.

Henrique closed his jacket and crossed his arms over his chest. "Why the hurry? The night is still young."

Pedro narrowed his eyes. "These letters are a threat to the country's political stability. People don't realize how close we could be to the turmoil lived by the Spanish."

"You are curtailing your summer holidays with Anne for patriotism? Tell me another tale. I know you too well."

Pedro's jaw locked, and his gaze flicked to the saber. The same that had hovered over Canastra's head and forced the man to spill his secrets. Henrique wasn't surprised. The Pedro he knew considered all options to get what he wanted, including violence.

The castanets resumed, their incessant clatter pounding on his skull.

Henrique would not back down, damn it. Either Pedro told him why he wanted the letters, or he would burn them. He tensed to stand.

Pedro clasped his shoulder, and their gazes locked. A second passed, two. The murderous glint left Pedro's gaze. Whatever battle he had raged inside his head, the peaceful side won.

"Anne loves Portugal," Pedro said between gritted teeth.

And Pedro Daun loved the British girl. "So naturally, you will save it for her." Henrique leaned back in the chair.

"I will do that and much more." Pedro's eyes hardened, and the grip on the glass turned his knuckles white. "She placed a knife against her own throat for me. In the arena last year, she thought my life was worthier than hers. She was wrong. But I won't let her change her mind."

Pedro would wear the shiny armor, not because he cared about old Portugal, with its rugged cliffs and rustic vineyards, but because of one person who lived in it. Wordlessly, Henrique removed the sheath of letters from his breast pocket. They still smelled of cheap perfume. Before, Luis's peccadilloes would have entertained him. Now he felt disgusted.

He passed the pile to Pedro. "You have the letters. I will take Isabel back to Lisbon."

"Not yet." Pedro stared at his glass. "Canastra has plans for Spain. You will stay here until we understand what those entail."

"You are insane. What of Isabel's security?"

"I think she would agree there is a time for sacrifices—"

"Bullshit. If it is not safe for Isabel here, I will—"

"Until we know Canastra's plans, it isn't safe for her anywhere. The border garrisons are active. If you wish to protect her, you must be vigilant. The duke's correspondence, his private talks—suspect everything." Pedro stored the letters inside his coat and stood. "I'll be close by."

The tavern crowd opened to let Pedro pass. Henrique cursed under his breath. His trip to Comillas had indeed turned into a Hydra of Lerne. No matter how many heads he chopped off, they returned to bite his ass. Dio strolled back to the table, a grin splitting his face.

Why was it so hot in here? Angrily, Henrique tugged at his cravat and removed the coat. A sheet fell from the inner pocket and landed near Dio's feet.

"You should have joined us. The girls were better company than the brooding Count of Almoster," Dio said, bending down to collect the paper. "What's this?"

Henrique rolled his shoulders. "It must have been among the letters."

"A death certificate?" Dio scrunched his face, and then his eyes widened. "I can't believe it." He lowered it slowly. "The date, the location, the name. This belongs to the friar. The one who cursed the Braganzas. For at least a century, kings and queens have been searching for his resting place."

Henrique took the paper from Dio's hand. It looked frail and ancient. Could it be true? The curse had been haunting the royal family for decades. He didn't like to believe in such nonsense, but the fact was, no firstborn of the royal house survived to assume the throne. Why had Canastra been keeping this?

Chapter 23

"A woman laughing is a woman conquered."
Napoleon Bonaparte

T he impromptu backstage buzzed with activity as dryads, nymphs, and satyrs hurried up and down, their pan-like harmonicas swaying from painted lips. Isabel rolled her shoulders. Soon it would be her cue. The last scene. Diomede's play delighted her. His tale of young Hercules was witty and held a core of morality.

Isabel peeked through the curtains as Alfonso delivered a soliloquy about what he should do with his life. He had spoken his lines with articulation, and the toga displayed sinewed arms, but something was lacking. Ever since Henrique mentioned Hercules, she could not help seeing his face whenever she thought about the hero.

She glanced at the audience for what must have been the tenth time, but Henrique wasn't on any of the velvet chairs her cousin had lined for the presentation. Neither was he near the Grecian columns supporting the ceiling. She bit her lip and tiptoed to inspect the shadows closer to the exit.

"Stage fright?" Dolly touched her shoulder.

She had been fabulous as Hera, performing the central part with humor and charisma. It had surprised Isabel, such theatrical talent.

Isabel kissed her cheek and tweaked her nose, now receding to its former glory. "I'm so proud of you."

"Lady Virtue is the perfect part for you. Break your tiara." Dolly beamed and skipped away.

The stage had been Isabel's cradle. From the moment she fluttered her eyes in the morning until she turned on her side and embraced her pillow, she performed. The country needed the perfect veneer, the groomed princess who quoted Rousseau, who could inaugurate a setting stone with dignity and be sent to diplomatic missions. At least this part of herself she performed flawlessly.

Henrique appeared from nowhere. Women around her giggled and pretended to cover their dishabille.

"Are you ready?"

Her lips parted as Henrique circled around her. Other men should be forbidden from wearing evening attire. They couldn't compare to Henrique in formal black and white. Tonight he had the red scarf around his neck, and the splash of color emphasized his blue eyes, making them magnetic. As if he needed more power. Shivers raced up her spine as his eyes took in her bare arms. The Greek gown woven with silver thread showed more skin than she'd ever exposed in her life.

Her mouth turned so dry she feared for her stage lines. "I thought only people involved in the production could be here."

He halted and touched a freckle above her elbow. "I am involved in the production."

Isabel stared at his lips. Sinful, they were, and so firm. She should've licked them when she had the chance. "How do you fit in a heroic play?"

"You can call me summer." After declaring such cryptic words, he passed a harness around her waist.

Isabel's breath caught. "Summer? The play is about the choice between virtue and vice."

"Indeed. It's time the cicada had a little push."

He so bemused her she only noticed he had strapped her to a ropy contraption when he guided her atop a makeshift stair. Even then, she was more preoccupied with his scent and how she could keep it inside herself.

They arrived at a wooden platform at least ten feet above stage level.

She would be above the stage when the curtains opened, facing the audience. Understanding of his plans dawned on her. Her stomach fluttered, and she held his arm. "What should I do?"

"Jump." The glow of stage lights played on the planes of his face. He bent to speak close to her ear. "Have a pleasant flight."

Slowly, he moved away from her, his expression an odd mixture of anticipation and worry.

She waited, brushing her ungloved hands against her bare arms. She barely recognized this Isabel, and yet, she didn't want to descend the stairs back to safety.

With a swoosh, the curtains opened. The light dazzled her. Her heart sped up, and the air solidified. Henrique demanded too much from her. Flight? It wasn't for her. On the stage, Alfonso sat on a throne, posing as Hercules. The rows of chairs were filled with aristocrats, their faces blurring into one flesh-colored mass. Her gaze flitted aimlessly, looking for purchase in a world that moved too fast.

Then she found Henrique.

The invisible threads stretched until they connected her with him. She placed higher trust in their bond than the ropes strapped over her waist. She took a fortifying breath and then two. Keeping eye contact, Isabel jumped. Airborne, her center of gravity tilted. Her tummy tingled, and laughter choked out of her.

While she floated above the stage, the audience cheered, awed by Henrique's creation.

All she could feel and see was Henrique staring at her. He made love to her with his eyes, but his lust did not reduce her womanly power. It enhanced it. He laughed as if her delight made him weightless.

She loved him. The realization arrived in a rush. Instead of alarming her, it made her soar and glide, unburdened by matters of state, by appearances, by playing a part. It was air, and Henrique, and those blue eyes staring at her.

Isabel missed her cue to speak.

Shaking her head slightly, she lifted her palm. "My name is Virtue. I came for you, Hercules. If you take the road to me, you will do great and noble things. Listen well, for nothing worthwhile comes without work. To earn the favor of the gods, you must worship the gods. Desiring the love of friends, you must do good for them ... and if you want your body to be strong, you must make it the servant of your mind and train it with effort and sweat."

Rafaela sashayed onto the stage, her dress displaying a naked shoulder, and offered Hercules a red apple. "My dear hero, I want to be your best friend. Follow me, and your road will be pleasant and easy. You won't know hardship, and all the sweet things in life will be yours. Forget wars and worries—your cares will be what food or drink you prefer and what sights and sounds most delight you. What touch or perfume most pleases, whose tender love you most enjoy, and what bed yields the softest slumbers."

"Lady, what is your name?" Hercules asked.

"My friends call me Happiness. Those who hate me call me Vice." Rafaela curtsied, and the audience laughed.

Rafaela clasped Hercules' hand. "The road to virtue is hard and long. Let me take you down the short and easy path to happiness."

Isabel inhaled to speak. "Choose me. Vice will lead you to despair. Stay with me, and I will lead you to happiness." *Choose me, Henrique. Stay with me.* If she thought it hard enough, he would listen. He mouthed something, but the noise of wood scraping startled her.

Hercules had risen from the throne. While he looked from Rafaela to Isabel, the audience hooted, some calling for him to choose vice. The women laughed. Isabel forced herself to pay attention. Just a few more lines and the play would end, and she could listen to what Henrique had to say.

Hercules cleared his throat and pointed his club in her direction. "I chose you, Isabel."

The audience cheered at Alfonso's faux pas, and they clapped when the curtains closed.

For a disconcerting moment, all was black. A rush of energy floated through her. As the crank of a pulley signaled her descent, she was lowered slowly, but her spine tingled as if she was ascending still. In the dark, she waited for Henrique to help her out of the contraption.

Hands circled her waist.

Isabel opened her eyes in time to see Henrique's retreating figure. Her breath caught, and she blinked repeatedly. In his place stood Alfonso, his enraptured face lowered to her.

"You were amazing," Alfonso said.

"Oh, I'm glad you liked it." Isabel tried but failed to keep the disappointment from her voice.

"Like it? You were exceptional. I will hire whoever created this to be my main engineer."

If he waits long enough to be caught, she thought bitterly.

Alfonso helped the backstage boy remove the harness from her waist and then escorted her out of the makeshift theater and into the conservatory, where the citrus trees were in full bloom. The cooling night air and the sweet scent of orange flowers tasted bittersweet. She watched again to see if Henrique would follow, but deep into her marrow, she knew he wouldn't. Hadn't he felt the same?

Maybe he did, only it was the thousandth time he did so, and he would reduce its power to some animalistic desire. But she would not deceive herself into discounting what happened. She had felt a higher feeling, and she would bet her brother's kingdom Henrique did too.

They trailed the moonlit path until they arrived at a fountain. The air was heavy with the scent of wet pavement and damp earth. A cicada struggled in the water, her spindly legs useless against the spray.

Isabel placed it gently on the fountain's rim.

When she lifted her head, Alfonso gazed at her strangely, his cheeks flushed. He still wore Hercules' costume, and his bare arms made her oddly uncomfortable.

He touched her cheek. "There are very few decisions I have carried out in my life, and none of them this important."

Isabel moved away from him, placing the fountain between them. "I'm sure this will change when you assume the throne."

An owl hooted to their left. She looked at the palace entrance longingly.

He followed her and, catching her hand in his, went down on one knee. "I want to cross the Ebro with you, Isabel. Will you be my queen?"

Isabel flew. Triumphant was her smile and her face fair as a cool wind on a sultry afternoon. Certainly, Henrique's enjoyment in her performance was because of the glimpses of skin under the diaphanous gown or for the rewards her joy would bring. Even as the rationalizing began, he knew it to be lies. He felt pleasure because she felt it. It wasn't perfect because she pended a bit to the side, and too many people watched. Still, it was addictive, this pleasure of hers. What else could he build for her to keep her smiling?

To what lengths had he gone? He, who scoffed at the differences between royalty and commoners, would found a new country just so he could proclaim her his queen. To make her happy. To bow to her every need. To be her subject, her executioner, her prisoner.

His pulse sped as he listened to her. Her cultured diction, spoken with all the consonants and vowels, breathed life into every word, warming his chest.

Then she paused, and her gaze found his. He sustained her look, like Hercules must have gazed at Mount Olympus, knowing there, hovering beyond a mortal's reach, lay his life's meaning. The time for denial had passed. He craved the meaning Isabel brought to his life even though it carried the promise of unfathomable pain.

As soon as she finished her performance, he would go to her. He would kiss her while the audience clapped their hands raw. He had so much to show her. Ropes and pulleys weren't the only way to fly.

As the curtains closed, he took a step forward.

Dio clasped his shoulder. "It pains me to admit this, you old fool, but you are a genius. Your contraption worked flawlessly."

"Save your flattery for the morrow. Now I—" His words died away as he spotted Alfonso approaching Isabel.

Muffled by the curtains, the audience clapped incessantly.

Dio linked his arm through Henrique's and tugged. "This calls for a celebration. I've been saving a bottle of my father's best brandy for the opening night."

Henrique planted his feet on the ground. Hands fisted by his sides, he watched Alfonso paw Isabel, helping her out of the harness. Every instinct he possessed clamored for violence.

Dio clucked his tongue. "If you had done your duty to the hostess and accepted Hercules' role, it would be you holding fair Virtue." He chuckled, oblivious to Henrique's murderous intentions. "They fit, don't they?"

Alfonso's besotted look washed down over Henrique with the force of a gale. With his precious *pundonor*, the prince offered dignity and entrance to Europe's leading families. All Henrique offered was clandestine passion.

What right had he to come in between the royal couple? Two princes of the blood. The schism between him and Isabel ripped Henrique's chest apart.

Anger curdled his stomach, and he turned away from the couple. "Where is the brandy?"

Chapter 24

"To Eros—You burn us." Sappho

Isabel's legs took her to the garden. The moon kissed the mowed grass, and jasmine fragrance lingered over the flowerbeds. Brushing her arms, she sped to the spot he favored. She wanted something from Henrique, a closure, a definition... She knew not which. A man should not look at a woman as he did and walk away.

A burst of nervous laughter escaped her throat. She had just received a proposal from the next king of Spain. Instead of pondering where her duty lay, she was ruining her slippers in search of a blue-eyed rogue. Craving his... His what? His passion? Like Ariadne and the women after her, Isabel expected more. Love. A future? Impossible. Her chest constricted until the air became scarce. It was best if she didn't love him. She'd never been in love before. She could be mistaken. This discomfort in the pit of her stomach every time he came near, this appeal to fluster and amuse him... This need to learn his opinion of everything? This admiration, this desire to have him succeed at his endeavors? Maybe this wasn't love.

He said passion and desire were but animalistic urges. Had other royalty not had to forbear such instincts? Her priority should be Alfonso's proposal. Instead of traipsing the garden, she should write to her brother, considering the implications for his reign.

A breeze kissed her cheeks, sweeping through the olive trees. Their silver leaves shimmered in the moonlight, adding a touch of myth to the summer night.

Henrique was there. Sitting on the bench underneath Eros' statue. He hadn't seen her. While the god of Passion aimed an arrow at his back, she admired the broadness of his shoulders and the scruff shadowing his chin and jaw. The maleness she found offensive before now pleased her better than Canova's craftsmanship.

Her throat closed, and words failed her. The image of the helpless cicada floated to her mind, beating her spindly legs, drowning.

He looked up, affected by the force of her gaze. "Did you enjoy flying?"

She ambled closer to the bench. "You would have known if you had stayed until the end of the play."

"Your royal beau has a way of materializing everywhere." He shifted, opening space for her.

Sighing, Isabel sat by his side. "I loved it. The flight."

Part of her wanted to tell him of Alfonso's proposal. To soothe her confusion. Strange how she came to rely on his opinions. Surrounded by watchful Spaniards, he had been her home port. The other part rebelled, afraid he might advise her to marry the prince like a dutiful princess should.

"Your engineering skills are superb."

He turned and stared at the Eros statue for a few heartbeats. Spirits scented his breath, and a new hardness shaped his jaw. "A set of cogs and pulleys... Theater tricks, nothing special."

If she were bolder, she would massage the pleats on his forehead and tell him how wrong he was. It bothered her how he dismissed his scientific pursuits.

"If this is a plot to make me flatter you, I must say you are succeeding. Shouldn't it be you fawning over my performance?" Isabel bumped his shoulder, her lips twitching into a smile.

He gazed at her then. This seriousness of him was too intense.

He touched her lips. "Have a care with your smiles, will you?"

Isabel stopped breathing. Something thick hovered in the air between them. She feared it. If either of them acknowledged it, it would change everything. She should say good night to him and go to her room.

Drums beat a staccato rhythm, grave and mysterious. It called to mind the flamenco's whirls and turns. She had the strange notion that beyond the palace's garden, a *torero* prepared to face a bull, and the beats were the pumps of the beast's heart.

Isabel shivered. "What is this noise?"

"It's a fiesta. A typical Spanish celebration. Just plain people, dancing to their heart's content."

A woman called her name, her steps shuffling closer. It was Sophie.

"Shouldn't you heed your chaperone?" His voice was cool, but his eyes—his eyes entranced her.

Her heart sped, and perspiration coated her arms. She could return to her room. Nothing needed to change. Still, change was as unstoppable as a bull crashing down the arena.

Isabel clasped his hand in hers. "Would you take me? To this fiesta?"

Henrique held her hand through the path leading to the village, his grip decisive and warm. They'd been holding hands since they left the garden. Isabel loved this holding of hands. Instead of fluttering her palm over a gentleman's forearm, a damsel needing guidance, she was his partner in crime.

They stopped by a stall selling tapas. Wine bottles lined the red cloth. An aging man with a waxed mustache offered her a glass. "Sangria?"

Henrique waved the salesman away, but Isabel held his wrist.

"I want to try whatever he is offering. Spanish wine, is it not?"

She was sick of the bland French wine served in Canastra's overlong meals.

"You don't drink alcohol, so..."

He was about to take the glass from her hand when she beat him to it. "I avoid spirits. Wine is fermented. There is a difference. You, above all else, should know it."

He merely lifted his brows as Isabel gulped the liquid. The sangria chilled her throat and swam on her empty stomach. He drank, too. A drop sparkled in the corner of his mouth. A bolder woman would taste that lucky drop. Hand in hand, they went farther into the village. Two-story houses surrounded a circular plaza, their front stairs interlocking at different levels and angles. The geometrical design mesmerized her.

"How lovely. It's like music in bricks," she said.

Henrique caressed the back of her hand with his thumb. "They block off the plaza and hold bullfights here, with watchers sitting on the steps."

Instead of bulls, villagers crowded the space, walking in circles. "What are they doing?"

"Courting. The men ramble clockwise while unmarried girls stroll in the opposite direction."

"How odd."

"It's groggily effective. I'll show you."

Isabel halted. "What if someone recognizes me?"

She still wore her costume, only a cloak concealing her skin from the night air.

He swept her with his gaze. "This has to go." He removed her tiara and shoved it inside her reticule.

When he started combing through her coiffure, Isabel caught his hand.

"I allow no one but Sophie to touch my hair."

He grinned. "Is it because she is a Republican? The only person guaranteed not to rob your crown?"

"How did you know she was a Republican?"

"She called me Citizen Henrique. I added two and two."

Isabel glanced away. "It's my scalp. It's... sensitive."

"I'll be gentle."

Isabel held her breath as Henrique unleashed her hair with deft but soft tugs. The tresses cascaded down her shoulders. She hadn't worn it down in society since she was assigned a personal maid at the age of ten. He massaged her scalp, and she sighed deeply. Then he placed his thumbs at the base of her neck, pressed up, and circled the sore spots from the pins. A moan escaped her lips, and she closed her eyes, leaning on him and listening to his heart drumming. If a person could inhabit a single moment for the rest of her life, reliving it for eternity, this would be hers—she would gladly take up residence in the luxury of Henrique's fingers.

"There, she's done punishing you for the night." He kissed her strands, his breath tickling the shell of her ear.

"Do you think a different coiffure will keep me incognito?"

"The hair, no. The crown? Definitely. But you are right. You need a finishing touch." He picked a hibiscus flower.

When he brought it close to her face, she held her breath, not unlike a bride who waits for her husband on her wedding night. How foolish of her. He wasn't denuding her. He was simply tucking a flower behind her ear. Yet, when he took a step away to inspect the results of his labor, Isabel felt naked.

"You will do. Now come, the courting awaits."

Henrique steered her towards the strolling girls. When Isabel saw the strangers twirling in circles, she planted her slippers on the cobblestones and gave him a pleading look.

He laughed and shooed her away. "It's not an intricate diplomacy affair. Just walk."

The folk song launched with an offbeat, the pipe crying out alongside an uplifting guitar. Isabel fell into step with the other ladies.

He winked and started in the opposite direction, his attire and bearing making him conspicuous among the other gentlemen.

A girl linked her arm through Isabel's and, laughing, pulled her into the gyrating mob.

Voices and music and shoulders and feet twirled with her. A bonfire threw cinders and sparkles high, illuminating smiling, weather-beaten faces. It all blurred when she spotted Henrique. Every inch a man's man, he strolled among the Spaniards, not seeing her, and when they crossed paths, she felt him touching her hand. A brief, too brief, touch. Her fingers twitched, and she closed her palm as electricity ignited her skin.

She hastened her steps, wanting to see him again. When they met, he caressed her cheek, a tender, chaste caress that left her breathless and overheated.

Her legs stopped, and before she was trampled, the girl by her side pulled her along. Isabel looked behind her, but she had lost him.

Isabel counted the seconds until she would meet him. She gave a complete turn, and he didn't appear. Her heart sped, and she went on tiptoes, trying to find him.

He circled his arms around her waist and lifted her from the ground. "Caught you."

Amid cheers and laughter from the twirling audience, he took her away from the plaza and into a shadowy alley.

Placing his hands on her cheeks, he stared down at her. Her skin tingled like she had rolled atop embers and entered a gelid cave. Isabel closed her eyes. When his wine-scented breath touched her lips, she lifted her face, a sapling searching for the sun's warmth. For an aching moment, she stood in a dark abyss. Waiting... and then he joined her. Isabel interlaced her fingers over his neck, her pulse hammering a flamenco inside her chest. Her legs became useless maypoles, unable to move, to do no more than keep her upright. Henrique kissed with the thoroughness of the scientist, the expertise of the rake, and the passion that was his alone.

He pulled away, breathing heavily. "Isa, Isa, Isa... this is—"

"Don't speak. I need, I need..."

He nibbled at her bottom lip and then peppered kisses over her cheeks. "What do you need, my siren princess?"

"I need another lesson."

She imagined many a maiden had been ruined by uttering much less. In silence, he guided her toward the palace. The incessant drums continued, like a desperate heart, giving the beat, excusing any behavior.

The way passed in a blur, and they were back under Eros' statue.

Henrique caught her in his arms and knelt over the grass. Kissing her deeply, he lowered her over the bench, a maiden sacrifice to the god of love. Inhaling the spice of wet earth and daffodils, she twirled her fingers through his hair, and tugged his head closer, thirsty for his kiss. His hand explored her torso, her stomach, her hip bones. Without a corset, his touch felt real, and yet, she wanted more.

Moonlight danced in his hair, and his face was dewy with the midnight mist. He drew up her skirts. He did it slowly, possibly giving her a moment to judge the sanity of her actions. How foolish. Her sanity still spun on the plaza. A soft breeze kissed her thighs as he revealed to the night sky places that had never seen daylight.

When he found the entrance to her drawers, she sought his eyes. She would have stopped him if his gaze was jaded, patronizing, or lewd, but he seemed... awed and affected like her.

He covered her mound with his palm and trailed his finger over her outer lips. Her hips buckled shamelessly, and he chuckled.

He found that delicious spot and brushed his finger around it, a different kind of courtship than at the fiesta, but with the same dizzying effect. It wasn't enough. Then he stopped. Isabel lifted her head to watch him. He changed position, now kneeling between her legs. The difference in height placed his face inches from her intimate parts. He caressed the fine hairs atop her mound, then sighed, her name a sweet chant on his lips. Isabel held her breath when he propped his weight on his elbows and moved closer.

"You are very pretty here." He kissed her there.

Abruptly, he slid his hands below her buttocks and lifted. Her legs fell to the sides of the bench, exposing her fully for his view. Her spine pressed against the stone bench, feet dangling without purchase. Heat rose to her cheeks, and she tried to wriggle away from him. He hushed her, and she felt his breath over her core.

"Henrique, I don't—"

"Shhh." Holding her firmly, he massaged her derrière. "Let me show you another way to fly."

The moist heat of his tongue lapped at her from her entrance to her little bud of nerves. A half moan, half gasp escaped her, and she lay back. He licked her outer lips, and then he penetrated her. Her body dissolved, becoming one with the cicadas, a creature with no tangents, boundaries, or thoughts, just a waterfall of feelings. He took her tiny spot of pleasure between his teeth, suspending her between this world and the next, poised at an abyss. She undulated her hips, offering herself to him, pleading for more heat, more friction, more. Then he sucked. All her energy floated there, wet and demanding, and she cried out as pleasure burst, igniting her nerve endings.

She closed her eyes, an arm flung over her forehead, panting.

Henrique petted her mound, the caress soothing. "Good God, Isabel, you are—"

Before he could define what had just happened, she laced her arms over his neck and pulled him atop her, shifting underneath him. The drums played a primitive rhyme of seduction. The pleasure he showed her left her exhausted but oddly empty.

She bit his earlobe. "I want more. The final lesson."

"Is this wise? You are tipsy..."

He was unsure. Of all the reactions she expected from him, indecision ranked the lowest.

A single glass of sangria hadn't muddled her wishes. "I'm not intoxicated."

"No? Lust is as intoxicating as any wine. I've been drunk on you since I saw you in your ridiculous Joan of Arc garb. I'm drunk on you now, drunk on your sweet breath, drunk on your scent. Drunk. And drunkards are famous for lousy decision-making."

Ignoring his reasoning, she licked his bottom lip and then his chin, tasting his brandy aftershave and the rough texture of his skin. Bolstered by his groan, she skimmed her palms over his back, tracing the ridges of his spine until she arrived at his waist.

Ending the kiss, he leaned his forehead on hers. "I promised you just a glimpse."

"A glimpse is not enough."

Why could he restrain himself so easily?

"Must we rush things? I don't want to do this on a bench, risking discovery." He sat, shifting away from her, his expression hidden by Eros's shadow.

The words 'I don't want this' rang in her ears. How foolish she had been. The prudish princess trying to tempt a rake. Her chin trembled, and she clutched her stomach. "Really, Henrique, for all your fame... You are revealing yourself to be a disappointment."

"It is not only your prince who has honor." His face hardened, and he stood up. "I will escort you back to your room."

Isabel smoothed her skirts down her unwanted legs, her cheeks heating with shame. "I know the way."

Chapter 25

"In friendship, as in love, we are often happier through our ignorance than our knowledge."
William Shakespeare

Isabel leaned over her dressing table, moonlight glowing over the hibiscus in her hair. Jaw clenched, she plucked it from her ear and replaced her tiara. The wire pierced her scalp. Cursing, she threw it away. Hibiscus and diamonds stood side by side on the vanity.

Panting, she splayed her hands over the wooden surface. Henrique's hurt expression haunted her. Stupid, stupid pride. Could she blame him for acting responsibly? He had been nothing but gentlemanly, and she had implied he was only worth his lust. Covering her face, she groaned. She had given him the treatment she despised men for. Isabel stared at her bed and then at the door. The clock struck the first chime of midnight. How could she sleep if she didn't apologize?

She tucked the hibiscus under her ear and crept out of her room. The way to Henrique's bedroom passed in a daze of empty corridors and dark passages. She tiptoed to the bachelor's wing, keeping to the alcoves and shadows formed by the heavy drapery. Rustling and rushed voices prompted her to hide behind a statue. In the dim light, she could make only a couple's outline, their hands interlaced.

Holding still, she waited. When the corridor was empty, she proceeded.

Flickering light spilled from Henrique's bedroom. She paused, imagining his surprise at seeing her again. The memory of his kiss was still in her mouth, and her skin tingled where he had touched it just minutes before.

Pulse speeding, she opened the door a slit. A candelabra burned atop the nightstand. Henrique was not alone. It took a moment for what she saw to make sense. He kissed Rafaela, her scantily clad body draped over his. A stab pierced her chest, the pain so acute she feared she would crumble. His proclamations of honor masqueraded for excuses. Henrique was a blackguard. And he broke her heart.

Chapter 26

"It seems impossible to repress Iberian blood at the age of twenty." The Duchess de Dino

Henrique closed his mouth against Rafaela's onslaught and held her at arm's length. "Stop acting. Your husband isn't here."

She laughed, her red lipstick now bleeding into her chin. "Why so tense? Your experiments? Are they giving you trouble? I can help." She moved behind him, her breasts crushing against his midback, and kneaded his shoulders.

Henrique stepped forward and waved to the open door. "Good night, Rafaela."

She pouted. "Let me stay... I'll make your night really good."

Henrique pinched the bridge of his nose. "I tire of your games. You love Canastra. Do nothing to cause regret in the morning."

"Do you see these?" She cupped her breasts.

"Hard not to," Henrique said dryly.

"I won't be like the other matrons who marry and spout a kid or two, then let their bodies go and become fat like pigs in a cornfield, secure that in this country, divorce is blasphemy, and though their husbands might take a mistress, no king or pope can take a wife from her home and children. I want more than a life of duty. I'm done waiting for Canastra. I want passion, and I want it now."

And he was the stallion waiting to perform? She better stay in line then. He massaged his temples against a wave of headache. Everything was askew in this place. The first time he'd acted with *pundonor*, he was rejected. Isabel wanted the rake, not the honorable gentleman. And it hurt. "The stud is closed."

"What a shame... Won't you make an exception? Both of us will be free. My husband plans a secret trip and will take your protégée with him."

Henrique froze. "Where?"

She tossed her hair and rolled her eyes. "Cordoba, Madrid, the fifth hell? I care not where."

Henrique grabbed her shoulders. "What does Canastra plan to do with Isabel?"

Frowning, she inspected him with sensual black eyes. "It is true, is it not? You are in love with her?"

Henrique released her and crossed his arms. He would take Isabel away from here on the morrow. To hell with the king and Pedro. "My relationship with Princess Isabel does not concern you."

She laughed, and the sound grated on his ears. "She might amuse herself with you for a while, but such a brilliant scientist should know... She won't marry you."

Henrique clenched his hands. He didn't need Rafaela to remind him of life's facts, damn it.

"Don't you see? Isabel is just like Canastra. She loves her duty above all else." Rafaela sneered and left the room.

Chapter 27

"Stronger than lover's love is lover's hate. Incurable, in each, the wounds they make". Euripides, *Medea*

Isabel opened her eyes to a room beset by dawn. A thick and pounding migraine assaulted her head, and she repented waking up. Memories of the night before crumpled her defenses, and she accepted her pain with a groan. She had hurt herself, and the fault was entirely hers. Hadn't she known all her life that passion led to disgrace? To think she could have ruined her reputation for that... that—for once, she could not find an epithet to call Henrique. Still, a treacherous part of her, the one who mutinied every time he came near, couldn't understand his betrayal. She rubbed her chest, trying to soothe the ache inside, telling herself it would soon fade.

If only she could believe in animal spirits as Henrique did. Why did women and men have to be so different? While men flew from attraction to attraction, never cooling their wings, women longed for the same love, their life's purpose diminished by a quest from myth—a man who gave constancy as he gave passion.

Sophie flung the door open.

"Mon Dieu, Dolly isn't here?"

"I'm certain she overcame her fears and decided to sleep alone."

"Her bed is made."

Isabel flinched. Sleeping after noon was Dolly's motto, and she would rather make merry than her bed. "Are you sure she isn't sleeping in her bedroom?"

The maid wrung her hands, her eyes downcast.

Isabel flung open the door to Dolly's room. If the chamber's stillness wasn't telling enough, then the ominous envelope atop the counterpane became doom's messenger.

With legs shaking and spirits sagging, Isabel opened the letter.

Your Highness,

You are right. I'm much more than an illustrious nose. I decided to follow my dreams.

I hope with all my heart you will understand.

With all my regard,

Dolly

Isabel lowered the sheet and stared into Dolly's empty armoire. She had eloped. Lady Dolores had ruined herself. Her brain searched for guilty parties and latched onto the most obvious culprit—Henrique. Why had she allowed him to convince her? Charles Whitaker, a man in love? A reformed rake? Impossible. She should have sent Dolly to her father the moment Charles arrived here. But no, she had permitted their interactions, even allowed herself to be convinced of his feelings.

"Do you think she went far?" Sophie asked.

"I don't know what they plan to do."

But Charles' best friend must be privy to their direction.

Isabel marched out of her room. Outside Henrique's door, Isabel paused.

She would not show him how his inconstancy had hurt. By God, she would not. She would ask for Charles's whereabouts, nothing more. Girding herself against his caressing eyes, she knocked.

Diomedes opened the door, unleashing a racketing noise from inside. His blond hair was disheveled, and purple lines marred his fair skin.

When he saw her, his eyes widened. "Yes?"

"I want to speak with him. Now."

"A second, if you please. I'll see if Viscount Penafiel is receiving." Diomedes closed the door in her face.

Isabel expelled air from her mouth. See if he was receiving? No one left a princess waiting. She tapped her foot, crossing her arms firmly in front of her chest.

Diomedes appeared again. "He asks your forgiveness, but he is otherwise occupied."

Isabel clamped her jaw so hard that her teeth hurt. "Tell him if he does not come here this instant, I will box his ears."

Diomedes gasped and vanished inside.

Isabel blew an impatient breath and glared at the closed door.

Diomedes returned. "He wants to know if you wish to offend him by telling him you want to box his ears."

"Offend? Of course not. I only wish to cause him unimaginable pain."

"If that is the case, then—"

Before he could shut her out, she barreled inside. Diomedes escaped the bedroom and her wrath, closing the door behind him.

Isabel inspected her surroundings and found her culprit at his worktable, in indecent shirtsleeves. Henrique had his back to her, pounding at something with a hammer, the sound of iron clubbing steel resounding like strident bells.

He glanced at her sideways and resumed the infernal noise. How dare he give her a cold shoulder? As if he were the injured party?

"I came to know the whereabouts of your acolyte," she said, raising her voice.

"I'm sorry, I can't hear you." His shoulders bulged with the force of his rams. The shirt was glued to his shoulders and chest. Any moment now, his laborer appearance would revolt instead of fascinating her.

"Then stop bashing."

He increased the speed.

Gritting her teeth, Isabel placed herself in front of him.

His eyes flared, but he quit. The silence pounded, reverberating over the empty room.

His expression was serious, and the shadow of a beard gave him a piratical appearance. "If you came to play Venus to my Vulcan, you are too late. The shop's closed for the day."

"Dolly eloped. She's ruined herself, and all because of your friend and partner in crime."

Henrique's eyes widened, and he rubbed his forehead. "But Charles' intentions were honorable. He loves Dolly."

"And you believed him? You, above all else?" Isabel could not keep the accusation from her voice.

Henrique lifted his brows. "Perhaps if you didn't hound the couple like Cerberus guarding the gates of hell, Charles would not have felt the need to flee."

Isabel stabbed his chest with her finger. "I forbid you to shove the blame on me. As we speak, your rakish friend has probably seduced Dolly, broken her heart, and left her alone to fend for herself. How do you think she will feel? Learning that after he gave her earthshaking pleasure, he returned to courting married women?" Her voice broke, and by the end of her rant, she was shaking.

"Isabel, are you all right?"

She placed her hands on her face, horrified to find her cheeks wet with tears.

He took her wrist and pulled her, trying to embrace her. After spending the night with her cousin, he wanted what? To amuse himself with her? A quick morning tryst to settle him for the afternoon?

"Don't touch me! Never touch me again, " she shrieked.

He stepped back, raising his palms.

Isabel used his confusion to flee.

She hastened through empty corridors and out into the garden. Her corset constricted her breaths, and her feet weighted too much, the ground stalling her progress as if made of wet cement.

Midway to the lawn, she stumbled upon a male chest.

"What's wrong?" Alfonso asked, holding her shoulders.

"He took her," Isabel babbled, tears streaming down her cheeks.

Alfonso rubbed her back and guided her to the kitchen. Among a crowd of ruffled servants, he brought her tea. Only when she regained her balance, he bade her speak. Sniffing, she told him about Dolly, who had a difficult childhood and finally found her confidence when a drunk libertine robbed her of a future.

"Do you think this *sinvergüenza* is after Lady Dolores's fortune?" Alfonso offered her his kerchief.

"Why, no... His father is wealthy and does not deny him anything." If the port trader had been less indulgent with Charles, he would have learned to respect propriety.

Alfonso frowned. "Is Lady Dolores' family unwilling to give permission?"

So many questions. Isabel pressed her fist against her forehead and shook her head. "Not that I know of..."

"Then why would he elope with her?"

"Why? Why! To ruin her, of course. To take advantage of her innocence and then leave her to fend for herself."

Alfonso nodded, and if her outburst surprised him, he disguised it well.

"If you are sure about this, I will lead the search party myself."

Chapter 28

"To me, he seems equal to gods, the man who sits facing you and hears you near as you speak softly and laugh." Sappho

An atmosphere of anticipation pervaded Canastra's palace tonight. The dining hall had been arranged with Byzantine splendor. Butterfly orchids adorned the vases and table centers. The chandeliers shimmered in blazing glory, spilling golden light over the marble statues. The Spanish aristocracy had donned their finery, the gentlemen's uniforms bedecked with medals and orders, and the ladies sported more jewels than they had space in their limbs to carry.

Henrique stood with Dio near the Grecian colonnades. Isabel had yet to appear. After blaming him for Dolly's disappearance, she avoided his presence. Henrique's gaze went to the top of the stairs again, hoping to glimpse the hoydenish princess. He preferred her outrage over this dratted distance.

Dio inspected the crowd with narrowed eyes. "Do you think they are eying us strangely tonight? At least more than their usual despise of foreigners?"

Henrique ignored Dio's fretting. "What maggot consumed Charles's brain? He'd planned to speak to Dolly's father. He had proposed to her. His intentions were honorable. Why did he change his mind?"

Dio crossed his arms and let out a sigh. "He could be as far as Liverpool. They were probably beyond reach before the ridiculous cavalcade this afternoon."

"Stop grumbling. After Alfonso decided to search for Dolly, it would have been strange if we had demurred, if not outwardly suspicious."

"And so we went. Instead of spending the siesta with my saucy maid, I had to comb the countryside until our asses were numb." Dio lifted his glass to his mouth. "Rafaela is flaying you alive. Someone's been naughty."

"Rafaela is her husband's problem." Henrique gulped a liberal amount of brandy. Between Isa's outburst in the garden and Rafaela's midnight escapade to his room, he had enough. He understood Rafaela's desperation with her passionless marriage, but he would not accept Isa's desire for a quick tumble on the grass. He wanted more from her. Christ. After seeing her flying, her joy... It was the first time he felt something different from a body's craving for sensual release. He felt a bonding of souls.

After dinner, he would take her to their secret spot under Eros and show her how deep his feelings were.

Dio groaned. "Don't look now. The dragon is prowling near."

Henrique hid his chuckle behind a cough. Lady Montijo had developed a less than platonic admiration for his friend. It was amusing to see Dio fending off her advances.

Trumpet in her right hand and her turban slightly askew, she latched herself to Dio's arm. "There you are." She leaned closer and whispered so loudly people around them stopped their conversation. "I have a problem that requires your youth, my dear."

Dio stiffened, his shoulders coming up to touch his blond curls. "And what would it be, my lady?"

Lady Montijo gave him a sly look and tapped his arm with her fan. "What a naughty, curious boy. I can't tell you now. Come to me after dinner."

Dio rounded his eyes. "But it will be way past my bedtime."

She licked her lips. "Poor baby. Auntie will put you to sleep."

Henrique didn't hear Dio's repartee. The trio of violinists struck the first notes of the *Heart of Granada*, and the assembly hushed.

Isabel appeared at the top of the stairs. Layers of white satin and silver thread embraced her torso and trailed to the floor like a moonlit wave. As she glided down, diamonds glittered on her cocoa hair and the hollow of her throat. She moved with the grace and the dignity of a true queen.

His gut tightened, and his mouth dropped open.

Lady Montijo rapped Henrique's forearm and said in her loud, deaf voice, like a person shouting from a cave into a strong wind. "If she isn't the most stunning princess I ever saw, I will eat up my turban. She will make a lovely bride."

Henrique groaned. He didn't need Montijo to express what passed through every male's head as Isabel crossed the ballroom. Their eyes met. He expected to see anger in her gaze, but he glimpsed confusion. Sadness even. Henrique started in her direction. Just as her joy had affected him, her hurt pierced him, their connection similar to the ones uniting atoms in a molecule. Before he could reach her, Alfonso was at her side, speaking close to her ear and escorting her to the dining room.

Henrique gritted his teeth and forced himself to stay away when every primal instinct clamored for him to pummel Alfonso back into exile. He didn't have to make a scene. He could wait to speak with her after dinner.

When the company settled at the lavishly decorated table, Alfonso stood. The Spanish aristocracy rose in unison.

Foreboding made the brandy churn in his stomach. All around him, people watched, excitement written clearly on their powdery faces. Why did he feel like the only one not privy to a joke?

He sought Isabel's gaze. She averted her eyes, interested in whatever French wine they had served tonight. Her face had the same color as the marble statues. The opposite of the brazen red of when he touched her.

Alfonso cleared his throat. His face was flushed, and he spoke with his chin up. "I'm sorry to make this announcement during such a convoluted period. As we speak, guards are searching for Lady Dolores, and her untimely disappearance will be accounted for."

Henrique scoffed. So that was what they decided to call Dolly's elopement? A disappearance?

Alfonso pulled Isabel to her feet.

Lady Montijo stopped harassing Dio and adjusted the trumpet to her ear.

Henrique's gut tightened, and he could not keep a scowl from his face as the Bourbon prince kissed Isabel's hand. For a second, Isabel's gaze found his. What he saw there curdled his blood. Regret dulled the emerald of her eyes. *What have you done, Isa?*

As Canastra lifted his glass, a villainous smile tugging his lips, and the footmen lined up the doors, their trays filled with champagne, Henrique knew. His stomach sunk, and he gripped the table to stay in his place.

"Still, I hope you all will find it in your hearts to appreciate our news, even in these trying times. With great honor, I inform you Isabel de Orleans, Princess of Portugal, has accepted to be my bride."

Chapter 29

"If I must lose because I am a woman, I want to lose like a man." Caterina Sforza, The Countess of Forli

Isabel focused on stitching the Portuguese flag. Shadows grew in her bedchamber, but the gas lamps were silent. The events of the past hours besieged her like a rioting crowd, but she refused to be affected by them. With gritty eyes, chest numb, she added carmine thread to the Braganza's coat of arms.

She told herself that accepting Alfonso's proposal had been the right thing. Seeing Henrique in another's embrace, and Dolly ruined by a rake, had shed her madness. Now, she saw her duty clearly.

Marrying Alfonso would bring stability to the peninsula. As Spain's queen, she would help him navigate the intricacies of political life. Her brother might grumble she didn't consult him, but he would understand she did the right thing.

Her chin trembled, and she shut her eyes. What if Alfonso didn't make her skin tingle and her heart flut-

ter? Isabel de Orleans wasn't meant for a life of passion. Passion was for brazen women like Rafaela. Flying wasn't for her. No, she had been raised for a life
of duty, protected within the walls of morality. Why
was it so hard to breathe? There was no crippling pain
inside those walls.

The needle slipped from her clammy hand, and she
pricked the pad of her finger. Numbly, she watched as
blood pooled on her skin. It was not blue, her blood.
A sob escaped her throat, and her chest shook.

Sophie entered her room and gasped. She dropped
a basket and kneeled at Isabel's feet.

"Here, let me take care of this." She picked up the flag
and shook the cloth. "See? No need to cry. You didn't
stain it. It isn't my France's tricolor, but your design is
beautiful. No one is better with needle and thread."

Sophie hung the flag over the back of the couch.
"Prince Alfonso is outside, but my lady is indisposed.
Should I tell him to come back later?"

Isabel cleaned the tears with a handkerchief and
pinched her cheeks. "I shall see him now. Thank you,
Sophie."

Alfonso stepped inside her bedchamber and bowed
deeply. "I apologize for his sorrowful state. I found the
sinvergüenza alone in the tavern. The Guardia helped
me haul him here."

The Guardia? But were they not a risk to Alfonso?
Isabel jumped to her feet.

Two officers of the Guardia Civil invaded the room.
Wearing blue jackets embellished with gold braids
and the coat of arms of the Spanish monarchy, they
cut an impressive figure. The plumed cockade atop
the tricorne wavered as they dragged a moaning man
inside.

Upon seeing her, they dropped the dead weight on
the Aubusson carpet. Placing a hand over their hearts,
they shouted, "*Viva la Reyna!*" Long live the queen.

So shocked was Isabel by their salute, it took her several seconds to recover her wits.

Her gaze trailed from the Guardia's impassive expressions to the man crumpled on the floor. It was Charles Whitaker. If he was alone, where was Dolly? Had he tired of her already? Left her for another woman?

Isabel fisted her hands by her sides. "Where is she? Where did you leave Lady Dolores?"

Charles lifted his face as if waking up from a bad dream. Tears coursed through his cheeks, wetting his red beard. She had never seen a man crying, and it constricted her chest. Her gaze flew to the Guardia and then to Alfonso.

Alfonso raised his palms. "For my honor, he was not touched in violence. When sober, though, he will have to pay for the slight to Lady Dolores."

At the mention of Dolly's name, a pitiful keening sound escaped from Charles' mouth.

"Please! Have you left her in some inn? She loved you, and—"

"Love? My dove doesn't love me."

"Don't place the blame on her. She—"

"She used me." Charles sighed and dropped his chin. "She told me if we didn't elope, she would leave me. We went to the station. I wanted to take her to her father to ask for her hand. Behind my back, she boarded a train to Paris."

Isabel gasped. "I don't believe you."

The Guardia advanced over to Charles.

Charles mumbled, oblivious to the threat. Trembling, he reached inside his coat and removed a paper. "See for yourself."

Isabel took the message from him. He gazed up at her, his eyes brimmed with raw hurt. Charles was heartbroken. She had judged him unfairly. Heart pain, it seemed, chose not gender. She had been wrong about that as well. Throat swollen with sorrow, she placed her hand above his shoulder. She owed him an apology.

Charles' face turned green, and Alfonso signaled the Guardia to remove him from the room before he could vomit.

Isabel's hand fell limply to her side. "Wait, I—"

Alfonso closed the door after the Guardia left. "They won't harm him unless I say so."

Was the Guardia supporting Alfonso? They must have because the prince's eyes showed a new light, and he had grown an inch. Still, Isabel couldn't process it now and slumped on the couch.

She read Dolly's note, and it all made sense at last.

Alfonso took it from her numb fingers. After scanning the lines, he crumpled the paper. "What an unnatural thing to do. Abandon her duties as a maid of honor to a royal princess. All to become an actress? A woman without morals?"

Alfonso must have believed her silence was due to shock because he knelt at her feet and held her hand. "It is better this way. My dear, you wouldn't want a corrupt sheep in your household."

The old Isabel would feel the same. This Isabel, this other version of her, was not so sure. Dolly dreamed of taking Paris by storm. Why should she bury herself inside her carapace and conform to a life of rigidity?

A tiny smile crossed her lips, and she hid it under her handkerchief. Lady Dolores had fooled everyone. Where did she hide such cunning? Lady Dolores, too, had chanced to fly. Isabel only hoped it wouldn't hurt Dolly as much.

Isabel looked at the heirloom ring crowning her finger and at Alfonso's austere expression, and an ache invaded her chest.

"Did you finish the flag?" Alfonso bent over the cloth. Frowning, he traced her precise stitches.

Isabel nodded. "As we agreed. And then you will—"

"I have *pundonor*, Isabel, and once I'm king, as promised, I will renounce any right to the Portuguese throne."

Isabel's smile was perhaps sadder than Charles'. Alfonso would be a qualified king for Spain. He wouldn't make her skin tingle or her heart pound, but he vowed fidelity. It would have to be enough.

Chapter 30

"Love as if you would one day hate, and hate as if you would one day love." - Bias of Priene

Henrique stood at the ballroom's fringes while the couple danced under the light of a thousand candles. Everything was correct in the waltz. At least a palm separated their chests. Alfonso led her into unimaginative steps, stiff as the stick in the mud he was. When he smiled at something Isabel said, the entire company sighed.

Alfonso had the right to smile into her eyes and bring her closer at every measure. He had the right to splay his hand over the small of her back and listen as her heart pulsed with the waltz's one-two-three. He had the right to her hand's weight in his and to square his chest as he paraded the most stunning woman around the ballroom. Alfonso had the right.

Then why did it feel so wrong?

A knot obstructed Henrique's esophagus, and no amount of brandy would make it recede. A lucid part of him tried to command his legs to leave the room and repel the pain, as any wounded animal would. But his skin had become bark, rigid, stuck in the same place like a gnarled oak. Thank God for it. Otherwise, the Spanish aristocracy would learn the mess within. He wanted to shout to them that the woman in Alfonso's arms was his and that, no, they could not have this particular princess, not for a ball, not for their political machinations, and not in blazing hell for breeding their next prince.

What had happened to his principles? Seek pleasure, avoid pain? She'd shoved her royal self into his beliefs, that's what. After her, pleasure and pain became the same, swelling and ebbing, scraping to show peaks underneath the physical. A deeper meaning to things.

Perhaps it was only he who saw it.

More fool him.

"Well, then. I can't say I'm surprised." Dio turned his back to the couple. "On to the card tables, shall we? All this royal sweetness is making me thirsty."

Dio's voice faded with the last strings of the waltz. Isabel's skirts twirled around her ankles and then stilled. Henrique stopped breathing. Alfonso leaned in, aimed for her cheek, and then kissed her lips. Isabel startled and pulled away. Even with the distance separating them, her eyes sought Henrique's. He crushed the brandy tumbler. His vision tunneled at the Spanish rooster, and a primitive urge gripped him to grab the prince by his lapels and shake the smile out of his Bourbon face.

The ballroom swirled around him. The guests' faces turned into mythological monsters, watching the tragedy unfold. Henrique hit the side table with his glass, sloshing liquid over the rim.

He advanced, a foreign bloodthirst fueling his moves.

A hand over his arm forced him to stop. Henrique eyed Dio with murderous intent.

"Are you sure you should congratulate her in your state? You've been drinking since last night's dinner."

Henrique panted. What would he do? Grab her like a Neanderthal and take her to his cave? Dio was right. He didn't belong here. With a last glance at the princess, Henrique strode through the French doors and into the gardens.

"Where the hell are you going?"

"To the tavern. Care to join me?" He had experienced enough pain for a lifetime.

"A Castilian maid might wash the breath of Lady Montijo from my neck. Good God, the lady is ferocious. But are you sure you should go?"

Henrique trampled the grass, not caring for Dio's tone. "I don't know what you mean."

"Self-deception isn't one of your poisons."

Henrique whirled and grabbed Dio by the lapels. The pent-up rage threatened to engulf him. "Stay out of this."

Dio's lips opened in a smile full of teeth. "I've known all along. You love her. That's why you have Hercules' club up your ass. Go after her. It's not too late."

Henrique released his friend, disgusted with himself. Isabel had used him. He had taunted her for keeping her passionate side on a leash, and she showed how wrong he was. What they shared meant nothing to her. She chose a royal prince. Whether for political reasons or sentimental ones, what was the difference? He had shown her his true self, and she chose another.

Henrique's long strides carried him to the brightly lit stables. Halting, he caught his timepiece. Half-past twelve in the morning. Why were all the torches burning?

Dio caught up with him. "As much as I love a good debauchery, I don't think—"

"Silence." Henrique lifted his hand.

The carriage house had trains of baggage being lifted to the coaches. Servants bustled about, carrying boxes and baskets.

Henrique intercepted a groom. "What is going on?"

"The royals leave for Madrid in the morning, *patron*."

One of Canastra's guards glared at the servant, and the boy lowered his hat and scurried away.

Dio lifted his brows. "Well, it seems our stay in Comillas has ended."

"The hell it has." The rooster would not take Isabel from here. Henrique was her escort. The king had entrusted him with his sister. He would not allow Canastra and Alfonso to steal the princess from under their noses.

Henrique stalked out of the stables.

Canastra's minions patrolled the house. A contingent of armed men had swelled their numbers. Henrique recognized the blue and gold uniform of the Guardia Civil. The hairs on the back of his arm stood on end. Canastra and Alfonso had gained the Guardia's support. What would Pedro Daun think of this?

Warming his heels, Dio panted. "Did they come for the ball?"

Henrique didn't know and believed the answer wouldn't please them. "Let's find Canastra."

When they arrived at the palace's entrance, the two guards eyed them disdainfully.

Outside Canastra's study, light spilled from the closed door. Henrique was about to twist the knob when voices from inside made him pause.

Asking Dio to be quiet, Henrique listened.

"You will face them in battle. You will conquer them with your courage. You will keep them with *my* cunning." Canastra's speech resounded with cheap rhetoric and political extremism, leaving a sour taste in Henrique's mouth.

"It's too soon for Madrid." Alfonso sounded shrill and out of breath. "Without the army's support, Aosta will repel us as he did with the Carlist forces."

"It is natural to be afraid. Battle is foreign to you—"

"I'm ready to die for Spain." Silence. "But I won't risk my bride."

Henrique gritted his teeth at the possessive note in Alfonso's statement. The clock struck the hour. Their conversation became hushed. Henrique shut his eyes, trying to hear.

"No cost is too high. We have come this far—"

"I've followed your advice since Sandhurst, and your support proved invaluable. But Isabel returns to Lisbon. After we conquer Madrid and I regain my throne, I will ask for her hand officially."

"No!" Canastra screeched. "I could have chosen any royal princess for you..."

Henrique locked his jaw. Canastra's blackmail finally made sense. He'd planned the betrothal from the start.

"But unlike the other European princesses, Isabel is more than a well-connected bride." Canastra's voice assumed the low, measured cadence of a preacher. "She is her brother's presumptive heir—"

"You go too far. Isabel's brother is young, recently married, and can no doubt sire many children before Isabel has to inherit," Alfonso said.

"What about the curse? No Braganza's heir will ascend to the throne unless they find the friar's grave. I assure you, they won't."

Alfonso scoffed. "I cannot believe it. You will resuscitate some moth-ridden myth?"

"I'm quite competent at resuscitation," Canastra said, and Henrique could see the sneer in his voice. "Why, if it wasn't for my powers, you would still be exiled."

"If my mother had not made you a duke, you would have no power."

"Perhaps Your Highness would like to try his luck with the old aristocracy then? Oh, wait, they are too busy fawning over the man who usurped your throne."

Silence.

Dio frowned. "What are they saying?"

"I think Alfonso is sulking," Henrique whispered. And so he should if he had to rely on such vipers as Canastra.

"If my strategy is unacceptable to Your Highness, we'll retreat. Wait for the army to support us. Perhaps one year or two. You hoped to return to Palacio Real, but Madrid will stay there. You can always go back to exile—"

"No!" A pause, heavy breathing. "No. What is your plan?"

Henrique suppressed a snort. What a wimp. And he wanted to marry Isabel? She would maneuver him better than he steered his automobile.

Canastra cleared his throat. Henrique could well imagine his feline smile. "We will garner the army with the promise of a united Iberian kingdom."

Dio sucked in a breath. Henrique signaled for him to move away from the door. He needed to hear the whole thing.

"I promised Isabel I wouldn't jeopardize her brother's throne," Alfonso said, but his voice lacked conviction.

"You worry yourself about wooing your bride. I will gather the army's support."

Henrique paced the expanse of his bedchamber. When the clock struck four in the morning, he kicked the ottoman, sending it crashing to the wall. Too fast. Things were happening too fast. Two hours ago, his valet had left to comb the harbor for Pedro's yacht. But even Almoster could not amass a force in such a short time. The muscles on his chest and shoulders were stiffer than the marble under his feet. The only thing worse than Spain putting its hands on Portugal was the prospect of Alfonso putting his hands on Isabel.

Dawn hadn't broken the night's darkness, but the palace was awake. Servants and grooms readied carriages outside. Isabel was closeted inside her bedchamber, guarded by Lady Montijo. The dragon had sent him away, refusing him a word with the princess. He could bet the old patriotic lady was in league with Canastra.

Dio entered his room, closing the door behind him. Henrique eyed his friend. "And?"

"Canastra sent Rafaela away. The scoundrel isn't taking any chances. Two guards hound your door. I told you the Spaniards had ulterior motives." Dio paced to the window and cast an alarmed look outside. Dropping the curtains, he groaned. "We must escape before they revive the inquisition and use our flesh for kindling. My flammability is uncertain, but with the amount of brandy you have ingested these past few days, I'm sure you will burn brighter than a fiesta bonfire."

Henrique ignored Dio's rant. Come the morning, Canastra and Alfonso would take Isabel to Madrid, and she would be lost to him forever. Portuguese independence would exist only in history books, soon to become a myth, like the country's great navigations.

Curse the princess for her gullibility. He brushed his chest, unable to soothe the pain inside. The image of her dancing in Alfonso's arms would haunt him into Hades. Henrique exhaled and dropped onto his bed. He tried to hold on to his rightful anger, but then...

The way she looked at him before the proposal... Had Henrique pushed her into this? Stirred her passions without committing himself? Kept silent when she needed more from him? Through the years, he had achieved a balance with women, allowing him to take what he wanted without giving false hope. But with Isabel, it was not caution that kept him from speaking, from accepting her offer, but fear.

The fear of showing too much of himself was nothing compared to the panic twisting his gut now. If he stayed in this room, arms crossed, Isabel would be carted to Madrid, out of reach, her life at risk, and if Canastra's plan worked, she would help destroy what her ancestors had fought so hard to achieve.

And yet... Canastra's machinations put Isabel's welfare back into Henrique's hands. The realization was like electricity coursing through his limbs.

Henrique stood. "I can't allow it."

Dio pinched the bridge of his nose. "If they know that we know what we know... We must leave. Now."

"I won't allow Isabel to marry Alfonso."

"What? The bacteria have infected your intellect. We are in Canastra's country and alone against his horde of political allies and gruesome-looking militia. What can we possibly do? For Heaven's sake, I'm a poet, and you are a scientist."

"Is it not part of a hero's quest to face formidable odds?"

Dio exhaled, lifting his palms. "Hero? It was a metaphor. Don't place this burden on my shoulders. This coat is brand new."

Henrique paced, his fists pressing against his temples. "We need a plan."

"You cannot deal with too much on your hands. Remember the three bugs?"

"Do you mind? I'm thinking."

Dio ignored his glare. "You were on a nature walk when you found a couple of rare bugs. You had to take them to the house. But on your way back, another turned up. Since you already had your hands occupied, you had the brilliant idea to put it in your mouth."

Henrique grimaced. He had forgotten the blasted afternoon. The Coleoptera secreted acid in his tongue, and he lost the sense of taste for a week.

Dio chuckled, shaking his head. "As any lady could tell, your mouth is a lousy place for safekeeping."

Henrique stilled. "Safekeeping. You are a genius. I cannot stop Canastra's plans, but I can spirit away a princess."

A shadow fell over the window, and then the glass opened to reveal a figure cloaked in black. Henrique had prepared to attack the newcomer when he recognized Pedro.

"Are you in league with Canastra and mean to scare us to death?" Dio drawled.

Pedro sheathed his pistol. "I came as soon as I received the message. Canastra caught your girl?" His tone was as sharp as a saber.

Henrique nodded, gritting his teeth. "Not for long. I'm getting her back."

Chapter 31

"Let me not then die ingloriously and without a struggle, but let me first do some great thing that shall be told among men hereafter." Homer, *The Iliad*

While Pedro vanished through the window to secure a carriage and fresh horses for their escape, Henrique armed himself with a cane, two pistols, and a saber.

Dio grimaced. "Next time you set up on a leisure trip, remind me to go the other way."

"The weapons are a last resource—in which case, I will use them. You are not to fire a gun even if an army charges us, do you understand?"

Dio nodded, his fair skin turning green.

Henrique eyed his microscopes and chemical bottles. His research would have to stay behind. The ether caught his attention. Before he could change his mind, he placed it inside his coat.

"My father would choke on his diplomatic medals. Steal the princess? What if Isabel resists?"

A flush rose over Henrique's face, and he cleared his throat. "Heroes have no such moral qualms. In Hercules' times, depending on the situation, any seafarer became a pirate or freebooter."

"When I called this"—Dio circled his finger, encompassing the room or the whole of Spain—"the hero's quest, I should have expected you would make me rue it."

Henrique grinned. "Too late."

"They will persecute us. These loyalists are modern-day inquisitors."

"When they realize the princess is absent, we will have crossed the border to Portugal."

Dio shook his head. "They must have a dungeon waiting. What if he peels the skin off his prisoners?"

Henrique grabbed Dio's shoulders and shook. "This is your chance to enter the hall of heroes. Side by side with Perseus, Atalanta, Hercules, and Achilles. Rise, Diomedes da Veiga, and claim your glory."

Dio didn't look convinced. Henrique could not blame him. Haranguing wasn't among his many skills. With a nod and then another, Dio followed Henrique out of the room.

Stealthily, powered by the righteousness of righting a wrong and accepting the weight of responsibility as if it had never found worthier shoulders, they set to the main house through gardens painted by the first blush of dawn. The only thing missing to complete his quest was his royal package. He counted the gallery windows until he found the one behind Goya's painting. When he flung his leg above the windowsill, Dio tapped his shoulder.

"Are you sure about this?"

"Now is not the time for doubt. Either you are with me, or you are not."

"Move your ass faster then. The Guardia is coming."

They entered the darkened corridor. A sharp inhale revealed the presence of a single guard. Henrique sighed, relieved the minion was alone. Before Henrique spouted an excuse, Dio clobbered the guard in the head.

"I've told you, no weapons," Henrique said as he sidestepped the fallen body to reach Isabel's door.

"Ouch." Dio shook his fist. "I didn't know my hands counted as weapons."

Henrique listened to the room's noises. Scurrying inside pointed to nervous preparations. Thank God they were not too late.

The loud, deaf voice of Lady Montijo reached them.

Henrique eyed his friend. "This is your turn."

"I have no idea what you mean."

"Yes, you do."

Dio frowned, his face bleached of color. "What if Isabel knows?"

"I thought she was like a little sister to you."

"A little sister with some twisted notions about duty. What if she decided Alfonso would be a better king than her brother?"

Had she? Henrique paused. He shook his head. His Isa? No matter. Grimacing, he pointed resolutely to the closed door. "We must do this for Portugal."

"Damn it, Henrique. When I spoke of sacrifice, I meant it poetically. After this, I will shun all my scientific friends. What a literal, life-threatening lot."

"I am your only scientific friend, and no, the disciples of Venus do not count as scientific people."

"You will owe me forever." Dio exhaled resignedly and knocked.

Lady Montijo answered after the fourth knock. Her little beady eyes lit up. "My Adonis at last."

"My... My, er... Aphrodite, the stars are shining brightly, and I was wondering if you would like to see them from the balcony, er... The full moon compels us...."

She waved her hand and scoffed. "Save the poetry for the chicks. I have better stars to show you in my bedroom." After interlacing her arm with his, she pulled him away from Isabel's door and into the unlit corridor.

Dio glanced at Henrique, his expression murderous. Henrique replied with a soundless chuckle and a mouthed thank you.

When the couple left, Henrique emerged from the drapery's shadows and proceeded to Isabel's room.

Isabel's dulcet voice came from inside. "Lady Montijo? Auntie?"

The little endearment set his nerves on edge. Whatever her part in this, Isabel was not a hostage.

Henrique entered. A flickering gas lamp illuminated her pristine bedgown, and an embroidery frame dangled from her hand.

Her eyes danced to his feet and back as if distrusting her senses. Then her pupils widened, shock bleaching her face. "Why are you here?"

All his logical replies failed him, and as footsteps sounded behind them, he did the unthinkable. Doused the Princess of Portugal with ether.

When he stepped out of the room, a limp Isabel in his arms, steel poked his ribs.

Henrique halted, cold sweat dripping down his temples.

"Are you toppling the monarchy, Citizen Henrique?"

Henrique exhaled, closing his eyes. It was only Sophie, thank God.

He hesitated, searching his mind for what to say to a Republican maid while spiriting away her mistress. He settled for the truth. "I'm trying to save it. Isabel is at risk."

She removed the knife and sheathed it somewhere in her apron. "I'm coming with you."

"Did you become a monarchist then?"

"No." Reverently, Sophie touched Isabel's cheek. "But she will always be my queen."

She had become his queen as well. So, who was he to judge? "Fair enough."

When Sophie stepped away from him, he noticed she had packed a suitcase and thanked her foresight. Together, they traversed the palace's dimly lit rooms. Sophie's nervous steps seemed too loud. Heart speeding, muscles straining, Henrique plodded on. For once, he was grateful for the resilience gained in the army.

When they arrived at Canastra's art gallery, he halted. The bastard's bedchamber was straight ahead. Henrique should barge in and show the treacherous duke where he could shove his plans. Henrique shook his head. He would jeopardize their escape if he stumbled anywhere near Canastra or Alfonso. Their chances were thin, even without him allowing his temper to interfere. Thwarting Canastra would have to be enough vengeance for now.

Sophie opened a glass panel leading to the garden. Dawn had colored the sky, the sea sparkling beyond the bluff. When he spotted the coach and four grey horses awaiting in the secret spot by Eros' statue, he almost dropped Isabel, so strong was his relief.

Dio held a horse by the bridle. He lifted a brow when he saw Isabel in Henrique's arms, but Henrique's expression made him refrain from ill-timed humor.

"So soon? How did you escape the Dragon?"

"I did like Odysseus with the Cyclops—"

"Please don't tell me you poked the lady's eyes—"

"Of course not. I snuffed the candles and locked her in her room. She is probably still looking for me inside."

Pedro opened the coach's door.

Henrique settled Isabel inside, propelling her head on the leather squabs. Breathing heavily, he rolled his shoulders, releasing accumulated tension.

Pedro wiped the blood from his gloves in a kerchief. "I will take her to the yacht. She can stay with Anne while I—"

"Isabel goes to Braganza with me. That is non-negotiable." Henrique's voice came out harsher than intended, and he exhaled. "My estate is just across the border. Close enough she won't be in the open for long, and Canastra won't dare cross into Portuguese territory."

Pedro narrowed his eyes, and for a second, Henrique thought he would object. But then he nodded. "Keep her safe until you hear from me."

Dante, Pedro's condottiere, shook a fresh jacket, and Pedro exchanged it for his blood-spattered one.

Henrique frowned. The man had throttled a few or many of Canastra's men to secure a carriage. While still in Spain, they risked capture, and Pedro worried about his damn clothes? "I never knew you to be fastidious."

"Anne is distressed already. I won't return to her covered in blood. Even if it isn't mine."

"What will you do now?"

"Alert the border garrisons. Prepare for war."

Henrique leaned against the carriage. "Let me guess, Anne hates Spanish paella?

"Anne hates no one." He looked up from his gloves, and his light brown eyes flashed. "I have no such scruples."

Pedro vaulted atop his stallion without bothering with the stirrups. The infamous black horse reared, hoofs pounding an invisible foe twice, and then they were off.

Henrique opened the carriage door for Sophie and helped her inside.

When Isabel's suitcase was settled as well, he turned to Dio. "Are you coming?

Dio's expression was somber, as if the gravity of the situation had at last sunk into his shoulders. "I'm off to Lisbon. My father could use a head start to this diplomatic hecatomb. That, and I don't want to be around when Isabel wakes up."

Henrique held the sleeping princess along hurried postilions, rocky valleys, and perilous mountain passes. When the coach crossed the border from Spain to Portugal, Henrique lowered his back to the bench, and a huge breath escaped his lungs. Canastra and his militia would not dare persecute them here. They were safe. Outside, the scenery changed as the Extremadura scorched plains gave way to Portugal's cultivated fields. Sophie dozed.

Isabel was heavy and warm, draped over his chest. Tawny freckles decorated her nose. He followed their intricate design like an astronomer watching the night sky until he found a constellation. He would call it Mistral, in honor of the Mediterranean wind. Nothing was ever the same after it passed with its cool, elegant breeze.

What would it take to have her sleep in his arms every day? He wouldn't know, would he? Not before, when she had been engaged to another, and not after a kidnap. One thing he knew for sure—he might get used to it, but he would always be awed by it.

The coach gobbled the distance with inexorable speed. A light drizzle clung to the window's glass as they crossed the River Tua and entered Braganza's land.

Isabel murmured in her sleep and turned, her cheek pressing too close to his heart. He propped her head on his coat and shifted away from her.

Through the bumpy miles, his liquor-rich, impulsive decision to abscond with a royal princess had filled him with a surge of righteous power. It was not only the right thing to do but the only one. At least in hindsight, he would make his father proud. Henrique would, after all, save the country's independence. But now, as the sun set beyond the hills he had known all his life, the excitement gave way to uneasiness. Under the shadows of his ancestral home, he could feel the accusing eyes of Saint Anthony from his perch atop the gate.

Liar, the Saint said. *You did it for her.*

To stump another bout of self-recrimination, he inhaled Braganza's wet schist scent as if it were Cuban tobacco, savoring all its nuances.

The hunchback porter, a relic from his father's time, jogged close and inspected the carriage's occupants. When he saw Henrique, he grinned. The old servant had not expected to see Henrique again, he said, pulling his hat. Henrique didn't expect to come back either.

The porter opened the rusty gate, as well as a flood of memories.

Henrique was five, sword fighting with his father and a short-trousered Luis, both boys listening to the sweeping stories about the castle's past. How the magnificent eye-sore was a vital point of defense and had changed hands from Portugal to Spain over the years until his eighteenth-century forebearers won the castle after repelling the Spanish invasion.

He was seventeen and leaving against his will for Mozambique to fight a war he neither understood nor cared about but went to anyway. How could he not? To show a lack of love for one's country was tantamount to heresy in the Penafiel line.

He was twenty-three, watching his father being buried without being able to say goodbye. He could have turned into a hater then, but Henrique never figured out the logic of hatred. He had always been a lover.

Henrique entered the castle, Isabel in his arms. She had yet to stir during the forty-mile carriage ride. He suspected exhaustion caused her heavy slumber. The wind whispered through the arrow slits. For a medieval jumble of rocks, the castle's acoustics could have made Mozart proud.

Weapons and crests decorated the walls. His ancestors' suits of armor watched his progress stoically. If the old Penafiel knights dared to mock his homecoming, Henrique would meld their scraps into spoons and fire pokers.

"Burglars! I told Mario to lock the front gates. I will tell the new owner to sack him. See if I don't."

Henrique groaned. Antonia, the housekeeper, marched near, her bundle of keys jingling from her waist.

"What is the meaning of this?" Her little gasp of recognition could only mean trouble. "Master Henrique." For a second, her black eyes softened, but only just. "Carrying women to the house? Have you no respect for your father's memory?"

Henrique sighed. "Do you love your country, Tonia?"

"Is this one of your pranks? Like when you brought a toad from the marsh and told me it was a prince, and I had to bathe the creature?"

Tiredly, Henrique related their adventure.

Fervent patriot that she was, she closed her gaping mouth with a loud pop and stood to attention. "Where will you accommodate her?"

"At the tower."

"The Princess Tower? But it's a—"

"I know what it is. It's also the safest place in the castle." It would keep strangers out and a familiar princess inside.

She nodded. "I will make the arrangements." After a crisp salute, she beat a retreat, her whistle sounding on the stone corridors as she assembled a brigade of servants.

As he carried Isabel up the hundred-twelve steps, he felt larger, like one of his medieval ancestors.

He crossed the threshold with Isabel in his arms and stopped, blinking repeatedly. The circular tower had been transformed.

"What happened here?" The room used to be a cloister, all naked rocks, and no comfort.

A faint blush colored Antonia's cheeks. "The Italian count said you allowed improvements."

Isabel would have his head at such improvements. Shrugging, too tired to take in the details of the extravagant decoration, Henrique lowered her atop the gaudy four-poster bed. She curled on her side, a sigh on her tempting lips.

There. He had done it. He had completed a hero's quest and came back with the prize. His conscience whispered that his labors were not finished, that this was him trying to vanquish the Hydra of Lerna. Each time he cut a head, he only made the problem worse.

He should leave. He needed to think.

Isabel moaned, her eyes moving under her purplish lids. Before he checked his actions, he took a step toward her and then another. Before he could control himself, he adjusted the pillow so she would be more comfortable and pulled in the quilt above her so she would not catch cold.

Isa, Isa... What have we done?

She felt fragile and totally at his mercy. His heart did a double measure and twisted with the force of the tenderness spreading to his chest. She was only flesh and tendons and bone and skin, yet how could she be so necessary to his constitution?

My Isabel. My prize.

A wave of exhaustion swept through him, and he eyed the mile-long mattress, a yawn escaping his mouth. Well, when in Rome...

A gentleman would leave and brave the stairs to his own room. She already thought him a *sinvergüenza*... And she hated when he proved her wrong.

He locked the door. After removing his shoes and coat, he climbed atop the bed. Her scent pulled him closer. He folded himself behind her. She gave a content sigh, and he fell asleep.

Chapter 32

"The tongue has no bones, but bones it crashes."
Greek Proverb

S he flew over a flamboyant tree, chasing its red petals. Then her wings folded like singed paper, and she dropped into warmth. Isabel floated and sighed in contentment, burrowing closer to the source. Lips met the skin below her ear, and a shiver danced down her spine. Henrique's scent filled her lungs, and she knew she was dreaming. A delicious dream she never wanted to end.

The sound of waves upset the haze. Why should the outside world intrude on her dreams? She wasn't ready to let go of Henrique's warmth. Not yet.

A screech made her eyes shoot open.

A gull had landed on the windowsill. Head cocked to the side, it stared at her.

"What's this ruckus about?" Henrique's voice, rusty from sleep, teased her nape.

Isabel scrambled from the bed. When her bare feet touched the stone floor, she noticed her dishabille.

Panting, she yanked the bedsheet and wrapped herself. A mistake. Now Henrique lay on his side, his chest uncovered, miles of bronzed skin displayed to the morning light.

A devilish grin lifted his lips, and he raised a brow, no doubt quite aware of his effect on her.

"They say married couples fight petty battles over bed covers, but one should know you would take matters too far." He rolled to his back, one arm flung behind his head. "Shut the windows, will you? I'm cold."

Isabel backed away, placing distance between her person and that indecent arrangement of muscles, sleepy lips, sinful blue eyes, and compelling scruff. "You! What are you doing here?"

Henrique sat up, his hair disheveled. "This is my house... so."

His house? Isabel turned slowly, holding the bedsheet to her chest. Naked stone walls surrounded her. A pond-sized copper bath stood indecently against floor-to-ceiling windows. Pillows of every color were strewed around the hearth as if waiting for their harem owners. The decoration combined medieval with exotic. Isabel shut her eyes. Was she dreaming?

She had been in her room, and a knock on the door had brought her to her feet. Henrique had appeared, his face set with determination. Memories of being tossed and jolted flitted through her mind, and before this, white teeth smiling at her from tanned skin. What did he do? And why? Could it be a plot to separate her from Alfonso? No. Not Henrique. He had a woman in every port. Why cart away a betrothed one?

"You drugged me and took me here against my will. You, you craven kidnapper, deceiver of—"

"There, there, no need for epithets." He rose and stretched his arms. "I could do no less for my country."

"Why interfere and bring me to this—What is this place? Your medieval seraglio?"

"I wish... This is my property, the very aptly named Princess Tower," he boasted, thrilled with himself.

Did he hold nothing sacred? Of course, considering a woman's feelings was beyond his rakish philandering, but had he no respect for church and country?

"You don't know the story? My ancestor used the tower to lock his wife so she would not meddle in his affairs—"

"Is this your idea of a joke? For taking me against my will, you will be charged with treason—"

"What in one country is called treason, in another can earn a medal." His voice turned gravelly, and the laughter left the corners of his eyes.

"Your actions don't deserve medals in any country. Unless you gave your loyalty to a nation of pirates."

"Your brother can be piratical when he wants to be. What about you, Isabel? Have your loyalties changed? Did your wish to be a Spanish queen overrule your love for Portugal?"

"Stop this instant. I forbid—"

"Was it the joined crowns of Portugal and Spain that lured you from my arms to Alfonso's?"

She lifted her hand to slap him, but he grabbed her wrist before she could connect with his cheek.

"I heard Canastra speaking with the prince. The second you grace Alfonso's bed, they will steal your brother's crown."

Isabel sucked in a breath. The walls blurred, and she fell on the mattress.

Henrique threw at her accusation upon accusation, and her head felt swollen with them. From the moment she had said yes to Alfonso, she had lived in a trance, wishing to turn back the clock, and if that didn't work, then at least she had hoped to speed time to a point when it didn't hurt so much.

"I didn't know," she whispered.

He stopped talking. The enormity of his claim descended over her shoulders, and Isabel covered her face with clammy palms. How could Alfonso do this to her? She gave him the flag, and he had promised to renounce any claim to the Portuguese throne.

She could not blame him, not really. Not even Canastra. The duke was an opportunistic aristocrat and would do whatever possible to grasp power. No, the fault was hers. If she had not acted so harshly... After she allowed passion in her life, all she fought to protect—her morals, her reputation—had come crashing down.

Henrique crouched at her feet. His warmth seeped through the bedsheet. She didn't move her legs.

He tucked a strand of hair behind her ear. "Do you love him?"

She looked away.

He pulled her chin back to him. His scent brushed against her, making it impossible for her to hide. She stared into his twinkling, earnest blue gaze.

"Don't you think I deserve an explanation? After risking my limbs to take you away from Spain?"

He caressed the pleats on her forehead, and it was hard not to lean into his touch. "Have I not proved myself a faithful patriot?"

"Faithful?" The hurt of witnessing him kissing her cousin pierced her anew, and Isabel flinched. "I was there. I saw you with Rafaela." She hugged herself, her body folding. Perhaps if she shrunk, she could reduce the amount of pain she could absorb.

Henrique stood and raked his hand through his disheveled hair. "You accepted Alfonso's proposal because of Rafaela?" He shook his head and expelled a most ungentlemanly snort. "The irony of ironies. The patriotic princess risking her country's independence because of jealousy."

Isabel's cheeks burned as a wave of heat incinerated her veins. "I request an escort, my tiara, and my clothes.

I'm leaving this ridiculous tower." She preferred to face the long journey back to Lisbon than spend another minute with Henrique.

His expression closed. "It seems Your Highness will have to make do with the current facilities."

Who was he to order her about? Isabel lifted her chin. "I would rather not."

"I will have to insist." He took hold of the key and opened the tower's door.

Isabel gasped. "You cannot keep me a prisoner."

"I prefer to call you a pampered guest, but suit yourself."

Isabel flung a pillow at the door. Henrique closed it just in time, and the pathetic piece of fluff sailed half a distance and sprawled on the floor, defeated. Huffing, her cheeks burning and her chest heaving, Isabel threw its twins, and when her ammunition ended, she grabbed the empty pitcher and hurled it. The porcelain shattered into a million pieces.

She screamed her throat raw. How preposterous. Henrique could not keep her here. She would get out, one way or the other. She raced to the windows. A five-story drop to a rocky cliff promised a harrowing fall. She inspected the walls and peeked behind the tapestries. Nothing. The circular tower was a perfect prison.

Porcelain shards cracked under her soles, and she bent to pick up the mess. Tears flooded her nose and throat, and she lowered herself to the floor. Her brother had trusted her to exert her influence, to move about the chessboard as only a queen could. Instead, she had allowed Canastra and Alfonso to outmaneuver her. Shame curdled her stomach and hunched her shoulders, her head weighing unbearably. Still, it paled compared to Henrique's betrayal.

The door opened, and Isabel hastily stood. Three maids marched inside, their white and grey uniforms spotless. They bobbed a curtsy in unison and set up about their duties. If they thought anything strange about having a lady imprisoned in her master's room, they gave no signal.

A diminutive woman in her fifties carried fresh linens, and the door closed behind her. From the ominous click, Isabel inferred someone outside had locked it.

She returned Isabel's stare with an astute one, her birdlike head tilted to the side. "Your Highness, may I introduce myself? I'm Tia Antonia, the housekeeper of the Braganza Castle and a proud subject of His Majesty."

Isabel thrust her chin forward. "If you know who I am, how could you condone your master's keeping me here?"

"The master told me... everything. I understand the princess is our guest until the country's independence is no longer at risk."

"I must return to Lisbon and speak with the king. I need to right this wrong."

"Sometimes a right is done by staying put."

"I can't stay under your master's rule. I can't." Her cheek flushed, and she moved to the window.

The housekeeper's steps sounded behind her. "I have known him since he was a baby. All that bluster? Only on the outside. Drove his papa crazy, he did. But Master Henrique has a heart of gold. I bet my old eyes it's eating his insides to keep you locked here. He could never watch another creature suffering without suffering himself."

The housekeeper bowed and turned to leave.

"Can you bring me the newspaper?"

"Of course."

Henrique's servants left. The room was again spotless as if her pique had not occurred. Sophie entered, carrying a tray. Isabel smiled. Thank God she was all right. Sophie set the burden on the table and rushed to her, and Isabel welcomed the fussing.

"Is he treating you well? Did you bring my clothes? My tiara?" Isabel would feel much more herself after she dressed properly.

"Yes, and yes—"

"Then I will change after breakfast," Isabel said, selecting an apple from the tray.

Sophie flushed, wringing her hands. "Citizen Henrique confiscated the valise. He told me you will be more comfortable in bedclothes, considering you won't go anywhere."

A rush of blood rose on her face, and she saw red. She would strangle him and keep doing it, even if he laughed at her efforts.

The housekeeper's voice replayed in her head. *He could never watch another creature suffering without suffering himself.*

Reluctantly, Isabel released the fruit she was about to sink her teeth into. A tiny smile appeared at the corner of her lips. If she could not leave, then she would make keeping her here impossible.

Chapter 33

"It is difficult to argue with the belly, as it has no ears." Greek Proverb

Henrique paced the antechamber leading to the tower. The maid had entered at least fifteen minutes ago, and the silence inside Isabel's room grated on his ears. Twenty-eight hours, and she still had not eaten or drunk. What was she up to?

He glared at the coat of armor decorating the hall. "What are you looking at?" His ancestors must be shaking in their graves, watching his dealings with this recalcitrant harridan with supernatural glee. He could see them, dressed in medieval finery, pointing their fingers at him and laughing. It was a fair turnabout. As a good sport, he had to admit it. The reason they locked their women instead of keeping them well-pleasured had finally been answered. The shrews didn't want to be sated and glowing. They much preferred to shrivel a man's private parts. Henrique's gaze lowered to the armor's codpiece, and he flinched.

Isabel had accepted the prince out of jealousy. He knew what it meant. She wanted *him*. Certainly not as much as he wanted her. Still, his hands tingled to open the door and show her. Heat arrowed through his chest and converged on his groin. Henrique snorted. What was he? An adolescent?

The maid left. All was silent inside his tower for a change.

He locked the door. "Has she eaten?"

The maid gave him a sullen look. She was new here, so she didn't dare to berate him for keeping the princess a prisoner, but the housekeeper teamed up with Sophie, and both had tried to upbraid him in the morning. Isabel had needed less than a full day to earn his staff to her side, and now he had to carry around the key to her room. Otherwise, Isabel would convince the servants to help her escape.

He couldn't let her out, and he couldn't allow her to starve. Unable to stay still and completely without a strategy, he opened the door and strode inside the tower.

Raising her retroussé nose to the ceiling, she crossed her arms over her chest, eyeing him as if he was the foe crossing her at a line of battle.

He shrugged and tried for a nonchalant tone. "Are you indisposed?"

Her lips tugged up, but the smile did not reach her eyes. "Since when does a jailor care for the prisoner's disposition?"

Henrique pressed his temples. "This is the third tray left untouched. What is your game, Isabel?"

"I demand my clothes, my tiara, and my freedom."

"Out of the question."

"Then eating is out of the question." Her voice dripped with challenge.

Henrique exhaled audibly. "Why must you be such an insufferable brat?"

She stiffened and gave him a cold shoulder. "Oh, I forgot you prefer your women to be more mature... Maturity only a husband can provide."

Hot white rage boiled in his gut. Henrique dropped the pretense. In three strides, he was by her side. He forced her to turn to him with both hands over her shoulders. It was like moving a stuck bolt.

"After you left the garden, I returned to my room. Rafaela was inside and willing, but I sent her away. She craves more passion from her marriage than the dutiful Canastra wants to provide... That night, she decided to—"

"Stick her tongue up your throat?" A sob escaped her chest, her eyes green pools of disdain and hurt. "Why didn't you let her?

He held her face. "Because after my tongue was inside you, it was ruined for every other taste."

Isabel gasped, and the hand she barricaded against him became limp. Henrique meshed their lips. She stiffened for only a second, and then her shoulders relaxed, and she was pliant in his arms. He deepened the kiss, and his heart pistoned out of control. A roar of relief and longing unfurled in his chest, and he pressed her closer. The kiss had no finesse, no delicacy, his tongue sweeping inside her mouth, clashing with her teeth.

He was conscious of the four-poster looming behind them. The pillows and soft coverlet exerted a magnetic attraction. Isabel was under his roof, using his bedrobe, involved in his arms. His, his, his. The possessive pronoun beat with his heart, unfurled through his veins, and pooled in his cock. He had half a mind to shut the door with both of them here and send the key flying through the window.

When she broke away, they were both panting.

"You must release me. It is not too late to return."

Henrique shook his head, his heartbeat ringing in his ears. After he confessed, after the kiss, she still wanted to leave?

She placed her chilled hands over his cheeks. "Don't you understand? I must speak with Alfonso."

His muscles tightened painfully, and he clenched his teeth. The hurt he felt when Alfonso kissed her lips burned in his stomach and spread to his chest. "You will never see that milksop again." His voice came out harsh and loud, and he pushed her away from him.

They eyed each other, again from different sides of the battlefield.

She lifted her chin. "Then you will watch me starve."

"As you wish, Your Highness." He grabbed the tray, sloshing juice from the jar, and strode to the exit.

Outside the room, he slumped against the closed door, the metal bars biting into his back. His breathing had yet to calm down. What devious hold did she have over him that she could explode his temper?

He had a headache from lack of sleep, his shoulders had more knots than a sailor's rope, and a damn hard-on would soon leave his balls blue. What the bloody hell was he supposed to do? He could not release her, but he could not endanger her health. What a rotten hero's homecoming.

Isabel lay on her bed, her lips tingling. The air crackled with promise and tension, not unlike the sea before a storm. She threw the gauntlet, hadn't she? She should be appalled. She was utterly at the mercy of a rake, now a rampant rake, but instead of dread, she felt a thrill of anticipation.

The desire glittering in his eyes... And then the rigidness of his shoulders and heat radiating from his body. Being well-versed in diplomacy, she wouldn't be far from the mark if she assumed the phase for innuendos and petty competitions had ended.

Animal nature. She hated it. Hated that it ruled over her morals, her upbringing, and her duties. Hated it brought her to her knees and transformed her into a creature of senses. And most of all, she hated that it was not unique to her. That every living thing felt the same.

Isabel rose from the bed. The sudden movement made her lightheaded, and her tummy growled. Princessing on an empty stomach was a hardship.

Perhaps her plan to starve had been too harsh. But what else could she do? Henrique had set guard outside her door, aware of her first attempt to co-opt his staff. She could not stay here forever. If Canastra threatened Portugal's independence, eliminating her from the scene might not be enough to curb his intentions. Her brother should be alerted immediately.

The door swung open, and Isabel straightened, dreading another confrontation with Henrique or a food tray. Either would damage her resolve. Instead, Tia Antonia sauntered inside.

The housekeeper removed something from her skirts.

Isabel perked up. "A Spanish newspaper?"

"Hush. I sent a lad across the border."

The headline occupied most of the first page: 'LONG LIVE SPAIN'S TRUE KING.'

For several heartbeats, she stared at Alfonso's pleasant smile. The newspaper made it all too real. The breath bursting in and out of her chest felt wrong, solid. Bringing the sheet closer, her clammy hands shaking, she scanned the news.

'General Espartero proclaimed Alfonso de Bourbon as Spain's true king. Fearing the army, the Duke of Aosta fled to his brother's court in Italy. Except for the Carlists' troops in the north, all the country regiments supported the general's manifesto. The young Alfonso XII waits in Salamanca, where the Asturias Frigate will take him to Madrid.'

Alfonso had gotten what he wanted. He would cross the Ebro back to his throne.

And after he arrived there, nothing could stop him. He had already gained the Guardia Civil, and with the army's support, his power would be unparalleled. Isabel's legs gave out beneath her at the enormity of the implications. Alfonso had given her his word only the day before. Visions of a barren land razed by war floated through her mind, and she flinched.

Isabel lowered the paper. "Salamanca is not far. I must go there."

"What can you possibly do?"

Isabel vaulted to her feet. Her legs couldn't stay still, and she trotted around the circular tower. Alfonso had what he wanted. He didn't need her anymore.

She stopped abruptly. "The marriage, the united crowns... It was all a bid to gain military support. But Alfonso earned it anyway. I must convince him to change his plans. I have to."

When the first powder kegs of war were ignited, opinions flared, bursting out of control. Monarchs retreated into corners from where the best diplomats couldn't rescue them. Isabel had no such restrictions. Her brother's words resounded in her mind. Like the queen in a chess game, she could move wherever she wanted.

Tia Antonia pursed her lips. "I don't know, I—"

Isabel grabbed the housekeeper's arm, assuming her most regal expression. "Listen to me. My country, my mother's legacy, and my brother's throne are at risk. And that is not the worst. Think about the people who live at the border. They will be the first to suffer if there is a war."

The housekeeper frowned and took a step back. "But—"

"This is all my fault." Isabel dropped her mask, allowing her face to show all she felt. "I have to make it right. Please."

The housekeeper's mouth gaped. "I don't remember the last time a *fidalgo* asked me please... but a princess?" She cast a furtive look at the door. "I can arrange a coach, and my son can escort you. But the key... Master Henrique doesn't let me hold it."

Isabel gave a curt nod. Tia Antonia was right. Henrique guarded it like a hellhound. But she couldn't allow a meddlesome, irresistible rake to jeopardize her plans. Whatever it took, she would get that key.

He stored it carefully in his waistcoat pocket every time he insinuated himself here. She needed a fail-proof strategy. She touched the pillows scattered above the bed. Why not put him to sleep? Wouldn't it be a fair turnabout? Isabel eyed the housekeeper sideways. While willing to help her escape, Isabel doubted she would approve of drugging her master.

Her glance circled the tower and landed on the fireplace. She could make the room so hot he would want to strip. No. What if she dropped water on his waistcoat? But then, he might leave to change, and she would lose her chance.

Isabel eyed the bed, and her cheeks flushed. If she could make him sleep by her side again... "I'll get it. Just ready everything for my leave."

She would not have to starve after all.

Chapter 34

"The only way to get rid of a temptation is to yield to it." - Oscar Wilde

Henrique climbed the steps to the tower, ignoring the suits of armor's silent reproach. His ancestors had the right to it. He had tried to be reasonable with Isabel, and where had it led him? Enough of such dysfunctional dynamics—good rake versus intransigent, morally stubborn princess. Henrique would march inside her bedchamber and demand her to eat. He would not give her a chance to work her wiles. He would lay down the rules.

Isabel understood rules. She lived by them.

Who was he fooling? He, a rule-maker? A rule-breaker—that was more likely. Ignoring the corruptive thought, he balanced the dinner tray on one hand so he could knock. What was he doing? Politeness would be his enemy tonight. He rolled the key, entered the room, relocked the door, and stored it in his pocket.

The air inside the tower was heavy with vapor and the scent of camellias.

The copper tub was empty, and so were the pillows strewed in front of the hearth. Where was she? Heart speeding, he gazed at the window. Impossible.

The bed curtains opened to reveal one shapely leg and then the next.

Cloth whispered over her torso, and then she stood, a vision in silk. Her hair was wet, dripping over the robe. Why wasn't she dressed? He mentally kicked himself for not returning her clothes. To better deal with Isabel, he should have been born a simpleton. The lack of a corset would make laying down the rules much more difficult.

She sauntered closer, pulling her hair atop her shoulder. In the soft glow of the setting sun, Isabel's hair unfurled, a cocoa cascade, each strand sighing and swaying in a sensual symphony. Henrique's gaze lingered, his longing finally unleashed.

Would he ever get used to seeing her glorious hair undone? If he were king, he would create only one law—forbid Isabel from painful chignons. The silk clung to her. By sheer willpower, he avoided checking the volume of her breasts. He gazed instead at her lips. They were soft, and when she perceived his regard, a shy tongue came out to wet them. That pink tip, less than an inch of tissue and membrane, got him harder than the tower's flagstones.

Henrique locked his jaw. He was in control. He laid down the rules. Not her.

Moving languidly to the chaise, her gaze brushed over his three-piece suit, and she fluttered her eyelids.

If he didn't know her better, he would think she flirted with him. What was her strategy? "Do you have something in your eyes?"

Her lips pursed into a pretty moue. "It's a side effect of being confined."

He set the tray on the table with an authoritative clink. "Your hair is dripping."

"Bathwater can produce such symptoms." She twirled a curl over her fingers once, twice, and then lowered it to the gaping cloth of her robe.

His self-control slipped, and he followed the lock. The silk covering her breasts was moist and transparent. Nipples the color of a dusky afternoon peeked at him. Warmth swirled inside his chest, and his mouth watered, an uncontrollable urge to taste them, first the right one, then the other, and then...

"If you allowed my maid to attend me, she would've dried my hair against the hearth." She caught said hair in a knot atop her head. The movement dislodged her robe, baring her arms and the curve of her left breast. She glanced at him sideways as if to make sure he had seen her bountiful charms.

His head jerked up. "Is this a seduction?"

Her sweet gasp was confirmation enough. He would be damned. The prudish princess trying to seduce the redoubtable rake...

She whirled away from him as fast as her legs would carry her, and then she wavered in place and would have dropped to her derrière if he had not caught her.

Ribs protruded from her torso. Had she lost two pounds? Three?

Gently, he settled her over the recamier. "Foolish, foolish girl."

She lay with her head lolling, lifeless, and Henrique's heart wrenched inside his chest.

He picked the truffle from the dinner tray and twirled it under her nose. She came to, confusion dimming her eyes.

"This ends now." His voice was low and explosive.

"Why should I eat?" She lifted her chin imperiously, but at least her cheeks had regained color.

That was the Isabel he knew. Seduction time had ended.

Her gaze shifted from his face to the dinner tray, caressing the food. A rumble interrupted their tense silence. It wasn't kind to point fingers, but he could swear it came from her belly.

Henrique cursed under his breath and paced away from the recamier. He couldn't think with her so close. He might be mistaken, and with Isabel, it was a fifty/fifty event, but what if the seduction had been a ploy to avoid her ultimatum while keeping her pride? He couldn't give up the chance to make her eat.

When Henrique turned to her, he had his grin back in place and shrugged. "We could play a game. If you lose, you have to take a bite."

She frowned, and for a second, he thought she would send him to hell. But then her eyes lit up. "It's hardly fair. Players should stand on even ground. You are dressed formally while I'm wearing a loose bed robe."

Henrique's pulse sped, and he feigned an interest in his fingernails. "Very well. If I win, you eat a morsel of my choosing. If you win, I will remove one piece of clothing."

Had her breathing turned shallower? She lifted her shoulder, and the robe slipped. "Why would I want that?"

Henrique couldn't take his eyes off her skin. "You are curious, Isabel. I remember the way you explored my chest in the garden and almost swooned when you saw me hammering the iron plaque, but if you prefer to disrobe yourself, then..."

She tugged the robe up. With her hair cascading down her shoulders to pool on the oriental carpet and her long legs resting over the carmine upholster, she looked like Venus awaiting mortals to sacrifice in her shrine. "What do you have in mind? Chess, cards?"

His gaze traversed the expanse of the tower. While the count had provided surfaces to tempt a couple into love play, he didn't bother with parlor games. "A trivia."

She narrowed her eyes. "The subject? I hope it isn't science. I will start at a disadvantage—"

"About myths. Greek myths."

She instantly perked up, her eyes flashing. Of course, she had a better classical education than many scholars he knew and would no doubt expect to give him a sound trouncing.

She tilted her head to the side. "The rules?"

"For each question you miss, you must take four bites. When I lose, I will remove a piece of clothing. The first to reply to three questions correctly wins the game. In the less probable event that you win, I will return your clothes and tiara. If I win, you will be civil and await Pedro Daun's arrival."

Henrique removed lint from his coat, pretending nonchalance when he wanted to force nourishment down her throat.

She nodded regally.

Before she could change her mind, he moved a low table to the hearth and placed the food tray atop it. The fire cast golden notes over the pillows, making the colorful silk resemble a lake. Isabel lowered her weight slowly into a half-reclined position, her legs folded beneath her. Despite the effort to cover herself, her toes peeked from the folds of her robe. She had lovely feet.

The scent of roasted lamb and spices rose from her dinner, and Isabel's throat moved with a greedy swallow.

Henrique sprawled by her left and ignored her protests that he was too close. What should be his first question? He wanted her to miss it, so she could have an excuse to eat. But she would see through his ploy. How outlandish that Isabel's cunning worked against her.

He cleared his throat. "Why did Eros forbid Psyche from looking at him?"

"He wanted to protect her from his jealous mother." She glanced into the fire, and her shoulders sagged. "Jealousy has a way of ruining everything."

Henrique didn't like the sadness in her voice and touched her foot. Her breath caught, and she tried to pull away, but he kept an easy caress, trailing his finger from her heel to her arch.

The next question came easily, as he had been experiencing it vividly since he met Isabel. "Who was the Greek king cursed by the gods to stand below an apple tree, and whenever he reached for the fruit, the branches lifted it from his grasp?"

Her eyes widened. She didn't know! Henrique wanted to scream in triumph.

She shifted closer to the table, and Henrique ceased her momentum to pull her across his lap. With a hand circling her waist, he kept her in place. With the other, he pulled lamb meat from the bone and offered it to her.

"No cutlery? Savage." She glared at him, her gaze devouring the meat.

Henrique fed her. She shut her eyes, her head falling on his chest. The little moan of bliss she let out resonated inside him.

The next time he offered her food, she closed her lips over his fingers. A bolt of lust speared him, so strong it left him intoxicated.

"Tantalus had been the king cursed by the gods to be forever tempted by the apples. The word tantalizing came from him." Henrique could relate to the poor mortal, for with each bite, he felt the temptation cursing through his bloodstream.

When replete, she drank the muscat wine and reclined over the pillows. She didn't bother to fold her legs beneath her. The robe slipped, revealing her knees and the creamy perfection of the top of her breasts. If she but opened her knees an inch, he would see the patch of brown hair above her mound. Rock hard, Henrique grabbed a peach and sunk his teeth into the fruit.

She gazed at him under sooty eyelashes. "What is the theme of Gilgamesh's myth?"

Henrique shifted closer to her. Before she could protest, he placed her foot on his lap. She lifted on her elbows, watching his movement with a furrowed brow.

He massaged it from the arch to her little fingers and back. He felt a knot under her sole and pressed delicately on it. She sighed, and her head rested over her shoulder.

Henrique brushed the robe further up her legs, caressing her calves. "Does it have one? I thought the gods sent a mythical friend to the unruly prince so he would stop claiming prima nocte rights on his subjects' daughters."

She had eaten. Henrique should leave the room before he did something they would regret. But her feet were not enough. He wanted more and tugged her closer until her thighs were atop his lap. A blush colored her neck and cheeks. He breezed a caress from her knee to mid-thigh. The robe opened further, revealing her pubic hair. He must be a masochist because he pulled her left leg slightly to the side. The robe gaped open, and the seam rested atop her mound, displaying the right petal of her labia. Henrique groaned, his fingers itching to reach her sex. Would she be moist for him?

"The theme is..." She paused as his hand came tantalizingly close to her heat. Closing her eyes, she licked her lips. "Transcendence isn't in heaven, glimpsed only after you reach immortality. It is found on Earth. By the deeds you leave behind."

He stilled his hand on her leg. Deeds? How he felt near Isabel had nothing to do with deeds. "Isabel—"

"You owe me a piece of clothing."

"Of course. Come get your war spoils then." He opened his arms but made no move to remove his coat.

She knelt in front of him. Henrique stopped breathing. Placing both hands above his chest, she burrowed her hands under his coat. Her scent invaded his nostrils, not of linen and silk and layers of garments, but of warm skin, soap, and a flowery fragrance wafting from her hair. She held his jacket close to her chest.

His head swam as if he had drunk a casket of port and caroused with Bachus all night. "How did Zeus seduce Hercules' mother?" He placed his hands on her hips.

"That's not fair. I never touched Ovid's erotic poems."

"Zeus fell in love with Alcmene, but the princess was faithful to Amphitryon, her husband. So, while he warred with a neighboring tribe, Zeus took the form of Amphitryon," Henrique said, tugging Isabel closer.

"How convenient."

Henrique stilled. "We should stop." He had gone too far already, damn it.

"No. I want to know the rest."

Henrique exhaled. "Zeus visited Alcmene. When she disrobed for him, he was so entranced the Earth went preternaturally still."

She gasped. Henrique placed his fingertips above her throat, not wanting to lose her tiniest reaction.

"And then?"

"Zeus loved her slowly, reverently..." Henrique lowered the right side of her robe and kissed her shoulder. When he did the same with the other side, the silk caught on her nipple, and he tugged it free. The folds piled at her waist.

Not even Apollo and his chariot could take him from her now.

His hands were unsteady when he breezed soft caresses over her breasts, chasing the freckles he somehow knew would be there. "Dawn came, but Zeus wasn't ready to leave, so he extended the night until he and

Alcmene were well and truly sated." Henrique rested his hands over her hip bones and brushed his thumbs up and down in a soft invitation.

"A night of myth." She breathed, her lips sweetly parted.

They were both on their knees, facing each other. The fire cast fairy lights over her drying hair and fair skin, a pagan goddess of old.

Everything in him stilled, and Henrique nodded. "A night of passion. No consequences, no guilt."

The idea took shape, solidifying inside him. They could have this night for themselves.

Sustaining eye contact, he released her waist and touched the back of her thighs. Her breath hitched, and he cupped her buttocks, pressing her against him. At the contact of his chest with her breasts, he groaned. He kissed her, penetrating her mouth with his tongue, tasting her warmth.

"If this is one of your games..." She pulled away, breathing heavily.

"A game? Christ, Isa, I want—" He traced the contours of her mouth and cradled her face with infinite care. "Passion is not one-sided. I want to kiss you, but I want to be kissed too. I want to caress your skin, and I want to be caressed. I want you to be vulnerable to me, but it makes me vulnerable, too. I want to revel with you, in you, for as long as our night lasts. I want to make you fly."

"One night."

"Yes," he said, extending his hand in invitation.

Green eyes flashed, and then she placed her palm atop his.

He stood paralyzed, transfixed, embedded in her gaze.

The deal was sealed. God help him. What a pair they made—a pearly princess and the luckiest savage in the world. Any control he had left flew away to cavort with the cicadas and stars.

He kissed her deeply, and she melted against him, warm and pliant, as if he had every right to embrace her. He tugged the sash of her robe, and the silk fell around her legs. All the reasons he should keep away from her crashed to the floor with the last folds of her robe. Fire glow danced over her skin. Henrique's befuddlement lasted three seconds before he embraced her.

He pulled away long enough to work on the folds of his cravat. Her fingers brushed against his as she removed his waistcoat.

Primly and nude, she folded the garment atop his coat.

The shirt almost ripped when he wrestled it from his body. His cock filled to bursting point, and he used all his willpower to focus on her. He picked her slight form in his arms and lowered her on the decadent pillows.

He bit her bottom lip, and her gasp thrilled him.

Fusing their mouths, he massaged her thighs from the back of her knees to just below her apex with slow, deliberate strokes.

"Henrique."

"Hmm?"

"Are we done kissing?"

"What do you have in mind?"

She huffed a little and wiggled her hips, her cheeks becoming red. He pulled her knees apart and opened her nether lips with his thumbs. The fragrance of her arousal rose in an intoxicating mist. They watched as he circled her clitoris, now standing proud and glistening. He knelt between her legs for a taste.

He loved her petals reverently, brushing his stubbled cheeks against the inside of her thighs. When a deep shudder raked her, he closed his mouth around her and sucked. Her small mews and moans and the timid pressure of her hands on his head hazed his thoughts.

When she trembled beneath him, her body arching with her release, he caught her to his chest and kissed her deeply. His cock demanded he mount her where they were, a sultan with his odalisque. No, damn it. He would make it right. The way to the bed passed in a blur.

With her auburn hair fanned over the pillows, the light caressing her skin, and her long legs soft and spread open in invitation, she tempted him beyond endurance. She opened her eyes and extended her arm to him. Henrique lowered himself by her side. He kissed her bottom lip and pressed it between his teeth, then he lowered his mouth to her neck and whispered everything he meant to do with her before their night ended.

He licked her breasts and sucked her rigid peaks. Pausing every few breaths to pace himself, he embraced her for the sheer joy of bringing their chests together, savoring her naked skin against his, inhaling her scent.

He measured her, using his hands, the scale of his lips, the breadth of his shoulders. After this night, he would have her imprinted on his very cells. He caressed and revered and coaxed her excitement until he could no longer keep from her.

Gently, he mounted her. His torso caged her chest, and they locked in a tender embrace. Panting, he guided himself into her entrance. She stiffened underneath him, and he murmured endearments. He lifted his head and sucked her breasts, pulling until she sighed.

When his cock reached her maidenhead, he froze.

"Isabel, I—"

She kissed his neck. "It's only a membrane, right?"

It was, and it wasn't. He was her first lover, and the idea thrilled and frightened him. "I have no kingdom to offer—I'm no prince—"

"You are Henrique, my obstinate protector, my reluctant friend, my cherished rake," she said against his lips, her soft breaths mingling with his harsh ones. "My chosen lover."

He rested his forehead on hers. "I'll never hurt you again."

Flexing his legs, he thrust. The barrier gave way, and he entered her. He wanted to howl and rut like a mindless beast, so blissful her sheath felt on his cock. A gasped moan was all the noise she made, and then she stilled, her eyes shut down forcefully.

Buried deep, he kissed her forehead, her eyelids, the tip of her nose.

Her lashes were wet and spiky, and her gaze traveled the length of his chest until it finally rested on his eyes. He tried to read the green depths. If she wanted to stop, by Zeus, he would, even if his balls writhed and fell like rotten apples. "Isa, Isa, is it so bad then?"

She licked his lips. "Are you always so chatty?"

Henrique chuckled and started moving in and out of her sheath. The friction of flesh on flesh was delicious. Pressure built into his lower back until his release roared from him in hot white waves.

Afterward, Henrique sighed, a naked Isabel in his arms, her soft sleeping sounds mingling with the creaking fire. An odd sensation swept through him, physical and yet transcendent. As if he had expanded to encompass much more than pain, pleasure, and matter. He became infinite, and just the right size to fit into her.

Living without attachments had detached him from life. Before Isabel, he was a cardboard cutout placed in the scenery for effect. With Isabel snug in his arms, his precious views dissolved like fool's gold when in contact with acid. Henrique buried his nose in Isabel's hair and inhaled her floral scent. His princess promised a wealth of pleasure and the possibility of fathomless pain. And yet, he could not bring himself to leave her side. One night would never be enough.

Chapter 35

"I almost wish we were butterflies and liv'd but three summer days—three such days with you I could fill with more delight than fifty common years could ever contain." John Keats

I sabel lay in bed, staring at the ceiling, her skin at once sensitive and numb. She had just given away her virginity, not as a wife, but as a prisoner. Too tired to think, she shut the censorship. During the long carriage ride to Salamanca, she would allow thoughts to beset her. Her heart fluttered against her ribcage like a trapped cicada. If only she could turn it off, too. Snuggling closer to Henrique, she closed her eyes, craving sleep's oblivion.

The rumble of waves outside combined with Henrique's breathing. Abruptly, he climbed out of bed and bent to the fire's dying embers. Isabel watched as light caressed the sinews of his back. He was a well-formed male. Bronzed and hard, as comfortable naked as in evening attire. It was brazen of her to stare, but she was no longer a maiden. Certainly, that entitled her to look her fill. So she opened her eyes wide, hoping his contours would burn into her memory. Muscles made golden by the fire's glow, Henrique was every inch a Greek god. She could well imagine Alcmene's breathless thrill at being visited by such a being. He padded back, his gaze eliciting a shiver in her cooling skin.

"You didn't need to bother with the fire. I'm not cold."

"I want to see you."

Isabel pulled the covers up to her chin. Surely, there was nothing new by now. He tugged the bedsheets, and Isabel was not fast enough to secure them. The linen brushed against her breasts, titillating as it exposed her. The mattress sunk under his weight as he stretched by her side. He had yet to touch her, but his gaze, serious and intense, singed her skin.

Squirming, Isabel covered her breasts. "Have you looked your fill?"

"Not in a thousand years."

Breathing the words into her lips, he pulled her arms apart and circled the flesh he uncovered with whispery caresses as if to gentle it to him. Whatever patch she protested could not be touched, he tickled, kissed, and licked. She was perspiring when he arrived at her inner thighs, her breathing shallow.

Would he leave her no place to hide? She must not allow him inside her heart. This one-night arrangement could not obliterate her duty. Trying to keep detached from the onslaught of his kisses, Isabel turned to her side, away from him. Undaunted, Henrique flung her onto her stomach and leaned over her, rubbing his furry legs over the back of her thighs.

Her duty. She could not forget her duty. Still, obligations were fluid and abstract, while Henrique, with his hairy, rough skin and sinewy limbs, was more real than king, country, court... everything.

Following the line of her spine, he trailed his finger between her buttocks and touched her entrance, a soft brush of his fingertips. "Are you sore?"

Isabel flushed. "You didn't hurt me when you—"

"Gave you pleasure beyond imagination?"

Isabel bit the inside of her cheek so as not to laugh. The man's conceit knew no bounds. "Well, if you must know, it was... wetter than I expected, and er... salty."

"Salty?" He growled against her neck and nipped her between her shoulder blades. "You wound me, wench."

She struggled, rubbing her naked breasts against the mattress. He flung himself atop her, kneading her waist and buttocks. His heat branded her thighs, and Isabel shuddered, a sensuous shiver blooming from the spot to her core.

"You slander my performance, but I'm as hard as a randy goat for you again." He thrust his hips against her derrière, and his hardness brushed against her entrance.

"Randy goat? I thought we were playing Zeus and Alcmene."

Another teasing thrust, this time penetrating her, just the tip.

"I'm very much flesh and blood, but when I'm inside you"—Henrique gave her another inch—"I feel close to the gods."

Her core tingled when he brushed against her, and she gasped. She didn't know there were other ways of making love.

"I shouldn't take you like a stallion mounting a mare. You deserve to be loved like a goddess."

Isabel stilled. If they did it like this, like mindless creatures, she wouldn't need to experience that intimacy again. Tilting her hips backward, she tried to lure him deeper.

He grabbed the indenture of her waist and paused above her. "You tempt me beyond words, Isa."

Flexing his knees, his breathing harsh, he buried himself to the hilt. Isabel screamed against the pillow. When she thought she would faint, he pulled her up against him into a kneeling position. A looming presence behind her, he grabbed her breasts, circling her nipples. Then he lowered his caresses to her stomach and finally to where they were joined. Isabel dropped her head against his chest, dizzy with pleasure. He massaged her wrists and pressed her spine until they were on all fours. He lowered himself atop her, his chest glued to her back. Isabel whimpered, breathless, her skin so sensitive she feared spontaneous combustion. The new position left her open to him. He possessed her with deep strokes. Pleasure built in a crescendo, but without looking into his eyes, it was hollow. She wanted more.

"I need—"

"What do you need, love?"

"You. I need you."

He flipped her onto her back. Hooking his hands under her knees, he came inside her. His eyes sought hers, and she allowed herself to be swept into the blue depths. The contact of their skin, heated and wet with perspiration, made her moan, and she clasped her arms around his neck. It assuaged something inside her, but it was never enough. She needed more.

He kept a steady, too-slow rhythm, touching her deeply for a spare second and then withdrawing completely. Isabel writhed on the bed, straining her hips, wanting more, wanting all.

Isabel cried out when he gave her a shallow thrust and pulled away. "Stay—inside. Please." She couldn't bear him gone for even the backlash of his thrusts.

Smiling, he kissed her mouth and thrust, burying himself inside her. "There. I won't leave you again."

He was so deep, he touched her soul.

Isabel burst into a thousand flames and whimpered, clasping her arms around him.

No, but I will.

One could get used to sleeping with Henrique. He was a natural source of heat. His aroma was clean, with a pleasant pine undertone. His purr was soothing, and his presence affected her in a way she couldn't understand, much less describe. It was as if... Every day and every night, she labored to arrive somewhere. With him, tucked against his chest, his heart beating against her spine, she arrived. In his arms, she realized how exhausting it was to be always in control.

She savored the predawn hours until sunlight crept into the tower.

Henrique rolled to his back, one arm flung over his face, the sheets tangled around his legs. His mouth was soft, inviting. She shifted closer, her hand tingling to brush away a few strands from his forehead. It had been a night of myth. A flutter started in her stomach, a feeling of emptiness. What would happen if—No, she would not think about it. A ray of sunlight invaded the arrow slit, drawing a line between Henrique and her.

The night was over.

She stood, her legs weighted by invisible greaves. Her chest was so tight, as if Sophie had fastened a metal corset over her bedclothes. It was best this way. She could not renege on her duties. The cold slabs covering the floor frosted her feet. She was not betraying him. They had an agreement. One night. No guilt, no consequences. That was what he wanted and what she needed. It was broad daylight now, and passion could not last beyond Eros' shadows.

After tiptoeing to the table, she picked up his coat and brushed it against her cheek, cherishing the texture. The key was cold and hard against her palm, and she stared at it, resenting the brass piece as if it were responsible for all her woes.

His voice, muffled by sleep, reached her. "Good morning."

Isabel slid the key into her robe pocket. Her gaze strayed to the door. If she darted to the exit, she could lock him inside before he chased her.

"Come back to bed."

Isabel turned slowly.

Henrique leaned on his side, naked beneath the sheets. The white cotton contrasted with his bronzed skin. He lifted a hand, palm up. His gaze was open and seductive. The memory of their night flooded her with heat.

Pressing her lips together, she cursed the light invading the tower. What if she closed the shutters? But it would still be day, and her country would still be at risk. "Our night is over." Her voice wavered.

He rose, his long, long legs hoisting his masculinity until he towered a head over her. Completely at ease with his nakedness, he walked until only her robe separated her from his warm skin.

Delicately, he placed both his hands over her shoulders and kneaded softly. "What if we made our night last forever?"

"Forever?" Isabel gasped, her gaze delving into his. A part of her wrested free and fluttered inside her chest, bumping against her ribcage. A part she had learned to guard since her infancy, a part she had forgotten existed.

He caressed her forearm and took her hand in his. He kissed her palm and placed it above his chest. His heartbeat thudded, alive and insistent. She could tell him about her plans... But how? The mere mention of Alfonso's name had put him in a rage. A sinking sensation spread to her chest, weighting her limbs. Myths would come true before he understood.

"It is not possible." She glanced away, staring at their rumpled bed.

"Nothing is impossible for Zeus." He smiled against her palm and licked.

Isabel's sigh came from deep inside her, a place only he reached.

"I'm not a woman from myth, and you are not a god." She touched his cheek. The grain of his stubble titillated her fingertips. "We are mortals. Would you not tire of me? You said it yourself... Monogamy is not in our nature."

Isabel turned away from him. She could leave his spell.

Henrique brushed his lips against her palm. When he looked at her, the blue fire was hers alone, hypnotic. There were secrets hidden inside its walls, secrets that whispered to her, and only her. Against her will, she lifted her chin, searching for his kiss.

"It happens infrequently, mind you," he said as he nipped her earlobe. "But you might as well learn of it now."

"Hmm?" She could not form words with him drawing circles over her forearms.

"There is the rare occasion when I am wrong."

He pulled her robe's cinch and bared her to him completely.

The brush of naked skin against naked skin immolated her denial. When he lifted her in his arms and carried her back to bed, she told herself they deserved another night, and she wasn't ignoring her duty... The housekeeper's son would come only tomorrow.

And then he bit the indenture of her waist, and her thoughts scattered.

Chapter 36

"If the butterfly wings its way to the sweet light that attracts it, it's only because it doesn't know that the fire can consume it." Giordano Bruno

Kneeling behind the Turkish bath the count had the foresight to install in the tower, Henrique washed Isabel's hair. The heat had relaxed her to the point of sensual languidness, but he was far from fooled. She had been about to flee this morning. The thought brought an emptiness to his chest, and he kissed the top of her head to dispel it.

She allowed him to pleasure her freely, but her mind was still locked behind a wall, unbreachable. While they talked about science and myths, and she asked questions about lovemaking that made him ravenous, they spoke not about the future.

But he wanted to.

It would take more than words to convince her, especially since he had hammered the point of infidelity ad nauseam. But there was never a woman he could not conquer. Granted, Isabel was different—cunning and intelligent, strong. Henrique glanced at the sunrays shining through the window. Not even she could stay immune to the outdoor wooing he had planned.

She relaxed her head over the tub's rim, and a contented smile left her lips. "I think Sophie will be miffed you stole her duties."

"Miffed? She is probably dancing up and down the stairs, relieved to the roots of her French braids."

Isabel laughed and sprinkled his face with water. "Is it such a hardship to serve me?"

He took her hand in his and kissed her palm. Then he placed it atop his cock. Her sharp intake of breath was a clear sign she understood just how hard it was.

"Sophie is an excellent lady's maid, but my princess will see the advantages of keeping me in the position."

"I don't know... Sophie is loyal."

"Hmm." He let go of her hand and leaned over the tub. "But can she do this?" He circled her nipples until they puckered, and then he lowered his hand under the water's surface. A groan escaped his throat when her legs opened for him.

She arched her back, her hips rising to meet him, and he grunted. Impatient now, he made her stand. The outing could wait. When he palmed her thigh and pulled her leg up, opening a path to her core, they both hissed.

Slowly, he tested her wetness with his fingers. She arched her hips into his hand, and Henrique withdrew.

She glared at him.

"You won't tumble me like a common heathen this time, wench."

Water glistened on her skin. Her eyes flashed green fire, and she bit her lip, watching as he folded a towel in two. Gently, he placed the sole of her feet on the tub's rim. With one leg up, Henrique exposed her to him.

"Look at you, so pink and pretty. I think you deserve a kiss." His mouth watered, thirsty for her secret taste. If he drowned in it, he would die a happy man. Holding her hips, he sucked her slowly, allowing her pleasure to build in waves.

She moaned and arched her back. Her flight came swiftly, her sheath clenching against his tongue.

"Please, Henrique, no more."

He wasn't ready to let go yet. "One more flight. For me."

This time, she bucked against him, and incoherent sounds escaped her mouth.

He rose and caught her in his arms before she collapsed. He was painfully hard, the exact opposite of his Isa, now soft and languid, liquid fire.

He placed her atop the table, and she blinked at his cock, jutting out against his stomach.

"Can I touch it?"

His pulse sped. "Absolutely not. Cocks are susceptible to yanking, as Priapus might tell if he still could talk. Your hands are deceptively strong." Henrique caught her wrists and kissed the pad of her finger.

His cock jerked to attention.

"He doesn't seem to mind." Tentatively, tenderly, she traced the head and stroked his length.

He held still, concentrating on not spilling in her hands. "He is simple-minded. His mind has a simple goal: to enter you."

Licking her lips, she measured him with her palms. "Though you are more proportioned than Priapus, I still don't understand how you didn't run me through with your mighty sword."

He grinned. "You will make him vain."

"More? Impossible." Her mischievous grin made his heart pound.

Leaning forward, he tasted her smile, licking the seam of her lips. She closed her eyes. He arranged her hair over her shoulders and leaned back to admire her. Naked atop the desk, her skin flushed from the bath, her

legs closed primly in front of her—she was his erotic
fantasies come true.

"You posed a valid anatomic question. We shall try to
answer it." He clutched her knees and slowly opened her
legs.

She didn't resist, her gaze following the contrast between his brown hands, so different from the cream of
her thighs.

Occupying the space between her legs, he wetted the
tip of his cock at her entrance and hissed at the pressure
on his spine. He pushed half his length inside her.

She gasped, arching her breasts. He accepted her offer, kissing and sucking the swollen tips.

"That's it, now be a good princess and take me all in."
He grabbed her buttocks, bent his knees, and thrust.
Bright points burst under his eyelids at having penetrated her so deeply. He rested his forehead on her
neck. She was breathing heavily, her sheath pulsing
against him.

"It is a measure of your eagerness that we must make
love standing up," she panted, her words ruffling the
scruff on his chest.

"It is a measure of how much I want you that I cannot
wait."

He should be careful with her. Yesterday, she was a
virgin. But when she licked his nipple, her little teeth
sinking into him, her heels digging into his flanks, a
mythic beast unleashed within him. He thrust savagely,
like a man possessed, like an animal in heat, like a
randy god. When the ripples of pleasure caught her,
she arched her back, her nails sinking into his shoulders. Henrique pushed inside her one more time and
exploded, a shuddering release that left him gasping for
breath, holding her tightly against his chest.

His legs threatened to give out on him, and before
he crumpled, he lifted her from the table. On the way
to the bed, Henrique paused, entranced by their joined

reflection, much like Narcissus gazing upon the pond. The Venetian mirror reflected his darkness to her fairness, her softness to his roughness. His mate in sensuality and intellect.

His hands, sun-bronzed and rough, seemed indecent against her lily-white buttocks, and the enormity of his action crashed down on him. She wasn't a lady he had stolen from a husband, but a princess he had taken from a country that loved and respected her.

As his gaze lowered to the place where his flesh met hers, a primal feeling took hold of him. She was his, damn the country. Only he could make her fly.

"Don't leave me yet," Isabel whispered, clinging to him.

His breath caught. "Are you sure you have not some peasant stock in your royal lineage? I never saw a lustier wench."

Without withdrawing from her tight sheath, he kneeled on the mattress and lowered his weight atop her.

"Look who is saying." She laughed breathlessly and brushed her fingers against his chest. "With your tanned skin and coarse pelt, you look the part of a heathen."

She lay beneath him, a contented smile on her lips, her eyelashes shadowing her cheeks. He kissed her eyelids and tasted the sweet, salty perspiration on her forehead.

His cock hardened by a sudden, savage rush of his blood.

Isabel's eyes widened. "Did you not just—"

"Indeed, quite vigorously."

Pinned under his weight, she strained her hips against him. "But you still feel quite ready."

"Not still. Again."

She gasped, her plump lips opening.

"If you are a nice peasant girl, this heathen will make you fly many times." He thrust, lodging himself to the hilt inside her sheath. Her breath broke, and she clawed at his biceps.

Henrique laughed and moved, savoring her warmth. Slowly, he retreated. When he returned, he let her feel his weight. The intense, gliding friction was heady, addictive.

"Henrique." Isabel breathed.

He doubled the pressure, filling her to bursting. If he seduced her with ecstasy, she would want to stay tonight, forever.

She quivered beneath him, her eyes heavy-lidded. Henrique drank from her lips, gliding in and retreating, the age-old rhythm of gods and beasts.

Her cries turned sharp, urgent, almost frightened.

"Sweet Isa, another flight, just one more."

"My wings are tired—can't—"

She could. He knew she could. One more time. Not enough. Forever. He placed his hand between their bodies, feeling the first shudders of pleasure course through her stomach. Her toes curled against his calves, and a keening cry escaped her lips.

He flicked her clitoris, and she ignited. "Hold on to me, Isa. This time, you will soar."

After they shared lunch, he helped her dress in her own clothes. A minor concession for her good behavior. The tiara sparkled atop the dressing table, and Isabel didn't place it atop her head. He stared at the forgotten diamonds, his eyes trapped in the light like a mesmerized feline. No. He would not consider her motives. It was too soon for her, for them. He felt her reluctance, and it wrenched his heart. Time was passing. If Pedro arrived before he convinced her to stay, then... What? He needed her to admit her feelings for him. With a sense of urgency gnawing at his insides, Henrique took her to his favorite spot, the wild garden patch behind the battlements.

He grabbed her waist and hoisted her atop the ruins of an ancient wall. She dangled her feet until her slippers fell with soft thuds on the grass, and then she leaned back on her elbows, the sun igniting golden streaks in her loose hair.

"You color this pile of rocks." He moved between her legs and caressed her calves.

"It's the Portuguese sky. Our blue is stronger, darker, and it makes every color spark." Her gaze swept over the castle's granite walls and the lush land surrounding it. "Your estate is so... ancient and alive, so filled with history."

"Even the tower?"

"Especially the tower." She smiled shyly, then looked at their entwined hands. "Why sell it?"

Henrique shrugged, uncomfortable. "The Italian count made an outrageous offer and—"

She touched his cheek. "The truth."

Henrique stiffened but didn't dislodge her touch.

"Is it the memories?"

"I can't blame them. All good. Fishing with my father, chasing my sister around the corn fields, flustering my mother with my escapades. But they are gone now..." He blew air slowly from his mouth and gazed at the tired crenelation. His ancestors had perched there for centuries, fighting to protect king and country. "Generation upon generation of Penafiel blood was spilled for the sake of this pile of rocks. I'll break the pattern."

He hadn't brought her here to tell her of his lack of love for his ancestral home—and now it was out, floating between them like a giant boulder about to strike his head. His teeth ground down, and he released her hand, awaiting a reprimand from her patriotic lips.

She placed her palm atop his. "You wanted to fly."

Startled, he glanced up. Her green gaze shone with understanding and warmth. He nodded and pulled her closer for a taste. The kiss was bittersweet as if their bodies knew something they didn't. Being with her filled him with a devastating joy that bordered on pain. He was suddenly unable to breathe unless she admitted she loved him and had no intention of leaving.

With the sun warming their backs, a soft murmur of water babbling on rocks, he caressed the side of her face and kissed her palm. "If Alcmene had confessed her feelings for Zeus, he would have fought heaven and hell to stay with her."

She glanced away, her expression closing. "Lecherous Zeus? I doubt it."

"Perhaps not... but in matters of the heart, it is sometimes expected the woman to acknowledge her feelings first."

"Is that so?" She shifted, dislodging him, and slid from the wall. Hair flying behind her, she raced toward the castle, her skirts brushing against the tall grass.

Henrique closed the distance between them. "Why are you running from me?"

She increased her speed, her breathing labored. "Really, Henrique, as a temporary lover, you are proving to be a nagging—"

Henrique grabbed her arm, halting her escape. "I don't want to be a temporary lover, damn it!"

She closed her eyes, and when she opened them, the green depths were replaced by steely determination. "Do you know what I want? I want friendship. I want respect. I want shared goals and to build a family. I want to set an example. I want to make a difference."

"I want you."

"I need more." She crossed her arms, her gaze sparkling with challenge and a question he had not expected to answer.

"I can do more. For you."

"Words, Henrique. How will I be able to believe in them? When they go against your nature? Do you think I forgot? You told me yourself. Monogamy is not natural." She hurled the words, and her eyes glittered with unshed tears.

He felt her slipping. The girl who laughed and soared with him was barricading behind her royal demeanor.

"I was wrong." Henrique pulled her into his arms and brushed his lips over hers, closing his eyes against the fierce wave of longing that shook him every time he breathed her scent. Conscious thought, motor coordination, sensory receptors—all shut down, his life energy demanding to fuse every inch of skin in his body with hers. His molecules had existed independently for thirty-two years, but now they required hers to achieve chemical stability.

"What if the mood passes and—"

"I wish this were a mood." He panted against her hair. "Moods are temporary. Moods sweep through a person harmlessly. A mood doesn't rearrange the structure of a man's cells. This? Us? Lifetime. Even then, my life will prove too short to live a love so long. I love you, you incredulous, shrewd woman. Curse your royal hide."

Isabel whirled on him. "This isn't fair. We agreed. One night, no guilt, no consequences." Her voice cracked, and she punctuated each word by stabbing her finger into his chest.

Henrique didn't move, didn't defend himself. He just stood—a boulder of a man, determined to crush all her defenses. Isabel panted, every breath a struggle. Why did he have to do this? Why change the agreement now? When it would wrench her heart to sneak out of his bed tomorrow?

"You want me here, pliable. You woo me like you do with all your women—"

He touched her cheek. "Woo? I've been trying to keep my hands off you, you stubborn princess, since the first second I laid my eyes on you. Half the time, I want to snap your pretty neck. The other half, I want to caress every inch of your skin. But what I can't do is let go."

"No, listen to me—"

"Do you think I welcome this feeling? If I could open my chest and extract it from inside, I would—"

"You are a scientist. You find a cure for this sickness."

"Eros' arrows have no cure."

"This is lust. You promised. One night, no guilt, no consequences."

He grabbed her shoulders and shook. "I love you, silly creature. I love you with love, with all the loves inside love, the divine, the human, the beastly, like Adam loved Eve, like Romeo loved Juliet, like Zeus loved Alcmene, like a stallion loves a mare."

He slanted his mouth over her and kissed her. Isabel didn't resist. How could she? When her heart sang, when her body rejoiced, when her mind burst under the onslaught of his touch?

Henrique's love loosened a thread in her chest, unleashing her restraint. She could be happy with him, she realized abruptly. Not the comfortable, proper happiness of duty she had envisioned for herself, but a giddy, exciting, joining of souls kind of happiness.

"Take me to the tower. I need you inside me."

The way blurred as they raced to the castle. The windy staircase robbed her breath, her composure, and she staggered through the threshold, hand clasped in Henrique's.

Clothes fell away to decorate the gaudy pillows, and then they were skin to skin. Her hunger for him surpassed anything she had ever experienced, and naked, they tumbled over the mattress. A manic force gripped her, and she bit his chest, shoving her hips against him. He shared her frenzy and entered her forcefully. She gasped at the friction. Shaking, trembling, she grabbed fistfuls of his hair and pulled him to her. He surged above her, pounding his hips against her. There wasn't laughter. Only the guttural cries of pleasure and pain, of flesh meeting flesh in search of oblivion, of harsh, never enough breaths. Promises died in her mouth, but her throat was sore from pleading, crying, begging for him to go faster, harder, deeper.

She would gamble anything to keep him, to be here with him—let morality die and the country explode, and she would not care.

The man she loved. She would leave the man she loved tomorrow. Whimpering, she ground her hips against him, wanting him to meld them like Vulcan fused two pieces of metal. If that failed, she wanted to enter him, sheltered by his sinewy strength, buried so deep she could never leave. If that was lost to her, she wanted him to pulverize her with the force of his mating.

She exploded, gasping for breath, her heart racing out of control. Henrique hummed to her, the tempo of his thrusts slowing until his invasion became a pressure deep inside her. He brushed the hair from her forehead and neck and caressed her bottom lip. His gaze held tenderness and the love he professed, and Isabel closed her eyes.

He rolled them until they faced each other by their sides. He caressed her back with long, soothing brushes of his palms and embraced her. With her head buried in the crook of his neck, she accepted his gentle love-making, just as he accepted her frenzied coupling. It was sweet, the friction barely there, his thrusts shallow and deep. Their chests glued together, too close.

Pleasure bloomed, leaving them both panting.

The sun was setting when he withdrew from her and pulled her to his chest, lazily touching her calves with her toes. Then he fell asleep, his leg thrown atop hers.

The ocean brushed against the shore, like rain trapped forever in an hourglass. Tears and perspiration had long cooled on her skin when the cicadas started their song. *Sing, my friends. This is your last night.*

It was fair of nature that after a cicada experienced life from the heights of flight, she didn't have to return to her burrow inside the earth.

While he purred in sleep, she twirled a curl of his hair in her fingers and said in a voice choked by emotion, "I love you too."

Forgive me.

Chapter 37

"Any moment might be our last. Everything is more beautiful because we're doomed. You will never be lovelier than you are now. We will never be here again." Homer, *The Iliad*

The muted tones of dawn pierced through the arrow slits. A scratch at the door cut through Isabel sharper than a scimitar. Though she had been waiting for it, the long night hours the only company for her conscience, it still startled her. Eyes gritty, throat sore, Isabel pulled her legs from beneath his and stood on the cold floor. She moved as if underground, dirt pressing down on her, invading her lungs. Like a fugitive, she dressed quickly, and placed her crown atop her head. The weight had increased tenfold since the last time she wore it. Hands shaking, she adjusted the letter to the left so Henrique would not miss it, resisting the urge to rip it. The medal had been a mistake. Why on earth did she place the gold piece inside the envelope? He had rejected it once. But the white paper filled with righteous justifications seemed too naked, too wrong.

The scratch again. The housekeeper, the car-riage—Salamanca.

A hurried knock.

The noise would wake him.

Yes. Awake, please. Keep me here against my will.

All her life, she had professed to be a patriot beyond reproach. Always choosing duty to the detriment of personal wishes. Scoffing when others rebelled against the strict demands of royalty life. Her gaze lingered on Henrique, his sharp, manly features now reposed, perhaps dreaming. She loved his wit, his intelligence, his tenderness, his lust. By God, how foolish she'd been. So righteous in her virtues when she had not been chal-lenged in her beliefs. Virtue was easy when it had no cost. When she had to choose between sleeping late or attending charity functions, wearing revealing gowns or maintaining her modesty, and opening herself to friendship and love versus keeping an aura of royalty... She took a shuddering sigh and swallowed a sob. This was hard. It was not fair. A choice between him and everything else.

If she remained in her lover's arms, no one would place the responsibility on her shoulders. But could she live with herself knowing she could have changed the fate of two nations? Could she enjoy this new happiness at the expense of thousands of her subjects? People who depended on her for moral support, for confidence, for stability?

Guilt-ridden if she stayed, miserable if she went.

Henrique had fallen in love with the courageous Is-abel. She cleaned the tears racing down her cheeks. Not a woman who placed herself above all others.

Chest so constricted that breathing became a struggle, she forced her legs to move past the pillows, the table, the bed. Him.

Trembling, she opened the door and passed the threshold to the other side. Unable to face the understanding in the housekeeper's eyes, Isabel turned the key.

Outside their heaven, everything was foreign. The coat of armor, the scent of iron and smoke, the servant's harsh breaths.

"Your Highness, the carriage awaits."

Chapter 38

"Ah, wretched me! That love is not to be cured by any herbs; and that those arts which afford relief to all, are of no avail for their master." Ovid, *Metamorphoses*

Henrique crumpled the note. Alone, locked in his own castle. His first reaction had been a jealous rage, wanting to rip the rocks, carve a way out of the prison she'd made for him. As the waves pounded at the shore, he realized jealousy wasn't the right emotion. At least, not jealousy for Alfonso. Since That first night in the garden, Henrique knew—Isabel was a martyr waiting to happen. It was there all along. Underneath the rusty breastplate lived a Joan of Arc, biding her time to save all. What a fitting choice for the prudish princess. Posterity veneered the woman warrior, the selfless saint, who sacrificed herself for the country. No one cared for the loved ones she left behind. A monster of a headache moved into his brain. If he had a drill, he would poke a hole in his skull and end the agony.

When the heavy oak portal screeched open, Henrique didn't lift his head. His father's housekeeper shuffled inside, her face haggard and yet sheepish.

He kept twirling the medal in his fingers. He didn't ask if she had helped Isabel. Of course, the old militant did.

"How long?"

"A few minutes past dawn."

By the sun's position, it was close to eleven in the morning.

"Who went with her?"

"Her maid, my son, and two of the retainers."

Henrique nodded. He knew Antonia's son. A clever, resourceful lad. Spoke Spanish and Portuguese. The castle retainers were all retired soldiers who had fought with him in Mozambique. She would be safe in her mad, ill-advised adventure. Thank God for that.

"My carriage?"

She gulped. "Yes, Your Excellency."

Henrique scoffed. "You never called me such before. Don't start now."

"The poor child. When she left... she was heartbroken. She only did so because she believed you wouldn't support her decision. So she sacrificed—"

"Stop," he barked. His jaw was locked so tight he might break his condylar bone. "I won't allow you to say she sacrificed her love for the good of the country."

"But she did, and you would go after her if you were not a stubborn, selfish boy."

No more *your excellencies* then? Henrique pinched the bridge of his nose. "Do you remember when Father sent me to Mozambique?"

She made a comical expression, half glare, half grimace. "Your father was a nobleman. It was different—"

"Different? He, too, sacrificed me for the country. I lost my entry at Sorbonne, my mother's last moments...." Henrique pushed away from the mantel, his voice harsh, metallic. "Now Isabel did the same. Should

I feel thankful? Noble? Should I coin medals and compose a song? When will the reward kick in? When? At least to take the edge off the pain? The bitterness?"

She didn't answer.

"No? Forgive me, but I want no part of her sacrifice," Henrique said, breathing hard.

Horses sounded beyond the gate. His heart picked up speed. Did she return? Panting, he went to the window. Pedro Daun's black horse crossed the bridge into the courtyard.

Henrique's shoulders sagged, and he shut his eyes. "We have visitors. Go see to their refreshments."

Henrique flung Isabel's excuses at the unlit hearth. Trying to keep his gaze from lingering on the bed and the broken promises, he descended the steps to his room. The chamber smelled of dust and fresh paint. He grabbed an old valise. It took only five minutes to pack the possessions he had brought from Spain.

Pedro strode inside. "How long ago?"

Of course, he already knew. Henrique faced him, his face blank. He would be damned if he showed Pedro any hint of his pain.

"Dawn. Not later."

Pedro nodded. "If we leave now, we can reach her before she crosses the border."

Henrique stilled, his breathing strained. He could chase her, bring her back, and keep her captive. Rafaela's prophetic words played again in his mind. *Isabel is just like Canastra. She loves her country above all else.*

Did he want to tie his fate to a woman who would always choose duty over him?

"She is headed for Salamanca. She took guards. You won't have trouble locating her." Henrique closed the suitcase.

Pedro held his arm. "I thought you had found your mate."

Henrique shrugged away the touch. "Your Anne was willing to cut her throat to save you. Isabel is more than willing to do the same. For Portugal."

"But—"

"I'm done." Done with the hero's journey, with his foolish, desperate need for love, for her. Done. "You go after her. I'm returning to Lisbon."

Chapter 39

"You will never do anything in this world without courage. It is the greatest quality of the mind next to honor." Aristotle

The carriage thundered along the rutted roads. Dust rose like smoke, stretching dirty fingers into the sky. Isabel kept her eyes open, focused on the landscape—anything to avoid her inner turmoil. Barren and treeless, there was hardly much to keep her attention besides dry streams crawling like snakes across the plain. The vastness imprisoned her, and she longed for the freedom of the tower.

They halted at a ramshackle port village. The streets were empty. No people, no animals, nothing. When Antonia's son helped her from the carriage, the heat hit her in the chest. "Where is everyone, Tito?"

"The *siesta*, Your Highness."

Sleeping. Everything was sleeping. Isabel wished she was too.

The small party crossed the lane toward the harbor. Though the huts had their windows closed, Isabel felt watched. As if Spain itself, with its weather-beaten face, hawkish nose, and glittering black eyes, peered at the insolent girl in their mist.

Adjusting the hood over her head, Isabel hastened her steps. The brick plaza, this one a very silent, drab one, opened up to a rocky beach. Spindly piers and narrow wooden docks reached the ocean but fell short of the harbor. It was easy to spot the royal frigate. It looked like a mother hen among the smaller chick-sized fisher boats.

The Portuguese flag, the one she had so naively sewed, flew alongside the Spanish one. Her heels sunk into the sand, and she missed a step. While Antonia's son went for information, Isabel waited with Sophie and Henrique's guards. Even though it filled her with dread and shame, she forced herself to look at the flag. It trembled in the gentle breeze, and she vowed to set things right.

When Tito returned, her skin felt taut, her insides brittle.

"I've secured a rowboat." He took her arm, guiding her to the breaking waves, and lowered his voice. "The Duke of Canastra is not with him."

Isabel sighed. Thank heavens. Without the duke's influence, she might convince Alfonso. Casting a baleful look at the soldiers patrolling the shore, she climbed atop the rickety boat. The hawks jostled them as they were rowed offshore.

The frigate loomed in their front, much larger than she expected. Barnacles stuck to the waterline, and ropes thudded against the masts. The flags were no longer visible from her viewpoint, but she knew they were there.

A rough-looking marine officer grinned lecherously at their small party.

Risking overturning the skiff, Isabel rose and lowered her hood, revealing her tiara. "I'm Isabel de Orleans, Infanta de Portugal. Take me to your king."

The smirk faded from the officer's expression, and he bowed deeply. "This way, Senhora Isabel."

Alfonso lounged on the frigate's deck. His lanky form was neatly encased in his country's military coat. His longish hair wiped the sides of his face as he stared at the ocean. She could bet his soul had already arrived in Madrid.

Isabel set her jaw and lifted herself to her full height. "You donned the uniform at last. It suits you."

"Isabel, thank god." His eyes widened and he shot to his feet. "Where were you? I have soldiers scouring the countryside."

Isabel pointed to the mast behind him. "The Portuguese flag doesn't belong on a Spanish Frigate." To give weight to her words, the cloth twisted and snapped with a gust of wind.

A flush colored his face and, turning away from her, he leaned over the railings. "Have you ever seen Spain's nautical bulls?"

Isabel swallowed an angry retort and followed the direction of his gaze. On the shore, scores of black oxen were harnessed to huge barges. The beasts, their coats gleaming with the harsh sun, were taunted and cursed by men wearing loincloths. Heads lowered, they advanced into the sea. A merchantman awaited to load their cargo.

The smell of oranges and brine cooled her cheeks, no doubt coming from the metal barrels they pulled. Braying, the poor creatures struggled with the weight but kept on, their bodies vanishing inside the surf.

Her hand came to her throat. "Certainly, they will drown."

"They've been at this for millennia. In Roman times, businessmen reared this breed of oxen to thrive in salt water. A crafty way to solve the problem of a lack of port. Centuries passed, and nothing changed. No ruler ever built one. The Spaniards pay for their politician's lack of vision with the sweat on their backs and the blood in their veins. That's why Spain needs me."

Isabel forced her gaze from the gruesome spectacle. She had believed in him the first time he had sweetened her with such talk. Now, he sounded hollow, false.

"I don't think it is fair when the ruling class hides their mistakes behind their subjects."

He smiled sadly, his eyes not quite meeting hers. "Canastra sometimes assumes control of things. I required the military to regain power. The country needs me."

The monotone of the words sounded almost like an apology. She didn't need an apology. Her desperate situation called for a true monarch.

Isabel took a deep breath. "Spain deserves a strong king, one who—"

"And it will have." He whirled and caught her hands in his. "Portugal as well. Your brother chafes under the responsibility. You said it yourself. With the peninsula united, we will regain the power of the Great Navigations. We will—"

"You don't believe that." Isabel didn't flinch from his touch and gazed into his eyes, hoping she could make him see the truth. "Portugal and Spain are as different as port wine and sangria. The people will fight against it. Both sides will suffer. There will be war."

"Canastra has no intention of a hostile invasion. He promised me—"

"Canastra has no scruples. He manipulated my brother into sending me to Spain." Why could he be so blind? Isabel pulled away from him. "He maneuvered you into offering for my hand to set up this scheme—"

"You shall not judge my supporters." His expression turned cold, distant.

"With Canastra as a supporter, you won't need anyone to bring you down."

"Enough. Canastra was the only aristocrat who didn't abandon me. You never had to fight for your rights."

"The army is already on your side. The Duke of Aosta is no doubt back in Italy licking his wounds. You don't have to do this."

"I'm sorry, Isabel, but I had to compromise." His expression closed, and he turned from her.

Her breath caught at the finality of his words. But what else could she do? She had argued with him as a princess, as a patriot, as a Christian, as a woman. Alfonso answered everything like a sulky boy.

She couldn't admit defeat. Heart speeding, she grabbed his hand. "Princes compromise. A king does what is right. A Spaniard shouldn't shed his *pundonor* when he sits on the throne."

A tick appeared on his jaw, and he fisted his hands.

Birds flew overhead, swooping across the water, their screeches too loud. The hull swung, and a wave of nausea rolled through her. She forced herself to stay still, staring at his handsome profile. Perspiration dampened her skin as she counted the rise and fall of his breaths. What had she done? The insult to his honor had been too harsh.

Alfonso whirled from her and bellowed words in Spanish. Too fast for her to understand.

A bulky man raced to them and saluted. She judged him to be the captain by the tricorn and braided epaulets.

Isabel gripped her skirts, her heart thudding painfully against her corset. Had he not told her a Spaniard couldn't allow an insult to go unanswered? Alfonso would toss her into the sea or lock her in the hold. As a war prisoner, she would never see Henrique again. Would he still hate her then?

Alfonso pointed to the mast. "Lower the Portuguese flag." Then he gazed at her, and his voice softened. "I will give it back to its owner."

Her legs faltered with the force of her relief, and she leaned against the railing for support.

She curtsied low, touching her knee to the deck in absolute deference. "Thank you, your majesty."

He lifted her and kissed her cheek, his longish hair brushing softly against her.

"Cross the Ebro with me. Be my queen."

Isabel startled. She could almost hear the voice of her mother inside her head. *You were born to be a queen.* Alfonso would have an enormous task, from forming a constitutional government to setting up a court. He would have to be wise beyond his years and fend off untoward advances. He was a boy still. All his teachings came from books and instructors with subversive intentions. What did he know of politics? Of intrigue? There could be others like Canastra.

With her training, Isabel could pave the way for his success. Even so, the words would not form. She could not marry him. Her heart belonged to another.

She pressed his hand affectionately. "Be wise. Trust your own judgment. Your kingdom will return stability to Spain, and I'll cheer you from my country."

Back on the beach, Isabel clutched the Portuguese flag to her chest, watching Alfonso's frigate leave for Madrid until it was a speck on the horizon.

"Where to, Your Highness?" Tito asked.

"To Braganza." Isabel shielded her eyes, straining her vision towards the south. The tower wasn't there. Just an expanse of wasteland mixed up with the colors of sunset.

Their small party had crossed the border back to Portugal when an army brigade forced them to stop. Her heart fluttered in her chest.

Someone opened the coach's door. The Count of Almoster shadowed the road, the sun glinting off his golden hair. He bowed slightly, his eyes accessing the interior. When he saw only Sophie, his hand left the hilt of his saber.

Isabel was acquainted with Anne's husband and inclined her head.

"War is imminent, Your Highness. The border is no longer safe—"

"I beg to differ, Count. I just spoke with the king of Spain." She smoothed the Portuguese flag over her lap. "I can assure you, he bears no ill will towards us."

He frowned and, with a nod, sent an officer scurrying away, no doubt to check the truth of her words.

"Is that all? Your officers are crowding the road, and I tire of the sun."

"Your Highness, if you are done with your ride, I would like to escort you to Lisbon."

"I'm headed to Braganza."

"I've just come from there." His expression softened, and Isabel wondered how much of her relationship with Henrique he knew.

A flush rose in her cheeks. "Is everything alright... with the tower?"

"Viscount Penafiel left this morning," he said and closed the door.

Isabel reclined on the leather bench, staring straight ahead. She listened as the Count of Almoster gave orders to begin the journey back to the capital as if the words came from another realm.

Sophie tapped her hand and sighed. "You will feel better when we reach home, Citizen Isabel. Being welcomed by your people has never failed to cheer you up."

Chapter 40

"Oblivion—what a blessing for the mind to dwell a world away from pain." Sophocles, *Oedipus Rex*

Isabel disembarked the *Rainha Frigate* and crossed the drawbridge to land on Lisbon's soil. It was hot and airless and muggy. The physical and mental oppression of the afternoon set up weights on her legs, and she had trouble placing one foot in front of the other. Since Pedro Daun had informed her of Henrique's desertion, nothing much mattered. What should have been a victory homecoming became a retreat to care for wounds. Two months since she saw the Tagus, Saint George's castle, the arches of the *Praça do Comercio*. Everything was the same, and yet it was not. Perhaps she had changed. She had flown, but instead of shedding the carapace, she had shed herself, and only the husk remained.

Sophie clicked her tongue. "This is not right. Citizen Pedro Daun sent word of your arrival. How come no one is here?"

Beyond the marina, only the palace coach awaited—no throngs of subjects waving scarves and going on tiptoes to glimpse their princess. No gas lamps lit the gloomy streets up the hill. No fresh flowers and boughs of rosemary festooned the windowsills.

They settled in the coach and slowly climbed to the palace. Close to the gates, a squalid crowd had formed. As the coach slowed to pass through her subjects, Isabel heard hisses and hoots. When a tomato hit the side of the carriage, Sophie yelped.

"Why are they behaving like a mob? Do you think Portugal is a republic now?"

Isabel shook her head and closed her eyes. She feared she would soon find out, but tiredness quenched her curiosity. All she craved was the closeness of her ladies and a respite from riotous emotions.

Isabel crossed the heavy oak doors of the Ajuda Palace. Her boots echoed over the empty marble vestibule. Only the sculptures were there to receive her, their faces austere. She didn't expect the queen to welcome her home, but Luis' absence pierced her heart. After what she had been through, she longed to lay her head on her big brother's shoulder and cry.

The servants kept their glances down while Isabel dragged her feet to her wing.

Before she could enter her morning room, Lady Philipa came to her.

Isabel leaned into her friend's embrace. When they parted, Isabel noticed she was dressed all in black, down to the veil of her bonnet. Dread swirled in her stomach. Death had visited the palace? Was that why everyone seemed so downcast? Her first thought was of her brother. But no, if the king had died, black crêpe would be covering the windows and portraits.

Heart speeding, she grabbed Philipa's shoulders. "Where are the other ladies?"

Lady Philipa glanced down, pressing the corner of her eyes with a kerchief. "Their families sent for them."

"Why?" The season would start soon. Families were returning to Lisbon from their summer houses.

"You don't know? Oh, dear." A single tear rolled down Philipa's cheek. She pointed to the escritoire, her mouth opening and closing without a sound. "It's tomorrow's newspaper."

A pressed sheet awaited there. The editor only sent an advance copy when he feared the news might displease the king. A sinking feeling plunged in her stomach as Isabel lowered her weight to her desk.

Her picture crowned the front page. In gaudy typography, the headline said: *Runaway Princess accepted a prince's offer and eloped with a viscount.*

Her eyes blinked rapidly, and a sob escaped her mouth. A heaviness expanded from her chest to her limbs. She forced herself to keep reading, even though her mind wanted to collapse.

"Princess Isabel de Orleans shed her morality as one exchanges the winter wardrobe. A summer spent in sin, financed by the public coffers."

Luis would set it to rights. The dreadful news hadn't been published yet. He had to. Had he not promised to hunt all the drakes in the lake so the hens could be left unperturbed when she was ten? Had he not ruffled her hair when she scraped her knees and listened to her music performances when she knew he wanted to be outside? Her arms ached to hug him and ask him to make it better.

Isabel sped through the corridors on the way to the music room. The queen and her ladies blocked the way. Isabel halted, her cheeks burning with mortification.

One of the ladies noticed her presence, and their dithering ceased. All eyes turned to Isabel. Forcing her chin up, she shuffled past them without meeting their superior gazes. Whispers of horrible Italian terms like *puttana* and *vergogna* followed her inside.

A stale silence pervaded the room. Her brother sat on his worn leather chair, the cello resting by his right side, his golden head bent.

Her heart leaped. A cry escaped her throat, and she raced to him.

He stood and raised his hand before she could reach him, his expression granite hard.

Isabel halted, her hopes crashing like a bird flying straight at a glass window.

"Is it true?" His voice was harsh.

Her cheeks burned under his scrutiny. She exhaled, and the air abraded her airways. "Not all of it."

"Which parts of it then? The affair with Penafiel? The trysts with that puppy Alfonso? The pagan revelry in the palace garden?" His face became red.

Isabel brushed away a stray tear. "The journalist distorted everything. I fell in love with Henrique—"

"I don't care to hear how my best friend seduced you." He flung the newspaper at the hearth and turned his back on her. For several seconds he gazed at the fire, his chest rising and falling irregularly.

"Please, Luis, you must understand--"

When he faced her, all traces of anger were gone. He adjusted his ruby studs and speared her with a demeaning stare. "I sent you to defuse a crisis, and you caused a scandal of geopolitical magnitude."

Isabel's chest caved at the cold reprimand. She would rather have the brother's anger than the king's displeasure.

The trip had turned into a disaster, but Luis had sent her there. Even knowing Canastra was a blackguard. "Your Majesty is right. I shouldn't have gone to Spain. It certainly wasn't my idea."

"The diplomatic mission was above your capabilities." He lifted his eyebrows, his mouth pressed into an unforgivable line.

Diplomatic mission? For whom? Luis only cared about his own skin. The realization pierced her in the chest. Her own brother and king. Isabel closed her eyes. "I know about the letters," she said, hating the weakness of her voice. "He blackmailed you, didn't he? So you sent me there, not knowing what his plans were. How could you?"

His mouth gaped, giving him the appearance of a bull fish. Glancing away from her, he brushed his nose. "The pressures of the throne, my popularity, I couldn't—You won't speak of it again. I forbid it."

"I was a pawn in Canastra's schemes to destroy Portugal, and you won't talk about it?"

"Talking won't make a difference. Our borders are already under martial law, and I swear, if the Bourbon tries to breach our Torres Vedras, I will lead the troops myself." He used a high pitch, a bravado she knew too well. He then pushed away from the mantel and went to the altar. Bending forward, he placed his forehead at the Saint's feet. "It's this curse. Perhaps an enemy gunshot will end my torment."

When he had spoken about the Braganza's curse in the past, she always felt sorry for him, but now, she could see it for what it was—another attempt to manipulate her feelings.

"Sheath your sword. Your wife will endure you for many years. Alfonso won't invade."

He straightened, a frown forcing his pale brows to meet atop his nose. "Impossible."

Isabel dropped onto the couch, her legs still tired from the journey. "I went to his frigate and convinced him of a monarch's honor. Alfonso craves stability and a chance to return home. Now that he sits on the throne, he doesn't need Canastra's schemes."

"Thank God." Luis sprawled by her side and closed his eyes.

The anger and worry visibly lifted from her brother's shoulders. He had denied her brotherly comfort, but she still needed the king's support. Only Dom Luis could salvage her reputation. He could speak with the newspaper owner and forbid the publication. "Will you summon the journalist here? Threaten him with libel?"

He tugged at his collar and looked away.

"You won't allow them to publish it, will you?"

"My interference won't matter. Do you think I can stop the dreadful pennies? The gossip will spread like wildfire."

The air left her lungs in a rush, and she grabbed his arm. "Then stand by me. The Society of Catholic Ladies' lunch is tomorrow. The gossip will die if you appear by my side and vouch for my character."

He tapped her hand affectionately. "The ministers called an emergency meeting yesterday. They forbade me to link myself to the scandal."

Scandal? If she had not spoken with Alfonso, they would have faced much worse. Isabel removed the flag from her reticule and passed it to him. "I gave you back your throne. Now I need you to give me back my reputation."

He eyed Portugal's colors as if she had presented him with a shroud. "The situation has been unstable. I cannot risk my popularity. I'm sorry, Bel."

Ice coursed through her veins, and she froze. Would he allow her to be vilified? Tears streamed down her eyes. "But I can't live here like this. I can't—"

She had already lost too much.

"You won't have to. I wired Aunt Rita in Bavaria. The court there is less rigid. At least until the scandal fades."

The scandal wouldn't fade. Not if the king turned his back on her and she escaped to a distant principality. It would be a declaration of guilt. The harsh winters, living among strangers... She could endure all. But never seeing Henrique again?

She clutched the flag to her chest, her voice a strangled whisper. "Don't ask this of me, please."

He placed his arm above her shoulder. It would have been better if he had kept his royal distance. The warmth of his touch hurt.

"Can you do this for me? For our country?"

Chapter 41

"I have seen only you, I have admired only you, I desire only you." Napoleon Bonaparte

Henrique swirled the port in his glass and eyed his friends. If they thought it strange he was drinking at ten in the morning, they wisely kept their silence. Pedro and Griffin exchanged worried looks. A fishy breeze lifted the cloth from the squalid table. The dockside tavern was a shitty place to say goodbye, except he had not invited them. Henrique glared at Dio, who had not only seen fit to ask their presence to cast him off but had also bought tickets to accompany him to London. As if he needed a babysitter, a bearded and overgrown one at that.

He sat facing the ocean. The city and everything in it stood behind him, and he wouldn't spare it a single glance. Still, the back of his neck burned. It was her. Isabel. The princess at the white palace atop the hill, her very own Olympus.

His luggage had been dispatched to the shipping company before the blasted trip to Spain, and he couldn't wait to join his stuff. What time was it anyway? When he retrieved his pocket watch, he touched Isabel's medal. Why hadn't he disposed of it? He told himself the journey had been rushed. He came to the docks straight from the road.

Charles zigzagged to the table and dissolved into a chair. His complexion had a green sheen, and his red hair was matted. That's what the human female did to its male counterpart, Henrique thought disgustingly.

Behind a lady's sweet looks and gentle caresses hid the ruthlessness of a mantis. They wooed the male with a single goal—chop off his head and feast over his brains. That wasn't fair of him. Comparing women with insects. The mantis was actually merciful, its technique fast and painless. What the human female did was much worse. She sucked the male's marrow and released his breathing carcass into the world.

Dio smiled nervously. "What a superlative day for sailing, don't you think? It invigorates a Portuguese to have the Tramontane wind blowing his coattails."

Henrique glared at his cup. "It is not the Tramontane. It's the Mistral. The day is only superlative in its dismalness. The sun is dismal, the cackle of the gulls is dismal, and this old rickety port is dismal."

Isabel's medal pulsed inside his coat, and he curbed the impulse to hurl it into the ocean.

Pedro clasped Henrique's shoulder and stared into his eyes. "Mozambique robbed us of too much. Never doubt you deserve happiness. Sometimes the best battle strategy is to lower the six-pounders and negotiate."

Griffin exhaled and pulled his eyebrows to his hairline. "This is pointless, Almoster. I told you. Our Dom Juan here isn't in love. Let him go in peace. Husbands from Lisbon to Oporto will enjoy the respite."

Henrique glared at the pretentious Englishman. Unable to come up with a suitable retort, he took another swig of port. He had loved Isabel like Paris loved Helen, like a peasant loves his wife, like a king loves his queen. But it was not enough. She loved her country better. Her duty.

Henrique tugged his neckcloth, cursing the propriety that was ever at odds with the climate. "Are you done meddling? Go back to your wives. I'm ghastly company today."

They ignored him, and a discussion erupted between the well-meaning bastards, with Charles offering a drunken ditty or two. Henrique covered his face with his hands and groaned. His black heart was a vessel of port and emptiness, lashing out, never settling. If there was an Entity above, he hoped It would shut up the noises and allow him to drown his sorrows in peace.

Dio raised his voice above the others. "Gentlemen, he can stay, or he can leave. If he stays, he should go after her. If he leaves, he should forget about her. Either way, he must snap out of this humdrum."

Henrique slapped his drink on the table, sloshing the liquid over the scarred wood. His breaths came in short bursts. "They can speak about it, but you cannot, Diomedes. This is all your fault. You and your myths. I embraced your hero's quest. I saved the country, and I brought back the riches. By all accounts, I should be living in heavenly bliss. Do I sound blissful to you? Because to me, it feels like hell."

Dio raked his finger through his blond curls. "Every hero needs to go through hell. Hercules had to enter Hades' realm to retrieve Cerberus. Dante had to search the *inferno* for his Beatriz. Only after the hero faces hell does he learn to be selfless and value what matters. Life is like a river—passion is the water, and duty is the rocky riverbed. Without the riverbed, water sloshes away in aimless pursuits. Without water, the riverbed is just a lonely, dry path."

"Stop. Not another word."

The ship's horn sounded. Henrique pushed to his feet as if bullet-ants had targeted his arse for their lunch. Briskly, he shook his friends' hands and boarded the steamer. Dio shadowed his steps, but Henrique ignored him.

The hours to cast off could not pass soon enough, and he paced the quarter-deck from aft to port and back, his speed increasing at each turn. His legs were charged as if voltaic batteries were strapped to the soles of his feet. He caught the pocket watch for the tenth time and cursed when he saw less than fifteen minutes had passed.

He tried to focus on the fish darting around the pilings, the masts reaching into the sky, the gulls flying overhead, but his eyes, damn their ocular muscles, always found the palace uphill. An Olympus guarded by milky white clouds. He bet she was there now, circled by her devoted ladies, bathing in men's blood and extolling all the advantages of choosing duty and trampling his heart.

With a groan and a tug, the ship cast its moors. The ropes were pulled taut and then released. The droning sound of the steam engine vibrated inside his ears and empty chest.

Dio put himself in his way. "Won't you go to the machine room? The first mate told me it has a hybrid converter, brand new."

Henrique wrestled his gaze from the palace and strode aft. "She robbed me of this as well."

"Are you sure science is your vocation? You should try the stage. You would displace Sarah Bernhardt with your dramatic streak."

Henrique glared at Dio. "If you are so offended by my performance, why are you following me?"

Dio threw his hands in the air and scoffed. "You wish to know why I follow you?"

"I believe it was exactly what I asked." Henrique grabbed the railings, his heart accelerating painfully with each yard the ship gained against the current.

Dio took a step closer, his eyes blazing. "I follow you now, just as I've done since we met. With you, I've drunk more in a night than Bacchus in a revelry. I've crossed frigid waters and the limits of morality. I'm here because you supported me when my family turned their back on me, and well, black sheep should flock together. And it's getting harder, I must admit, but I'm here because I care for your miserable hide. Because of all the men I've known, you are the most brilliant, and the most stubborn, the bravest—and the least willing to confront his demons. You are generous with your friendship, your money, your vast knowledge—but you are awfully selfish with your heart. So for Christ's sake, take your face out of your arse. Isabel didn't leave you because she wanted to spite you or because she loves you less than you love her. She left to avoid war."

Henrique shook his head, shutting his eyes with enough force to bury his eyelashes in the skin below.

Dio grabbed his arm. "Stop pacing for a second. Would she be the woman you admire if she had allowed Alfonso to sail without trying to convince him to desist?"

An anguished howl burst from Henrique's throat. "Don't you think I know all this? It's eating my insides and messing up with my legs so I cannot stay still. I screwed up. There's no other word for it." He knew the instant Pedro left the tower, he had made a colossal mistake, and it was killing him. The Isabel he loved wouldn't always sacrifice their love for duty, but he could depend on her to always do what was right. "I'm a blackguard."

"And she is a brilliant, courageous woman. No better consort for my Portuguese hero..."

Dio went on speaking, but Henrique ignored the words. One passenger leaned against the railing and opened a newspaper.

As if Henrique had conjured the image, Isabel's picture stared at him from the black and white page. His thoughts scattered.

He grabbed the sheet and barked when the owner objected.

Dio grinned. "I knew you two blockheads were fated to be together. When we arrive in Liverpool, I'll help you write the perfect love letter to soothe my little surrogate sister's temper. A few of my inspired verses will wipe out your desertion."

Henrique shoved the newspaper on his friend's chest and removed his coat. His shoes came next.

Dio's mouth gaped open. "You can't mean to swim back. It is at least half a mile against the current."

"We've swum longer."

Dio shaded his eyes, glancing at the port. "The river is frigid and fast. The ocean tide is rising, and the Tagus is treacherous in the high tide."

Henrique stood with feet braced apart, eyes focused on the palace. "We've crossed the Hellespont."

"You will lose your position in Oxford. The dean threatened to hire a replacement if you didn't arrive in one week."

"There are chairs in other universities."

"She might never forgive you."

"She shouldn't. You are right. I'm a selfish ass, but I cannot allow her to be ruined."

Dio nodded, his eyes conspicuously humid. "Spoken like a true hero." He leaned over the railings and eyed the Tagus churning beneath them. "There's nothing to it, just water and fish. I'm coming with you."

Henrique shook his head. "You helped me this far. This I'll have to do on my own."

Henrique hugged his friend tightly and pounded his back with hearty slaps. He pulled away from him, holding him at arm's length, and fished inside his pocket. After opening Dio's palm, he placed Isabel's medal atop it. There wasn't a worthier recipient.

"What's this?"

"A recognition for services rendered to your country and to this ornery mule. Thank you, Diomedes da Veiga. I could not hope for a better friend."

Dio brushed the back of his hand over his eyes. "What will you do?"

"I'm needed at the palace. Duty calls, so to speak."

The sun shone brightly, coloring the Tagus with a brilliant green. What a lovely day to grow up. With a parting glance at Dio, he focused on Mount Olympus and leaped.

Henrique flung the door to the dispatch room and sloshed inside. His clothes had dried up during the Americano tram ride from Belem to the Ajuda Palace. Still, his shoeless feet left wet prints on the parquet.

"Sir, the king is occupied." The secretary placed himself in Henrique's way.

Henrique sidestepped the scrawny sycophant. "He will make time for old friends, won't you, Luis?"

The king sat in his customary chair. A Goliath-sized man faced him, feathers and elaborate shells decorating his head. By his attire, he was a Mozambique chieftain.

The secretary lifted his palms, his face flushed. "Sire, I tried to prevent his excellency from barging in, but—"

"Fine, João, escort the Nkosi outside."

Both men left, the secretary closing the door silently.

Luis chuckled. "Can you believe the chieftain asked me for a cannon and a six-pounder? Shoot crocodiles, he said he wants. Says the nasty animals are a plague in the Zambezi River."

"They are called Crocodylus Niloticus, and they are not a plague. He probably wants the guns to blow up his neighboring tribe. I'm here to talk about Isabel."

"By the saints, man, lower your voice. I'm trying to avert a scandal and keep our friendship, but if you assume your deeds, I will have no alternative but to—"

"Export her like an unwanted commodity?"

"What do you suggest I do? You ruined her, didn't you?"

Henrique looked into Luis' eyes. "I took her maidenhead, yes. But if you imply that a man can ruin a woman of Isabel's caliber with his dick, then you are inflating our masculinity. It would take much more than a cock to ruin Isabel, but since I read in the newspaper that she is, indeed, ruined, then it was another instrument wielded by males—a crown."

"How dare you?" Luis' voice became high-pitched. "I sent you to Spain to protect her, and you seduced her, my own sister."

"You plunged her into a viper's nest."

Luis' face became blotched. "I had no choice."

Henrique took a shaky breath. He wanted to punch the king's head until there would be no hope of removing his blasted crown. But violence would serve only his temper. To help Isabel, he needed to use politics, not his fists.

"You have a choice now. You can go there and tell the press, the court, what Isabel did. Tell them she saved the country from a senseless war. Tell them she sacrificed her—her reputation for the country."

The king flushed, and a glimmer of sadness flickered in his pale gray eyes. If he didn't know the man for over twenty-five years, he might call it indigestion. "I can't. She tied up my hands. The reporter had pictures... The queen and the ministers put their differences aside and aligned in this. They strongly opposed me linking myself to her. It would reduce my popularity—"

"Forget about those idiots who hail themselves as ministers. Be a man, for Christ's sake, and protect your sister. She did the same for you."

"Not everyone can flaunt rules like the *bon vivant* Henrique Penafiel. Some of us have obligations to the country. If only you were a patriot—"

"If being a patriot means sacrificing a hero for public appearances, then I don't want to be a patriot. If this country, the country of Camões, of Vasco da Gama, of Eça de Queiroz, of The Avis Dynasty, will burn a true hero, it does not deserve my patriotism."

"Isabel accepted the need for exile. Tomorrow, she leaves to stay with our aunt in Germany."

His insides rebelled, and his hands turned into fists. Henrique had hoped Luis would prove honorable. But *pundonor* was in short supply these days. Henrique nodded, and as if he didn't have a care in the world, he strolled to the altar.

Luis watched him, his face tilted to the side.

Henrique dusted the image's feet and lit the single candle. "Really, Luis, you shouldn't neglect Saint John. He might never remove the curse."

Dom Luis eyed him with unease.

"Wouldn't offering candles and prayers directly to the offended friar's grave be more effective?"

"My mother, my grandfather. They spent their lives searching for the friar's mausoleum without luck."

"Is that so? Then this is your lucky day."

Luis stopped breathing.

Henrique removed seaweed from his soggy shirt. "I have the location of the friar's resting place."

The king went pale. "Impossible."

"It was with the letters from your Spanish mistress. Canastra didn't want to take any chances with your manipulation. Shrewd of him. Placing you between the cross and the bed, so to speak."

"Damn it, Henrique. Show more respect."

Henrique shrugged. "You want to save your future heirs? I'm more than happy to oblige. But first, you will rescue Isabel."

The king hesitated for three seconds, and then he nodded.

Henrique grinned, already turning to leave. "Always a pleasure doing business with you. Expect the location as soon as I get hold of my luggage. It might take a while, but then, the friar is not going anywhere. After two hundred years, I dare say he enjoys holding a grudge."

"What, then, you will run and tell her? Isabel asked me to protect her yesterday, and I... I had to deny her."

"You are her hero. Let's keep it so."

Luis clasped his hand. "You didn't ask, you arrogant blackguard, but you have my blessings."

Chapter 42

"Time, as it grows old, teaches all things." Aeschylus, *Prometheus Bound*

"I'm going with you," Lady Filipa said, holding the mirror so Isabel could apply rouge to her face. "You can't face the Catholic ladies alone."

When Isabel inspected the results, her shoulders sagged. The two red circles above her cheeks made her pallor more noticeable.

Isabel put the makeup away. "No. It would taint you if you stood by me now. I won't allow you to be ruined."

Even with all the windows closed, a chillness pervaded her bedchamber. The chests lined up to cart her belongings made the once cheerful space gloomy.

Philipa lowered the mirror to the dressing table and smoothed her lavender gown. Dressed in mourning tones and with her hair pulled up unmercifully from her circular face, she seemed older than her twenty-two years. Was it Isabel's fault she had matured before her time? Her impossible demands of morality? And all for what?

Philipa bit her lip. "If I had gone with you, I would've prevented you from—"

"Falling in love?" Isabel doubted. Henrique and her were like *torero* and *toro*, racing on the opposite sides of an arena. The impact had been fated. And if she was honest with herself, she didn't regret meeting him and being privy to his brilliance and outrageous humor. She could not regret allowing him to see her without her carapace. And she couldn't regret the memories of the tower. No, those she would keep to warm her during the long, cold winters in Bavaria.

Sighing, Philipa leaned closer, and a new light appeared in her caramel eyes. "Do you think you might forget him?"

"I don't know." So far, she had failed miserably.

She had tried to forget him when she was angry. She tried to forget him when she was sad. She tried when despondent, when irritable, when frustrated, when irrational... She didn't try it when happy... The occasion didn't present itself. Since she left the tower, happiness had been elusive.

With the suaveness of a raging bull, he had hacked a place inside her chest. The cavity was only furnished by his presence. In fact, it was only lit, aired, perfumed, adorned, and filled with laughter when he was near. When he was far, it was empty. And the emptiness hurt.

"It is time." Anne Daun glided inside, a confident smile lighting up her face.

Isabel embraced her friend. "Are you sure you want to do this?"

Anne nodded. "My husband's reputation is enough to scare even the most prudish matron, dear. I won't leave your side."

Isabel nodded, her throat clogged with tears. Together, they moved to the morning room. Midway, she paused, her stomach churning.

She should have canceled the Catholic Ladies' gathering. Her ears burned, and she feared she was not strong enough to face the disapproval lined in their eyes.

Anne pressed her hand and gave her a firm nod.

When the footman opened the door, the conversation skittered to a halt. The gloomy day made the blue silk covering the walls a sickly gray. The candelabra was unlit, casting spider-like shadows over the assembly. At least the fear that the women would not appear had been unfounded. The room was crowded.

All her other fears were genuine. The ladies had dressed in black, with mantillas hiding their hair. Murmured disapproval rose in waves and circled the room.

The austerity would have pleased Isabel before. Now, more than the shame at their resentful stares, she felt sorry. Sorry for making it fashionable to reside inside a carapace. Never realizing the carapace brought no protection, no contentment, just a self-inflicted restriction that strangled happiness and true freedom. All her life, she had wanted to be an example for women, and now that she knew the kind of role model she wished to be, she had become a pariah. Mothers would turn her story into a cautionary tale, forcing young ladies further into their carapaces.

Their agenda for the meeting was to increase the orphanage's funding. Still, when the Duchess of Beira rose, requesting permission to speak, Isabel knew the reprimands would start and cringed at the disgust written on the older woman's harsh features.

Before the duchess could utter the first disparaging comment, the door opened. All seats were occupied. Who might it be?

Luis entered the room, his marshal's uniform gleaming as if illuminated by an inner light. The crowd hushed.

He was so handsome when he wanted to be, so regal. He strode across the room and stood behind Isabel. The doors were flung open, and several courtiers, diplomats, and ministers thronged the space. Even the queen and her Italian retinue came. The women tittered in their seats as if they needed to go to the water closet, sighs of admiration bursting from their parted lips.

A heavy hand, her brother's hand, settled over her shoulder. It was all she could do not to crumble. Slowly, she realized what he came to do, and she sagged against the chair, glad for the layers of whalebone and stiff cloth holding her upright.

His voice rose in the most pleasant bass, and he spoke strong words like 'mistake, above reproach, vouch for her reputation, our very own hero'. If it all sounded a little farcical, she guessed it was only to her practiced ears. The ladies in the room sighed and glanced at her at all the appropriate pauses.

Luis' peeked at the door. She looked in the same direction, and there she saw him. Just a flash, but he was there. Henrique. Her heart halted for five seconds and then squished painfully. She didn't expect to see him again, and there he was, more handsome than Zeus.

The king stopped speaking. The room burst into applause. In a trance, Isabel allowed her brother to pull her to her feet.

Isabel pressed his hand. "Thank you."

He kissed her cheek and bowed, then moved back graciously. The Duchess of Beira hugged her, and a queue of courtiers awaited to congratulate her.

She had come full circle from a persona non grata to a national hero, yet she could not muster the will to care. All that mattered was reaching the brooding male at the fringes of the salon.

Isabel went to her toes and started to make way among the crush of people, absently nodding and smiling. When she finally arrived at the door, he was no longer there.

Chapter 43

"I am not afraid of the darkness. Real death is preferable to a life without living." Vasco da Gama

T he well-wisher's words barely grazed her conscience. The sounds of laughter, claps, and clicking glasses were muffled. Isabel couldn't process what had happened, her brother's change of heart, her change of fortune, what it all meant. All that pierced the fog clouding her thoughts was that Henrique was in the palace and that she must find him. On rubbery legs, she disengaged herself from the throng. She knew where he would be.

The secret door gaped open. Instead of moonlight spilling from the glass panels, sunshine warmed the carpet above the threshold. Isabel halted, waiting for every part of her to catch up—the princess, the woman, the warrior, the peasant, the timid and the bold, the moral and the passionate.

Collecting all the pieces of herself, she crossed into the garden.

A soft breeze ruffled the grass and the daffodils. The sky was the blue of myth. The pond reflected the acacias, a mirror for dragonflies. Heart speeding, she scanned the willows.

Henrique sat among the flower beds, his back to her, an arm flung over his knee. Warmth radiated from her chest, a burst of energy so strong it dazzled everything that was not him. Weak, dizzy with relief, with joy, she lowered her weight by his side. She held to the grass blades, restraining herself from curling close to him, from tasting the sun on his lips.

"It was you," she whispered.

"No, it was—" He didn't finish. He raked his fingers through his hair and kept his gaze on the lake. Then he sighed. "No more lies. Yes, I spoke to Luis. But we agreed he wouldn't tell you."

She peeked at him, and her breath caught. Not only had he saved her from scandal, but he also had planned to keep it a secret. He did it selflessly, not trying to gain her favor. Instead, he had tried to protect her image of her older brother. For that, he had been too late. Luis had already shattered her trust. "Thank you."

Was that why he came? To shield her from scandal? Her chin dipped down, and she took a shuddering breath, her throat clogged by unspoken words. Did the invisible threads bonding them die? Now, a rift was in its place, filled with uncomfortable silences and unshed tears. Pain bloomed in her chest, exquisitely acute, the pain of being close and unable to touch. Cleaning up her tears, she shifted to leave.

He held her hand. Isabel stopped breathing. He turned to look at her for the first time, and the emotion she saw in his blue eyes drowned her. The bond shimmered into life, snapping into place, thread after thread.

She opened her mouth to speak, and her words collided with his.

He touched her lips, silencing her. "I'm a selfish bastard. Forgive me?"

"I love you, too." A laughing sob escaped her throat, and she flung her arms around his neck. "I should have said it before I left, and it's been choking me ever since."

He pulled her into his lap. Isabel kissed him desperately, holding both sides of his face to keep herself grounded in reality, afraid he would vanish.

"Shh. I'm here now. I won't leave you again."

The excitement, the travel, the dread, the fear of losing him, of war, crashed down on her, and she cried against his neck. He massaged her back in the soothing way she loved so well.

"My brave, beautiful princess. My fierce Joan of Arc."

"I'm not fierce, and the heavens know I'm not brave. When I had to leave you, it was the hardest thing I've ever done. It tore me in two."

He cleaned her tears and kissed the top of her nose. "You showed me patriotism comes in different shapes. Canastra's patriotism is greed for power. Luis' is self-interest. For Pedro Daun, it is love, but not for the country. To Alfonso—"

"I know you hate him, but he loves Spain. I convinced him to desist by appealing to his *pundonor*."

Henrique kissed her fingers. "His *pundonor* is another name for vanity and pride. Do you know who is the only being I know who possesses true *pundonor*?"

Isabel shook her head.

"You." Before she could reply, he caressed her cheek. "It wouldn't be a sacrifice if it didn't hurt."

Isabel closed her eyes and nodded. Nestling in Henrique's arms, she exhaled a contented sigh. She had never allowed herself to consider a future with him. But now, the possibilities opened to them, and she rolled them over in her mouth, savoring their taste. Tart, forbidden, their improbability was the stuff of myths, legends, and quests for king and country. She decided she rather liked it. Yes, she would keep him. It would unleash hell on their heads—her brother would be against it, even Parliament. The press might condemn the alliance. Let them try to separate them—she was more than ready for this fight.

Then she sat up straight. "What about your plans to leave Portugal? Your desire to be valued for your scientific work? I couldn't forgive myself if—"

"Some prudish princess showed me I love Portugal, and if I'm not recognized for my work as a scientist, then the work will have to be reward enough." He shrugged and grinned one of her beloved Henrique's smiles.

She brushed her nose against the folds of his shirt and caught a distinct smell of brine. Only then did she notice his state of undress. No shoes, no coat. "Why are you wet?"

"I came from the river."

"You swam the Tagus?"

He nodded, looking smug, gorgeous, and none the worse for the dunk.

She glared at his unrepentant face. "You could've been killed. Turned into food for the fish." Or worse, for a saucy fisherwoman.

"Nonsense. What would happen if the hero refused the call of duty? How many delicious princesses would fall prey to hungry mythological creatures? I could not allow it, could I? Those creatures from myth are notorious for their bad digestion, and princesses are too difficult to swallow."

Laughing, she swatted his arm. "I will let this pass, just this once, mind you, since a Tagus crossing will be a delightful addition to our myth."

"What myth?"

"The myth of our courtship, of course. Our grandchildren will be entranced by the perils and adventures I endured to save the country and gain the heart of the most handsome male in the kingdom." She tapped her chin. "Hmm, what should I call it? *Isassey*, like Homer's *Odyssey*, or *Isabelyad?*

"Impudent wench. You will steal all the credit?" He slapped her buttocks.

Isabel squealed. "How dare you slap the royal rump, sir?"

He tackled her to the ground, rolling atop her. Her back met the grass, unleashing the rich scent of wet earth. After sleeping so many nights alone, his weight was delicious, precious, and warm.

Grinning, his blue eyes crinkling at the corners, and he tugged the hem of her dress, exposing her stockings to the elements. "You are right. I'd much rather kiss it."

They laughed and tasted each other's lips, and then he cradled her face. "Before we embarked on our adventure to Spain, I was drifting. Life had become a pleasure ride. From the first day I met you, you've put me on a track toward something. I thought it was Dio's idea of a hero's quest. It was not. You brought meaning to my life, Isabel. Do you know what is the truth about myths? People don't need myths to give meaning to their lives when they have love."

"A princess lives to inspire." Her eyes filled with tears, and she grinned. "All my life, I feared the only way to defeat death was to live a life of duty, leaving a legacy for others. Now, the only person I wish to live my life for is you."

He kissed her, a kiss to seal fates. They rolled playfully, their bodies renewing their acquaintance. When Isabel wrestled her weight atop him, caging her arms above his head, her hip bumped into something stiff.

It was a gift box. The rickety wood had two holes above it and a bow made of twine.

"What is inside?"

Blushing, Henrique tried maneuvering her away from the gift. "It's nothing."

Isabel lifted herself from atop him and kneeled over the grass. She poked the box, and an angry shuffling came from inside.

Henrique looped his arm around his bent knee and, lowering his chin to his chest, he gazed at her from below his eyelashes. "I enlisted help in case I had trouble securing your forgiveness."

Heart speeding, Isabel opened the lid and gasped. Two downy creatures, not larger than her tiara, lifted their beaks in unison, staring at her through beady black eyes. "You brought me a couple of ugly ducklings?"

Henrique reached inside the box and scooped them in his hands. Gently, he placed them on the grass and pushed them in the pond's direction like a mother hen. While they watched the chicks waddle to the pond, the sunset glinting through their gray feathers, Henrique pecked her cheek.

"They are not ducks."

Startled, Isabel looked at eyes so blue as to be transparent. They hid nothing from her beyond an invitation to dive into its depths. Luckily, she now knew how to swim.

"No?"

"They are swans, and swans mate for life." He kneeled at her feet and kissed the back of her hand. "Princess Isabel de Orleans, will you marry me?"

Chapter 44

"Until you spread your wings, you'll have no idea how far you can fly." Napoleon Bonaparte

S ix months later...

The last rays of the sun touched the university tower as the bell tolled at the end of the sixth class. Through her bedchamber window, Isabel watched students flocking about the square, their black mantles flowing behind them like raven wings. With a sigh, she closed the shutter. Henrique would return home, and she had made no progress. On Tuesdays, he had fewer classes and never stayed at the laboratory later than six in the afternoon. The scent of spring clung to the city's ocean breeze, and soon, they would move to England for the season. Not that they were not proud of Henrique's position here. Coimbra was every bit as prestigious as Oxford. The oldest school in Europe, founded by her ancestor, King Diniz, in the thirtieth century. But Henrique was eager to expose the results of his research in Britain, and she would love to meet her royal cousins and show off her scientist husband.

"Come, Sophie, let's get this done."

The maid eyed the new garment with distaste and shook it from the box. The dressmaker's craftmanship was superb, Isabel had to admit. Form-fitting, the tailored jacket was made of striped tweed lined with black silk. The problem was the cycling skirt. If she could call it that.

"Are you sure you wish to wear it, Your Highness?"

"Sophie, when I was a princess, you balked at calling me Your Highness... But now that I'm no longer one, you decide to use the honorific." As a blessing to the marriage, her brother had granted them the title of Duke and Duchess of Braganza. At first, she feared she had robbed Fernando's legacy. But Henrique believed her late brother would be happy if his lineage were kept alive. Even Pedro Daun, who had been Fernando's closest friend, had written to her saying that after the courage she showed in Spain, he could not think of a better bearer of Fernando's name.

The maid huffed. "Your Highness will always be a royal princess to me. But a trouser?"

Isabel sighed. "Ladies want to try the bicycles, but long skirts make it unsafe. Many had accidents when their hems caught in the chain."

Sophie seemed resigned as she helped Isabel fasten the new garment over her waist. "I never knew Your Highness to be interested in bikes."

Isabel watched her reflection in the mirror. The bloomers, as the English called it, had no excess cloth, making her feel naked.

"I'm not. But I have the means to keep a landau, a vis-à-vis, coachmen, and four carriage horses waiting for my pleasure. What about the thousands of women who don't have the same privilege? The bicycle provides them with a respectable form of transportation."

It gave women freedom. And free women were happy women.

The door swung inwards, and Henrique strolled inside her dressing room.

Her heart sped, and she grinned. "Don't you ever knock?"

"It would be contra-productive, now, would it not?"

"Why is that?"

"If my goal is to glimpse you in dishabille, knocking would ruin the surprise factor."

Sophie blushed furiously and, muttering in French, hurried out of the room.

"What are you wearing?"

"These are bicycle bloomers. Do you approve?"

"Absolutely not."

"Why?"

He took his hat off and flung it. It sailed and landed perfectly on the peg. He removed his gloves and great coat and moved slowly towards her. A frisson started in her belly at his nonchalant approach.

"Like all libertines, I am extremely conservative. Are you ready to start a scandal? I can see the headlines. Duchess of Braganza is seen flaunting her derrière in Coimbra's main street."

"It's for a worthy cause." She swatted his arm and watched her reflection, twisting this way and that.

Was it really so scandalous?

He placed his brawny arms around her and kissed her neck. Their eyes met in the mirror.

Playfulness gone, he became serious. "Your effort is commendable. I'm sure when you wear these"—he placed both hands over her hips—"they will become fashionable."

After their marriage, she had regained her popularity and even increased it. "Thank you."

"I'm not finished." He bit her earlobe. "I love a juicy scandal. If you wish to make a Godiva-like tour around the palace, I will be in the front row as you cycle buck naked. But I don't want you to do anything that makes you uncomfortable."

How did he do it? Make her love him even more? Her heart was about to burst with love already, yet he surprised her at every turn. Be it by making her laugh when she felt gloomy or supporting her when she didn't know she needed support.

"I love you."

He grinned. "Does that mean you will bicycle in the nude? For my eyes only?"

"Not a chance," she said against his lips and brought him in for an open-mouthed kiss.

He circled his arms around her and cupped her derrière. The absence of petticoats and crinoline made contact much more satisfying. The new clothing certainly had its merits. Isabel moaned as his hardness connected with her core and ground against him, letting her body speak its needs.

He removed the breeches, and soon they were both naked and straining against each other. He threw her playfully on the bed. With a dramatic sigh, he jumped by her side, shaking the mattress and scattering the pillows.

"Come, wife, let's see how you ride. You will need to awe the ladies into adopting the bicycles. Or at least not to fall flat on your arse."

Isabel bit his chest.

"What?" He caressed her curves, tugging her atop him until she straddled him. "I'm terribly fond of your royal rump."

She lowered herself to his hardness. Pulling her hair over her shoulder, she splayed her hands over his chest, relishing his rippling muscles.

He lengthened inside her, and her mouth opened as languid pleasure sluiced inside her. She nibbled his bottom lip. He groaned, and his hands traveled from the indenture of her waist to her hips. He caressed her derrière with a light touch, sending tingles dancing down her spine, and then he touched where their bodies were joined.

Holding her hips, he pressed her down, forward, and backward. Her mouth opened in a wordless O, and he traced her lips, his touch like a drop of water in the desert. She closed her lips and sucked his fingertip.

He lifted his hips. "Move, Isabel, take all your pleasure. I'm yours."

Isabel did.

Slowly at first, getting used to him. His broad chest and taut abdomen were too close for her to resist, and she leaned over him, caressing his nipples. She closed her eyes as the heat of him pulsed inside her. She could lose herself with him, drop her mask, and be Isabel. Her hands grabbed her own breasts. They were swollen and heavy, and she delighted in his heated looks. But it was not enough. She increased the tempo, grinding against him. Perspiration covered her brow, and she whimpered in frustration.

He touched her mound and spread her outer lips atop his hardness. She watched him, mesmerized by the place where their bodies joined.

"This is—it feels as if I'm conquering the world."

Henrique grinned, the rakish smile she loved. "I like it, too. I lay back and enjoy my bounty."

"Yes, my reposing rake."

Henrique frowned, grabbing her waist, and pressing down. "Reposing? Rampant is more likely. Perhaps it's time we changed our epithets... I don't think Prudish Princess will do, not for a lusty wench like yourself. What do you feel about Hungry Heroine?

Isabel laughed. "Comes to mind a paunchy Athena."

"I have the perfect one." He flipped her and came on top. "Love of my life."

When she started to tremble, he increased the tempo of his thrusts. His body loomed above her, and she embraced him, marveling at his strength. Only her hands felt like her own, exploring the ridges and sinews of his spine. He kissed her, a warm, open-mouthed kiss that murmured tenderness into her throat. He drove inside her, one, two times, and she burst, pleasure consuming her. The bonds that connected them turned strong and stronger still. Then he shouted his love so loud the Olympian Gods must have heard him.

Epilogue

Lisbon, Fall of 1873, Ajuda Palace, Prince John's Baptism

"The challenge which Hercules faced is still with each of us today — to wrestle with our limitations and the monsters within us, to overcome our flaws and failings and then, like Hercules, to go on and become something extraordinary." Philip Matyszak

Henrique led the all-male procession, exiting the palace's vestibule and emerging on a sunlit courtyard. The deafening cheer pierced his ears. Lisbon had come out en masse to fete their prince. They started gathering after the first cannon blast yesterday. And by the time the hail had reached ten, the salute reserved for a male firstborn, the streets became a revelry. The housemaids, the tanners, the shopkeepers, the port traders, the bakers, the sweeps. They all came, one after the other, some shyly, some loudly, some drunk, some sober, some gracious, some pushing, some bragging, some laughing.

Isabel had attended Queen Maria Pia's labor all night. By the message she sent him, the queen would have loved to witness the crown's renewed popularity. However, while she had recovered, she could not attend church as she was still impure, whatever that meant. Henrique couldn't understand the intricate costumes involved in a child's baptism. All to give the baby a name, and since it was born in a royal crib, it would be a mile long, and after the priest uttered it once, it would be forgotten.

Henrique shaded his eyes, trying to spot Isabel among the women's procession. They left the queen's apartments from the opposite side of the castle, and they would meet at the entrance to the chapel. He had spent thirteen days and seven hours away from his wife, and he shook from head to toe like a mooning adolescent. If only the train from Paris had not run late. He would have arrived the day before yesterday and made love to Isabel before this carnival. Instead, he had to stay with the king and his gentlemen, pouring liquor down their throats while the queen poured out the country's next king. A fair division of labor, he might add. As a result, he was randy, he was moody, and he was without a care for the senseless procedures about to take place.

Dio covered his eyes. "I shouldn't have sipped that last glass of port. It burned right through my stomach's coat."

The fault always rested in the last, not in the dozen first. "Then you better ready your stomach's waistcoat. It will be a long day."

Dom Luis's son squalled as he was carried to the chapel by his fussing father. The king had out-drunk and out-bragged all his gentlemen. Griffin had succumbed first, as he stubbornly refused to eat. Still, Dio, Pedro, and Henrique had fought tenaciously. To no avail. The gloating king had spent the entire night extolling the prowess of his manhood and the values of his firstborn. With a blazing smile on his ruddy face, not once did he speak of the curse. His relationship with the queen improved dramatically.

"Don't you love a christening? The ritual originated in the Middle Ages, from the myth of—"

"Save your breath, Dio."

Dio grinned. "What? I thought the godfather routine would inspire you to start a family."

"I already have a family." He and Isabel formed a perfect couple, mathematically, physiologically, and spiritually. Why would he want to spoil that?

Speaking of his family, where was she? Gravel crunched under feet as they kept their sedate pace. Would it be a breach of protocol if he burst out in a sprint?

When they turned at the fountain, the male procession came face to face with the ladies. She was there. Resplendent in an emerald dress, her hair swept up, a delicate diadem circling her head. Their eyes met. His heart drummed a fanfare. Her lips parted, and then the sweetest, loveliest smile lit up her face. Henrique released a pent-up breath. Had he breathed at all since he left her at the train station? Apparently not. A nagging voice inside his head worried she might realize her mistake when she chose him to marry. Now, it went blessedly quiet. She had missed him as well.

When they entered the palace's chapel, he could finally walk down the aisle by his wife's side. Henrique pulled her into an alcove and tasted her lips. His heart leaped when he felt her little mews and how her body melted against him.

"You smell like a barrel of port wine."

Henrique grinned. "I taste like one, too." Somehow, the retort sounded better in his head than said out loud.

She chuckled and adjusted his cravat with deft tugs of her competent hands. He wanted to do sinful things with those hands.

"Do you know what to do?"

He frowned, biting the inside of his cheek to smile. "Must godfathers do anything?"

She shot him a disgruntled stare.

"I have it right here." He removed a list from his pocket. "Place salt on the infant's lips, exorcize the devil, answer 'yes, the prince believes in God', dump said poor child in the water, dry him, return him to his father, make love to wife."

She smoothed down his lapels. "You are incorrigible."

"But you love me."

"Immensely. Now try to behave."

He entered the aisle, cradling his wife's arm in his, chest stuffed, his feet light. He wanted to shout to the court lining up the pews that, yes, this stunning, once-in-a-lifetime princess was his wife. When they arrived at the altar, he couldn't keep his eyes from her, his gaze traveling the freckles on her shoulder.

Santiago, his face overly red, cleared his throat. Even after ten years, Henrique still choked every time he saw his friend in the cassock. Santi fidgeted with the bell and rearranged the chalice several times. Henrique could not blame his nervousness. Performing a prince's baptism in front of his king, foreign dignitaries, and the whole Court of Portugal was no easy feat.

The king lifted the prince for all to see, and then, with liquid eyes, he passed the country's hope to Henrique's arms. By God, it was the size of a shoe. He had no recollection of babies being so small.

He gazed into the child's face. The prince's eyes had the color of opal stones. For a tense second, everything stilled, the choir, the *oohs* and *ahhs* of the old ladies, the crying of older children. Henrique could not breathe. He felt the child would speak to him, and worse, he wanted to hear his thoughts.

"Hello, little guy."

The prince grabbed his finger, and Henrique's chest squeezed. "If you ever want to learn about cars, and engines and bacteria, your uncle knows all about it. You will be good, won't you? Yes, you will, and if ever you need advice, I'll give you the gold location. Your aunt. She is the wisest woman I know."

Henrique's eyes met Isabel, and a tiny tear had made its way to the corner of her lips. When she smiled, the drop caught the light of a thousand candles.

"I love you," she mouthed.

When the wet nurse came closer, arms outstretched, he reluctantly relinquished the tiny package.

Isabel pulled her arm through his, and it was over. People started retreating from the chapel.

"Do you want to stay for the banquet?"

"Absolutely not." He placed her gloved hand above his forearm and directed her toward the palace. He knew of a shortcut to the secret garden.

"What do you wish to do?"

"Let's make a baby."

The End

Also by Giovanna Siniscalchi

The True Purpose of Vines

A headstrong Portuguese winemaker meets her match in an arrogant Englishman who threatens her beloved lands. When the wine plague strikes her vineyards, they put differences aside to find a cure, blind tasting their way into an intoxicating passion. "True Purpose of Vines - An intoxicating blend of romance, Portuguese history, and winemaking lore." *Kirkus reviews*
https://www.amazon.com/dp/B09W6CL8RQ

The Wedding Surprise

An overly rational Englishman attends his superior's wedding. When a meddling godfather risks the ceremony, he must ally with a passionate Portuguese to save the day. Can he put logic aside to embrace love? "When you stop following love, it follows you back... and it will meet you in the most unexpected manner. Witness the heartfelt and beautiful love story of Edmond and Elise from "The Wedding Surprise," a brilliant work of Giovanna Siniscalchi. A perfect bedtime read!!!" *The-BigReads*
Join my book club and download this delightful novella for free! https://BookHip.com/QNJCNVJ

The Taste Of Light

Pedro Daun, haunted by a secret past, seeks solace in his vineyard. Anne Maxwell, a dreamer with dawn in her eyes, arrives in the Douro hoping for love's embrace. Fate intertwines their destinies, placing them in a race against time and deceit. Love's complexities unravel, proving that even in the midst of conspiracy, redemption and forgiveness can bloom. Will Pedro let go of his past and allow Anne's light to guide him? Dive into a tale of intrigue, love, and the taste of light that can shine through even the darkest shadows. "Mind, body, and soul of characters like Jamie and Claire Fraser of Outlander." *The Historical Fiction Company*
https://www.amazon.com/dp/B0BMMBJD4B

Let's keep in touch!

Don't miss out on exclusive character photos, contests, updates, and more! Follow me on social media for all the latest news, behind-the-scenes glimpses, and a chance to connect with fellow readers. Let's embark on this exciting journey together!

https://linktr.ee/giovannasi niscalchi

Afterword

Dear readers,

I hope you enjoyed "The Truth About Myths." I'd like to provide some insights into the blend of historical fact and fiction that shapes the narrative. While the novel is a work of imagination, many elements are drawn from the rich tapestry of history that Portugal and Spain share.

The Braganza curse was a genuine belief, fueling superstitions and shaping the destiny of the royal line. The absence of a male heir to inherit the throne was indeed a prevailing notion, and history stands as a testament to the Braganza legacy.

The historical tug-of-war between Portugal and Spain for independence is an enduring backdrop. The crown's dance between countries echoes both nations' events and aspirations. Dom Luis's principled refusal of the Spanish crown is rooted in the very essence of Portugal's fight for autonomy.

Dom Alfonso XII's exile and eventual return to the Spanish throne are factual. After he became king, he married his cousin. The love match surprised and enchanted anyone who visited the Palacio Real in Madrid.

Isabel's spirited character is an homage to the remarkable princesses who wielded influence across Europe, shaping destinies amidst battles and intrigues. Henrique, in turn, finds his inspiration in the Viscount of Vila Real, an advocate for knowledge and advancement in nineteenth-century Portugal.

And, of course, the iconic Princess Tower is a landmark of Braganza in the north of Portugal, still alive with its ochre stone walls and gruesome legends. (It's worth a visit on your next trip to the country!)

Additionally, I want to share my deep fascination with monarchy in the nineteenth century. It was an era that witnessed a transformation of power dynamics, where kings lost political power due to the constitutional monarchy. Yet, amid this shift, the intrigues of families and royal lines intensified, to the point that every royal family was related and backstage politics held as much sway as on stage. Exploring this dynamic backdrop, where personal desires intersect with the responsibilities of the crown, has been a remarkable journey.

If you enjoyed "The Truth About Myths," please consider leaving a review. Your feedback not only means the world to me but also serves as a guiding light for future readers.

Again, Thank you for being part of this journey and for your ongoing support.

Warmest regards, Giovanna

About Me

My name is Giovanna Siniscalchi, and I have two passions: History and Romance. My goal as a writer is to transport readers to Portugal, where they can watch the sunset through majestic umbrella pines, taste bold wines, and sway to the sound of a Fado.

I research every detail of my novels, hoping to make you treasure my grandparents' country as I do. I grew up reading sweeping romances like Gone With The Wind and Count of Monte Cristo. What I love most about reading a novel is the sensation of having experienced something special. My goal is to recreate this feeling. You won't find instant love in my books. My characters need to grow and overcome their flaws before they can experience true romance. I have a loving husband, who still is my hero, and two amazing kids.

As you embark on this journey through "The Truth About Myths," I invite you to be a part of its legacy. Your thoughts, feelings, and experiences with this story matter immensely. Reviews are the lifeblood of any author, and your words have the power to shape the destinies of future readers. Whether you found joy, laughter, tears, or simply a momentary escape within these pages, I implore you to share your thoughts with others. Your review is not just a critique; it's a beacon guiding fellow adventurers to explore the uncharted territories of this book. So, please, take a moment to leave your mark on the story, and know that your support means the world to me. Thank you for being a part of this incredible journey.

Made in the USA
Middletown, DE
06 April 2024

52683223R00222